AGE OF SHIVA

AGE OF SHIVA

JAMES LOVEGROVE

SOLARIS

First published 2014 by Solaris
an imprint of Rebellion Publishing Ltd,
Riverside House, Osney Mead,
Oxford, OX2 0ES, UK

www.solarisbooks.com

ISBN: 978 1 78108 181 5

10 9 8 7 6 5 4 3 2 1

A CIP catalogue record for this book is available from the
British Library.

Designed & typeset by Rebellion Publishing

Printed in the US

THIS IS A confession.

This is an apology.

This is an origin story.

This is the tale of ordinary people who became extraordinary, became heroes, and the price we all paid.

It's completely true.

I know.

I was there.

1. KIDNAP IN CROUCH END

I STEPPED OUT of my flat to get my lunchtime sandwich and cappuccino, and never went back.

There was a coffee place round the corner from my house. It styled itself like one of the big chains, calling itself Caffè Buono and boasting baristas and leather armchairs and a Gaggia machine, but it was the only one of its kind in existence and it never to my knowledge opened any other branches. The sandwiches were all right, though. The coffee too.

I didn't notice the jet black Range Rover with tinted windows prowling after me as I sauntered along the street. It was spring. The sun was out, for a change. I'd been slaving away at my drawing board since breakfast. Daylight on my face felt sweet. To be among people – the usual milling midday Crouch End crowds – was pleasant. My work was a kind of solitary confinement. It was always good to get out.

I was thinking of a plump, tasty BLT and also of the plump, tasty new barista at Caffè Buono. Krystyna, her name badge said. From Poland, to judge by the spelling and her accent. Farm-girl pretty and very friendly. Flirtatious, even. It was never likely that I would ask her out, she being at least fifteen years younger than me, but seeing her brightened my day and I chose to think that seeing me brightened hers. If it didn't, she did a very creditable job of pretending it did.

I moseyed along, a million miles from where I was, and all the while the jet black Range Rover was stealing ever closer to me, homing in from behind, a shark shadowing its prey.

I was coming to the end of my latest commission – another reason I was so preoccupied. I was on the final straight of eight months' solid work. Five pages left to go on a four-issue miniseries. Full pencils and inks, from a script by Mark Millar. I liked collaborating with Millar; he gave the bare minimum of art direction. Usually he offered a thumbnail description of the content of each panel, with a caption or two to fit in somewhere, along with an invitation to "knock yourself out" or "make this the best fucking picture you've ever drawn." So few restrictions. Happy to let the artist be the artist and do what an artist was paid to do. I was fine with that.

But it had been a long haul. I was slow. Had a

reputation for it. A stickler; meticulous. Notoriously so. Every page, every panel, every single line had to be exactly right. That was Zak Zap's unique selling point. You only got top-quality, ultra-refined product, and if you had to wait for it, tough titties. I'd been known to tear up a completed page rather than submit it, simply because a couple of brushstrokes weren't precisely as I'd envisaged they'd be, or the overall composition was a fraction off. Just rip that sheet of Bristol board in half and bin it. Three days' effort, wasted. And I'd rage and fume and yell at the cat, and then maybe neck down a few beers, and then next morning I'd plonk my backside down in front of my drawing desk and start all over again.

Stupid, but that's how I was.

It was why Francesca left me.

Not the tantrums or the fits of creative pique. She could handle those. Laugh them off.

It was the pressure I put on myself. The sense of never being good enough which constantly dogged me. The striving for unrealisable goals. The quest to be better than my best.

"It's not noble to be a perfectionist, Zak," Francesca told me as she packed her bag. "It's a kind of self-loathing."

I was within spitting distance of the coffee place, just passing the Louisiana Chicken Shack, when the Range Rover drew alongside and braked.

The doors were already open before the car came to a complete stop.

Men in suits bundled out.

I glimpsed them out of the corner of my eye. They were Hugo-Boss-clad barrels in motion. My first thought was that they must be bodyguards for some movie star. Someone famous, over in the UK from Hollywood to promote the release of his latest action-fest, had had a sudden hankering for southern fried chicken, and his security detail were forming a cordon so that he could go in and buy a bucketful. Will Smith, maybe. Bruce Willis. The Rock. One of those guys.

And then I thought, *In Crouch End?* This wasn't even the fashionable end of Crouch End. This was the crouchy end of Crouch End. And no movie star in his right mind, however hungry, would want to sample the battered scrag ends of battery hen they served at the Louisiana Chicken Shack.

And then the nearest of the men in suits grabbed hold of me. And then another of them did too, clamping a hand around my elbow and whispering in my ear, "Don't shout. Don't struggle. Act natural, like this is nothing out of the ordinary. Otherwise you'll regret it."

Then, loudly so that passersby would hear, he said, "All right, sweetheart. That's enough now. You've had your fun, but it's time to go back to the Priory. Your management is paying all that money for your rehab. They don't want it wasted."

With that, they dragged me towards the Range Rover – literally *dragged*, my heels scraping the kerbstones. I was helpless, inert, a flummoxed idiot, no idea what was going on. Even if I hadn't been warned to act natural, I'd have been too dumbfounded to resist or protest.

It happened so fast. Just a handful of seconds, and suddenly I was in the back seat of the Range Rover, squashed between two of the suited goons, and the car was pulling out into the traffic, and I wasn't going to have that BLT or that cappuccino today and I wasn't going to cheer up Krystyna with a smile and she wasn't going to cheer me up either.

2. KNUCKLEDUSTER RING, HILLBILLY MOUSTACHE AND FRIENDS

THERE ARE MOMENTS in your life when you do what you have to, simply because you're too scared to do anything else.

I was no Jedi knight, no master of kung fu. I hadn't been in a fight since secondary school, and that was more of a pathetic bitch-slap contest than anything, and besides, I lost. Now I was in a car with four blokes, each of whom weighed twice as much as me, each of whom had a shaven head and no-bullshit mirrored sunglasses and seam-straining muscles and looked as though he could snap my neck just by breathing hard on me.

Compliance was the only logical course of action. I wasn't going to karate chop my way out of this predicament. I didn't have super powers like the

characters in the comics I drew for a living. No
eye beam to blast a hole through the car roof. No
webbing to truss up my kidnappers. No frigging
Batarang. I was stuck, a victim, panic-stricken,
hyperventilating, only human.

They could kill me, these men. Were they going to
kill me? Who were they? What did they want with
me?

We had driven perhaps half a mile before I finally
found some gumption and piped up. "Piped" was
the word; my voice sounded like a piccolo.

"You must have the wrong man," I said. "I haven't
done anything. I'm nobody."

"You Zachary Bramwell?" said the goon on my
immediate left, who wore a gold sovereign ring so
large it could easily double as a knuckleduster.

It didn't really seem to be a question, which was
why I said, "Yes."

"Then we've got the right man. By the way, you
got a phone on you?"

"No."

"I'm going to check anyway." Knuckleduster Ring
ransacked my pockets, finding nothing but lint and
loose change. "Left it at home, eh?"

I had. I nodded.

"Good. No need to confiscate it, then. Now shut
your trap."

I shut my trap, but after another mile I couldn't
keep it shut any longer. My anxiety wouldn't let me.

"What was all that stuff about 'the Priory' and my
'management'?"

"What do you think? To make it look like we were staging an intervention."

"Oh. But you *are* sure you've got the right Zachary Bramwell, not a different one? Same name but, you know, minus the substance addiction issues?"

"Hundred per cent."

"So where are you taking me? Who do you work for? Are you cops? The government?"

Knuckleduster Ring smiled. The goon on my right, who had the type of drooping moustache favoured by bikers and hillbillies, smirked. The guy driving the car actually laughed, like I'd cracked a joke.

"Nah," said Knuckleduster Ring. "They pay shit."

"Private contractors, you could call us," said Hillbilly Moustache. "Available to the highest bidder."

"Well, who is that, then?" I said. "Who in God's name has it in for me so badly that they've hired you to snatch me off a London street in broad daylight?"

"Christ, this fucker talks a lot," said the fourth goon, who was the spitting image of Knuckleduster Ring and could only have been his identical twin brother. "Can't I give him a crack upside the head? I don't want to listen to him jabber all the way."

"Unharmed, intact," said the driver, who I reckoned was the boss of the outfit. He had a diamond inset into one of his upper incisors. "That's the brief. But," he added, "maybe you should think about quietening down, Mr Bramwell. My boys have a pretty low threshold of tolerance for nonsense, if you know what I'm saying. Here, I've got an idea.

How about some nice soothing music? Help us all chillax."

Diamond Tooth switched on the radio, tuned it to Classic FM, and there we were, tootling along the North Circular, me and this quartet of brick-shithouse abductors, listening to a sequence of plinky-plonk sonatas[1], with comments from the nerdy posh announcer spliced in between. At one point Knuckleduster Ring's twin brother raised his hand off his knee and started stroking patterns in the air as though conducting an orchestra. It was ridiculous, and I might have thought it funny if I hadn't been trying so hard not to soil my pants.

We drove for an hour, leaving London behind. We headed northbound up the M1, turning off somewhere before Milton Keynes and then wiggling around in the Buckinghamshire countryside on A-roads and B-roads until I was thoroughly disorientated and couldn't have found my way back to civilisation even with a map.

In my head Diamond Tooth's words – "Unharmed, intact" – rang like a church bell, offering solace and hope. Whoever my kidnappers' employer was, he didn't want me hurt. There was at least that.

Or could it be that he didn't want me hurt until he himself got his hands on me? I was the pair of box-fresh sneakers that no one else could touch and that only his feet could sully.

I racked my brains, thinking of people I'd pissed

---

[1] Vivaldi? Haydn? One of those guys.

off during the nearly forty years of my life so far. It wasn't exactly a short list. I'd aggrieved more than a few editors in the comics biz with my propensity for handing in work at the very last minute, or else blowing the deadline completely. I'd hacked off my previous landlord but one with my complaints about mice droppings in the kitchen and mould on the bathroom walls, but those were legitimate gripes and he had no right to be upset with me for pestering him about things he was duty-bound to fix. I'd left behind a trail of women who to a greater or lesser degree found me lacking in the attentive boyfriend department, up to and including Francesca, who had stuck it out with me the longest but had ultimately come to the same conclusion as the rest: that I wasn't worth the time, trouble and effort. And then there was that financial advisor at the bank who I'd lost my rag with, just because he told me I wasn't in a "reliable occupation with regular income" and therefore didn't deserve to be offered a more preferential mortgage rate. In hindsight, I shouldn't have swept his pot of ballpoint pens onto the floor of his cubicle and told him to stick his flexible variable rates up his backside. It was petty and childish of me. I should have done the mature, manly thing and thumped the tosser.

All these people and others had cause to dislike Zak Bramwell. They might well wish to curse me under their breath and think ill of me during the long watches of a sleepless night.

But hate me so much as to have me brought to

them so that they could inflict prolonged and nefarious revenge upon my person at their leisure? And at great expense, too?

I didn't think so.

Who, then? Who the hell was I being taken to meet?

I couldn't for the life of me rustle up an answer.

Finally the Range Rover arrived somewhere. And by "somewhere" I mean the middle of nowhere.

To be precise: a disused, dilapidated aerodrome that had once served as a US airbase during World War 2 and subsequently the Cold War, and was now a collection of grass-covered hangars, mouldering Quonset huts, and sad, sagging outbuildings.

An air traffic control tower with smashed-out windows overlooked a shattered concrete runway criss-crossed by strips of weed.

And on the runway stood the most extraordinary vehicle I had ever seen.

3. THE *GARUDA*

MOST OF YOU reading this will be familiar with the *Garuda*. How can you not be? You'd have seen it on TV or the internet, maybe been fortunate enough to watch it in flight, zipping overhead with scarcely a sound. You'd no doubt have been startled the first time you clapped eyes on it, perhaps a little in awe, certainly impressed.

Back then, virtually nobody knew about the *Garuda*. Maybe no more than a couple of hundred people in total were aware that it existed.

So imagine my feelings as the Range Rover bumped out onto that runway and pulled up in front of this sleek metal angel with its folded-back wings, its downturned nosecone, its jet vents, its high-arched undercarriage, its rugged spherical wheels, its all-round air of lofty magnificence. It didn't seem to be standing on the ground so much as perching, a forty-ton bird of prey that had briefly alighted to survey the lie of the land.

I was gobsmacked, all the more so in those shabby surroundings. The incongruity was striking. It didn't belong here in a disused Midlands aerodrome. It belonged somewhere in the future, perhaps docking with a space station in near Earth orbit.

I think I fell a little bit in love with it, there on the spot. And bear in mind, this was before I had any idea what the *Garuda* was capable of, all the things it could do.

The goons hauled me out of the car and lugged me over to the aircraft, from which steps unfolded like a carpet unrolling. A door opened, so smoothly it seemed to melt inwards, and a woman emerged, extending a hand to me in welcome.

I can't deny that things were suddenly looking up. She was quite beautiful. She was Asian – Indian, if I didn't miss my guess – with almond-shaped eyes and soft features. Her hair was pure black gloss and her figure was full, just the way I liked. I wasn't into the skinny, self-denying type of woman. I preferred someone who ate and drank with an appetite and wasn't guilt-ridden or ashamed.

Her dress was smart and immaculate, from pale blue silk blouse to hip-hugging skirt. Her makeup was subtle but effective. Her nails were varnished chocolate brown.

I think I fell a little bit in love with her, too. Maybe

I was just glad to see a face that was utterly unlike the hard, expressionless faces of the four goons. Maybe it was a relief to meet someone who looked friendly and wasn't acting as though I needed to have my head stove in.

"Aanandi Sengupta," she said, introducing herself. "I hope you've had a pleasant journey, Zak. Sorry if it's been a bit... abrupt. Our employers are not patient men. When they want something, they tend to reach out and grab it. Often without asking permission until afterwards."

"Ahem. Yes, well..." I felt scruffy and uncomfortable in front of the crisply turned-out Aanandi Sengupta. I hadn't shaved that morning, I was in my oldest, baggiest sweatshirt and jeans, and there were ink blotches on my fingers as I shook her hand. I was a mess, and she was as far from a mess as one could be. "Can't say they were the finest conversationalists I've ever met."

I glanced over my shoulder as I said this. The goons were keeping their distance from the aircraft, standing at ease, soldiers relieved of a duty. I was passing from their care to Aanandi's. And don't think I was unhappy about that, but I also figured I had no choice about getting on the plane. If I turned and made a run for it, Diamond Tooth, Hillbilly Moustache and the twins would be on me in a flash. I could walk aboard willingly or I could be frogmarched aboard with my arm twisted up between my shoulderblades. Either way, I was making the flight.

"Come on in," Aanandi said. "I promise I'll answer every query you have, once we're wheels up and in the air."

"Every query? Because I have loads."

"Almost every. Some stuff is off-limits for now. All right?"

"Fair enough."

The main cabin was spacious and fitted with large, plush seats; about a dozen, all told. Shagpile carpet whispered underfoot. I caught a whiff of a fragrant scent – incense?

"Make yourself at home, Zak. I can call you Zak?"

A woman like her, she could have called me anything she liked.

"How about a drink? Coffee? Tea? Something stronger?"

My body was crying out for alcohol. Something to de-jangle the nerves. But I settled for mineral water. I had a feeling I ought to remain *compos mentis* for the time being. Whatever wits I had, I needed to keep them about me.

The water came in a cup with a plastic sippy lid, like a takeaway coffee. This should have struck me as odd, but didn't. So much else here was off-kilter, what was one more thing?

Aanandi hit an intercom button. "Captain? We're ready for takeoff."

She sat beside me. She buckled her lap belt and I followed suit and buckled mine. Through the window I saw the Range Rover depart with its full complement of goon, veering out through the broken gateway it had come in by. I gave it a little farewell wave.

The aircraft began to move, those ball-shaped wheels rolling along within armatures that clutched them like talons, and then, before I even realised, we were airborne. The abandoned aerodrome shrank below. England disappeared. Within moments we were soaring among the clouds, our climb so steep it was all but vertical. Other than a plummeting sensation in the pit of my stomach, there was little to tell me we were actually in ascent; our rise was smooth, turbulence-free and eerily quiet.

"What *is* this thing?" I asked Aanandi. "It's like something out of a Gerry Anderson show."

"It's the *Garuda*. It's the only one of its kind; a multi-platform adaptable personnel transporter, equally at home in five different travel environments."

"It's ruddy quiet, is what it is. My bicycle's louder."

"I don't know the technicalities, but the engine design incorporates sound reduction technology way in advance of anything else currently on the market. The turbofans have the highest conceivable bypass ratio and feature multilobe hush kit modification baffles. And of course the cabin is comprehensively soundproofed with layers of porous absorbers and Helmholtz resonators."

"That's an awful lot of jargon for someone who says she doesn't know the technicalities."

Aanandi gave a brief, self-effacing smile. "I listen well. I pay attention. I have a good memory."

"Your accent," I said. "American?"

"Born and bred. Second-generation Indian from Boston."

"And who are these 'employers' you mentioned?"

"That I can't tell you, Zak. Not yet. You'll find out in due course. What I can tell you is that you're under no obligation to co-operate with them. You're under no obligation to do anything. I'm pretty sure you'll want to be a part of what's happening, once you learn what it is, but there's no coercion involved. We're after willing recruits, not slaves."

"It did seem like I was being pressganged," I said.

"Not so. Those four were perhaps a little insensitive and overenthusiastic, I imagine, but they had to get the job done quickly and with minimum fuss. Like I said, we work for people who are not patient and have no time for messing around."

"Well, where are we going? Is that one of the queries you *can* answer?"

"Certainly. The Indian Ocean. The Maldives."

"Seriously?"

"Is that a problem?"

I looked at her. "Normally I'd say no. Who wouldn't want to visit a tropical paradise? Especially when someone else is paying for the ticket. But... You can see it from my point of view, can't you? I'm in a super-duper fancypants James Bond aircraft, with someone I've never met before, being flown halfway across the world. How long does it even take to get to the Maldives? Twelve hours?"

"Ten by conventional means. In the *Garuda*, a third of that."

I shot past that little nugget of information. I was in full spate, mid-rant. All the outrage and disquiet of the past hour was pouring out, and not much was going to stem the flow. "And there I was, not so long ago, just walking down the street, minding my own business. I still can't help thinking this is a case of mistaken identity. You've picked up the wrong Zak Bramwell. What the hell would anyone who can afford a plane like this want with someone like me? I draw comic books for a living, for heaven's sake. I don't have any practical skills besides that – and it's not even *that* practical."

"You are Zak Zap, though," Aanandi said.

I winced a little. The name sounded dumb, coming from her. Even dumber than usual. "That's me. I know, I know. Pretty lame. I was young when I chose it. Teenager. Seemed cool then. Now I'm stuck with it and there's not much I can do. Too late to change it."

"The same Zak Zap who drew the *Deathquake* strip for *2000 AD*, and did brief but well-respected runs on *Fantastic Four* and *Aquaman*, and recently illustrated Robert Kirkman's *Sitting Ducks* miniseries for Image."

"Yeah. Don't tell me you're a fan."

"I'm not. But the people I work for are."

"Oh." I digested this fact. It sat pleasantly in my belly. "Right. And, er... Am I going to some sort of convention? Is that what this is? Maybe a private one?"

"Not as such."

"I just thought... I mean, I've done Comic Con.

Plenty of others, too. Crap hotels, mostly. Teeming hordes of cosplayers and fanboys. Pros all hunkered down at the bar trying to avoid them. I thought this might be the same deal only, you know, classier."

"Afraid not."

"Shame." The professional freelancer instinct kicked in. "But you say there's work involved? Actual paid work?"

"There could be," said Aanandi, "if you want it. Very well paid."

I was beginning to like the sound of this. I was still unnerved and discombobulated. It had not been an ordinary day so far, and the dread evoked by my "kidnap" had yet to subside. But work was work, and I was never one to turn a job offer down. I could hardly afford to: plenty of comics artists made a pretty decent wage, but they were the fast ones, the guys who could churn out a book a month, twenty-odd pages bang on schedule, no sweat. As I've already established, that wasn't me. My financial situation was definitely more hand-to-mouth. I'd never been asked to draw any of the mega-sellers; *Fantastic Four* had been in the doldrums when I was assigned to it – and then fired six issues later. And as for *Aquaman*... Who the hell buys *Aquaman*? I only took the gig because I was short on cash at the time and I liked drawing underwater stuff. [1]

---

[1] There'd never been any great fan-love for the King of the Seas with his daft orange and green swimsuit and his power to exert mental control over, er, fish. After my brief tenure on the title, no one liked him much more than they had before.

So I didn't have a steady stream of backlist royalty revenue to rely on, and no editor with any sense was going to hire me to do *Superman* or *Amazing Spider-Man* or any of the other DC and Marvel flagship titles. Readers wouldn't stomach the indefinite delays between issues or the inevitable rushed fill-ins by other artists. They'd desert in droves.

So somebody was interested in employing me? And was flying me to the Maldives for the job interview?

I can handle that, I thought.

I felt a flush of smugness, the kind you get when your talent is recognised, when you're acknowledged as being skilled at what you do. The pardonable kind. A sort of giddiness overcame me. I undid my lap belt, thinking that a victory stroll up and down the cabin aisle was in order, a moment by myself to clench my fist and go "Yes!" under my breath.

"I wouldn't do that if I were you," Aanandi advised.

Too late. I was already on my feet. And then I was off my feet. I was somehow standing without standing. My toes were in contact with the carpet, but only just. The giddiness wasn't an emotion, it was a genuine physical sensation. I was bobbing in the air, a human balloon.

"What the hot holy...?"

Aanandi took my wrist and pulled me back down into my seat. I refastened the belt, tethering myself.

"I would have warned you," she said, "but you had so much to say."

The empty cup floated free from the armrest tray.

Tiny sparkling droplets of mineral water poured from its lid aperture like reverse rain.

I glanced out of the window.

We were high up.

Oh, God, so fucking high up. I could see the curvature of the Earth, the horizon line of pale blue sky giving way to the blue-blackness of the void. Continents were small enough that I could blot them out with my hand. Cloud forms were rugged Arctic snowscapes.

"Space," I breathed. "We're in fucking space."

4. MIRAGES

"Point-to-point suborbital spaceflight," said Aanandi. "The *Garuda* arcs above the planet in a steep parabola, using helium-cooled air intakes to help it achieve hypersonic speeds."

"Hypersonic? You mean we broke the sound barrier and I didn't notice?"

"Why would you? You can't hear a sonic boom on board the aircraft that's making it. It's the outer edges of a pressure wave spreading behind us, like the wake of a ship. It's audible only if you're outside it."

Duh. I felt like a complete dunce next to Aanandi. Good thing I found smart women such a turn-on.

"And we're weightless? Like astronauts?"

"Not quite," she said, catching the cup before it could fly out of reach. "Something as light as this cup will float. You and I are just buoyant. It isn't true weightlessness because, at a hundred kilometres up, we're not in true orbit. In fact, what we're doing is just free-falling without ever hitting the ground. How are you feeling?"

"Weird. This is the coolest thing I've ever done, and I'm shitting myself at the same time."

"But not unwell? Stomach okay? No nausea? There are sick bags if you need one."

"I'm fine," I said. "I've never really done travel sickness. Lucky that way."

"I puked like a dog my first couple of times," Aanandi admitted, "but I've gotten used to it since then. Dramamine helps. And the *Garuda*'s a friendly fellow. Never gives you a rough ride if he can help it."

"*Garuda*. Where do I know that name from? Isn't there an airline called Garuda?"

"Garuda Indonesia, yes. It's named after a mythical bird. As is this. Buddhists regard the Garuda as a divine avian creature, but to Hindus, Garuda is more than that. He's Vishnu's mount. Whenever there are demons or serpents to be fought, Vishnu summons him and rides him into battle. His form is much like that of an eagle, but with human features, such as arms and legs."

"You're just a mine of information, aren't you?"

"Actually, Hinduism is my area of true expertise," said Aanandi. "I majored in Asian religions at Yale and wrote my doctoral thesis on mythopoesis in the Hindu tradition. Mythopoesis," she went on, anticipating my next question, "is the study of myth-making and how it adapts over time to meet changing cultural and historical circumstances. I've published several books on the subject and lecture about it all over the world. I've even been called the leading authority."

"An over-achiever," I said with a comedy eye roll. "I hate you."

"You're well respected in your field too, Zak. I don't read comics myself, but from what I know about you, your work is highly praised – and prized. Pages of original art by you fetch several thousand dollars."

"Much of which goes to the dealer in commission. That or it's early stuff that I sold for a pittance and some eBay scalper makes a mint off it and I don't see a penny."

"You've been nominated twice for an Eisner Award and once for a Harvey."

"Didn't win, though."

"You've drawn for Warren Ellis, Grant Morrison, Garth Ennis, Brian Michael Bendis..."

"Rubbing shoulders with the stars."

"What people seem to like about your artwork most of all," Aanandi went on, "is the design sense. The way you draw buildings, machinery, backgrounds, costumes. Especially costumes."

"That, I have to confess, is something I enjoy doing," I said. "Dreaming up nifty costumes. It's the one part of the job I really love. Just going crazy and inventing something that looks brilliant and is memorable and hits the mark. I mean, superheroes, intrinsically they're a bit silly. The whole concept of someone putting on spandex and going out and fighting crime – you can't take it seriously. But given that basic absurdity, there's no reason why you can't let your imagination fly and make the characters look exciting and dramatic and fun. Take Batman. If you saw him coming down the street in the real world, you'd probably laugh. In context, though, on the comicbook page, his outfit works. It's absolutely right. He's scary and badass and you wouldn't fuck with him. It's all about the visual, you see. Draw a superhero properly, and he becomes credible. Give him the look he needs, and everything else takes care of itself. That's the magic of comics. Oh. I'm boring you. Nerd talk overdose."

"No. No." Aanandi had just stifled a vast yawn. "Not at all. It's been a long day, is all. We set out at first light this morning, my local time. So it's evening for me now and it'll be midnight before we get in. You don't mind if I grab a quick nap, do you?"

"Go right ahead."

"Is there anyone you'd like to phone? Maybe you need to straighten out your domestic affairs, cancel the newspaper, whatever."

"I would, only I left my mobile back at the flat. I was literally just popping out for five minutes."

"That's all right. There's a sat-phone handset beside you. See it?"

"Why do I need to phone someone anyway? How long am I going to be away?"

"It depends. Not that long, necessarily. What about your cat? Someone should probably feed him."

"You know I have a cat?"

"Zak, if you haven't realised by now, there's pretty darn little my employers *don't* know about you. You've been thoroughly vetted. Just don't tell anyone you call where you're headed. Or, more importantly, what you're heading there *in*. Got that?"

"Okay."

I dialled my neighbour's number. I wasn't that much bothered about my cat, Herriman. He was a real Six Dinner Sid, known at most of the houses in my street and welcome in several of them, where titbits and even full-blown meals awaited him. He would never starve.

I felt enough of a duty to him, however, at least to make a show of seeing that he was looked after while his ostensible owner was away. Mrs Deakins, who lived on the floor above mine, was always prepared to nip downstairs and refill his bowl. She also liked to snoop around my flat, I knew. She was the archetypal busybody, forever poking her nose into other people's affairs, and after her visits I always found stuff had been moved around, piles of magazines shifted, cushions out of place, that sort of thing. Me being an artist, she assumed all I did was drink, take drugs and hold licentious parties, and I'm convinced she was checking my flat for evidence every time she went in to feed Herriman.[1]

---

[1] Once, when I went to New York for a week of publisher meetings, I deliberately didn't tidy away a half-smoked spliff,

Mrs Deakins was out, so I left a message. Then I contemplated phoning Francesca. Hers was the only other number I knew by heart. In the old days you remembered countless phone numbers, didn't you? They imprinted themselves on your brain through repetition. Then mobiles and contact lists came along, and we lost the knack fast. Didn't need it any more.

Why ring Francesca?

Because it had been less than a month since she'd bailed out on me and taken home the few belongings she kept at my place. Because the wound was still raw but there was something compelling about probing it and feeling its shape and sting. Above all because I was on an adventure of some kind, I wanted to share it, and she was the person I'd grown accustomed to sharing with; she was the one I contacted whenever I had exciting news and couldn't wait to tell it to somebody. It had been ingrained in me, during the two years we were going out. It was still hard to shake. Whenever I said to myself, *Wow, this is cool*, it would be closely followed by, *Must let Fran know*. And I was stuck in that pattern even now, even after Francesca had made it clear that she wanted nothing more to do with me, that she had wasted too much time on me and there had to be someone else out there for her, a man who would actually give a shit about her and not be so self-absorbed, so consumed by his own needs, that he barely noticed her unless it

---

just left it sitting in an ashtray so that Mrs Deakins could have something to confirm her worst fears. You have to throw a dog a bone every so often, don't you?

was convenient for him. I longed to hear her voice. I missed her. And all that time when we were together I had hardly paid her any notice, taking her for granted. Irony, no?

I didn't ring her. Perhaps this was the time to make the break finally. Jetting through the ionosphere, sitting in my tin can far above the world like Major Tom. Let the slender fragile thread of connection snap once and for all and move on.

Aanandi was fast asleep when I next turned round to look at her. I rested my forehead against the small cold window and gazed out.

I stayed that way for the next four hours, and saw the terminator between day and night creep towards us and pass below, the countries becoming black shapes outlined by sparks of electric light, the seas turning into soft dark gulfs of nothingness. Mesmerising.

Aanandi woke up when the captain announced over the intercom that we were commencing our descent.

"Another half-hour," she said. "Are you hungry?"

"Starving," I replied with feeling.

"Sorry. Can't really serve food in microgravity. We'll get you something as soon as we land."

"Sounds good to me."

As the *Garuda* dropped towards the Earth, I felt heaviness settle back into my body. It was a bit like pins and needles.

Ten minutes out from our destination, the captain's voice echoed round the cabin again. This time he wasn't so silkily businesslike. There was an edge to his tone.

"Folks, it, ah, it appears we've drawn a bit of attention. Signals chatter from Masroor airbase indicates there's been a launch. Couple of PAF Mirages have been scrambled and are heading on a course to intercept. We're altering our approach vector but there's not a lot we can do to avoid them, to be honest, if it's us they're after. I'll keep you updated."

"Shit," I said. "What does that mean? Mirages as in fighter jets?"

"I wouldn't worry about it," Aanandi said. "This has happened before. The Pakistan Air Force likes to keep tabs on us. They're exceptionally inquisitive. They know the *Garuda* isn't some commercial flight, and its suborbital trajectory puzzles them and concerns them. They're paranoid about anything that comes near their borders and isn't following a standard flight path through established air corridors."

"But they won't shoot at us or anything, surely."

"Hard to predict. Try not to think about it."

"Too damn late."

"We'll be fine. It isn't the first time." She patted my hand. I would have been reassured, had her palm not been hot and slightly moist. Aanandi herself was not as calm as she wished me to be.

The next few minutes were gnawing anxious agony. I peered into the blackness outside, searching for the telltale flash of aircraft navigation lights, perhaps an afterburner glow. I spotted a flicker in the far distance, but Aanandi reckoned it was just a jumbo bound for Karachi.

I gave a little jump when the captain next spoke over the intercom.

"We've definitely picked up a tail," he said. "Eleven miles behind and closing fast. Likely the intention is to spook us, in which case the best plan is not to act spooked. They've no real reason to attack. It'll probably just be a flyby, to let us know they're watching, rattle our nerves. I've hailed base anyway and informed them of the situation. Let's see what those fellas can do about it, eh?"

Up until that moment I had had our pilot pegged as an American, but his pronunciation of "about" – *aboot* – suggested he must in fact be Canadian. Somehow, irrationally, this was a reason to be hopeful. I couldn't see a Canadian acting rashly or foolishly and endangering our lives. Canadians were safe and sensible and never took risks. I clung to the stereotype like a shipwrecked sailor to a lifebelt. Our captain would get us safely to the ground without a hitch, purely because he came from a country famed for its boringness. Talk about clutching at straws.

Less than a minute later, the sleek, hunched silhouette of a fighter jet drew alongside the *Garuda*, at a distance of, I estimated, a quarter of a mile.

Another joined it, on the other side of us.

Both Mirages kept pace, matching the *Garuda*'s gradual rate of descent. Their lights strobed busily, hypnotically, illuminating the contours of their wings and the ugly payloads that hung beneath.

I glanced at Aanandi.

She smiled.

"It's going to be all right, Zak. Trust me."

I wished I knew her well enough to believe her.

Then the Mirages withdrew, pulling back, out of sight.

Returning to base, I thought, *mission accomplished.*

Relief flooded me like chilled champagne.

"Ahem," said the captain. "Hate to say this, folks, but it's not looking good. Couldn't raise either of the PAF pilots on the radio. Hailing them, but they're flat-out refusing to respond. And now they seem to be lining up behind us in formation so as to..."

"To what?" I asked, not that he could hear. I wasn't anywhere near the intercom button.

"Yeah, ah, seems like we now have a semi-active radar target lock on us," the captain said. "They're carrying Sidewinders, so... Better hang on back there, eh? This might get bumpy."

5. THE CAVALRY

SPHINCTER-PUCKERING, KNUCKLE-WHITENING, GUT-CHURNING
terror.

*We're going to die. They're going to shoot us out
of the sky. We're going to die.*

The *Garuda* went into a nosedive, and pathetically
I assumed the brace position just the way flight
attendants tell you to during the pre-takeoff safety
spiel. No practical use in the event of the aircraft
blowing up, but if my head was between my knees
at least it would be easier to kiss my arse goodbye.

We plummeted, the captain pouring on speed.
I had no idea how fast a Mirage could fly, or a
Sidewinder missile for that matter. I had to hope
that the *Garuda* was faster than either. Otherwise
this was just some pointless stunt, a desperate, futile

attempt by Captain Canuck to evade the inevitable.

We bottomed out of our kamikaze plunge with a juddering, teeth-rattling lurch that shot me bolt upright. G-forces pressed me into my seat hard enough, probably, to leave a permanent Zak-shaped impression in the upholstery. Someone was screeching like a girl, and I assumed it was Aanandi, but, embarrassingly, it turned out to be me.

Now the *Garuda* was scooting along at low altitude. How low? I glimpsed the glitter of moonlight on water not far beneath the wingtips, less than fifteen feet. The crazy thing was, the ocean seemed to be getting closer. The captain was bringing us right down until we were brushing the wave tops, and I was no aeronautical expert but I didn't reckon this was a very sensible plan of action. The *Garuda* wasn't a seaplane, as far as I could tell. I'd seen wheels but not pontoons. Ergo, landing on water did not strike me as viable or advisable. Wouldn't we just sink?

Besides, we weren't decelerating, the flaps weren't down, no reverse thrust – nothing to suggest we were landing at all. So what was the purpose of the exercise?

"Okay," said the captain, "hold tight, everyone."

Then we were bouncing along on the sea's surface like a skimming stone. I dug my fingernails into the armrests, expecting that at any moment the *Garuda* would flip and go cartwheeling end over end, disintegrating piece by piece until there was nothing left of it but scattered smithereens.

Instead, it settled onto the water, coasting like a powerboat. Plumes of sea foam sprayed up over the wings.

"Wrongfooted those PAF boys with that manoeuvre," said the captain, "but we haven't shaken 'em off. They're coming down for a closer look, and the targeting radar lock is still active. We're going to have to lose them once and for all, and that means reconfiguring."

"Reconfiguring?" I said to Aanandi with a frown.

"Wait and see."

"Good news is, the cavalry's on its way," the captain added. "Couple of minutes out, inbound. It's going to be tight but I think they might make it in time to help."

One of the Mirages thundered by overhead, then went into a sharp banking turn to come around.

Meanwhile a succession of tremendous whines and rumbles shuddered through the *Garuda*'s frame. I saw the wings retract, telescoping inwards until they were a fifth of their original span, more like fins now. Then what appeared to be a pair of turbines folded out from recesses in the fuselage. Their fans started to turn. All the while we lost speed, the jet engine powering down.

"This is..." I started to say, but in fact I didn't know *what* this was. It was something, certainly.

The Mirage returned for a second flyby, shooting up afterwards into a perpendicular climb.

"His buddy's at five o'clock, zeroing in," said the captain. "Looks like it could be a kill run. But if you'd care to take a gander out of the starboard windows you'll see a sight to gladden your hearts."

Out there, a pinprick of light glimmered on the horizon, growing fast.

"The chariot," Aanandi said with satisfaction.

"We're submerging in ten," the captain said. "You may have just enough time to catch the fireworks first, though."

The approaching light resolved into the flare of a rocket engine, propelling a kind of open-topped airborne sled in which two figures were visible. One manned the controls. The other rode behind, legs braced and apart for balance. They must have been doing two hundred miles an hour, yet the standing figure didn't appear to be having any trouble staying upright. More than that, he didn't appear concerned in the least.

And he had a bow in his hands.

If ever there was a time to exclaim "What the fuck!?" this was it, and I did.

The chariot shot past.

The bowman unleashed an arrow, a streak of silver in the gleam of the full moon.

There was a burst of golden orange, the unmistakable bright cascade of fuel igniting.

Then water bubbled up over the *Garuda*'s windows, rising like ink, blotting out the sky.

We plunged into the depths of the Laccadive Sea, the *Garuda* humming happily to itself, quite at home.

6. THE TRINITY SYNDICATE
GRAND HOSPITALITY PROJECT

I STEPPED OUT from my room onto the patio, into a billow of humid morning air. In the shade of an awning, breakfast had been laid out for me. Hot coffee. A huge bowlful of fresh pineapple, mango and papaya. Porridge. Bacon and eggs under a domed steel lid.

I ate and drank like I hadn't seen food in weeks.

Just yards from where I sat lay a white beach caressed by blue wavelets. A leatherback turtle was lugging itself across the sand, making for the shallows. A pair of scarlet-clawed crabs were engaged in some kind of turf battle or mating ritual, tangoing back and forth amid the coarse shoreline grass, pincers locked. Brown, nondescript little birds fluttered onto the table, hoping to snaffle some scraps.

In the light of a new day, the events of the previous evening seemed distant, incomprehensible, almost surreal.

Had I really been in an aircraft that doubled as a boat and trebled as a submarine?

Had we really come under attack by Pakistan Air Force planes?

Had I really seen someone armed with a bow and arrow take out a Dassault Mirage in midair?

I could scarcely believe any of it. If someone had come to me with a story like that, I would have told them to lay off the wacky baccy for a while.

Yet all I had to do was turn round, my back to the beach, to know that it was all true.

Behind me loomed a mighty, outward-curving building, a giant edifice occupying almost the entirety of one of the lesser Maldives at the far northern end of the island chain. It was steel and concrete and tinted glass, narrower at its base than at its summit, flaring like a conch shell, with barely a straight line anywhere in its architecture.

This, of course, you will all know as Mount Meru.

At the time, though, it had another name, a much less evocative, more prosaic one. It was known as the Trinity Syndicate Grand Hospitality Project. It was – or so everyone had been led to believe – a gigantic hotel complex, the largest and most ambitious undertaking of its kind, a billion-dollar attempt to create a kind of static cruise ship, an isolated and self-contained venue for leisure, entertainment and relaxation. It was touted as a Mecca for wealthy vacationers who wanted a combination of high-end luxury resort and the balminess of the tropics, Las Vegas but with breezes and ocean views.

I had seen pictures of the complex in the news media, both computer-generated artist's impressions of how it would look when completed and work-in-progress update photos. I think I might have marvelled at the sheer audacious folly of it and reckoned I'd never be able to afford to stay there in a month of Sundays even if I'd wanted to.

It was beautiful, no question. An aerial shot I'd seen showed how the building radiated out in seven concentric layers. The petal-like rings rose towards the middle in an inverted funnel shape. They were divided by courtyards and gardens and connected on their upper levels by walkways and skybridges.

Some of the solutions to the technical problems thrown up by the complex's construction were spectacular, too, such as driving dozens of steel-and-concrete monopiles half a mile deep in order to create foundations which could support the immense weight of such a structure. Without them it would have crushed the stack of compressed coral it stood on and sunk beneath the waves like Atlantis.

The Trinity Syndicate Grand Hospitality Project was also entirely self-powered, using the photovoltaic properties of the paper-thin solar tiles – alternating layers of graphene and transition metal dichalcogenides – with which every exterior surface apart from the windows was covered. Electricity was abundant and free.

And now I was staying there myself, as a guest – or a something, I wasn't yet sure what. But I had been given a set of clean clothes which fit and were made of light cotton, just right for the climate, and I'd had an amazing super-hot multi-nozzle shower before coming out for breakfast, and I'd shaved, and now I was eating heartily, and I felt, in a word, resurrected.[1]

My upbeat mood was in no way diminished by the arrival of the lovely Aanandi.

"How are you feeling, Zak?"

I patted a belly that resembled an expectant mother's. "Gloriously stuffed."

"Ready for a meeting?"

"What? Now? Who with?"

"The bosses. The Trinity Syndicate. Busy men, like I said, but they've made time to fit you in. They're eager to say hi."

She led me through the complex's outer ring in a clockwise direction, up and down a number of staircases. The place had that new-building smell, all freshly poured concrete and just-dried plaster. Pot plants glistened. Slabs of slate and marble gleamed.

What I was seeing now confirmed the impressions I had gathered the previous night: if this was a hotel, it was the oddest one I'd ever been in. There was no reception or main lobby that I was aware of. The communal areas seemed more like rec rooms at an office, full of low chairs and discreet soft furnishings,

---

[1] Like Jesus. Or Superman after Doomsday killed him.

with drink dispensing machines, flatscreen TVs and table football. There were staff, Maldivians all of them, but their uniform was informal – T-shirts and sweatpants bearing a three-heads logo that was a bit like the biohazard symbol – rather than the trousers and ties that were regulation dress for employees at a posh hotel.

We passed people who I took to be fellow "guests" like me. They were a motley assortment, ranging from pudgy bespectacled boffins with Doc Brown hair to smoothly efficient and smartly groomed city types who could only be dabblers in the dark arts of corporate public relations.

In short: hotel, shmotel. This was no more a resort destination than Disneyland was a concentration camp. The Trinity Syndicate Grand Hospitality Project was a front, hiding something utterly other.

Finally, after a lengthy indoor trek, Aanandi ushered me into a conference room. One wall was an unbroken, floor-to-ceiling window, showing me two equal fields of flat colour, the aquamarine sea and the cerulean sky, like something Rothko might have painted in one of his mellower phases. That triple-head logo was embedded in the ceiling as a quartz mosaic, and repeated in the pattern of the carpet.

"I'll leave you here," Aanandi said. "They won't be long."

"Any advice? Handy tips for dealing with them?"

"Be honest. Don't lie. Smile. Be yourself."

"Oh, shit. I'm doomed."

"You'll be fine." She gave my shoulder an

encouraging rub. "Don't forget, they want you, Zak. You're not auditioning. They're the ones who need to be schmoozing you, not the other way round. You're in the driving seat."

I was alone with the Rothko view and the whisper of the air conditioning for several minutes. Then three men filed into the room via a side door, not the one Aanandi and I had used.

I recognised the first of them straight away: Dick Lombard, Australia's pre-eminent media mogul and only one of the best known and most reviled faces on the planet. Lombard owned television stations, movie studios, internet giants and publishing companies on every populated continent, and was famous for his trenchant opinions, which were right-wing bordering on neo-Nazi. To his supporters he was the "Wonderful Wizard of Oz." To his opponents, a far greater proportion of humankind, he was Satan from Down Under, a capitalist Beelzebub born and baked in the infernal heat of the Outback, a rapacious Antipodean Beast who would not be sated until he had bought up every last media outlet in the world and controlled the flow of information into every single household.

He was a hulking presence in the flesh, far taller than I'd have given him credit for, with a lantern jaw and weathered leathery skin. He had been raised on a cattle station, destined to spend his life as a jackaroo rounding up livestock on horseback, until both his parents died within months of each other and he decided to sell the farm and buy a local radio station with the proceeds. That was forty years and countless hostile takeovers ago, but there was still a squint in those eyes that spoke of red dust vistas and searing sunshine.

Lombard took point. He greeted me with one of the firmest handshakes I'd ever experienced, pumping my arm like he was cranking the motor of a vintage automobile as he said, "G'day, mate. Glad you could make it. I realise we didn't give you much of a choice, but it's appreciated anyway. Dick Lombard, of course."

"Of course," I said.

"And allow me to introduce my partners – not partners in the civil-ceremony sense of the word, I hasten to add; I'm no fudge packer. Scrawny Yid-looking bloke with the flash clobber and the rimless glasses is R. J. Krieger. From Texas, believe it or not. And he swears he isn't Jewish but I know a Red Sea pedestrian when I see one. Look at that nose."

Krieger's handshake was firm, but, mercifully, it was nowhere near as metacarpal-grindingly painful as Lombard's.

"Howdy," he said, in a deep cowboy voice that could not have suited him less. His suit was a thing of sleek grey beauty, his shirt and tie sheerest silk. "Pleased to meetcha."

"And the brown chap's Vignesh Bhatnagar," said Lombard. "Don't be fooled by that chubby cherubic little face of his. Looks all meek and mild, like he should be giving sermons and diddling choirboys on the sly, but he's a merchant of death."

Bhatnagar heaved a rueful sigh, clearly used to his colleague's blunt humour, if not amused by it.

"Hello, Zak," he said in cultured Oxbridge tones with the faintest trace of an Indian accent. "Try to ignore Dick's casual racism and homophobia. He means nothing by it. He's harmless. It's just Dick being a, well, a dick."

I wasn't sure whether I should laugh or not, so to be on the safe side I didn't. Krieger did, while Lombard himself let out a low chuckle which sounded not dissimilar to a growl.

"Old joke, Vignesh mate," he said. "Old joke. Heard it a million times."

"Doesn't make it any less funny. Or true."

"Maybe not to a curry-eating turban-botherer like you. He sounds sophisticated, Zak, but he's only a couple of generations away from shitting beside the railway track and wiping his arse with his bare hand."

"And you're only a couple of generations away from deported convicts," said Bhatnagar. "Let's not get into ancestry, eh?"

"I'm a self-made man," said Lombard, puffing himself up. "Where I come from has nothing to do with where I've –"

"Perhaps, guys," said Krieger, putting himself between the two of them, "we could save this for another time. We're *all* self-made men, okay?"

"You aren't," said Lombard. "Your daddy was in oil."

"And he gambled away every penny he earned, leaving his family dead broke with nothing except debt."

"Still sent you to boarding school and Harvard. You had advantages."

"Whatever. I'm just concerned that we're giving Mr Bramwell the wrong impression, bickering like this not two minutes after we came in. Zak, pay us no mind, y'hear? Just a bunch of middle-aged rich guys joshing around. We're here for *you*. It's you we're interested in, you we've brought five thousand miles to see us."

"No, if you lot want to keep tongue lashing each other to see who's got the biggest dick, you go right ahead," is what I shouldn't have said but somehow did. I don't know what came over me. I think I was trying to ingratiate myself with them, be one of the boys.

At any rate, an awkward silence fell, and I couldn't help but feel that with that single sentence I had just done myself out of what promised to be a fairly lucrative commission. All for a cheap quip about fellatio. Talk about blowing your chance.

Then Lombard laughed, and the other two chimed in, and I sensed I'd got away with it. I even thought I had gone up in their estimation a little.

"So you'll be wondering," Lombard said, "what am I doing here and what the hell do these three larrikins want with me?"

"Something like that," I said. "Don't get me wrong, the trip was exciting. Four bullyboys dragging me into a car. Outer space. Nearly getting turned into a fireball by a Pakistani warplane. Thrill a minute. But what it's all in aid of – that's the big question, isn't it? And why me?"

"Put simply," said Krieger, "we need someone to draw for us."

"Draw? Draw what?"

"My older son's into comic books," said Lombard. "Dick Junior. He's bloody college age and he still reads the damn things, though apparently that's 'cool' these days."

"Comics aren't just for kids!" I said brightly.[1]

The three of them looked at me like I was some kind of fucking weirdo – as they had every right to.

"Yes, well," said Lombard, "Dick Junior tells me you're one of the top doodlers in the biz. Raves about your stuff, he does."

"As a humble 'doodler,' all I can say is your son has impeccable taste."

"We need you for a project, Zak," said Bhatnagar. "We need your input. Your design brain. Your artist's eye."

"Colour me intrigued."

"We're prepared to reward you."

"That's good to hear."

"Handsomely."

"Even better."

"Enough to cover what's left on your mortgage and leave you financially secure thereafter."

"Enough to...?"

How did they know how much my mortgage was? And then I thought, *According to Aanandi they know everything there is to know about me, so why*

---

[1] It was the slogan that used to appear on DC's direct-market covers in the 1980s in place of the UPC symbol.

not that? And then I thought, *They're talking about a shitload of cash, aren't they?*

"But time is pressing," Bhatnagar went on. "You'd have to be able to start more or less straight away."

"Like today straight away?"

"If possible."

"But…"

"We've got you all the equipment you'll need," said Krieger. "We've a studio ready for you. Desk, drawing board, pens, brushes, a computer, all top spec. Phenomenal natural light."

"But I have sort of a deadline I need to meet," I said. "I'm in the middle of something already."

"We can sort that for you," said Lombard. "Just so happens I own the company that owns the company that's going to publish your next series. Tell me who to phone directly to get you an indefinite extension on the deadline. All ridgy-didge, no problem."

"We're really keen that you can do this for us," said Bhatnagar. "I know it's short notice, and I'm sorry, but we've had to shorten a deadline of our own. Certain parties are getting interested in us. Too interested. We're drawing unwelcome attention from various quarters, and we're having to bring things in well ahead of our planned schedule, so that we're not pre-empted in any way."

"What do you mean, pre-empted?"

"I can't explain. Not 'til I know you're onside and part of the team. There are things we have to keep secret – even if they're no longer as secret as we would like right now."

"Anything to do with what happened last night?" I asked, cunningly putting two and two together. Not that it was that tricky a piece of arithmetic. "The Mirage and the two men in that 'chariot'?"

"Very much so. But that's just the proverbial tip of the iceberg. This is something big, Zak. One of the biggest somethings there's ever been. The repercussions will be immense, the consequences world-changing. We'd like you in on it. Would you like to be in?"

"Give me a clue. Just a hint. What's going to sell it to me?"

The three members of the Trinity Syndicate exchanged glances.

"In a word," said Lombard, "superheroes."

"You what?"

"You heard. Real-life superheroes."

"A super team, to be precise," said Krieger.

"Like in the comic books," said Bhatnagar, "but in the flesh."

"Powers. Armour. Weaponry. The works," said Lombard.

"And we'd like you to design them for us," said Krieger. "Come up with the costumes, the accessories, the colour scheme, the insignia. Work out how they should look."

"Me?" I said.

"You're the go-to guy, that's what everyone in your line of work says. You've done revamps of some of the classic characters and generated several brand new ones. This is right in your wheelhouse, son."

"What do you say?" said Bhatnagar. "Interested?"

"Have you offered this to anyone else?" I asked. "Frank Quitely? Alex Ross? Dave Gibbons? Jim Lee? Come on, you must have."

"You're the only one, Zak," said Lombard. "Top of the list. First refusal."

"Well, shit. I don't know. This is so sudden. Right out of the blue. Superheroes? Really?"

They nodded in unison.

"Can I see?"

"Thought you might say that," said Krieger. "What do you reckon, Dick, Vignesh? A demonstration for Mr Bramwell? No harm in that, surely."

"Wasn't last night good enough?" said Lombard.

"Ah, but Zak hardly saw anything," said Bhatnagar. "It was dark, and over in no time. Right, Zak?"

I shrugged. "I'm not even sure what I saw. Did one of the planes blow up? What happened to the other one?"

"Best you don't ask," said Krieger.

"But if you downed their planes, isn't that like an act of war? Won't there be reprisals?"

"Let's just call it a diplomatic incident and leave it at that. We've been up half the night making phone calls, soothing brows. The lid's back on the pot – for now."

"It's a risk, showing him anything more," Lombard said. "Can we trust him? What's to stop him blabbing?"

"Zak knows we know where he lives," said Bhatnagar. "Besides, he tested well in the psych evaluations."

"I have?" I said. "When did I do those?"

"You didn't sit any actual tests. We worked up a full personality profile based solely on your online presence and records, especially your activity on social networks. You scored highly in the compliance section."

"Meaning I'm a pushover."

"More or less."

I didn't have the balls to argue with that. Which proved that the psych evaluation was pretty much on the money.

"Whatever happens, you're not leaving this island without signing a confidentiality agreement," said Krieger. "And believe me, the clauses in that are tight enough to make your eyes water."

Lombard pondered, then decided. "Ah, what the hell, why not? Doubting Thomas here needs proof? Let's give it to him." He yoked an arm around my shoulders and hugged me to him as though we were drinking buddies at the pub – although it felt somewhat like a headlock as well. "I have a good feeling about you, Zakko mate. I think you're going to be one of us. You're going to fit right in."

7. THE MAN-LION AND THE DWARF

IN A COURTYARD between the seventh and sixth rings of the complex, two men approached.

They were a study in contrasts.

One was African, long-limbed and tall, seven feet if he was an inch.

The other was Caucasian and short, three feet if that, a dwarf.

The African had a regal bearing and a shock of frizzy hair like a lion's mane. His fingers were tipped with nails so long and pointed they resembled talons.

The dwarf had an easy smile, but an air of self-importance, too. I knew him from the TV. He was an actor. He'd featured in a BBC sitcom, and a Channel 4 documentary about the trials of being a little person in showbusiness. His name escaped me just then.

Both men wore plain black jumpsuits and combat boots. They greeted the Trinity Syndicate with nods, the tall man deferential, the dwarf not so much.

"Zak?" said Bhatnagar. "This is Murunga Kilimo and Tim VanderKamp."

"Tim VanderKamp," I said to the dwarf. "Yes. That's who you are."

"Yeah, yeah, him off the telly," said VanderKamp, sounding slightly bored. "BAFTA-nominated. Winner of a *People's Choice* Award. Also an Olivier for my Macbeth at the Young Vic. And you are...?"

"Zak Bramwell. Better known as Zak Zap."

"Daft name."

"Not a comics fan, I take it."

"Why would I be? I'm not eight years old." VanderKamp turned to the three men. "Who is this loser anyway? Is he why you asked us to meet you here?"

"Zak's going to be working on costumes for you," said Lombard, although I hadn't agreed to it yet.

"Sewing them?"

"No," said Bhatnagar, "designing them. We hope."

"Oh," said VanderKamp, unimpressed.

"We'd like you and Murunga to show him what you can do," said Krieger.

"Like performing monkeys, you mean?"

"Like indentured employees of the Trinity Syndicate," said Lombard, with a broad grin full of latent menace, "who'll do whatever's asked of them by the blokes who sign their paycheques."

VanderKamp shot him an insolent glare. There

was a very large ego packed into that very small body.

But he knew which side his bread was buttered on. He turned to Kilimo.

"Why don't you go first, Murunga? I need a few moments to prepare."

The African gave a bow of consent. "How do you wish me to display my skills as Narasimha the Manlion?" he asked the Trinity trio.

From the back of his waistband, under his cream-coloured linen jacket, Krieger drew an automatic pistol.

He levelled it at Kilimo. "I'm a Texan. We tend to settle matters with guns."

He cocked the hammer and snaked his forefinger round the trigger.

Kilimo, staring down the barrel of the pistol at point blank range, was admirably unperturbed. Me, I was alarmed just being *near* a gun. I cringed away from it.

Lombard and Bhatnagar lodged their fingers in their ears. I copied them, just in time, as Krieger loosed off a shot at Kilimo.

Who was no longer standing in front of him.

Who was, indeed, nowhere near us.

Krieger looked up. We all looked up.

Kilimo was clinging to the side of a second-storey balcony. His fingers were dug into the fabric of the building like climber's pitons.

Krieger drew a bead on him and fired again.

The bullet ricocheted off the spot where Kilimo

had been holding on. He wasn't there any more. There was only a set of gouges.

Krieger spun. Kilimo was now on the opposite side of the courtyard, even higher than before, hanging upside down from the base of a skybridge. He had leapt faster than the eye could follow, covering a distance of some thirty feet in a single bound.

My jaw was halfway to my chest by this time. It would drop still further in the coming moments.

Kilimo alighted back in front of us before Krieger could get off another round. The pistol seemed to vanish from the Texan's grasp. Next thing I knew, Kilimo was holding it out to its owner, partly dismantled. He had the bullet clip and the slide in one hand, the rest of the gun in the other.

"Thank you kindly, sir," Krieger said, taking the pistol from Kilimo and reassembling it. "That'll be all."

Kilimo stepped back. His expression was impassive. He wasn't even out of breath.

"Masai warrior," Bhatnagar confided to me. "Used to hunt lions, but there's been a number of conservation programmes started up in the Serengeti lately, using Masai tribesmen to monitor the prides rather than decimate them. Murunga was a part of that, before he came on board with us."

"And here comes Dopey," said Lombard, pointing. "Or is it Grumpy? It certainly isn't Bashful."

VanderKamp reappeared, now naked save for a pair of very baggy Lycra shorts.

"Not the prettiest sight," Lombard added in a

murmur. "A fucking bare-arsed dwarf in a black diaper."

I'm not ashamed to say I sniggered.

"I suppose you want me to go all Vamana now," VanderKamp drawled.

"If you'd be so good," said Bhatnagar.

VanderKamp scowled in concentration. I swear to God he looked like someone trying to take a dump, straining against a constipated lower colon.

And then he grew.

Muscles warped. Skin distended. I heard a *creak* and a *crack* like a falling tree, as bones elongated and gained mass and density.

VanderKamp swelled to the size of an average man, and just kept on going. Tendons writhed like snakes. Veins engorged to the thickness of vines. He grimaced and grunted. This was not a pleasant procedure, clearly.

Now he was ten feet tall and proportionately wide.

Now fifteen feet.

He topped out at twenty-five, a genuine giant. The shorts had become a tight thong restraining a set of genitalia so large it still makes me shudder just thinking about them.

VanderKamp reached for a palm tree planted close by. It was only slightly taller than he was. With a booming growl he wrenched it out of the soil, braced the trunk across his knee, and snapped it in two. Then he waved the halves above his head like a caveman brandishing a pair of clubs.

"Let me have war, say I," he intoned, megaphone-loud.[1] "It exceeds peace as far as day does night; it's spritely, waking, audible, and full of vent. Peace is a very apoplexy, lethargy; mulled, deaf, sleepy, insensible; a getter of more bastard children than war's a destroyer of men."

He dropped the broken tree.

"Is that all right?" he asked his three bosses archly. "Seen enough? Any notes on my performance? Or can I return to my dressing room?"

"Fine, thank you," said Bhatnagar. "You may go."

VanderKamp turned and strutted off, shrinking with every step until by the time he reached the exit from the courtyard he was back to his original squat dimensions, waddling rather than striding.

The Trinity Syndicate were all looking at me expectantly.

I groped for a response.

"That was... just... fucking... I did see all that, didn't I? I wasn't imagining any of it? It actually happened? One guy moved like greased lightning, the other *grew*?"

"Now are you convinced?" said Lombard.

"Well, yeah. Super powers. People with actual, honest-to-fuck super powers. How?"

"That's not important right now. What's important is, do you want the job?"

I laughed, hoarsely, perhaps a little hysterically. "Are you kidding? Does the Hulk wear purple trousers?"

---

[1] *Coriolanus*, Act IV, Scene 5.

Blank stares.

"That means yes, I'm in," I said. "Just tell me where to sign."

8. WHAT WOULD JACK KIRBY DO?

FOR THE NEXT fortnight I worked like I'd never worked before. I was no shirker to begin with, but for those first two weeks I put in hours that were downright ridiculous, twelve a day, often more. I stuck to my usual method, tried and trusted. I'd rough out a pencil draft, hand-ink it with brush and technical pen, then scan the result into the computer, polish it up, add grayscale and colour and effects overlays and whatever else, and hey presto, bingo-bango, job done.

I loved every fucking minute of it.

Perhaps I should rewind a little. At the very least I should fill in some background detail. I'm an artist, not a writer. I tell stories with pictures, not words. This business of stringing sentences together is still pretty new to me. I'm not sure I've got the hang of it yet. Bear with.

Dick Lombard you know. But what about his two accomplices? I should fill you in on them, at least in brief.

R. J. Krieger had made his fortune in biotechnology. He owned a couple of dozen laboratories worldwide and had registered around three hundred patents. GM crops were his forte, but he was involved in gene therapies and other medical applications of DNA manipulation as well. Not long before I met him, scientists on his payroll had made a breakthrough in creating stem cells that exhibited a heightened resistance to anti-cancer drugs, thus improving the success rates of courses of treatment, and another breakthrough in synthesising an artificial human growth hormone to help children with restricted physical development.

So, depending on your viewpoint, he was either Albert Schweitzer or Victor Frankenstein, all wrapped up in a drawling "aw, shucks" down-home package, a Southern gent with his hands on the building blocks of life.

As for Vignesh Bhatnagar, the "merchant of death" label wasn't undeserved. He was one of the world's most successful arms dealers, with extensive contacts and contracts in every trouble spot around the globe. He supplied weapons to dictatorships and insurgents, oppressors and freedom fighters, tyrants and rebel militias, admirably even-handed in his distribution of the tools of war. For him there was no good or bad, no right or wrong, no politics, no sides. There was only the buyer. As long as the bank transfer cleared, he didn't care who he sold what to.

But he wasn't merely a middleman. Bhatnagar manufactured as well as dealt. He prided himself on being able to offer ordnance that no one else could, exclusive items which were superior to most of the product available on the market and therefore commanded premium prices. These included grenade launchers with programmable targeting and range-finding, portable railgun rifles, cluster munitions with "smart" bomblets capable of distinguishing friend from foe, and recoilless electrical guns that could fire over 100,000 rounds per minute.[1]

So that was the Trinity Syndicate. Lombard, Krieger, Bhatnagar. Three plutocrats, each a genius in his own way, rich beyond imagining, masters of all they surveyed. Men who were as close to being gods as it was possible to get. Divine thanks to their wealth, their power, their status. Not subject to the same laws as you or me. Set apart. Unassailable. Untouchable. An elite.

And I'd been hired by them to work exclusively for them.

The studio they gave me to use was every comics artist's dream. For a start, it was mostly glass, and was flooded with steady equatorial sunlight all day long. Then there was the equipment: a fully adjustable glass-topped Futura drawing table, an ergonomic

---

[1] Let's face it, he was an Indian Tony Stark, but without the alcoholism or the goatee.

stool to go with it, and an iMac with a twenty-seven-inch screen, Intaglio graphics software, a Wacom drawing tablet and a Xerox DocuMate scanner. The art supplies were top-drawer, too, from Dixon Ticonderoga pencils in every hardness to Strathmore vellum Bristol board, from brushes tipped with Kolinsky sable to the whole spectrum of inks from good old Windsor and Newton, from kneaded rubber erasers to the most comprehensive set of French curves I had ever seen. I was in "doodler" heaven. I even had my own cappuccino maker sitting right by my desk, and if I wanted anything else to drink, or eat, all I had to do was pick up a phone, dial an internal extension, and within a quarter of an hour one of the Maldivian domestic staff would have brought whatever I'd ordered.

Don't tell anyone, but given those circumstances, I'd have done the job for free. Getting paid a six-figure sum was just the icing – the very thick, delicious icing – on the cake.

I was creating the costumes for the Dashavatara, the Ten Avatars.

My brief was this. The Trinity's superhero team were based on the Ten Avatars of Vishnu, from Hindu mythology. They derived their power sets, their weaponry choices and their skills from the ten incarnations which, according to the Vedas, the great god Vishnu assumed one after another when he descended into the realm of mortals to combat evil.

Why the Trinity had chosen Indian gods as their theme, I had no idea, not then. But the more online research I did for the costumes, the more I could see it was a rich seam to be tapped. Hindu gods did seem to have super powers and behave like crimefighters, whizzing here and there, righting wrongs, battling baddies, brawling with monsters and the like. Reimagining these ancient deities as bang-up-to-date superheroes – why not? Weirder things have happened. Stan Lee strip-mined the Norse sagas for his spandex take on Thor, after all, while Wonder Woman's origin and background draw deeply on Greek myth. There was a noble precedent for this.

So I was given photos of the faces of the Dashavatara for reference along with their vital statistics, and was invited to dress them up as devas – Hindu deities – but the look was to be modern, hip, slick, sleek, ultra-cool. The costumes had to be practical but dramatic, hard-wearing but striking.

It was one of those design jobs that I just loved to get my teeth into, fusing the old with the new, the traditional with the on-trend.

Aanandi was on hand to help. Another huge bonus. She was the resident Hindu-mythology consultant at Mount Meru, there to offer tips and advice on the whole project to anyone who asked, but, during the early stages of the costume designing process, she was almost exclusively mine. I'd spend a good couple of hours of each day going over the preliminary and interim sketches with her, batting ideas about, and flirting in my not terribly subtle way.

We could, for instance, be figuring out how to shape Varaha the Boar's helmet in order to accommodate his wickedly long tusks, and I might make some wisecrack along the lines of "It's not the size of the tusk, it's what you do with it," and she would give one of those laughs that women give to say they don't mind you being smutty but really you should have grown out of it by now.

Or, we might be discussing how Parashurama the Warrior should stow his battleaxe when he wasn't using it – on his back or by his side? – and Aanandi would tell me the legend of how, when Parashurama was a boy, he decapitated his mother with an axe at his father's request, because she had entertained lustful thoughts about a group of male nature spirits passing by, and I replied that there was nothing wrong with lustful thoughts and I had entertained quite a few of them myself in my time but I didn't deserve to get my head chopped off for it; or anything else chopped off, for that matter.

I took to calling Aanandi my "mythtress," and she took to pretending she didn't mind that I called her that. We had fun in that studio, the two of us, me probably more than her, but we did. I slipped into a creative groove, that soaring feeling you get inside when inspiration just keeps on coming and you're operating at peak efficiency and it seems you can do no wrong, and Aanandi was right there with me.

The first question I always used to ask myself when coming up with an image for a superhero was, "What would Jack Kirby do?" As a matter of fact it's the first question any self-respecting comics artists should ask himself or herself every single day before starting work. Kirby, rightly dubbed the King, was the man who defined how superhero comics should look. He codified the rules. He set the standard. The rest of us are just his followers, his acolytes, and "What would Jack Kirby do?" is our mantra.

But Kirby, aside from everything else, had a particular knack for a costume. Consider the Fantastic Four's utilitarian blue uniforms. Consider the star-spangled chainmail of Captain America. Consider the bonkers traffic-light bodysuit of Mister Miracle. Form follows function in every case. One glance tells you how the FF are a unit, a family, parts of a whole; how Cap is a patriot but also a knight; how super-escapologist Scott Free is all about the garish misdirection of the carny performer.

I channelled the spirit of Jack and poured it out onto paper and screen. My Ten Avatars of Vishnu were Hindu through and through. The bottom half of Matsya the Fish-man's flowing swimsuit had a suggestion of a dhoti kurta about it, while I sheathed Rama's bowstring-drawing arm from wrist to shoulder in golden bracelets and armlets. Kalkin the Horseman wore a version of jodhpurs, while I kitted Parashurama out in a kind of Mughal Empire chainmail armour. Yet, at the same time, I made the costumes as futuristic and outlandish as Kirby would have. I imagined him standing at my shoulder, cigar clenched between his teeth, saying in his gruff Lower East Side accent, "This mayn't be how Indian gods usually look, but damn it, this is how they *oughtta* look!"

It was my brainwave to give the Dashavatara individual numbers, worn as chest emblems, the numerals contained in circles and hanging from a horizontal bar, typeset in a Sanskrit-style sci-fi font of my own devising. I wasn't sure the Trinity chaps would go for this. Maybe they'd think it a bit tacky, a bit low-rent, kind of too obvious, too football team. But when I submitted the number emblems to them via the Mount Meru intranet for their inspection, the response was a hearty, three-for-three thumbs up.

Thus the Avatars were given a set of universally recognisable insignia which reflected the sequence in which Vishnu had manifested as them over the ages:

1 matsya the fish-man
2 kurma the turtle
3 varaha the boar
4 narasimha the man-lion
5 vamana the dwarf
6 parashurama the warrior
7 rama the archer
8 krishna the charioteer
9 buddha the peacemaker
10 kalkin the horseman

It was Aanandi who pointed out to me that there was a correspondence with evolution in that running order. Vishnu made his first appearance as an amphibian, then as a reptile, then a mammal, then a human-mammal hybrid, then a kind of proto-human, and so on through levels of increasing social and martial sophistication. The Vedas, she said, weren't only anthologies of myths. They were commonly regarded as scientific and historical textbooks as well. In fact, some Hindu scholars argued that these religious scriptures contained specimens of knowledge dating back to a millennia-old prehistorical civilisation, long gone and forgotten. Possibly even a civilisation founded by extraterrestrials with technological capabilities far in advance of our own.

I chuckled at that, and so did Aanandi, although not as derisively as me.

9. THE GREAT UNVEILING

By THE END of that two-week flurry of activity the costume designs were finalised, approved, signed off on. I was knackered.

There was no resting on my laurels, though. The costume department got to work – a group of a dozen seamstresses and dressmakers drawn from the world of movies, most of them Hollywood professionals with impressive credentials and even an Oscar or two under their couture belts – and I remained involved through the countless tweaks and alterations that followed. Not everything I had drawn was practically feasible. In comics, if a character's outfit defies logic, it doesn't matter; it's comics. The laws of imagination are in effect, not the laws of physics. Catwoman's skintight PVC catsuit would restrict her movements when leaping across Gotham City rooftops and probably be biting painfully into her crotch by the end of a hard night's burgling. Thor's bulky cape would get in the way when swinging his hammer. The hood sometimes worn by Green Arrow, to remind readers of Robin Hood, would severely limit his peripheral vision and make it easy for enemies to sneak up on him from the side. But no one's bothered by any of that when they see it on the page. In comics, image is all.

Our Dashavatara, however, needed not to have to worry that they were going to trip over dangling cloth or be unable to draw a weapon smoothly. There could be nothing in their costumes hampering them or inhibiting them in any way.

For example, the mane-like headdress I gave Narasimha was, as originally conceived, too long, too shaggy. We tested it out on a volunteer model, and the fibres kept flopping forwards, getting in his eyes, especially when there was a strong breeze. So they had to be shortened, and the headdress ended up more like a ruff than a mane.

Kurma's turtle armour was another headache. It had to be lightweight but durable, able to withstand substantial punishment, so the Trinity drafted in a technician from one of Bhatnagar's R and D labs who was developing an experimental carbon nanotube reinforced polymer for use in bulletproof vests. The polymer, it turned out, wasn't easy to work into complicated shapes, and my grandiose plans for the armour, reflecting the Mughal Empire stylings of Parashurama's, had to be streamlined and simplified. The design ended up much blockier than I had envisioned, more like a spacesuit than a shell, albeit with distinct turtle-esque traits. Compromise, compromise, compromise.

As for Vamana, how do you fashion a costume that fits someone when they're three feet tall as tidily as it does when they're twenty-five feet tall? The answer is: with difficulty. Lycra will stretch only so far before snapping. I just hadn't considered this when coming up with my design. So it was literally back to the drawing board for me. Liaising with the costumiers, I figured out that segmented leather panels interspersed with sections of folded elastane would give Vamana just enough growing room. There was an element of caterpillar about the end product, and an element of concertina too, but it worked, which was the main thing.

Did I mind any of this extra tinkering and tailoring? Did I hell. Perfectionist, remember? Anything to get it right.

I hope all this behind-the-scenes nitty-gritty is interesting. I suspect it may not be for everyone, and for that reason I'm going to fast forward to the day the Dashavatara first stepped out in their finished costumes. It was also the day they saved New York.

10. REAL LIVE SUPERHEROES

THE TRINITY CALLED an assembly of Mount Meru's key workers, in whose number, flatteringly, I was included. We gathered on the esplanade at the island's western tip, near the docks. Here was where ferries, cruise ships and seaplanes were supposed to moor and deposit their cargoes of tourists, except of course that would never happen because the whole "hotel" concept had been nothing more than a a cover story. This place was never ever going to be a leisure complex. This was Mount Meru, the mythical axis of the cosmos, that sacred peak shaped in rings with the material world at its outer edge and Brahma's sublime, ineffable heavenly city at its summit. This was the Avatars' base of operations, their Fortress of Solitude, their Avengers Mansion, their Tracy Island.

While we waited for the great unveiling, Dick
Lombard delivered a speech. He thanked us for
our hard work. He apologised that we had had to
redouble our efforts in recent weeks and that many
of us had had to pull all-nighters in order to meet
the revised, accelerated schedule, which was due to
circumstances beyond anyone's control. The results,
he assured us, would be worth the bloodshot eyes
and the torn-out hair and the caffeine poisoning.

"This is a great day," he said. "Historic, even.
Today you are going to see, for the very first time,
something that up until now people have only read
about or watched movies about. Something that
has existed purely in the realms of fantasy. We've
achieved it through science, technology, imagination,
and good old-fashioned graft. The world has been
crying out for this. We're going to give it to them.
The official public announcement isn't for another
week, but here, for your delight and delectation, is
a sneak preview. Ladies and gentlemen, I present to
you... the Dashavatara!"

They emerged from indoors, one after another in
ascending numerical order, at five-second intervals, a
neatly choreographed entrance parade. Matsya first,
with his glossy turquoise skin and his flared gills.
Kurma with his sturdy, quasi-chelonian[1] armour.
Porcine Varaha. Leonine Narasimha. And on and
on. Rama looking haughty with his sleek recurve
bow. Buddha, serene.

---

[1] "Turtle-esque."

They were monstrous and absurd and alarming and beautiful and disconcerting and splendid. Lombard led a round of applause, the rest of us joining in, some enthusiastically, some more nervously. Here and there, a cheer.

I myself had no idea, at that time, how the Avatars had been created. Perhaps I should have asked, perhaps I should have been more curious, but I had been too caught up in a hurricane of creativity, and too dazzled by the lure of filthy lucre, to care. Men had been *remade* somehow. It was the only explanation that made sense, extraordinary though it was. Krieger's boffins had applied their gene modification knowhow to the question of gifting humans with super powers, and had succeeded.

Now, I beheld the fruits of our labours; not just my own, everyone's at Mount Meru, creatives and test tube jockeys and costumiers and armourers and number crunchers, the lot of us. The Avatars stood together in a huddle, amused by the reception they were getting, bemused by it too. They looked good in their new outfits. They looked right. Ego alert: I had come up trumps. From a purely aesthetic standpoint, I'd nailed it. The costumes were different in each case but there were design elements common to all of them, not least the numbers. They were self-evidently a team.

I gave in to a little fanboy thrill, an inner *squee* of geeky rapture. Not so long ago I had witnessed for myself what Narasimha and Vamana could do. I had also witnessed, back on that the day I first arrived on the island, Rama and Krishna in action – although it had been just a glimpse, scarcely even that.

Imagine what ten of them were capable of.

Superheroes.

Real live superheroes.

Gods on Earth.

Lombard continued with his speech. He was telling us how each of the volunteers for what he called "theogenesis" had been selected with care. Each had a particular speciality which made him right for his role as an Avatar. Each was keen to work for the betterment of mankind, and fight for it too.

There would have been more. Lombard loved the sound of his own voice. But then someone scurried out from the complex, a personal assistant or PR guy, one of the Trinity's smartly suited flunkies, our resident Armani army. He had an iPad in his hand and a worried frown on his face. He tugged Bhatnagar's sleeve and showed him something on the tablet's screen. Bhatnagar paled and drew Krieger's attention to the iPad. Krieger also paled. He tapped Lombard's shoulder.

"What?" said the Australian, breaking off testily. "What is it? You better have a ruddy good reason –"

"It's happened," said Krieger. "We thought it might, and it has."

"An asura," said Bhatnagar.

"Fair dinkum?" said Lombard.

"It can't be anything else," said Krieger.

"Where?"

"Manhattan, of all places."

I turned to Aanandi, who was nearby, and said, "Asura?"

Her expression was tight and grim. "Demon."

"You're shitting me."

"I wish I were." She hurried over to the Trinity to confer with them. Around me people murmured and exchanged looks. They seemed as much in the dark as I was.

Had she really said *demon*?

"Ah, everyone, if I could have your attention," said Lombard, hands raised. "Really. Shut your flaming gobs, will you? Okay. There are reports coming in – from one of my own news networks, as it happens – of ructions in New York. It's looking pretty much like an asura. Which sort, Aanandi?"

"A rakshasa, I think," said Aanandi. "Unless it's just some maniac on the loose. But I don't think it is."

"A rakshasa is attacking commuters on their way to work in Manhattan. Now, we, well, we sort of suspected we might have to face something like this. Maybe not so soon, but still. We've generated gods" – he indicated the Avatars – "and that was bound to create some sort of blowback. No coincidence, just karmic balance. Gods appear, so demons come crawling out of the woodwork. It's a contingency we've anticipated and prepared for. Fellas?"

He was addressing the Dashavatara directly now.

"Hate to do this to you. You've barely put on your glad rags, and already we're asking you to go out there and get busy."

Parashurama took a step forward from the others,

snapping off a sharp military salute. He was a broad-shouldered man-mountain, massively muscled, almost as wide as he was tall. I've seen bodybuilders less statuesque than him.[1]

"Sir," he said, "we are ready. This is what we were meant for. What we've trained for all this time. Let us go."

Lombard was mightily gratified by this response. "Do you speak for all ten of you, Parashurama?"

Without even turning round to check, Parashurama said, "Yes."

In next to no time the *Garuda* had been fuelled and prepped for takeoff, the Dashavatara were aboard, and the multi-platform adaptable personnel transporter was leaving its hangar and hauling out to sea, jet engine burring. It whisked off across the water and then was up, up and away, leaping aloft to commence its slingshot journey across Africa and the Atlantic to America.

---

[1] *Secret Origin:* His real name was Tyler Weston, and he was a Harvard valedictorian and an alumnus of West Point, joining the 3rd Ranger Battalion immediately afterwards as a second lieutenant. His father had been an enlisted man, and his grandfather. The army ran through his veins like magma through the Earth's crust.

11. A RAKSHASA AT GRAND CENTRAL

DOZENS OF US were gathered in one of the rec rooms, glued to the television. It had been four hours since the *Garuda* left. The Dashavatara were due to be touching down on the US East Coast any moment.

There were techies present and backroom boys and all sorts. Some of the domestic staff mingled among us, chattering to one another in mellifluous Divehi.

Aanandi, however, was nowhere to be seen. She had gone off with the Trinity to help oversee the Avatars' departure, and when she didn't return, that was when it dawned on me that she ranked higher in the pecking order than I had thought. My assumption had been that she was a minion, more or less on my level, a fellow underling, but it seemed she was close to the inner circle, if not inside it.

I felt disappointed about this, and obscurely threatened too. The disparity in our status ought not to be a stumbling block. It wouldn't prevent anything of a romantic nature developing between us. Would it? Then again, maybe this explained why, even though we had been getting on well together, I hadn't been making any real headway with her. That or my smouldering sexual allure was just not compelling enough, which was inconceivable.

The TV was tuned to a 24-hour rolling news channel, Lombard's very own US-based Epic News, which had first broken the story of the horrific assaults on commuters alighting from early-morning trains at New York's Grand Central Station. The reporting was confused. No one had a clear idea what was going on. The police had cordoned off an area a block wide around the rail terminal, and Epic News's on-the-spot correspondent, Melody Berkowitz, stood just outside a barricade of sawhorses and yellow tape, reiterating again and again the few facts she knew and speculating wildly about the rest. She was TV journalism at its rhinoplastied finest.

"What I can confirm," Berkowitz said, gripping the microphone, "is that at least twenty-two commuters are dead so far. Those are the known casualties, but I should stress that it's only a provisional figure and could easily rise. Their assailant – and we believe it's just the one man – has been leaping out from hiding to carry out vicious onslaughts on victims chosen apparently at random. It's suspected he's using the below-ground tracks, of which there are around a hundred arranged across two levels, to conceal himself and move about unseen. To be honest, information is hard to come by at this present moment, but we are hearing rumours that – and I still can't believe I'm saying this – that cannibalism may well be involved. It's almost too horrible to think about. I have with me NYPD spokesperson Armand Dominguez. Mr Dominguez, is there anything you can tell Epic News viewers about what's going on inside Grand Central?"

The camera operator pulled back for a two shot, revealing a portly, luxuriantly-coiffed Latino.

"Well, Melody," said Dominguez, "the situation is still fluid right now. What I can say is that the station has been evacuated of all rail users and Metropolitan Transportation Authority personnel, we have managed to extract the casualties, and we've got several dozen uniformed officers in there right now combing the premises, hunting the suspect, who seems to have gone to ground since the initial wave of attacks. We're confident we can have this wrapped up within the hour."

"But the site covers nearly fifty acres. That's a lot of ground to cover, a lot of places to lurk."

"We're confident we have the manpower for the job."

"And the stories we're hearing about cannibalism in the attacks – do you have any comment to make on that?"

"Not at this time," said Dominguez.

Berkowitz's scalpel-sharpened nostrils flared. "EMTs I've personally spoken to claim that the bodies of the deceased show signs of being partially eaten. Tooth marks."

"Again, I can't comment on that at this time. It's a fluid situation and these are the kinds of statements that can't be clarified or verified right now."

"Do you think this could maybe be the handiwork of a deranged mole person – a subway dweller who has, as it were, gone off the rails?"

"I am not in a position to confirm or deny that as a possibility. Someone is committing a spree killing, that much I am at liberty to say, and we will stop him."

The transmission cut back to the studio, where the anchorman began conducting a phone interview with an eyewitness, Lamorne Wilson, who ran a bakery concession on Graybar Passage, adjacent to the station's main concourse.

"Yeah, I saw something all right," said Wilson. "Only I ain't one hundred per cent sure *what* I saw, you with me? I was, like, opening up the shop, same as I do five-thirty AM every morning, and suddenly there was this screaming, this woman running across the concourse, running for her life. She was this Filipina, I seen her before. Overnight cleaner would be my guess. She usually came in round 'bout then to catch the train home. And this – this *thing* was chasing her. Jesus, man, its skin was black, but not like my skin's black, not African-American black, black like coal, black like oil, shiny, and its eyes glowed like flames, all red and huge. It was mean-looking, and it went kinda on all fours but it flowed as it moved, sort of like it was flying. I'm not crazy. I saw what I saw. I'm on the air, and I know millions of people are listening, and I'm telling you, and them, I ain't crazy. This was some sorta ... I gotta say it: monster. Seriously. A monster."

"No one's doubting your integrity, Lamorne, or your sanity," said the anchorman, Brett Bowen, a man so smug even his hairstyle seemed pleased with itself. "But are you willing to consider that it was just someone in a suit? A Halloween costume, perhaps?"

"No, man, no. That weren't no someone in a suit. It had these long fangs, like werewolf fangs, and a mouth way bigger than a mouth has any right being."

"They can do amazing things with special makeup and prosthetics in movies these days."

"It weren't no creature-feature monster," Wilson insisted, sounding justifiably irked. "It jumped on that woman and dug those fangs into the back of her neck, and then it kinda wrenched its head away, sideways, taking part of her neck with it. God, that was an awful noise, the flesh and stuff tearing. And she was still screaming – in agony, not in fright, now – and it had her pinned to the floor, and then it began – oh, man – began munching on her. I just ran, dude. Ran as fast as I could. Hightailed it. Got the hell outta Dodge. 'Cause no way was I gonna step up and fight that thing and help that lady. 'Cause the lady was as good as dead and I'd have been as good as dead too."

"Yes, well, forgivable, in the light of your evident distress," said Bowen, who then did that classic anchorman thing of frowning and cocking his head as he received an urgent instruction from the production gallery via his earpiece. "Ah. Seems we're going to have to terminate the interview there. We have breaking news from another corner of Manhattan. One of our Epic News traffic 'copters is on the scene, sending us these images. What are we seeing here?"

What we were seeing, in a shaky aerial shot, was the *Garuda*, which had just alighted on the East River immediately below Roosevelt Island.

"Appears to be some kind of, uh, aircraft," said a baffled Bowen in voiceover. "Anyone know what type? It's new to me. On the water. Is that a crash? Has it crashed? Anyone? Do we have anyone who can identify that aircraft? Folks, I don't categorically know what we're looking at here, but our traffic 'copter pilot tells us this vehicle, whatever it is, entered New York airspace just moments ago and set down in the river, or came down, we're not sure which, but we're relaying these images to you of what appears, maybe, to be a plane crash – or maybe not, because I'm not seeing any wreckage floating. Lots happening in New York City today. We'll keep you posted. Stay tuned, and we'll be right back with more Epic News after these messages."

The channel cut to a commercial for toilet bleach, and then the TV screen flickered and dissolved into static. An "ahhh" of dismay rippled around the rec room. Then a fresh image appeared on the screen, this one grainy and jittery. It showed silhouettes of people in a dimly-lit environment, their heads mostly, accompanied by muffled conversation.

One of the *Garuda* ground support crew twigged. "They've patched us into a live feed, from the Avatars. This is... Rama, most likely. Yeah. You know he's got that headband thing? Mini camera implanted in that. Him and Parashurama and Krishna all have one. Kurma too, I think. We're getting first-person footage of the Ten in *Garuda*'s loading bay, about to go out into the field. Holy shit. This is going to be awesome."

"Rama-vision," I said. "Rama-o-rama." Aanandi would have found it funny, had she been there. Francesca, too, only I wasn't thinking about her nearly so much these days.

Brightness flooded the screen as the hatch of the loading bay behind the *Garuda*'s main cabin opened The camera revealed an expanse of river and a stretch of Manhattan shoreline; FDR Drive, the trees of Peter Detmold Park, the high-rises beyond.

There was a lurch. The Avatars were aboard their sky sled, Krishna's chariot, with blue-skinned Krishna himself at the front manning the controls, guiding them steadily out onto a platform on the *Garuda*'s starboard flank. Matsya and Vamana were visible in the foreground, the latter mugging for the camera, giving peace signs and sticking out his tongue.

VanderKamp had always annoyed me on screen, bigging himself up and boasting about his thespian triumphs. You can hardly blame a dwarf for having "little man" syndrome, a pathological need to make up in personality what he lacked in stature, and there was no denying that VanderKamp was an accomplished actor who had not allowed his size to stand in his way, even to the point of tackling the great Shakespearean tragic roles such as Lear and Macbeth, to acclaim. But did he have to be quite such an obnoxiously bumptious fucktard?

"Hey, Klaus," the dwarf said to Matsya.

The Fish-man glared down at him through slitted eyes. "We are on duty, Vamana," he said in sibilant tones and with a marked German accent. "We will use our Avatar codenames at all times when in public."

"Yeah, sorry, Matsya." Vamana smirked. "Good point. Onstage. Don't break role. But this is great, isn't it? Action at last."

Matsya had nictitating membranes, under-eyelids that slid sideways across his eyes. He blinked them at Vamana. "Perhaps you are excited. But a rakshasa, if that is what we are facing, is nothing to be taken lightly. Recall our briefing with Aanandi? As with any asura, it is the sworn enemy of all devas, and it will not go down without a struggle."

"So there you have it," Vamana said to Rama's camera. "The team's pet amphibian has spoken. 'It vill not go down vizzout ein struggle, ja?'"

His sniggering was lost in a burst of noise as the chariot abruptly shot free of the *Garuda* and hurtled out over the river. The microphone in Rama's headband camera picked up nothing except the buffeting of the wind and the rumble of the chariot's rocket engine. There was, though, a quite clearly audible sigh from Rama, and I could have sworn I heard him mutter "*salaud*" under his breath. Rama was a Frenchman,[1] and if he thought Vamana was a – rough translation – wanker, then I couldn't fault his judgement... and I wanted him to be my friend.

The chariot streaked above the City That Never Sleeps and swooped to an elegant landing on 42nd Street just inside the police cordon, beside the Park Avenue Viaduct.

Immediately, inevitably, a score of New York's finest dropped their doughnuts and sprang into action. The Dashavatara were surrounded by a ring of cops, all with sidearms drawn and yelling out a barrage of contradictory commands: "Drop your weapons!" "Stand down!" "Hands on your heads!" "Hands where I can see them!" "Identify yourselves!" "Step out from the vehicle!" "Do not move!" "Stay where you are!"

This was Buddha's moment to shine.

"My friends," he said to the police officers, "my dear friends, there's no need for such hostility. We come in peace. We're here to help."

Even muffled and distorted over Rama's headband mike, that voice was remarkable. Calm, measured, persuasive. Like chocolate dipped in honey and

---

[1] *Secret Origin:* He was Jean-Marc Belgarde, gold medallist in the men's recurve event at the FITA Archery World Cup three years running, and also winner of the Longines Prize for Precision trophy for scoring the most bullseyes during a single competitive season.

sprinkled with sugar. As Buddha continued to speak, reassuring the cops that the Avatars were a force for good and meant them no harm, I felt soothed myself. A sensation of warmth and wellbeing flowed through me. I wanted to hug someone. I wanted someone to hug me back. I could see others in the rec room experiencing much the same thing. A couple of IT nerds slipped an arm around each other's shoulders. A big beefy guy on the onsite security team discreetly wiped away a tear. I began thinking that harmony was such a wonderful concept, and conflict so futile. Why couldn't we all just get along? The world would be a far better place if everyone could only appreciate that despite all our differences we were all the same, just people. War, war is stupid. I hope the Russians love their children too. Ebony and ivory. All we are saying is give peace a chance.

And if Buddha's words were having that effect on me at a distance of nine thousand miles via a satellite linkup, what were they doing to those New York cops standing just yards away from him?

"So put away your guns, why don't you?" he said. "Be reasonable. Show understanding. There's no need to fear us. We are your friends. We wish this carnage to end as much as you do, and we're here to make that happen."

The police officers holstered their pistols, with puzzled frowns, as though they couldn't quite figure out why. They offered one another apologetic smiles and shrugs, and the most senior of them, a sergeant I think, said to Buddha, "Our people have engaged the suspect. We've heard firearms discharge over the shortwave, and we're awaiting further communications. There may be nothing for you to do in there. It could all be over."

"We'll take a look anyway."

"You're welcome to. Just be careful, all right?" The sergeant tipped his cap to the Dashavatara with the stern, avuncular air of a B-movie beat cop who had just delivered a caution to a gang of rambunctious teenagers.

In return, I-Can't-Believe-It's-Not-Buddha just smiled benignly.[1]

Leaving Krishna minding the chariot, the rest of the Dashavatara made their way through the station entrance below the statue of Mercury, and ventured along onto the main concourse, with the four-faced clock above the information booth and the astronomical fresco arching overhead. Parashurama was in the lead, Narasimha just behind him. Kurma dogged along at their heels. Rama took the rear, bow raised, an arrow nocked and ready to fly. The onscreen image veered left and right, up and down, as he quartered his surroundings, scanning for targets. The bow and arrow remained in shot, a fixed constant.

The concourse was deserted, eerily empty given that it was midmorning Eastern Standard Time.

---

[1] *Secret Origin:* Prior to becoming an Avatar, he had been an ascetic yogi and professional life coach, Mohinder Dasgupta from Bangladesh. He had packed on the pounds since donning the mantle of Buddha but still moved with the lightness and nimbleness of a trim, limber man.

Visible on the Tennessee marble floor and on the double staircase were pools of blood and gobbets of torn flesh. The bodies had been carried out by the paramedics.

Narasimha knelt by one, dipped his finger in, sniffed the fingertip, and then licked it.

That brought noises of disgust from several people in the rec room.

"Gross," said someone.

"More lion than man," said someone else.

Narasimha straightened up. "I can taste it. It is in the blood. In the *fear* in the blood. Whatever did this was no human being. It was not of this world."

"Asura," said Kalkin. "Must be. Straight out of the pits of Yamapuri."

"It may come from Hell," said Rama, "but we can always send it back there."

"Tighten up, people," said Parashurama. "You know the drill. Stay together. Keep your wits about you."

The Dashavatara moved deeper into the station, descending to the subterranean track levels. There, they encountered the first corpse: one of the police officers who had been sent into the station to flush out the killer. The woman was decked out in tactical vest and NYPD cap. Her gun had been drawn but lay several yards away from her – along with her hand and forearm. The rest of her was an even less pretty sight. The tac vest had protected her about as much as a silk waistcoat would have. She had been gutted like a fish.

A couple of the Maldivians left the room, murmuring imprecations to Allah. One of the IT nerds felt light-headed and had to lie down. The rest of us continued to watch in appalled fascination.

There were more corpses strewn along the platforms. It had been a cop slaughter. Tattered blue shirts were soaked purple with blood. Everywhere there was evisceration, dismemberment, decapitation, not to mention the omnipresent bite marks.

Parashurama toe-nudged the spent shell casings that littered the floor. "At least they got off some shots, for all the good it did."

The tracks perspective away from the brightly lit platform, narrowing into darkness. The Avatars peered along them, wary, alert. Only a couple of trains had pulled in. The rest had been stalled further up the line once the attacks started.

"Matsya?" said Parashurama. "Those big eyes of yours picking up anything?"

"My vision is superior underwater," said Matsya, "but in air, no better than yours. Rama has the sharpest eyesight of any of us."

"Even I cannot see in the dark," said Rama.

"Hush!" Narasimha had a hand up. He was swivelling his head this way and that, his nostrils widened as far as they could go. "There are so many strong smells. Oil. Metal. Concrete. The blood and entrails. But I think..." He pointed, and his voice dropped to an urgent growl. "There. It knows we are here. It is coming towards us. So fast."

"Everybody," Parashurama barked. "Defensive positions."

The Dashavatara formed themselves into a circle, and then there was a scuffling, a screeching, lots of yelling, chaos. In the rec room we got glimpses of a black humanoid shape, like a mannequin carved from jet, moving swiftly, a glossy blur. One moment it was on Varaha's back and he was shaking frantically from side to side, trying to buck it off before it could sink its hideous fangs in. Next, it was grappling with Narasimha, the two of them locked in a furious embrace, both snarling and spitting. Then it was pounding on Kurma's armour, trying to tear through the nanotube polymer plates. A large fist batted it aside – the fist of Vamana, who had grown to his full height. All the while, Rama was calling out, "Get clear! I cannot make the shot if you don't all get clear!" And then he hissed, "*Merde!*" as, drawn by his shouts, the black thing had turned and made a beeline for him. It filled the entire screen, and there were panicked yelps in the rec room, as though the rakshasa was coming for *us*, as though it was somehow going to squeeze out from the TV and launch itself into our midst.[1] Glowing red eyes traced lens flare spirals. Above all the ruckus there was an audible *twang*, and then the beast was lurching away from the camera, an arrow protruding from its black hide somewhere in the abdominal region.

It was hurt, but it didn't seem any less deadly for

---

[1] A bit like the ghost girl in *Ring*, but without the scary long hair.

that. It rounded on Kalkin, who had a wickedly curved talwar in either hand. He slashed both sabres in an X pattern across the rakshasa's chest, and it reeled, keening horribly. Sticky, tarry blood spattered the platform and Kalkin's face.

The rakshasa scuttled down onto the track and limped off. It had had enough. These devas weren't easy pickings like ordinary humans were.

Parashurama gave chase, his battleaxe held high. He swung. There was a *chunk* sound, like a hatchet cleaving wood, only louder and wetter. The rakshasa let out a high-pitched shriek that reminded me of the blood-curdling noise urban foxes made when fighting in my garden, and then Narasimha sprang forth, straddling the creature's back, talons out. His *coup de grâce* blow severed the demon's head clean from its neck at a single swipe.

The image steadied. I could hear Rama panting. Vamana was looking startled and dazed, his head bowed beneath the ceiling. Varaha was feeling himself all over, checking to see that he was uninjured. Kalkin was saying, "Did we get it? Tell me we got it."

Buddha joined Parashurama and Narasimha down on the track. He approached the rakshasa and uttered what sounded like a prayer in Bengali. Switching to English, he said, "You are gone. You have acted only as your nature compelled you to. We bear you no ill will for that. You were savage but necessary, and your cycle through life will lead you to purification and oneness with the heart of creation eventually, as it does all of us."

"Yeah," said Vamana, shrinking down. "Or, to put it another way – you've just been deva'ed, you piss-ugly piece of shit."

12. THE SCOOP OF A LIFETIME

YOU CAN'T HAVE missed the footage of the Avatars' first public interview, such as it was. Even if you missed it as a live broadcast or repeated endlessly on Epic News and other channels for days afterwards, once it was up on YouTube it got about a kajillion hits worldwide. I'll bet there were monks in remote Himalayan lamaseries who watched it, families on Micronesian atolls who debated it for days afterwards.

The Avatars emerged from Grand Central victorious, lugging the rakshasa's remains with them. Melody Berkowitz and crew were waiting to pounce. Berkowitz, sensing the scoop of a lifetime, vaulted the police barricade and hustled across to them as fast as her Jimmy Choos would allow, holding her microphone out like a cattle prod. The questions came thick and fast: "Who are you guys? What is that thing you're carrying? Where are you from? Are you maybe superheroes?"

Cops closed in on Berkowitz, ordering her to get back behind the cordon. Buddha raised a hand and begged them to leave her be. He wished to speak. He wished to address the world.

The cops, once again in thrall to Buddha's voice, backed off. The Epic News camera operator, who was less intrepid than the onscreen talent and had stuck to the civilian side of the cordon, zoomed in for a close-up.

"We," said Buddha, "are the Dashavatara, the Ten Avatars of Vishnu. Our purpose is this: We wish to help. Whatever threats rear their heads, we will deal with. Whatever sinister powers endanger the safety of humankind, we will confront. Wherever innocent lives are in jeopardy, we will be there. It's that simple."

"Vishnu..." said Berkowitz, struggling to place the name. "So you're... gods?"

"Some might call us that."

"And this is what was attacking those people?" Berkowitz gestured at the dead rakshasa, which Parashurama and Narasimha were loading onto Krishna's chariot.

The camera operator tried to get a clear shot of the asura, but all he managed was a blurred glimpse of its flailing limbs as it tumbled out of sight into the sky sled's rear deck.

"A rakshasa," said Buddha. "A demon. Bloodthirsty. Driven by rage and hunger. Unrestrained by conscience. Ignorant of the sacred duties of dharma. Its only instinct is to slaughter and feast. That one was the first since the days of the scriptures to manifest in the mortal realm and wreak havoc. It will in all likelihood not be the last. There will be more of its kind to come, and worse, alas."

"But rest assured, we will stop them, as we stopped that one," said Kalkin.

"Yeah," said Vamana. "Kicking monster arse, that's what we Avatars do. Like Ghostbusters but thirty times cooler."

"Wait!" exclaimed Berkowitz. The Dashavatara had begun boarding the chariot. "Don't go yet. The Epic News audience – the world – deserves to know more about you. What are your names?"

"You can look that up," said Krishna.

"Google, Wikipedia," said Varaha, in his dry, drawling New Zealander accent.[1] "It's all there."

"For the time being all you need to know," said Parashurama, "is we're on the right side. Our siddhis – our powers – are in service of American citizens and the peoples of all nations."

"Will you be fighting terrorism?" Berkowitz asked as the chariot's engine began to cycle. "Going after Al Qaeda? Bringing peace to the Middle East?"

---

[1] *Secret Origin:* He had once simply been Stevie Craig, a committed Kiwi eco-activist who had been kicked out of several green organisations for being too radical. Now, as Varaha the Boar, he was the Avatar of Vishnu most closely associated with the Earth, its protector and upholder.

"I advise you to step back, ma'am," Parashurama said.

The chariot lifted off, and the hurricane downwash from its tilted rocket forced Berkowitz to retreat several paces. Her hair was thrown into chaos, whipping about her face. She kept lobbing questions at the Avatars, even as their transport roared out of earshot. The camera followed the chariot all the way down East 42nd Street until it was no more than a dot on the horizon, then resumed on Berkowitz, who was trying her best to fix her dishevelled coiffure.

"Well," she said, breathless, "I can't begin to describe the magnitude of what we've just seen, but I'll try. The Ten Avatars of Vishnu – gods, we're told, but they look like bona fide superheroes to me. And they fight demons. Slay demons. *Demons*. It's a lot to process. Everything, and I mean everything, has changed in an instant. This isn't the world we woke up in this morning. I'm... I'm finding it had to put into words. They're out there. They're here. Holy cow." She was lapsing into stunned inarticulacy. "Viewers, you have just witnessed something extraordinary. Unprecedented. We've entered a new era. Avatars. Superheroes. Whoa."

13. DOUBLE-PAGE SPREAD MONTAGE

WHAT I SHALL do now is the prose equivalent of what we in the artist biz call a montage.

In a comic this would be a double-page spread, a series of tableau images segueing one into the next without panel borders, straddling the staple fold. The captions would carry the reader's eye across the entire composition, making sure every section got its equal share of attention.

This montage is of the Dashavatara during the days immediately after New York, as they jetted around the planet battling one Vedic bad guy after another.

Here's them in Moscow taking on Kumbhakarna, a huge horned demon with Hulk-like musculature and Herculean strength. Kumbhakarna has been busy snacking on any Muscovites he can lay his hands on, snatching them up and biting off their heads like human Peperami sticks. The Avatars have pursued him halfway across the city, down into the Metro and up again, and are facing him in a final standoff in Red Square, with St Basil's Cathedral and the Kremlin wall forming a scenic backdrop to the action, church and state in all their pomp. Kumbhakarna, blood dripping from his mouth, is tearing up granite paving slabs and hurling them at his pursuers like missiles. His body is quilled with Rama's arrows. Varaha is charging at him, head down, tusks to the fore, ready to deliver the fatal blow which will disembowel the monster and end his rampage.

And now here's Paris in the spring, but we're far beneath the avenues and boulevards, in the city's maze of sewers and catacombs, because there is a nest of vetalas down here, slimy, nocturnal vampiric types, all snaggle teeth and pulpy albino axolotl flesh. They have been coming up through manholes during the wee small hours and dining on denizens of the Pigalle, Paris's red light district, pouncing on lap dancers, prostitutes and punters alike in the street, hauling them down below and draining their blood. Narasimha has led the Dashavatara to the nest thanks to his tracking skills and hyper-acute sense of smell, and Parashurama and Rama are making short work of the creatures, as is Matsya, who drags the vetalas down into the foetid waste-lumpy water and holds them under until they drown.[1]

---

[1] Lovely way to go. Couldn't happen to a nicer set of demons.

Here's another scene showing Matsya in his element. It's Venice, and Duryodhana, a villainous eldritch king, has been subjecting the city to a reign of terror. Armed with a massive mace, he has been cutting a swathe of devastation through *La Serenissima*, smashing down delicate, venerable Venetian buildings left, right and centre, a one-man demolition crew. The local authorities have been unable to prevent him or even catch him. Every time he runs into opposition he dives into the nearest canal and swims off underwater. Duryodhana is capable of holding his breath indefinitely. Luckily, Matsya is at home in an aquatic environment, can swim at speeds of up to twenty knots, and can see in watery murk as well as you or I can in broad daylight. He's as strong as a great white shark, too. He wrestles Duryodhana to the surface and onto dry land, where Krishna takes over. He and Duryodhana have history. They were on opposing sides on the battlefield during the war between the Kaurava brothers and the Pandava brothers, as chronicled in the *Mahabharata*, so it is fitting that Krishna again defeats him now. He grabs Duryodhana's mace handle and hauls him up high in his chariot, Duryodhana too stubborn to let go of the weapon. When they are at an altitude of several hundred feet he drops him, and Duryodhana plummets, landing on the Campanile in St Mark's Square and becoming impaled on its pyramidal spire. The bell tower, already suffering badly from subsidence, shudders under the impact. Cracks appear, and it collapses in a heap of red brick rubble, its five bells clanging mournfully as it falls. An architectural tragedy, but at least Venice is spared further ruin.

Here's Rahu, a shape-shifting asura, on the loose in the *favelas* of Mexico City. Rahu can adopt any humanoid form he wishes, but his transformations cannot fool Narasimha because his scent remains constant and is distinctively noxious. He has even at one point assumed the guise of a ten-year-old girl and feigned abject terror, but Narasimha's nose never lies. The shanty houses of the slums are flattened as Rahu finally morphs into his true shape, of a dragon with hooded eyes and an abnormally huge head, and engages the Avatars in a knock-down, drag-out fight. Vamana, at full height, begins strangling Rahu while Parashurama slashes at his body with his axe. Kurma is protecting some street children from becoming collateral damage. He shields them with his armour-clad body as a corrugated iron roof comes crashing down. Rahu, tail lashing and thrashing, dies.

And here, last of all, is Adi, an asura with serpentine attributes – scaly skin, reptilian eyes, lipless mouth – and a penchant for rape. He has been prowling the seedier corners of Bangkok, not just the Patpong district where the strip clubs are but the Khao San Road where the rundown backpacker hostels are. He has been violently molesting female tourists, sex workers, even ladyboys – he's not picky – leaving them with horrific injuries, but he receives his comeuppance at the hands of the Dashavatara. Buddha tries to talk him into surrendering peaceably, but his silver tongue seems not to work on Adi, who responds with a hiss and an insolent flicker of his own forked tongue. So Kalkin steps in with his talwars, slicing Adi to shreds, rending him limb from limb.

End of montage.[1]

It was a big deal, the Avatars' first appearance and early battles. All around the world the news wasn't about much else. Phone camera recordings of the Ten taken by members of the public fetched silly prices, networks outbidding one another to buy up every scrap of footage they could for broadcast, however wobbly or fragmentary. Same went for still snapshots and the print media. "Feeding frenzy" doesn't even begin to cover it.

Pundits and commentators queued up to give their opinions. On Twitter, nobody tweeted about much else. Roughly five hundred Facebook pages dedicated to the Avatars were set up within the first twenty-four hours.

The mighty Stan Lee himself, brainfather of the Marvel Comics universe, was so in demand as a talking head that he rented an outside broadcast van and stationed it in the driveway of his West Hollywood mansion, so that he wouldn't have to pinball around Los Angeles calling in at one TV studio after another all day long to talk superheroes.

---

[1] Interesting. That passage took me about an hour to write, and you perhaps three or four minutes to read. Whereas, if I'd drawn it, it would have taken me at least two days and more likely three, and you'd have looked at it for twenty, thirty seconds, a minute at most, before turning the page. There's a whole different creative-effort-to-audience-attention ratio between prose and art.

Western theologians were consulted, and most of them pooh-poohed the notion that the Avatars were genuine deities, while a minority attempted to reconcile the Avatars' godlike abilities with the existence of a monotheistic Creator, arguing that it must be all part of God's ineffable plan.

Hindu scholars cheerfully and gleefully explained the Avatars' mythological background and discussed their respective siddhis. They seemed to have no problem with the idea of gods from their religion being incarnated on Earth and re-enacting the motifs of the Vedas in a new guise. As one of them said, "Hinduism has evolved constantly over four thousand years, changing as different outside powers have invaded India and exerted influence, from the Persians to the British. Its core texts sprang from the collective consciousness of countless generations of Indians. It's more a worldview than a faith. So these Avatars do not present a dichotomy. They are not blasphemous. If they really are what they seem to be, they are merely Hinduism's latest model, Hinduism in an age when secularity and empiricism rule, an age when we accept only the real, the tangible, the concrete. They are postmodern Hinduism in the flesh."

14. PARANOID IN PARADISE

MOUNT MERU WAS the eye of the storm, the calm centre of the whirlwind. The Dashavatara came and went, travelling wherever their missions took them. The rest of us carried on about our business.

Some of us had more to do than others. I myself was pretty much redundant by this point, but since no one had suggested I should go home, I stayed. A call to Mrs Deakins confirmed that Herriman was okay. In fact, the blasted cat seemed to be thriving in my absence. Everyone on my street was aware that he was currently ownerless, and so everyone was looking after him. "He's getting rather fat," Mrs Deakins informed me. "If this keeps up he'll have a hard time getting through the catflap."

To occupy my days, so that I wasn't completely

at a loose end, I sketched possible upgrades for the Avatars' costumes. If their image ever needed freshening, I'd be ready. I also polished off the last few pages of the Mark Millar miniseries. It seemed daft not to finish the commission, seeing as I had the time.

Otherwise: plenty of swimming, sunbathing, reading, snoozing, boozing. The sea around Mount Meru was just beautiful, warm and calm and pellucid, like liquid glass, and there was a reef a couple of hundred yards off the sandbar promontory at the island's western tip that was fish-spotter heaven. I'd float above it, mask and snorkel on, looking down at thousands of finny creatures, from tiny electric-blue things no bigger than a paperclip to iridescent six-bar wrasse, all skittering around their coral metropolis beneath my hovering shadow. At times I felt like Godzilla terrorising the inhabitants of Tokyo. At other times I just felt like God.

One evening I heaved myself out of the sea to find Aanandi on the beach. I'd been in the water for an hour and a half and was as wrinkled as a prune. I flopped down next to her on the sand, heavy-limbed and near exhausted.

"Hello, stranger."

"Hello yourself," Aanandi said. "Want one?" She had a cooler with her, full of Tiger beer on ice.

"Don't mind if I do."

I uncapped the bottle and drank. I was glad that I'd been wearing a t-shirt while swimming in order to avoid sunburn. Aanandi did not need to behold the pallid frame of an Englishman who spent far too much time indoors and did not know the meaning of the word exercise. In particular she did not need to be exposed to his puffy midriff and budding moobs.

"How've things been?" I asked. "I've hardly seen you since it all kicked off."

"Good," she said. Distantly, distractedly. "Good."

"This is a lark, isn't it?" I said. "I mean, here we are, support team for a bunch of actual superheroes. The world out there is going nuts for them. Some people even think they're gods. We know better. They're not devas, they're very naughty boys." The Monty Python reference was lost on her. "How long's it going to last, do you reckon?"

"How long what?"

"Until people cotton on to the truth."

"No idea. It doesn't matter anyway. That's not part of the..."

She tailed off. I realised she was quite tipsy. There were at least three empties lying next to the cooler.

"Part of the...?" I prompted.

"Nothing."

"No, what were you going to say?"

"Nothing," she repeated, more insistently.

"Oh. Okay." I let it go. What did I care? It was her I was interested in, way more than the Trinity or the Dashavatara.

We gazed out to sea for a while. The sun was setting fast, turning water to flame.

"I'd like to draw you sometime," I said. "You have a great profile."

"Oh, for fuck's sake," Aanandi sighed. "Is that one of your pick-up lines? Is that how you get girls? 'Hey, look at me, I'm an artist, I'll draw you.' Could you be any cheesier?"

Guilty as charged. I'd pulled with that line, or tried to pull, on more than one occasion. Who wouldn't be flattered when offered the opportunity to be immortalised on paper? It was a date without any of the usual pressures or expenditures of a date.

"Yeah," I admitted sheepishly. "I must be a little rusty. Not working?"

"You think? Maybe if I was a Zak Zap fan I'd have gone weak at the knees, but I'm not and I haven't."

"I thought you liked my work. That's the impression I've been getting."

"You're talented, no doubt, but it's not as if I'm actually into comics. I have a life."

"Ah. Well. I see." I got to my feet. I had no idea why Aanandi had turned all snarky like this, why she'd soured on me, but I did know that there was nothing to be gained by my sticking around. "Thanks for the bev. I'm sorry I'm not important enough for you to talk to any more. I thought we had a, you know, a connection, you and me. Obviously I was wrong."

I'd gone three paces when she said, "No. Wait. I'm sorry. Come back."

I hesitated.

"I'm in a mood, I admit it," she said. "And your huffy passive-aggressive self-pity is not attractive. But still. I could do with company."

"All right," I relented. "But my fee is another Tiger."

"Done," Aanandi said, fishing out a fresh bottle and patting the sand beside her.

"I'm wondering why I'm still here," I said after downing half the bottle. "I've done my bit, haven't I? There isn't really any reason to keep me around."

"I'm wondering that, too," she said, adding quickly, "Kidding, I'm just kidding. I guess the Trinity think they still need you."

"Either that or they've forgotten about me."

"It's perfectly possible. As you can imagine, they're crazy busy right now. They've launched the Dashavatara. There's endless maintenance and management to be done."

"That was all very corporate-speak."

"They're corporate men. I spend a lot of time with them. Their influence must be rubbing off."

"But you make it sound like this is all some sort of grandiose business scheme. Isn't it about saving the world? Protecting humanity from danger?"

"Do you think that, Zak? Honestly?"

"I'd *like* to think that altruism lies at the heart of it. After all, I'm a superhero buff. Superheroes never fight crime for the money or the glory. They do it out of a sense of responsibility. It's a vocation. But maybe I'm naive."

"Do you have any inkling how much Lombard, Krieger and Bhatnagar have spent on this?" She jerked her head backwards to indicate Mount Meru.

"I'm guessing 'a lot.'"

"The technical term for it is, in fact, 'a buttload.' And they're not the types to just throw away huge sums of capital. They're going to want to see a return on their investment."

"They want to monetise the Avatars somehow?" I said. "How? Action figures, movies, licensing deals, lunchboxes, that sort of thing?"

Aanandi gave a hollow laugh. "You *are* naive. It's actually quite charming." She uncapped two more Tigers and handed me one, even though I hadn't finished the one I was on. I was building up a decent buzz. She, I could tell, was starting to reel. Her eyes were losing focus and her speech had developed a slight slur. She was getting herself drunk in that way that people who don't want to think too hard about their lives get themselves drunk. "I don't know if I haven't been wasting my time here."

"What, with me, on this beach?"

"No, Mister Ego. At Mount Meru. Maybe I'm not cut out for this job. I just... I couldn't resist. When they asked, when they told me what they were doing... I loved the myths, you see. My pop used to tell me them on his knee. Every night, those were my bedtime stories. Hindu folk tales. How King Kaushika tried to steal the yogi Vasistha's cow, only he ended up seeing that Vasistha's lifestyle was better than his own and so abandoned his kingdom to become a yogi himself instead. How mischievous Krishna hid the cowherd girls' clothes while they were bathing in the river, and how his foster mother accused him of eating earth and he opened his mouth and showed her the entire universe inside his throat. How the sage Rishyashringa made it stop raining and King Lomaharsha sent his daughter Shanta to seduce him and take away his chastity so that he lost his power and the drought ended. When I was really little I used to think my dad was making the stories up himself. I must've been about nine or ten when I finally learned they were taken from the *Upanishads* and the *Brahmana* and the *Mahabharata*. He'd sit there speaking in his thick accent, and I'd sit there listening with his beard tickling my head, and I loved it. I loved it all. And that's why I so wanted to be a part of this, because it would make it real, those stories, and I know my poppa would have loved to see it. Only now..."

"It's not what you expected."

"It's so much less. So much cheaper. So much more cynical. I can't explain. There are things you don't know and shouldn't know, Zak."

She turned to me, her eyes glistening, tears bright in the rays of the sinking sun.

"You really should leave," she said. "I'm telling you this as a friend. As someone who likes you and respects you and doesn't want to see you get sucked into something you may not be able to get out of. It's too late for me, probably. I'm in too deep. I'm compromised. You're not, not yet. Quit while you still can. Just tell the Trinity you're done, time to go. I can't see them objecting. Part on good terms with them and go back to your life and enjoy the money you've made and don't think about any of this any more."

"You're serious."

"As cancer."

"But... What *is* going on here, Aanandi? What am I missing?"

She tried to rise. She failed twice but managed it the third time. "I can't tell you. Won't. For your own good. Just take my advice. Please, Zak."

She sealed the request with a clumsy kiss on my forehead, and then she was gone, shambling down the beach with the beer cooler tucked under one arm, and I just sat there, puzzled and nonplussed, watching her walk off.

I had been given a warning. Unambiguously.

But about what?

Doubts were niggling at me. As though I'd sensed all along that something was off-kilter at Mount Meru, that the whole setup here was fundamentally unsound, but I had chosen to ignore my misgivings until now. The phrase "too good to be true" came to mind. And "gift horse."

With the Dashavatara, the Trinity were perpetrating a kind of lie, letting people believe they were one thing when they were actually another.

In which case, what else might they be lying about? Aanandi seemed to have been hinting that there was more than met the eye here, that there were secrets to be worried about. Was that why the Pakistani planes had harassed the *Garuda*? Did the Pakistani government have intelligence about Mount Meru that was giving them cause for concern?

The sun swelled and bloated. A palm swayed nearby in the cooling onshore breeze. Waves lapped at my feet. My brain churned.

Suddenly I was not happy at all.
Nothing seemed right.
Paranoid in paradise.

15. THE OZYMANDIAS SOLUTION

THERE'S A SEQUENCE in *Watchmen* – the graphic novel, not the movie – where a bunch of writers, artists and scientists are on a remote Pacific island, working on what they have been led to believe is a Hollywood movie featuring some kind of spectacular special-effects alien creature. It turns out that what they've instead been doing is creating the giant tentacled psychic monster thing which Ozymandias, the book's messianic nutjob baddie, uses at the end to shock the US and the USSR out of their brinkmanship and pull the world back from imminent nuclear Armageddon. Before that, though, the freighter on which the writers, artists and scientists are having a wrap party is blown up, killing them all. They are witnesses to Ozymandias's plan, potential liabilities.

They could blow the whistle on his audacious hoax, and so they must be got rid of.

This scenario played on continuous repeat in my head. Could it happen here? Were the Trinity ruthless megalomaniacs like Ozymandias, and once we Mount Meru minions had fulfilled our purpose would we too be cold-bloodedly eliminated?

Leaving the island was nigh-on impossible. Other than the cargo seaplane which brought supplies twice weekly from Malé, and of course the *Garuda*, there was no form of transportation on or off. What's more, nobody I knew of had actually left. I presumed this was because nobody had asked to or been invited to yet. Would consent be granted if anyone did want to go? Were we all being kept here in a gilded cage, *Prisoner*-fashion? Were we sitting complacently like sheep, happy in our pens, blissfully unaware of the coming slaughter?

I spent days in a state of dire anticipation, wishing I had never read *Watchmen*.[1]

I suppose I could have gone to the Trinity and let them know I was thinking about escaping, although of course I would call it "heading homeward." But here's the thing. They were pretty much inaccessible. They had apartments at the hub of Mount Meru, in its tallest central section. They ran the show from there and seldom ventured out into the complex's surrounding rings, at least not any more, not since the Dashavatara had gone public. They'd been in the

---

[1] See, kids? Comics *are* bad for you.

habit of popping over to visit us lowly subordinates, show their faces, rally the troops, once a day on average. But not now. Now they were remote and hard to reach. Even the odd email I sent them went unacknowledged.

And the inner reaches of the complex were *verboten* to the majority of the workforce, including me. Past the middle ring of the seven you needed a special swipe card to gain access. I found this out the hard way while roaming one afternoon. At the far end of a skybridge I came to a door that wouldn't open. I wrestled with it for a while, which drew me to the attention of a security officer, who politely but firmly steered me back the way I had come, saying I didn't have the appropriate clearance to go any further. I would have got snitty with him if he had been a twat about it, but the guy was niceness itself, which kind of spiked my guns. I enquired who *did* have clearance, and he told me it was above his pay grade to know the answer to that and above mine to ask.

Naturally, knowing there were parts of the island where certain members of personnel weren't entitled to go fuelled my paranoia. The obvious, reasonable explanation was that the Trinity had cards they wanted to play very close to their chests. They couldn't have everyone on the premises knowing everything they were up to. It wasn't sound business sense. All corporations compartmentalised, especially those with crucial proprietary interests they wanted to protect. Coca-Cola and their ingredient "Merchandise 7X," for example, or the

Chartreuse monks and their recipe of herbs and flowers, or Disney and Uncle Walt's cryogenically frozen head. The Avatars and theogenesis were the Trinity's. I could see why they'd prefer not to have random bods like me tramping through the hush-hush corners of their empire, intruding where we didn't belong, potentially stumbling on trade secrets we could sell to their rivals.

But I didn't like being excluded, and I really didn't like the feeling that the Trinity were pursuing some sort of hidden agenda, especially if it was one that might lead them to copy Ozymandias's method of tying up loose ends. Ignorance, in this instance, was *not* bliss.

I began identifying people who might work in Meru's inner recesses. Some of the computer techies, for instance, I was sure spent their daylight hours in the third ring. They were secretive about what they did, and had a slightly superior air. But then so did a lot of programmers.

One of them turned out to be a comics reader and a fan of my work, so I sounded him out, quizzing him casually about what he did. He wouldn't be drawn. He just kept shrugging and saying it was a job, nothing more. I even drew him a sketch of She-Hulk in a lingerie-clad lesbian clinch with Storm out of the X-Men, since he confessed that this had been one of his masturbation fantasies as a teenager.[1] He

---

[1] If memory serves, I had She-Hulk looking out from the page and gave her a speech bubble that read, "Come and join in, big boy, if you're ready." Classy, eh? But also a doff of the cap to John

was delighted with the gift, but it didn't get me any further. The ingrate.

Another guy, some sort of nurse or medical orderly, was similarly tight-lipped. I cornered him in one of the bars and bought him a drink, but every time I steered the subject round towards his role at Mount Meru he just brushed it aside. "I'm just here in case anyone gets hurt," was all he would offer. "Avatars, humans, whoever. They get broken, I help fix them." He then asked me if I was single, and I went into a tailspin of embarrassment. Talk about misinterpreted signals.

It was frustrating. Everyone was being so damn discreet. No one was letting slip even the smallest clue. These people knew more than I did, but they weren't sharing. Probably they were getting paid big bucks not to, or else they'd signed confidentiality agreements with penalties even more swingeing than the one I'd signed.

So I did something I am still not proud of.

I nicked Aanandi's swipe card.

I didn't plan to. I am not that much of a schemer. I certainly never went to her room with the express intention of purloining the swipe card. Until I spotted it on the floor I wasn't even aware that she had one, although why shouldn't she? Let's just call it a crime of opportunity.

I knocked on her door, toting a six-pack of Tiger from the canteen. My aim was nothing more than

---

Byrne's run on *Sensational She-Hulk* which had the character constantly breaking the fourth wall and addressing the reader.

to have a drink and a chat with her. Maybe I could get her to open up a bit more about the Trinity and their overarching goal. Maybe I was hoping to get her squiffy, lower her defences, then put the Zak Bramwell moves on her. I wouldn't be sorry if either approach got a result. I swear, though, that I had nothing devious or treacherous in mind.

No answer to my knock, so I tried the door handle. Perhaps she was in the en suite bathroom having a shower. "Coming in!" I announced. "Only me!" The door wasn't locked, you see. So, arguably, my stealing the swipe card was all her fault. If only she'd been a little more security conscious.

Her room was empty. It smelled of fragrance and the overall spring-freshness that women's rooms tend to have. It was tidy, too: the bed made, the clothes put away, not a chair or trinket out of place. A far cry from the malodorous, unruly pit I'd allowed my own room to become.

There were framed photos on the vanity unit, one of a bushily bearded Indian man with kindly, soulful eyes, another of the same man next to a graceful woman in a sari and headscarf with a bright red bindi on her forehead, he kissing her cheek, she hugging him. Aanandi's father and mother, had to be. They looked a sweet couple, very much in love, very much unlike my own argumentative parents whose marriage had ended when I was eleven in a divorce so acrimonious that neither of them even spoke to the other for the next five years. I envied her them.

There were no sounds from the bathroom. I was conscious of being where I shouldn't be, trespassing. I knew I should get out of there in case the rightful resident turned up and caught me.

But I couldn't go just yet. I stayed, looking round at Aanandi's things in a creepy, slightly stalkerish manner. I studied the books on her shelf, mostly textbooks on Hinduism, including two she had authored herself, *The Field Of Truth: A New Perspective On The Bhagavad Gita* and the catchily titled *Brahma's Lotus: Eastern Tradition Through Western Eyes*. I lingered beside her laptop, then accidentally-on-purpose hit a key so that her desktop popped up onscreen, although there was nothing of note there, just the usual icons. I even, God help me, checked in a couple of drawers in the hope of snatching a glimpse of underwear.

I realise this makes me seem like a pervert, but I'm not – I was simply doing what any red-blooded heterosexual male might have in those circumstances. I justified it to myself by telling myself that I was getting to know her better, covertly gleaning extra info about her which I could use to my advantage later.[1]

Then my gaze happened upon the swipe card, which Aanandi had left under the desk chair.

Did I say "left"? Clearly she had dropped it by accident. Most likely it had slipped out of her pocket the last time she'd sat down to work at her laptop,

---

[1] Which doesn't, I appreciate, make it sound any better.

and she didn't even know she hadn't got it on her right now.

I reckon that was what prompted me to pick it up and shove it into my own pocket: the conviction that Aanandi had already in a sense lost the swipe card and so would not be suspicious if she returned to her room and couldn't find it. Had it been sitting somewhere obvious, somewhere it was meant to be – on the bedside table, say – then I wouldn't have touched it. She would notice, would realise someone had snaffled it. As things were, I stood a decent chance of getting away with the theft.

No, not theft, I insisted to myself. I was merely taking temporary custody of the swipe card. I would put it back when I was done with it.

I crept out of the room and tiptoed down the corridor, super-furtive, like a spy. No one saw me.

The swipe card had Aanandi's photo on it.

It stated that she was Clearance Level Beta.

It was mine.

16. CHINATOWN NAGA
AND THE SHUJAU SIEGE

FOR TWO WHOLE days I didn't use the swipe card. Didn't dare. It sat in a drawer in my room, radiating a terrible guilty heat. Every time I went near its place of concealment I could feel its presence register on the internal Geiger counter of my conscience.

I knew what I ought to do was give it back to Aanandi and be shot of the damn thing. I could even miraculously "discover" the swipe card and earn myself a few brownie points. *Honestly, Aanandi, it was just lying there on the beach, half buried in the sand...*

But then my thoughts kept cycling back to *Watchmen* and the island's hidden, forbidden layers.

A couple of times I bumped into Aanandi and nearly owned up to my crime on the spot. I would have made a terrible secret agent. Although we didn't speak for that long on either occasion, the harder I tried to avoid using the word "swipe card," the closer it edged to the tip of my tongue. To keep from spitting it out, I repeatedly spun the conversation off in random new directions, no doubt leaving her with the impression that I had turned into a babbling loon.

Did Aanandi seem unusually distracted? Like someone who had lost something important such as a Clearance Level Beta swipe card?

Not so as you would notice. She came across as though nothing untoward had happened. Maybe she had already logged the swipe card as missing and obtained a replacement. Maybe she hadn't had to use it lately so still didn't realise it wasn't tucked safely away wherever it was meant to be. Either would account for why she was so apparently unflustered.

Come the morning of the third day I knew it was shit or get off the pot time. By now there was a very good chance that Aanandi would have noticed the swipe card's absence. In which case, she would have taken steps to get it cancelled, rendering it useless to me.

Two things happened that day that made up my mind.

The first was the Dashavatara taking a casualty while on a mission.

They were fighting a naga in the scenic setting of downtown Los Angeles. The conflict raged through the streets, sending Angelenos and sightseers fleeing in all directions. The naga, ten feet tall and bright green, was as quick as any snake, and as elusive. Every time the Avatars seemed to have it pinned down, it slithered out of their grasp and retaliated ferociously. Its humanoid upper body had enough strength to throw a car; its serpentine lower half propelled it along like living mercury.

The Dashavatara pursued the naga from Little Tokyo to the Civic Center to El Pueblo to Chinatown. They finally cornered it on the central plaza there, but the naga broke free from their corral. A pitched battle ensued along the pedestrianised streets, among the bazaars, jewellery stores and eateries.

Narasimha was in the thick of it, growling, as was Varaha. Parashurama kept swinging at the naga with his axe and missing; the creature was too fast. Between them, Avatars and naga, they caused untold millions of dollars' worth of property damage in the area. One pagoda-style dim sum restaurant was practically obliterated.

Eventually, almost out the other side of Chinatown, Vamana snatched the naga up by its tail, whirled it like a hammer thrower and flung it headlong into the West Gate. The landmark structure was more or less destroyed, collapsing into a rubble of camphor wood and shattered neon tubing. The naga, however, shrugged off the impact and launched itself back at the giant Avatar. Vamana shrank to normal size just in time, and the half-man/half-snake hurtled over his head and struck his teammate behind him.

This was Kalkin, who happened to be busy

shepherding an inquisitive I-Ching fortune teller back into his shop. He didn't see the naga coming.[1]

The naga collided with Kalkin and managed, while he was still reeling, to sink its fangs into his shoulder. The Horseman bellowed in pain and slashed backwards at the creature with one of his talwars, splitting its face open to the bone. The naga recoiled in a fury of hissing. Venom spurted from its maw, blood from its brow.

Rama shot it through the eye with an arrow, but the naga was still not quite done. It lunged again for Kalkin, who was on the ground, floored, rolling around in a paroxysm of agony. Kurma thrust his armoured self between them. Feet planted, he withstood the full brunt of the naga's attack. It rebounded off him, straight into the clutches of Narasimha, who unhesitatingly tore the monster's soft throat open.

The naga went down gargling on its own blood, its tail coiling and knotting.

Narasimha proceeded to pull it to pieces like a Christmas turkey. His face was distended in a leer of loathing, a primal disgust. By the time he was finished the naga looked like the floor of a particularly unhygienic abattoir. You could barely tell if it used to be man or snake or what.

Buddha knelt at Kalkin's side, scowling with concern. Kalkin's face was puffing up and turning black, foam poured from his mouth, and he was shuddering, going into convulsions.

---

[1] Neither did the fortune teller, which some might say shows a surprising lack of clairvoyance

Krishna descended in his chariot, and Parashurama loaded Kalkin aboard.

There was a hurried, anxious discussion among the Avatars. Should Kalkin be taken to a local hospital, Cedars-Sinai perhaps? Or should he be transported back to Mount Meru?

Parashurama was adamant. "People, there are established protocols. In the event of casualties, it's immediate medevac back to base."

Matsya raised his voice to object. It was seven hours from here to Mount Meru and Kalkin might not last the journey.

Parashurama interrupted him. "No buts. We can dose him with amrita in flight, which should help keep him stabilised. What we cannot do is allow a bunch of ER docs to tend to him. They have no idea what they're dealing with. The guys at Meru do. Avatar physiology is not normal physiology. Also, we operate under strict need-to-know conditions, and there's a heck of a lot about us that civilian medics do not need to know."

"Maybe we should put it to a show of hands," said Kurma in his soft Swedish accent.[1]

"This is not a goddamn democracy, Lindström!" Parashurama snapped, before instantly correcting himself: "I mean Kurma. We are combatants. We have orders. We follow them. That's all there is to it."

The *Garuda* was parked off Long Beach, in San Pedro Bay. The chariot got there in minutes, with all

---

[1] *Secret Origin:* Real name Eric Lindström. Caver, mountaineer, long-distance skier, all-round Nordic daredevil.

ten Avatars on board and the remains of the naga too. The *Garuda* itself was airborne not long after.

At Mount Meru, the Avatars' return was awaited tensely. An emergency medical team were on standby at the slipway from the *Garuda*'s hangar. For hours a nervous atmosphere prevailed. Updates on Kalkin's health kept filtering through, relayed from sources higher up. He was doing okay. He was holding on. The amrita was doing the trick.

What amrita actually was, I hadn't the foggiest, and nobody I asked knew either. Some kind of special Avatar medicine, was the general assumption. Until Parashurama had mentioned it on air, none of us in the lower ranks had ever heard of it.

When the *Garuda* was less than an hour out, a second crisis arose.

One of the domestic staff, a chef called Shujau, had locked himself in his kitchen and was threatening to turn on all the gas rings and blow himself to kingdom come, along with several of his colleagues and a large section of the complex.

The security team responded by shutting off the electricity to the kitchen at the mains and the supply of propane from the external storage tank.

Shujau, undeterred, set all of his workmates free save for one, a female dishwasher whom he had been holding hostage at knifepoint.

His demands were as simple as they were untenable. The Dashavatara must halt their activities immediately and permanently. They were an abomination, he declared, an affront to the

Prophet and to the One and Only God, praise be to His name. They must deny that they were gods themselves. They must renounce all claim to divinity and submit to the will of Allah. If not, Shujau would slit the dishwasher's throat, then his own.

It might appear that Shujau had become radicalised. That was how the security team read the situation, at any rate. They assumed he had not been properly vetted during the screening process, had somehow kept his extremist tendencies hidden from his interviewers. A Human Resources error. The upshot was a fundamentalist terrorist in our midst.

In hindsight, though, I think the likelier explanation is that Shujau just went a bit nuts. He had been on the island too long, and had gone stir crazy. He was, like many Maldivians, a devout Muslim and had been having trouble reconciling the Avatars' avowals of godhood with his understanding of the Qur'an. He had wrestled with this dilemma until finally he couldn't take it any more and flipped.

The security officers tried reasoning with Shujau through the kitchen door. They promised him that if he let the dishwasher go there would be no repercussions. Shujau would be allowed to leave the island and nothing more would be said about the incident.

Shujau refused. He didn't trust them, he said. They would surely kill him.

In truth, that was pretty much what the security guys were planning to do, should things turn really ugly. They had the Trinity's permission to resolve the hostage crisis by any means necessary, and several of them had accessed the onsite armoury to equip themselves with handguns. The Trinity insisted, however, that lethal force be used only as a last resort.

The negotiations through the door dragged on, Shujau becoming ever shriller and more stubbornly entrenched. Eventually the security team had heard one too many panicked cries for help from the dishwasher. In a pincer movement, a group of them broke through the grille on the serving hatch between the kitchen and the dining area, while another group kicked the door down and barged in.

Shujau was on the brink of drawing the carving knife blade across the dishwasher's throat, when one of the security officers tagged him with a taser and electrocuted the fuck out of him. After that Shujau didn't do much except wriggle on the floor and wet himself.

All this chaos and confusion was a sign; a sign that said, "Now's your chance. You're never going to get a better one. While everyone's distracted and flapping around with their knickers down, now is the time to grab that swipe card and use it, see how far you get with it, find out what you can."

So I did.

17. A COLLAGE OF DEVOTION

I AM NOT by nature an intrepid person. You've probably worked that out by now.

What I am, though, and have always been, is someone who resents being taken for a ride. I have a perilously low bullshit threshold. If a publisher was ever slow paying off an invoice or a contract contained a few too many ambiguously worded clauses, I had no problem making a fuss about it. I like to deal fairly with others, on the condition that they deal fairly with me. Muck me around, try to bamboozle me, and you'll get my hackles right up.

So that, I think, is how I found the nerve to penetrate the inner recesses of Mount Meru. My motivation wasn't curiosity or even courage. It was righteous indignation, a sense that someone was not being straight with me, that the Trinity were pulling a fast one.

Righteous indignation is not the same thing as bravery. I was scared as hell sneaking through to the fourth ring of the complex while everyone else was preoccupied with the Avatars' return and the Shujau kitchen siege. I was shitting enough bricks to build a second Westminster Abbey.

I made it to one of the locked doors without being spotted. I'll say this for Mount Meru: no CCTV cameras. Not a one. The Trinity didn't spy on their workers. To that extent, our overlords trusted us underlings.

I inserted the swipe card into the slot. There was no numeric pad, no PIN code to enter, thankfully. Slide swipe card through, wait for little LED light to flicker from red to green.

Which it did.

I couldn't quite believe it.

I heard the *clunk* of a bolt withdrawing electronically.

I depressed the handle.

I was through.

This ring of the complex, I quickly gathered, was all about the technology. It was decked out in the plain, functional style of an IT department: long sterile hallways, low-level lighting, with the hum and the ozone tang of electric current strong in the air. I imagined the headquarters of Apple or Facebook might look something like this, clean and uncluttered, an abundance of space as if to emphasise the increasing miniaturisation of computer hardware. *Hey, check out all that square footage we* don't *need any more*.

I passed doors marked Systems and Data Core and suchlike. I tried to act confident, like I belonged, in case I ran into anyone. It wasn't easy. I wanted to skulk, hug the walls, cast surreptitious looks all around.

One room seemed to be the ring's hub of operations. It was huge, amphitheatre-shaped, with a raised viewing gallery at the rear where I halted and took stock.

Dozens of plasma screens formed a curved wall, towering over a raked floor dotted with workstations. A handful of technicians were manning their posts, all seated with their backs to me, facing the screen wall. I thought of Mission Control at Houston, and the War Room in *Dr Strangelove*, and, damn it, Ozymandias's bank of televisions in which he divines the trends of the future like a wizard scrying into his crystal ball.

Each screen showed clips that were either live or recorded, I couldn't tell. They were all different and yet it didn't take me long to discern a common theme.

Worship.

Not just any kind of worship, though.

Hindu worship.

Shrines decked with offerings – fruit, flowers, jugs of water.

Idols of blue-skinned, multiple-armed deities wreathed in incense smoke.

Temples being visited by flocks of pilgrims dressed in a myriad of bright hues.

Families bowing before pictures tacked to the living room wall.

Businesspeople in the workplace tending ritually to statuettes set in alcoves.

Individuals with sacred cotton threads slung over their shoulders, sending up prayers.

Orange-garbed priests officiating at ceremonies.

A bride having her feet washed with milk and honey.

A corpse being cleaned and shaved in readiness for cremation.

A spring festival in a dusty village square, petals and coloured powder being hurled about by riotous laughing crowds.

Bathers dunking themselves in the hot-chocolate waters of the river Ganges.

A dreadlocked sadhu, skeleton-thin and covered in ash, adopting yoga postures that would cripple a cat.

Some of the clips were news feeds. Others were amateur camcorder jobs. Some were international broadcasts. Others were private uploads.

It was a vast, ever-changing collage of devotion. Everywhere it showed Indians of all ages and backgrounds attending to their religious duties. It spoke of a billion-strong nation whose faith interpenetrated their lives at every level. It ran the gamut from elaborate mass occasions to simple personal rites, from heaving throngs in public spaces to private daily acts of self-purification and mortification, from choral chants to solitary meditative mantras, from the joyous to the solemn.

It was dazzling and bewildering and in its way quite moving.

But, for me, it also raised a massive question.

Why?

What was with all these screens? What did the Trinity get from assembling hundreds, possibly thousands of scenes of Hindu worship in one place? What purpose did it serve?

I couldn't fathom it. There had to be a connection between this and the Dashavatara, clearly, but what was it?

One of the techies called across to the other, "Dude, where are we at, download-total-wise?"

"Just shy of five terabytes."

"That ought to be enough. Time for the three C's."

"Affirmative. Compress, classify, cache. And after that it's beer o'clock."

They were wrapping up for the day. That was my cue to move on. I could have stood and gawped at the screen wall for hours, but I didn't want one of the techies turning round and looking up and spotting me.

From the fourth ring to the third.

This one housed the Avatars' living quarters. They had sizeable individual suites, plus a gym, a swimming pool, a sauna, recreation rooms that made the well-equipped ones on the outer ring look paltry by comparison, and indoor and outdoor dining areas furnished like five star restaurants. I couldn't help but feel a tad jealous. The Ten were getting rock-star treatment, the full-on lap-of-luxury lifestyle. I wouldn't have minded a bit of that myself, even if it did mean I'd be obliged to keep jetting off at a moment's notice to put the smackdown on some grotesque supernatural beastie or other. The pros, in my view, well outweighed the cons.

My dissembling skills were put to the test as I walked past a spa outside which a pair of very pretty Maldivian girls sat on deckchairs. Both were in tunic and trousers and could only have been masseuses, although their lavish makeup and long, manicured nails hinted strongly that they were of the "happy finish" variety. Underneath their uniforms lurked some considerably skimpier and less formal clothing.[1]

They broke off from their conversation in Divehi to look at me, smiling with a touch of curiosity.

I smiled back and waved the swipe card at them, my thumb covering the picture of Aanandi. "Lovely evening, ladies," I said, and one of them nodded while the other turned back to the celebrity tittle-tattle rag she was reading. She pointed out a picture of an Indonesian soap actress to her companion and said something bitchy that made them both titter.

Phew. I had managed that far better than I'd expected to. Not in the Nick Fury super-spy league yet, but I had earned my basic covert operative credentials.

---

[1] That may just have been my foetid imagination, but I don't think so.

Onward to the second ring, and I was beginning to feel cocky. This was going well. In fact, it was a piece of cake. The swipe card was like an access all areas pass at a gig. It was allowing me to get as close to the stars of the show as I could wish. I doubted it would work for the innermost section of the complex, the Trinity's private sanctum. If there was a Clearance Level Beta, then there must be a Clearance Level Alpha, exclusive to Lombard, Krieger, and Bhatnagar. But that didn't matter. The second ring, surely, was where the truth lay. There, between the Avatars' accommodation and the Trinity's, I would learn what our bosses didn't want the majority of us to know.

And I did.

Boy, did I ever.

18. GODS IN SPANDEX

THE SECOND RING was a warren of laboratories. Through small windows inset into doors I peered at workbenches laden with biochemistry apparatus: centrifuges, beaker shakers, incubators, dry baths, microscopes and other machinery whose identity I would only learn later.[1] The equipment was all high-spec, to my layman's eye, cool white and gleaming with newness. Screensavers cycled on idling computer monitors, the Trinity Syndicate logo gently dodgeming.

There was also a room whose door did not have a window but did bear the spiky biohazard symbol

---

[1] Things like cell lysis homogenisers, spectrophotometers and gel electrophoresis analysers. I can reel off the names. Just don't ask me what any of them's actually *for*.

and a sophisticated-looking code lock. It was marked simply "Treatment Chamber," with a small plaque insisting that entry was for authorised personnel only and that Level A hazmat suits were mandatory beyond this point. I shrank back from this door, as well anyone might, given the warnings festooning it.

You didn't have to be the Dark Knight Detective to deduce that this Treatment Chamber was the place where theogenesis happened. Here, people were subjected to a sophisticated DNA manipulation process devised by R. J. Krieger's geneticist boffins and remade into Avatars. They went in ordinary and came out siddhi-wielding superhumans.

It was the stuff of science fiction, and I might have had trouble believing theogenesis was possible if I hadn't seen the evidence with my own eyes. What was surprising, in fact, was how easily everyone was taking the notion in their stride, not just me but the entire world. Superheroes were here. They had been created. It felt somehow... *inevitable*. For decades, comics had been defining and celebrating superheroes. You might even say that we had, as a race, been preparing ourselves for the day when paragons in form-fitting costumes would walk among us, combating evil, doing good. We had been psyching ourselves up for it through illustrated stories, fertilising the soil with the pop-culture mulch of cheap pulp fiction – and now they'd arrived. Science had made them, the same science that gave us vaccines and pacemakers and cochlear implants, improving lives on a daily basis. Science had advanced to the point where it could offer the ultimate improvement, super powers. The comicbook writers' dreams of incredible speed, heightened reflexes, extraordinary strength, enhanced senses, and all the rest, had been brought to fruition, through gene tinkering, and it was almost as though it was past due, as though we'd been waiting plenty long enough. Superheroes? About bloody time.

And superheroes tricked out as members of an established pantheon of gods? Why ever not? Gods were the ancients' superheroes, after all. Hercules performing his Labours, Thor battling Frost Giants, Quetzalcoatl the Feathered Serpent locked in constant rivalry with his were-jaguar brother Tezcatlipoca, Gilgamesh and Enkidu defeating lion-faced Humbaba and other monsters, demigod Cuchulainn defending Ulster from its foes by warping into a dreadful ogre-like warrior form at the height of his battle frenzy, Sun Wukong the Monkey King who could travel thousands of miles in a single somersault and transform magically into seventy-two different objects and animals, not forgetting that fellow from Nazareth who did some nifty magic tricks with wine, food and aquatic pedestrianism...

I could go on, but enough for now. We had been telling ourselves tales about super beings and their outlandish feats for centuries. Comicbook superheroes were just the latest iteration of an age-old trope. They were gods in spandex, and the Trinity had exploited this association to give their own superheroes a pre-established identity, a recognisable theme. Saved them from having to come up with a whole new one from scratch, didn't it?

I was mulling over these thoughts and trying to link them back to the wall of Hindu worship I'd seen in the fourth ring, and I was doing this so intently that I wasn't concentrating on anything much around me. I had become complacent. When I heard footfalls approaching round a corner, I didn't react as sharply or as smartly as I might have. Earlier I had breezed past the two, ahem, masseuses. I could see no reason why I shouldn't be able to pull off the same stunt again.

The man who appeared at the end of the corridor was short, balding and dressed in chino shorts and a breathtakingly ugly Hawaiian shirt. He was frowning through his bifocals at the tablet in his hand, but when he noticed me he didn't just give me the once over and carry on. He stopped in his tracks and his frown intensified to a scowl.

"Who are you?" he challenged. His accent was Russian, Eastern European, something like that, thickly guttural.

"It's all right." I flourished the swipe card, again cunningly obscuring the photo with my thumb. "I'm allowed to be here. Clearance Level Beta."

"That isn't what I asked, my friend," said the man, whom I'm going to call the Professor for the time being. "I have asked who you were, and I am asking it again. Name?"

"Uhh..."

Here's a handy tip. When someone – particularly someone who belongs somewhere where you don't – demands to know your name, the most useful response is not "Uhh..." You'd be far better off giving your actual name, or failing that a made-up one, and straight away, soon as you're invited to. "Uhh..." would suggest you're having to think about your answer, which in turn would suggest you're trying to avoid the truth or fabricate a lie. That, then, arouses suspicion.

"Let me see this," the Professor said brusquely, and before I could pocket the swipe card or, I don't know, swallow it or something, he had snatched it from my grasp and was squinting at it. "You are not Aanandi."

"Um, no. No, I'm not."

"So what the hell are you doing here, with her swipe card?"

"That's a very good question," I said, "and the explanation is –"

And I turned tail and started running.

The Professor was an oldish geezer, didn't look to be in great shape, potbellied from too many hours sitting on his backside fiddling with his test tubes. I didn't think he was going to give chase, and I was right.

He didn't have to. A couple of taps on his tablet interface, and an alarm started to *whoop-whoop*.

He also didn't have to give chase because he still had my, or rather Aanandi's, swipe card. I charged up to the nearest door back to the third ring, and couldn't open it for the simple reason that I had nothing to insert into the relevant slot. You needed a swipe card to travel both ways through the complex, outwards as well as inwards.

To summarise: I was buggered. Without the swipe card there was no hope of escape.

Or was there?

I gatecrashed into a lab, an unoccupied one on the edge of the ring. The alarm continued *whoop-whoop*ing, a discreet but insistent sound, loud enough to raise a commotion in this building but not be audible beyond. I scrambled over to the windows and fumbled with the catch on the nearest of them. Just as I got it undone, the Professor appeared in the doorway, accompanied by two security officers.

"That is him!" the Professor yelled. He jabbed a finger at me, quite unnecessarily seeing as I was the only other person present and there was no one else he could be referring to. "Improper clearance. No right being here. Not one of my assistants. I have never seen him before in my life."

I thrust the window open as far as it would go, which was about forty-five degrees, and stuck a leg out. Straddling the sill, I began squeezing myself through the gap. The security guys were dashing towards me.

Have I said that I was on one of the upper storeys? Perhaps I should have mentioned it. At the time, I myself had forgotten. I wasn't thinking straight. I just wanted to be out of there.

I swung my other leg over the sill, and then, guess what?

I fell.
Quite a long way.
Onto quite a hard surface.
Knocking myself unconscious for quite a while.
I know, right?

19. AN ELEVENTH MAN

I CAN MAKE light of it now, but it was a drop of some twenty feet, and my fall was broken by a shrubbery of strelitzia, but not so much by the flowering plants themselves as by the stone surround of the raised bed they were planted in. I felt a tremendous thwacking *crack* at the back of my head, and that was it. Lights out.

The first sound I heard when coming to was voices. They were talking low and urgently. About me.

"Cut him loose," said one. "Pay him off, let him go, make sure he doesn't forget about the gagging clauses in his contract. That's my first instinct. But failing that... We *have* been talking about expanding the line."

"Agreed," said a second voice. "Let's make him the offer. He's a suitable candidate, maybe even the ideal one, and he's right here under our noses. It'd save us having to search for anyone else."

"Or c) none of the above," said a third. "He's been a nuisance, and nuisances are like dog shit. They need to be bagged and binned."

The last was Lombard speaking. The other voices were Bhatnagar and Krieger.

I prised open my eyes. Pain was spiking through my skull, but it was someone else's pain, someone else's skull. Everything seemed fuzzy and glowy. I was ripped to the tits on some kind of wonderful medical-grade analgesic, and it took me some time to grasp that I was lying on a bed and not simply hovering in midair. It took me a little longer to register that the room I was in was a hospital-style single occupancy ward, a sickbay somewhere in the second ring.

The Trinity's voices faded in and out of intelligibility. At some point they became aware that I was awake. They peered over me, their heads like balloons, wafting and bobbing.

"Zak," said Lombard. "Zak, Zak, Zakko. Three words: what the fuck?"

"Uh, I, uh..."

"Pinching Aanandi's card. Breaking in. Poking around. Strewth, what was going through that pinhead brain of yours, mate?"

"I, ummm..."

"We have security systems for a reason. Some things are classified because they're not safe for any old drongo to know. Why couldn't you be content with what you had? Why'd you have to go snooping? What is *wrong* with you?"

"Er, you... I..."

Articulacy wasn't going to be possible right then. I had to accept that. The drugs were doing a fantastic job of keeping pain at bay, but they'd shrunk the language centre of my brain to the size of an amoeba.

I had no choice but to let Lombard rant on. He was halfway between angry and despairing, like my mother that time when I was seventeen and borrowed her car to drive to a convention in Birmingham where the great Frank Miller was guest of honour.[1] Lombard used more swearing than my mother had, but otherwise it was little different. More had been expected of me. I should have been better than this. I should have thought twice.

Once he was done chewing me out – and I was so away with the fairies, it made little impact – Bhatnagar stepped in. He struck a more conciliatory note, but in essence he was telling me I was finished at Mount Meru. I had crossed a line. Breached a trust.

---

[1] And by "borrowed" I mean "took without permission" and by "drove" I mean "wrote off on the A38 near Edgbaston." I couldn't afford the train fare on top of the con entry fee, and my mother refused to drive me there herself – "A two-hundred-mile round trip just to meet some long-haired American druggie?" – so taking the car seemed like the right thing to do even though I only had a provisional licence, because, after all, Frank fucking Miller. When was I going to get another chance to meet the genius behind *The Dark Knight Returns* in person and show him my portfolio? Of course Mum was relieved when I called from a payphone to tell her that I was alive and unhurt, but she was furious, too, quite understandably, that her beloved Golf GTi was totalled and I had broken the law. "Of all the stupid, reckless, irresponsible...!" etc., etc.

"We should be giving you your marching orders," he said. "Unless..."

He moved aside to make way for Krieger.

"My colleagues both have a point," said the Texan. "That was an asshole move, Zak. Truly. You're lucky we don't take legal action, sue you for industrial espionage or anything we like. We can have you in jail so fast, you'll be bending down in the shower to pick up the soap before you even realise where you are. But we don't want to do that. We wouldn't be in this room, we wouldn't be troubling ourselves to talk with you, if we didn't have something else in mind."

However pharmacologically stupefied I might have been, I could tell that what was coming next was important. I strained to pay every bit of attention to Krieger's words.

"You see, the Dashavatara took a hit yesterday in LA," he said. "Kalkin's going to be fine. That's the good news. The bad is that it's shown they're vulnerable – more so than we anticipated. We foresaw the odd injury, but with Kalkin it was touch and go. The docs here struggled. We came *this* close to losing the guy. And it's too soon, way too soon in the show, for us to be a man down. Ten can't become Nine. It won't look good. It won't play well."

"Superheroes have to last," Bhatnagar chimed in. "They can take their licks but they have to persevere. It's part of the paradigm."

I would have nodded but was afraid of what this might do to my head, which felt as fragile as an eggshell, so instead I grunted in agreement. It was true – indomitability was a crucial ingredient in the superhero recipe. Superheroes could be hurt, they could appear to die, they could even genuinely die, but they always had to come back, to keep slugging, to conquer the foe. That was what made them better than us and worthy of our adoration; not their powers per se, but the dogged, unflagging dedication with which they used them.

"What we need," said Krieger, "is backup. A reserve member. Someone we can trot out should the worst happen."

"A twelfth man, like in cricket," said Bhatnagar. "Only in this case, an eleventh."

"Me, I'm not in favour of the idea," Lombard grumbled. "Tampering with the original concept – it doesn't sit well with me. The Ten are ten because the mythology says there are ten of them. We start screwing around with that, who knows where it'll end up?"

"But the mythology is quite explicit," Bhatnagar insisted to his colleague. "There is room for an eleventh. I explained this to you. Rama is well known for having –"

"Let's not get ahead of ourselves," said Krieger, butting in. "Zak doesn't have to know everything just yet."

"Sure, no, not everything," I slurred. "'S cool."

"We reckon you may have the right credentials, Zak," said Bhatnagar. "We've been at pains to match each selectee to the Avatar he becomes.

Parashurama is an ex-soldier. Krishna, a cowherd in the Vedic tradition, was an actual cowherd before theogenesis. Kurma – a speleologist, resilient, unafraid of confinement and tight spaces. Kalkin – once a professional equestrian. We call it 'vocational determinism.' Type reflects type. It makes the change from base state to Avatar smoother and more... *organic*, for want of a better word. More logical. An evolution rather than a metamorphosis."

"Your profession, your background, your interests, should suit you well to being the deva we have in mind," said Krieger.

"Hold on," I said, but it came out as "hol' ah." Meaningless.

"I still disapprove," said Lombard, adding with a disgruntled sigh, "But the other two are keen, so what can I do? The Trinity's a fucking democracy, worse luck."

"When you're a little more compos mentis, Zak, perhaps we'll talk again," said Bhatnagar. "We just wanted to, as it were, plant the seed."

They departed. I tried to urge them to stay and explain further, but it was no use. I even raised a hand to grab Bhatnagar's arm, or thought I did, but the hand seemed to go nowhere. I looked at it and saw that it was attached by a cannula to an intravenous drip – as good as a shackle.

Time passed, and I dozed fitfully, and between dozes I wondered whether the Trinity had even been here. Could be I had dreamed their visit.

Medical staff came in at intervals to check on me,

examine me for signs of concussion, feed me. I had a call button so that every time the pain started to swell I could summon someone to adjust the IV's delivery of blessed relief and send me back to doped-up la-la-land.

One morning, after a couple of days of this, I awoke to find Aanandi at my bedside. I was feeling less groggy than before. The splitting headache was more or less gone, and with it the need for the analgesic.

"Hi," I said.

She smiled in greeting, but I can't say she looked happy.

"So," she said, "an upper-storey window. Genius."

"I panicked."

"They were worried you might have given yourself a subdural haematoma."

"I hit my head. No vital organs there."

"I'll say. Because only a brainless moron would have used my swipe card. *My* swipe card."

"I know, I know."

"Where did you get it?"

I recalled the excuse I had concocted in the event that I was going to return it to her. "Found it. On the beach."

"No. Really."

"Your room."

"Thought so. I knew someone had been in. You can tell. There's a slimeball in the PR department who's obsessed with me. A real pesterer; all paws and bad breath. I suspected it was him. Never occurred to me it might have been you."

"Sorry. The door wasn't locked."

"It is now, always. I won't be that careless again. Do you have any idea how much trouble I got into? Security thought I'd lent you the swipe card, like we were in cahoots. I had to protest my innocence 'til I was blue in the face. I'm not sure they don't still think I helped you."

"I'll make it right," I said. "Promise."

"Don't do me any fucking favours, Zak."

It hurt to have her so pissed off at me. If we'd ever had any bond between us, I had severed it with my deceit. Whether that was permanent... Well, that wasn't up to me. It could only be mended from her side.

I took heart from the slightly softer tone she then adopted.

"Listen. Word is, the Trinity are giving you a second chance. A very special second chance."

"So it seems."

"I think you should take it. I think you *have* to take it. They can seriously mess your shit up, those three. I think this is the classic 'offer you can't refuse.'"

"Do you know why? Why me? Why now?"

"I guess they'd prefer to have you in than out. Golden handcuffs. It's the neatest solution to the problem."

"The problem being that I've seen too much?"

"You haven't seen all that much, but what you have seen is enough," Aanandi said. "But it's also about timing and opportunity."

"They want to theogenise me. Deva-fy me."

"Yes. They need a pinch hitter, just in case."

"Baseball reference." I whisked a hand above my head. "Totally wasted on a Brit."

"It's a sweet deal, Zak. Though I'm not saying you shouldn't think carefully about it. You should. As carefully as you've ever thought about anything. What could you gain? What do you stand to lose?"

"I have a choice?"

"Not much of a one, but yes."

"Krieger seemed to imply that the alternative is being bought for a packet of cigarettes by the boss of B-wing."

"Worst-case scenario. They want you off-balance, intimidated. You've ticked them off, and nobody gets off lightly with ticking off the Trinity. But they're businessmen too, first and foremost. They're playing hardball. They can't help themselves. It's ingrained. It's how they get their way."

"Is this part of the sales pitch?" I asked. "You being here now?"

"You mean did the bosses send me in to sweet-talk you?" Aanandi half smiled. "Maybe. Maybe I came of my own free will. Does it matter?"

"Obviously not to you, because I'm the thieving bell-end who swiped your swipe card and landed you in the shit."

"That you are. Why in hell should I care what you do next?"

"But if you *were* someone who cared, what would your recommendation be? I mean, being honest now, not just toeing the party line. What would you do in my shoes?"

She shrugged. "Way I see it, Zak, you're a fan of superheroes. Always have been. You loved them as a kid. You still love them as an adult. You love them so much that you spend your life drawing pictures of them. Now someone is telling you they're willing to turn you into one. If it were me, it'd be a no brainer."

"And," I said, "as we've already established, I *am* a no brainer. One more question. Is it reversible? Theogenesis? If it doesn't agree with me or I decide I don't like it, can I go back to being just me?"

"Not to my knowledge. As far as I'm aware, it's a one-way ticket. Once it's done, it's done, and you just have to live with it. None of the others have seemed too worried about that."

"It's a hell of a commitment, though. A hell of a change."

"You scared?"

"No. Actually no." I sounded surprised, even to myself. I was already more than halfway to making my decision.

"To think," said Aanandi, "just a few days ago I was advising you to get out while you can. Now look at you."

"I know. I kind of wish I'd listened."

"Well, too late." Her smile was rueful. "You're in it now, up to your neck. The alternatives are sink or swim. If it were me, I'd start doggypaddling."

20. THEOGENESIS

THEY WARNED ME it wouldn't be pleasant. They never said just *how* unpleasant. Which was just as well, because if I'd known how grim an ordeal theogenesis was going to be, I would never have consented to go through with it.

A pair of orderlies came for me. Both of them were sheathed in pale blue hazmat suits, the material of which rustled and squeaked as they wheeled me on a gurney to the Treatment Chamber. By this point the propofol I had been given had really kicked in, and I was off my face, feeling limp, loved-up and wonderful.

Inside the room, the Professor was waiting. I'd learned that his name was Gennady Ivanovich Korolev, and he was a biochemist from Yekaterinburg with a list of qualifications, prizes and accomplishments as long as your arm. His speciality, aside from being spectacularly surly and wearing eye-watering shirts, was the use of protein cage structures – virus-like particles – for the packaging and targeted delivery of gene therapy drugs. He had explained to me earlier how, through a process called bioconjugation, he was able to link small molecules to proteins which became self-replicating when introduced into the host body. In this instance the host body was me and the small molecule was a reverse transcriptase enzyme which resequenced specific DNA strands in the telomere regions, causing chromosomal alteration and enhancement by means of wibble-wobble gobbledygook blah blah blah-di-blah... He had lost me somewhere around "bioconjugation," but happily he had a succinct, *Reader's Digest* version to hand.

"You have heard of 'god particle' in physics, yes? Higgs Boson? I have developed something similar. A 'god virus.' I infect you with it, you become god. Simple."

Put like that, it did sound simple. Yet also daunting, and I had plenty of questions. How safe was the process? Were there failures as well as successes? If so, what was the ratio of one to the other? What were the odds on me ending up a mangled, distorted mutant reject rather than a sleek, glorious deva? And assuming it did work and all went according to plan, what if, afterwards, I changed my mind and wanted to go back to being just plain old Zak Bramwell again?

Professor Korolev's response had been a hefty shrug and a liver-lipped scowl. "You wish to back out? Too late. You have made pact with Trinity. You have signed release forms. Decision is made. The time for second thoughts is past. No use being coward. Face up to your commitments like a man."

Not big on the bedside manner, this guy. Not one for the morale-boosting pep talk.

The propofol infusing my bloodstream had made all my fears vanish – *poof!* – in a cloud of euphoria, and now the orderlies were hoisting me from the gurney to a steel table with a moulded indentation of a human shape in it. I shivered at the metal's chilly touch. The orderlies attached a dozen dry electrodes to various parts of me until I was sprouting wires in all directions like some sort of cyber hedgehog. They then fastened fleece-lined Kevlar straps tightly across me, buckling them at the side.

"I can't move. Is this a bondage thing?" I tittered hysterically.

Professor Korolev appeared at my side, also in a hazmat suit. His bifocals glinted through the Lexan faceplate. "Is for your own good. So that you do not harm yourself with the thrashing about."

"Not harm," I mumbled. "Thrashing. Gotcha. It's a good thing you're all covered up, you know, prof. Can't see whatever Hawaiian monstrosity you've got on underneath. Be thankful for small mercies."

"Says adult man naked except for Joker underpants," Korolev replied. "Maybe you should be one wearing hazmat suit, huh? For mental health of others."

"*Lucky* Joker underpants. Never leave home without 'em."

"Lucky. So you wear on dates?"

"Without fail. Make a girl laugh, she'll go to bed with you."

"Is plan, I suppose. But if she laughs when seeing underpants, probably not best timing."

Through the faceplate and the bifocals I caught a hint of a twinkle in Korolev's eyes, a glimpse beneath his permafrost of grumpiness. Blame the propofol, but I found myself warming to him.

The table was swung up on a central axis until I was perpendicular. The orderlies rolled me towards a tall plexiglass tube that stood in the centre of the room, thick as a column in a Greek temple. At the press of a button, the front half of it swung outwards on hinges. The orderlies stationed me inside, then stepped back. The tube closed with a pneumatic sigh, sealing me within.

Korolev's voice came through via a speaker. "You are ready, Mr Bramwell?"

"Not ready. Braced, perhaps. Hey, this must be how a goldfish feels in its bowl." I gaped my mouth a couple of times, goldfish-fashion.

"*Dolboeb*," Korolev muttered.

"I heard that. I have no idea what it means, but I heard it and I think it's not nice."[1]

"I am commencing sequence to introduce vector virus. It comes in aerosolised form. Introduces itself

---

[1] It's *fuckhead*, if you must know.

into body most efficiently that way. Even penetration of membranes all over."

Through the plexiglass I watched the Russian biochemist prod at a rubber-sealed computer keyboard, taking time over it to compensate for the clumsiness of his gloved fingers.

"You will hear hissing, then see vapour. Stay calm. Breathe deeply."

Vents in the base of the tube began to whirr. Then, with a mechanical sibilance, mist began billowing in around my feet, wreathing slowly upwards. It bore a bluish tinge and smelled bitter, like salt marshes and lime zest.

If not for the propofol, I might have started panicking. I'd never been good with enclosed spaces anyway, and the rising vapour intensified my claustrophobia. Contrary to Korolev's instructions, I held my breath. It was instinctive more than anything. Meanwhile, beneath the blanket the sedative had laid over my thoughts, a faint, small voice was quailing: *Are you sure about this? Are you sure? Are you really sure?*

Finally I had to inhale. The vapour flowed down my throat and into my lungs. I coughed and spluttered. It was icy and acrid, like breathing in a vodka shot.

The vapour continued to rise and thicken, obscuring the Treatment Chamber from view. The last I saw of Korolev, he was bent over his computer, monitoring my vital signs. The orderlies, meanwhile, stood back watching me with curiosity. One of them

I recognised as the guy whose approaches I had rebuffed at the bar. He offered me a thumbs up as the vapour completely filled the tube.

Cut off, alone, I gradually adjusted to the taste and feel of the vapour.

This isn't so bad, I thought. *What was everyone so stressed about? I can handle this.*

Then the pain slammed into me.

It seemed to come from nowhere and everywhere at once. It wasn't localised. It was *everything*, every part of my body, from inner organs to muscle fibre, from bone marrow to skin.

My limbs convulsed. Uncontrollable shudders coursed through me. I could feel my flesh squirming, as though there were pythons inside, coiling and writhing. My nerves were red-hot filaments.

My temperature rose steeply. Perspiration broke out all over me, dripping into my eyes. My stomach cramped, and bile burned the back of my throat.

What came next was a long, gruelling continuum of racking spasms, relentless nausea, wave upon wave of pain, and intermittent stretches of blissful blackout.

At some point extractor fans came on and the tube was vented clear. A sluicing rain came down from above, reeking of chemical disinfectants. After that, I vaguely recall the orderlies, still in their hazmat suits, switching the table back to horizontal and transferring me onto the gurney, then trundling me from the Treatment Chamber to another room. I was still riding storm surges of pain.

The orderlies rolled me into a coffin-like machine. This, I had been informed beforehand, was an Induction Cocoon. Not much larger than an MRI scanner, it was a tunnel of inward-pointing flat panel display TVs. The screens surrounded me entirely and played clips on a constant loop.

Over and over, kaleidoscopically, I was exposed to footage from a range of sources. Kids' cartoons, mobile uploads, movie sequences, blog videos, news reportage, documentary archive. All with one subject.

The hungry monkey leaps for the sun, mistaking it for a mango.

Hilltop temples in numerous locations, all believed to be the birthplace of a certain deva.

The deva, as a baby, accidentally dropped on a rock by his mother, the rock shattering, the baby unhurt.

The deva, as a child, mischievously swapping around yogis' personal effects.

The deva in fire, immune to the flames.

The deva hurtling across water like an arrow in flight.

The deva escaping from a fish monster's jaws.

The deva at Rama's side, battling a ten-headed demon king.

The deva freeing a cloud spirit, who has been cursed to inhabit the form of a crocodile.

The monkey, red-faced, enormously agile.

The monkey deva.

This was who I was going to be.

Through the shakes, through the fever sweats, through the scrim of pain, I watched worshippers coat idols of the deva with vermilion powder, ring a bell and chant to him. I watched them offer him new-moon prayers along with gifts of betel leaves, flower garlands, fried lentil cakes and butter.

Their voices intoned his name, the name of a god, my name-to-be.

Hanuman.

Hanuman.

Hanuman, Hanuman, Hanuman.

21. THE LOTUS ON THE LAKE

I DON'T KNOW how long I was inside the Induction Cocoon, bathing in the radiance of charged plasma, marinating in the welter of Hanuman imagery. Time has no meaning when you're in constant sickening agony and you're in an enclosed space without clocks or windows.

My body kept doing these herky-jerky twists and wrenches, like it was being manipulated by a particularly sadistic chiropractor. I felt it didn't belong to me any more. It was a runaway vehicle helter-skeltering down a hill, and I was strapped in, helpless, along for the ride and praying it wouldn't come to a messy end. Everyone all right?

And from all sides there was Hanuman. Hanuman, in countless different guises and interpretations.

Hanuman – trickster, deva, helper, strongman. Hanuman, agile and invulnerable, a true Hindu superhero.

I soon lost track of who I was. Who was I? Was I Zak? Was I Hanuman? Where did Hanuman end and Zak begin?

Had I been dropped on a rock as a baby?

Had I fought demon kings and liberated captive cloud spirits?

Had my life as Zachary Bramwell been nothing more than a dream? Had I imagined it all? Had I only thought I was a man with a semi-respectable career as a comics artists and a poor track record with women? Had I, deep down, really been someone else all along? Someone who could leap like lightning and whirl like a dervish? Someone brighter, faster, better?

Then came calm. A whiteness like a landscape after a blizzard, pure, silent, still. Uncertainties faded. Questions were quelled. I floated in a never-never of simple *being*. I was sure of nothing except that I was where I was, and where I was was where I was supposed to be. I can't help but think that this is how a foetus in the womb must feel. That state of utter belonging, cushioned and cosseted. Nothing to think about, life reduced to sheer essence.

The lotus.

All at once it sprang into my mind's eye.

A lotus flower on a lake, its stem reaching down through the brackish water, its root entrenched in the muddy bed.

Its petals, clenched at first, but gradually unfurling.

The lotus opening like an eye widening in comprehension.

The centre of all things.

The navel of creation.

The spirit of truth.

I gazed at the flower for a minute and a millennium. It was exquisitely white, its sevenfold layers of petal symmetrical and without blemish.

The lotus arose, enlarged, enfolded me. I was in the heart of it, adrift in soft nothingness. I wasn't scared. I had never been more content. All was light. Brightness. Weightlessness.

Who was I?

Zak Bramwell?

Hanuman?

It didn't matter. What was the difference?

22. BEING HANUMAN

THE FACE IN the mirror was definitely mine, only not. There had been changes.

The skin was redder, for one thing. My complexion was naturally pasty.[1] I'd developed a bit of a tan since arriving at Mount Meru, or at least turned a few shades less pale. Now, though, I boasted an earthy ochre hue, not unlike a Native American.

My cheekbones had filled out, too, and my brow was more pronounced, a deep overhanging ridge.

I was still me but, well... simian. Not like something out of *Planet Of The Apes*. In fact, there was a touch of the Hollywood actor Ben Stiller about my features now. Handsome, but in a monkeyish way.

---

[1] I have my father's Scots ancestry to thank for that. Also for my ginger-tinged hair.

"Hanuman," I said to myself, trying the name out for size. "Hanuman is what I am called. I am Hanuman."

"You are," said Korolev, who was studying me studying myself. "It can be disorientating, seeing reflection for first time after theogenesis. But the mind adjusts. As with plastic surgery patient, acceptance soon comes. Self is what self appears to be."

"Well, I am a bit weirded out," I admitted. "But it's not as freaky as it could have been. I mean, look at Matsya. All scaly and fishy. How long did it take him to come to terms with that?"

"Not so long at all. No time. Funny thing. He loves it. As Klaus Gottlieb, aquanaut and oceanographer, sea creatures were his life. He admired them – their grace, their variety, their ability to swim underwater unaided, not like him with clunky scuba gear. I think he liked them more than people. Antisocial, that was him. Always being called 'cold fish.' As Matsya, he has become all that he wanted to be. So, not much problem getting used to new look. He is more comfortable in his body than he ever was."

"And *my* body..." I took a step back from the mirror to bring my torso into view.

I was lithe. Lithe in a way that I hadn't been since my teens, before I was old enough to drink beer, before I settled into a sedentary profession, day after day sitting on my arse at the drawing board. I had a serious six-pack, where for many years there had been a doughnut of middle-aged flab. I had chiselled pectoral muscles. My arms were no longer stringy tubes of macaroni. They had what the gym bunnies all crave, definition.

I was a whole lot hairier than I used to be. There was that. A mat of the stuff covered my chest. My forearms had tufts starting a centimetre long at the wrist and rising to several inches at the elbow. My eyebrows were shaggier, too.

But it seemed a small price to pay for the overall improvement in my physique. I looked as I might have done had I been careful about my diet and exercised intensively for a year – and all I'd had to do was stand in a tube of blue mist for a while.[1]

I turned round to inspect the rear view. No tail. Thank fuck. I'd have had real problems with having a tail. That would have been a body modification too far.

"How do you feel, generally?" Korolev asked.

"Pretty damn good, all things considered. Energised. Like a kid again. Like I could do anything."

"Shall we put it to test?"

"How do you mean?"

"You are Hanuman. Do you know what Hanuman can do?"

"Sort of. Not exactly. No. I think I do, but then I also think I can play guitar and I only know four chords."

"Then how else you find out? You practise. You test."

---

[1] Oh, and go through a purgatory of excruciating pain. Let's not forget that.

"Okay. What do you have in mind?"

Half an hour later, we were outdoors with three of the Avatars: Rama, Parashurama and Vamana.

Parashurama and Vamana were guarded and sceptical.

"They're letting just anyone sign up?" said the Warrior.

"A week ago this bloke was fiddling about with drawings," said the Dwarf. "Now he thinks he's a deva?"

The Archer was somewhat more welcoming. "Let's give him a chance," Rama said. "I like the look of him."

"You would," said Parashurama. "He is your sidekick, after all."

Sidekick? Yes. Rama and I did have a history of partnership. I'd seen it in the Induction Cocoon. No, more than that, I knew it. Deep down I *knew*. I knew that Hanuman had helped Rama conquer the ten-headed demon king Ravana. I knew that Hanuman had gone in search of Sita, Rama's wife, whom Ravana had abducted and was holding prisoner on his island kingdom Lanka. I knew that Hanuman had been chased off the island by Ravana and his demon horde, who set fire to Hanuman's tail. I knew that Hanuman, immune to burning, had swished his tail back and forth, setting all the buildings on the island alight. I knew that Hanuman had mobilised an army of monkeys to build a bridge from India to Lanka which Rama crossed with his troops. I knew that Hanuman had fought side by side with Rama during the final pitched battle against Ravana, which resulted in victory for Rama and the rescue of Sita.

I hadn't been there, I hadn't done any of these things... and yet I had. Hanuman had, and I was Hanuman. And the fight with Ravana was just one of the many adventures I had shared with Rama as his loyal companion. As, yes, his sidekick.

So that was me, then. Robin the Boy Wonder to Rama's Batman. Bucky to his Captain America. Bullwinkle to his Rocky.

Somehow I didn't mind. It felt right. It felt preordained. It was the way it had to be.

What I did mind was that Rama had just unshouldered his bow and nocked an arrow. And was aiming it directly at me.

"Is this any way to treat your – ?" I began, and then Rama let loose the arrow and it was flying through the air.

I had never known an arrow move so slowly. It twanged away from the bowstring at normal speed but decelerated almost immediately, as though piercing an invisible wall of jelly. I watched it approach, feeling a sort of bemused fascination. I could even see the feather fletchings rippling and the shaft rotating as the arrow inched across the twenty feet between Rama and me. It was a simple thing, stepping out of its path. A feat on a par with avoiding a pensioner in a mobility scooter.

Rama sent another couple of arrows my way before the first reached me. Hitherto I'd marvelled at the uncanny speed with which he could shoot, reload from his quiver and shoot again. He could loose a dozen arrows in a handful of seconds.

Yet now he seemed inordinately leisurely-paced about it, as though he was barely trying. The second and third arrows sailed along their flight paths at protracted intervals. I counted my heartbeats between each. Seven at least.

Having dodged the very first arrow and then the first of the subsequent pair, I thought I would have some fun with the third, so I snatched it from midair and lobbed it back at Rama. A look of alarm crossed his face, and I sensed I had made a mistake. What if his reflexes, so rapid in matters of bowmanship, weren't as good when it came to evading missiles?

Parashurama's battleaxe descended with an almighty *swoosh*, chopping the arrow in half before it could rendezvous with Rama. As the two pieces fell harmlessly to the ground, the axe changed direction and swung towards me, scything at my head. I reared away, bending over backwards so that the blade cut only thin air.

Parashurama adjusted his stance and grip in order to bring the axe down vertically. He was grinning but his eyes were deadly serious. For all that this was a kind of hazing-the-newbie ritual, the Avatars weren't pulling their punches. They were playing rough, playing for keeps.

I somersaulted out of the axe's way. The impact of the blade shattered a paving stone.

Parashurama was fast. With him there was none of the time dilation I'd experienced with the arrows.

He was operating at the same heightened rate that I was. He recovered his footing and sprang at me with the battleaxe held aloft.

Instead of evasive-manoeuvring again, this time I leapt to meet him. I danced higher off the ground than he did, so high that I landed a foot on his shoulder and used him as a stepping stone to propel myself even further into the air. Parashurama crashed to earth. I came down light as a feather.

We pivoted to face each other.

"I have no idea how I'm doing this," I said. "It's mental. It's like it's the most natural thing in the world – and completely fucking *un*natural at the same time."

"You get used to it," Parashurama said. "You never stop being aware of it, but you stop noticing. If that makes any sense. Now stand still for a moment..."

He attacked, axe to the fore. I, of course, did not stand still. I'm not stupid. I darted to the nearest palm tree and shinned up the trunk to the top as easily as a – I'm going to say it – monkey.

The tree had a crop of young green coconuts at its crown, and these said just one thing to me: *ammo*. I plucked them one after another and flung them down at Parashurama like cannonballs. He sliced each one to pieces before it could hit him. The coconuts exploded in a spray of water and yellow pulp, some of which spattered Korolev, who was spectating nearby.

"My shirt!" he cried in dismay. "Is vintage Aloha from nineteen-fifties. Dry clean only. Very delicate."

"Looks better now, if you ask me," I said. "You've improved me; I'm returning the favour by improving your shirt."

"Ha ha, not very funny, I think."

"May not be for you, but me, I'm laughing my *arrrruuuullllp*!"

A pair of giant hands had clamped around my torso and hoisted me off the palm tree. Vamana. I'd been so busy mocking Korolev, I hadn't noticed Vamana sneaking up from behind. As much as a twenty-five-foot-tall dwarf can be said to sneak.

Vamana held me up in front of him, suspended by my wrists.

"Not so hilarious now, is it?" he sneered. "Struggle all you want, monkey boy. You're not going anywhere."

"Struggle?" I said, going limp. "Who's struggling? I'd much rather just hang, dude."

"It takes more than a bit of ballet and chucking some coconuts to be an Avatar. It takes sweat, dedication, talent, a few hard knocks... You can't just waltz in and grab it. You have to earn it."

"Aren't you confusing being a deva with being a diva?"[1]

"God, what an annoying little turd you are." Vamana brought me closer to his face. "I'd snap you in two like a wishbone if I thought I could get away with it."

"Don't bother, your breath is killing me as it is,"

---

[1] I'd been sitting on that pun for ages. Couldn't wait to use it.

I said, wincing and cringing aside. "Don't they sell mouthwash in giant-size bottles?"

Vamana bared his teeth in indignation, and it was just too tempting a target to resist, so I kicked him. Right in the upper incisors.

He recoiled, dropping me. Thrashing backwards, clutching his mouth, he collided with an outdoor table and chair set. His feet tangled up in them and he fell flat on his backside with a thunderous *thump*.

He was up again in no time and raging towards me.

Korolev could see the situation was turning nasty and barked, "Enough!"

Vamana ignored him and continued to make for me. He swiped at me with clenched fists, each as large as a beer keg. He wasn't anywhere near as quick as Parashurama, or as me for that matter, so I had no trouble staying unhit. I kept taunting him as I pirouetted again and again out of his reach. Lots of heightist gags. "Tall order." "It's a small world after all." "Oh, no! Enormous Oompa-Loompa on the loose!" Which only infuriated him further. Which made him attack with even greater frenzy. Which meant Korolev's repeated instructions to stand down were all the harder for him to heed.

Eventually Rama stepped in, putting himself between me and Vamana. His bow was drawn taut, arrow aimed unerringly at Vamana's eye.

"Calm down, Vamana. Don't make me shoot you."

"You wouldn't dare," the Dwarf growled.

"Try me and see."

"I'll swat you."

"Not before this arrow enters your brain."

They faced off for a good thirty seconds. Vamana was the one who blinked.

"This is not over," he said to me as he began to shrink to normal size. "Not by a long shot."

"Bite me, munchkin," I replied.

Vamana started to grow again, almost as if anger was inflating him, but Rama's arrow was still trained on his eye. Reluctantly, sullenly, he resumed shrinking.

As Vamana sloped off, escorted by Parashurama, Rama turned to me.

"You should not antagonise him," he advised in his lilting French accent. "Not if he is to be your ally someday. Hatred between comrades-in-arms does not win battles."

"Can't help it. Guy rubs me up the wrong way, or I do him. One or the other."

"Well, as for me, I am impressed." Rama stowed his bow over his shoulder. "You are fast. You are agile. You improvise well. You amuse. I look forward to working with you."

He extended a hand, and I would have shaken it, but all at once I was woozy, and the world seemed to be heaving up and down like a ship in heavy seas. I had to sit on my haunches and put my head between my thighs. It was the only way to make everything stop swaying and lurching, and even then it wasn't wholly successful.

"Korolev. Korolev!" Rama called out. "Hanuman is unwell. It looks like a siddhi crash."

Korolev came plodding over. "*Da*, is siddhi crash all right. He has overexerted. I should have realised. Too soon. Metabolism is still adjusting. He needs amrita dose. Help him up. Follow."

23. FAITH ENERGY

"Amrita," Korolev said, withdrawing the hypodermic from the crook of my elbow and sticking a cotton wool pad onto the injection wound. "Consists of tweaked fibroblast cells taken from salamander. Promotes growth of connective tissues and nerves, like in salamander which can not only regrow lost tail but also other parts like retinas and intestines. Using siddhis causes progressive physiological damage, especially if body is unaccustomed and unprepared. Like running marathon without proper training first. Drain on body's repair systems leads to symptoms you are experiencing – nausea, dizziness. Amrita is quick fix. Rejuvenating cocktail."

"Like a vodka Red Bull in a needle," I said.

Korolev deadpanned me. "Were you always wiseguy?"

"You bring it out in me, professor. I just love to see your face light up with that winning smile of yours."

The amrita swiftly took effect. I could feel it coursing through me. In the hypodermic it had been an innocuous-looking pale pink serum; inside me it was a warm golden glow that spread from my arm to my chest and onwards and outwards until it suffused me completely. My head cleared. The world's pitching, yawing motion settled down, the "waves" calming.

"It is the one drawback of being a deva," Rama said. "You become exhausted very quickly when in action. You can overtax yourself if you are not careful. A half-hour of full siddhi usage is the safe maximum. More than that and you are in danger of doing yourself permanent harm."

"Amrita helps," said Korolev, "but is not cure-all. Do not rely on it if you suffer catastrophic siddhi crash. It may not be enough. Better not to run risk in the first place. Start to feel weak in combat, withdraw. Do not carry on. At worst, result could be respiratory failure and cardiac arrest."

"Don't overdo it, or die," I said. "Gotcha. I knew there had to be a catch. You don't get something as cool as this without strings attached. With great power comes great drawbacks."

Rama patted my shoulder. "You are learning already, my monkey. Tell me, when you were in the Induction Cocoon, what did you see?"

"Apart from the Hanuman Channel, you mean? Nothing, really." I paused. "Unless you're talking about the lotus."

"The lotus is precisely what I am talking about." Rama looked satisfied. "Did you hear that, Professor Korolev? Unprompted, he mentions the lotus. It can't be coincidence."

"What about the lotus?" I asked. "What's it signify?"

Korolev grunted something in his mother tongue. You didn't have to speak fluent Russian to understand what he said. It was basically an elaborate *harrumph*.

"Each of us Avatars saw the lotus while in the Cocoon. It wasn't on any of the screens. It came from within, an image in the mind's eye only. The lotus is the crucial symbol in Hindu mythology. It is central to everything. It is known as 'padma' and it represents purity and divinity. The Vedas say that Brahma, Creator of Mankind, was born inside a lotus which arose from Vishnu's navel. The flower itself stands for the expansion and development of the soul. It is rooted in the mud of mundane things but rises above. It hardly seems to touch the water it floats on – that is how ethereal it is, how apart from the rest of existence. It is a state of oneness with the universe, of godhood."

"Blimey, have you been talking to Aanandi? This is just the sort of thing she loves to spout off about."

"As a matter of fact I have. I am quoting Mademoiselle Sengupta as best I can. I consulted her

on the subject of the lotus after I became curious
about it. Why would all of us devas see it during
theogenesis? It cannot be just some random delusion
or hallucination. We would not all have shared it if
it was. It must have manifested to us for a reason."

"Namely?"

"Do you know, Hanuman – Zak – precisely how it
is that we are Hindu gods and not any other kind?"

"Perhaps now is not time," said Korolev. "You
stray into classified territory, Rama."

"*Bouf.*" Rama puffed out his cheeks. Pure Gallic
couldn't-give-a-flying-fuck. "I think Zak is past that
now. He is a deva and has a right to know this."

"But Trinity..."

"Forgive me, Professor Korolev, but since when
do you care what the Trinity think? You are their
employee, but not their slave. As long as they keep
funding your research and paying you, you are
happy to work for them, but you are not some
lapdog, obedient to their every whim. Are you?"

"*Nyet, nyet, nyet,*" Korolev said, as dogmatically
as Khrushchev banging his shoe on the table at the
UN.

"This is not Soviet Russia, after all."

"Do not talk to me about Soviet Russia. I am old
enough to remember Soviet Russia. Old enough to
remember bread queues and bad cinema. Old enough
to remember my father disappearing to gulag for
two years and coming back a husk, with many toes
lost to frostbite. Just for making joke in bar about
Brezhnev counting medals on chest instead of sheep

to go to sleep at night." He looked at me. "And you wonder why I do not find anything funny."

"Hardly surprising if that's the standard of humour you grew up with," I said.

"The point," said Rama, shepherding us back on track, "is that Zak is Hanuman now, one of us. We know the truth, so why not him too? The Trinity will no doubt reveal it to him in due course, but why should he have to wait?"

"Cannot hurt, I suppose," begrudged Korolev.

"We are Hindu gods," Rama said to me, "not just because we were designed that way or because the Dashavatara are a convenient, ready-made superhero team. We are Hindu gods because the Hindu faith powers us."

"Huh?" I said, articulately.

"The footage shown to you in the Induction Cocoon is drawn from current Hindu religious practice. It is worship in electronic form, distilled, compacted, refined to its essence. Dick Lombard culls it from various origins using his media empire. With his TV stations, his satellite and cable services, and his internet interests, he has 'eyes' all across the planet. But recently, in this region, in India especially, he has been growing his market share, and in fact has gained a near monopoly. Little is broadcast around here that he doesn't have access to or owns outright. He has algorithms and search bots programmed to hunt through his networks, seeking out anything that involves the Hindu gods, which is then retrieved and routed to Mount Meru through satellite uplinks.

Lombard harvests it and stores it like wheat, and then it is fed to us as part of the theogenesis process."

"Is soil you sprout in," said Korolev. "Fertiliser that makes you grow."

"Hindus' worship is what gives us our shape and function," said Rama. "Hinduism is a living, thriving religion. 'The world's most popular form of polytheism,' as Aanandi described it to me. Did I pronounce that right? 'Polytheism' is a very difficult word for a Frenchman."

"Even I can't say it, and I'm English," I said.

"How many people are there in India?" Rama asked Korolev.

"Over one billion," said the biochemist. "One and a quarter, I think."

"And it is they who have made us. They who supply us with our siddhis and our deva characteristics. We are supported by one and a quarter billion individuals and their beliefs. They do not realise it, but every time they make an offering or perform a ritual, they are empowering us. Charging us up."

"Like a kind of living battery," I said.

"*Exactement.*"

"Shit. Is that really true?"

"To me, the lotus visions confirms it," said Rama. "It is an acknowledgement of the change we have undergone as devas. It is proof that we have been transformed as much by spirituality as by science, that we *are* gods, or at least the living incarnations of gods. No disrespect to *monsieur le professeur* here and his skills, of course."

"I am not so sure," said Korolev. "Is possible to explain theogenesis in purely non-metaphysical terms. Induction Cocoon, for example? Simple rerouting of neural pathways through intensive neurolinguistic conditioning. Process alters brain's chemistry and reinforces belief that you are deva."

"And how about the transfer of power to us from the Hindu faithful?"

"I have hypotheses. Quantum entanglement. Interaction through morphogenetic field. Something just a notch or two above us on the Clarke magic/ science spectrum."

"That sound you hear is the sound of straws being clutched," said Rama to me.

"However theogenesis works," Korolev declared, "what is true is that it does work and my science has made it possible. If I have harnessed spirituality through biochemical principles, then is to my credit. Is triumph of intellect – using religious faith as tool, bending it to my will in laboratory. I have fashioned men into vessels that are capable of receiving and storing the power of worship. Is kind of energy source, and I have turned you devas into conduits for it."

"He says that, but it wasn't *all* his doing."

"Bah." The Russian gave a dismissive shake of the head, like a terrier killing a rabbit. "So Krieger helped. So what?"

"More than helped, as I understand it. Krieger came up with the basic theory, *n'est-ce pas*? And supplied the fundamental building blocks for your, what is the name? God virus."

"Who is builder? Man who brings bricks to site or man who places them on top of one another to make house?" Korolev was the picture of defiant pride, thumping his chest, jutting his jaw. "Amrita at least is all mine, that cannot be denied. Except name, which comes from Bhatnagar, after so-called nectar of Hindu gods which gave them their immortality."

"So Krieger's more than just the man with the MBA?" I said. "He knows the stuff he trades in?"

"He is a biochemist of some repute," said Rama.

"Or someone who makes lucky discoveries," Korolev muttered, mostly under his breath. "Which is not same thing."

Back then, this remark sounded like nothing more than the bitchiness of professional rivalry. Only later would I learn what Korolev had really meant by it.

"This may sound like a stupid question," I said, "but what if Hindus stopped believing? Would our siddhis not work then?"

"That will not happen," said Rama. "How could it? Religion is core to their lives. It is something they engage in every day, without fail. A billion-plus people would not just suddenly give up their faith."

"Existence of Avatars only makes it stronger," said Korolev. "Hindus are more ardent than ever, now that they see their gods in flesh."

"Also, there have been converts. Hinduism is growing faster now than at any time in its history."

I'd heard about that. Since the Dashavatara went public, new Hindu temples had opened up in all regions of the world, and the existing ones were packed with newcomers, full to capacity and beyond. Pilgrimages to India were being undertaken by all sorts, not just the hippies and airy-fairy tie-dyed mystical types that you'd expect, but hardnosed businesspeople and arch-rationalists, men and women who had had their materialistic worldview completely overturned. Foreigners thronged the banks of the Ganges, descending the stone-stepped ghats and washing themselves in the silty waters. Faith tourists were flocking to Srirangam in Tamil Nadu, Akshardham in Delhi, Jagganath in Orissa and all of the religion's other principal holy shrines. Christians, Jews and Muslims were abandoning their solitary, aloof almighty in droves and prostrating themselves at the altars of gods who demonstrably existed, gods who didn't demand blind trust and obedience, gods who were irrefutably flesh-and-blood and having a tangible and beneficial impact on the world.

"Is positive feedback loop," said Korolev. "The more Avatars do, the more worshippers Hinduism gains. The more worshippers Hinduism gains, the more faith energy there is to fuel Avatars. Win-win situation."

"And the asuras?" I said. "Does belief create them too?"

Rama shook his head noncommittally. "Asuras seem to be a law unto themselves. We're not even sure where they sprang from."

"Lombard said something about karmic balance. The whole yin-yang thing. You order gods, demons come as an unavoidable side dish whether you want it or not. Like those salady bits you always get with your Indian takeaway."

"Is theory," said Korolev.

Again, there was a subtext here, but one I would recognise only in hindsight.

"Yes, perhaps asuras do gain their power, their existence, from belief," said Rama. "But that, too, works in our favour. With every asura we defeat our worldwide popularity increases, and so consequently do our siddhis grow. I have observed it in myself. During our most recent missions I have been even quicker with my bow, even more accurate. My marksmanship is such that it sometimes astounds me. It is as though I can *will* the arrow to its target. I only have to glance at what I wish to hit and the arrow goes there. I am barely aware of releasing the bowstring, and I no longer consciously think about variables such as wind speed and direction. It is automatic now, beyond instinct. I almost feel I could find the bullseye with my eyes shut."

"You're saying this is just the beginning?" I said. "I'm going to keep getting free upgrades?"

"While Hinduism continues to spread and prosper, yes."

If I had any last lingering qualms about becoming a deva, they were now dispelled. It was as though I'd been handed the keys to my very own Ferrari, and I didn't even have to pay for the petrol.

I couldn't wait to take my new sports car self out for a proper spin.

24. DELEGATION FROM NEW DELHI

I DIDN'T HAVE to wait that long.

The following day Mount Meru received visitors. A pair of seaplanes decanted them at the docks, where they and the Trinity greeted one another with plenty of gladhanding and obsequious backslapping. A huge banquet was laid on outdoors in an open-sided marquee, and the visitors took full advantage of the hospitality, troughing down on swordfish steaks, mahi-mahi curry and dressed crab, along with Maldivian specialities such as garudhiya[1] and thinly sliced strips of screwpine.[2]

They were a dozen-strong delegation of

---

[1] A clear fish broth. Yummy.
[2] Crazy name, crazy-looking fruit. Like a Mandelbrot set in plant form.

bureaucrats from India. Among their number were senior politicians, including the Cabinet Secretary and the Minister of External Affairs. There were a couple of high-ranking spooks: the Director General of the Defence Intelligence Agency and the Deputy Director of the Intelligence Bureau. There was also a smattering of military top brass, notably the Chairman of the Chiefs of Staff Committee and a ramrod-spined official who oversaw defence procurement for the country's entire armed forces.

After the last chunk of flatbread was used to sop up the last smear of curry sauce, but with the champagne still doing the rounds, we devas were ushered out and introduced personally to the Trinity's guests. Our instructions were to mingle and hobnob, not say or do anything controversial, just be friendly and polite.

It was quite startling the way the Indian VIPs acted around us. These were top-echelon representatives of government, secret service and military, used to commanding respect, yet they fawned over us, head-bobbling like crazy, offering us namaste after namaste, almost genuflecting. They were like Bollywood fans meeting their silver screen idols. I swear that the Deputy Speaker of the Lok Sabha, the lower house of parliament, nearly fainted at the sight of us. In a flash she was reduced from dignified elder stateswoman to breathless, hand-fanning schoolgirl.

"So amazing," the Minister of External Affairs kept saying. "So amazing."

We put on a siddhi display for them. None of us

particularly wanted to – it seemed cheap – but the Trinity insisted, and they were our paymasters, our benefactors, so how could we really say no?

Matsya swam out to sea, breasting the waves like a powerboat. He dived under for a while, and then resurfaced and came back to shore lugging a four-hundred-pound yellowfin tuna. The giant fish writhed in his clutches, its bright golden dorsal and ventral fins flashing in the sunlight, but Matsya held on tight and it couldn't break free. Once everyone had had a good look, he released it, and the tuna thrashed away as fast as it could through the shallows, seeking the sanctuary of deeper waters.

Kurma showed off the impenetrability of his armour by inviting Vamana, at full size, to hit him hard on the head. Vamana pounded away like a steam hammer, and the paving stones beneath Kurma's feet cracked, but the Turtle himself remained unbent and upright, weathering the blows. Kurma's siddhi was the ability to absorb untold amounts of shock and pressure. His armour afforded protection against penetrative wounds, but the man inside was extraordinarily durable too. The density of his skeleton and musculature was so great that, Korolev reckoned, he could survive being crushed inside a car compacter.

Narasimha and Parashurama did their thing, sparring with each other at blazing speeds.

But it was my double act with Rama that brought the house down. I skipped around finding objects to toss into the air. Rama shot them. Be it cloth napkin or empty magnum of Dom Perignon, I hurled it aloft and he either shattered it or pinned it to a wall. I juggled three tablespoons – *with my feet* – and Rama pinged all three in turn. I balanced on a dining chair while his arrows snapped the legs off one after another until finally I was left perching on tiptoe on the chair's back, the whole thing poised at an acute angle, with just the last remaining leg holding it up. When Rama shot that leg too, what was left of the chair fell to the floor, but I wasn't on it any more. I was dangling upside down from one of the marquee's horizontal roof struts. Again, this was courtesy of my feet, which only that morning I had found out were fantastically prehensile. It was like having a second pair of hands attached to my ankles.

All of the above was improvised. It just came naturally to the two of us, as if it were a routine we had rehearsed together for years. I felt entirely in sync with Rama. You know that thing where you meet somebody for the first time and you instantly become firm friends? Like you've known each other all your lives, or maybe knew each other in a past life? You almost don't need to speak, you're so attuned to each other's wavelength? That. That was me and Rama. Rama and Hanuman, the Vedic Dynamic Duo.

Afterwards, when the applause had died down and the mingling resumed, Aanandi sidled up to me. It was the first time we'd spoken since my elevation to the ranks of deva-dom.

"So," she said. She appraised me up and down, an eyebrow cocked. "Hanuman. It figures."

"Oh, don't pretend you had nothing to do with it, Aanandi. I know you. I bet you're the one who proposed I should be the monkey god. This has your fingerprints all over it."

She blushed ever so slightly. It was very fetching. "Vignesh and I talked about it a while back." She nodded towards Bhatnagar, who was deep in conversation with the Cabinet Secretary, both speaking Hindi. "It was his idea that there should be a Hanuman on the team. He used to read comics about him as a kid. There's this publishing imprint in India called Amar Chitra Katha. It's been going for decades and it does comic-strip retellings of the great epics. Hanuman had his own series, and it was Vignesh's favourite. Once the Dashavatara were up and running, creating a Hanuman was always his next goal."

I recalled that Bhatnagar had been watching my acrobatic antics just now more keenly than most, and I had noticed a childlike delight on his face as I cavorted and tumbled. His wife and two sons were with him, and he had kept pointing me out to the boys and making excited comments. They, being in their teens, acted as though they couldn't care less. One of them barely took his eyes off his smartphone.

"And you encouraged him to choose me for the job," I said.

"I didn't *dis*courage him, put it that way. He wondered aloud who'd be a suitable candidate, and

I jokingly suggested you. He, also jokingly, agreed. But I think somewhere inside him he was thinking, 'Well, if the opportunity ever presents itself...'"

"And then you helped persuade me to agree."

"You didn't take much persuading, as I recall."

"With hindsight, I shouldn't have needed *any*."

"You like how you are?"

"Who the fuck wouldn't? Look at me. I look great, even with the monkeyish add-ons. I *feel* great."

"You do look great." Aanandi gave me another once-over. "Not that you didn't before. But this is like Zak deluxe. Zak after a total makeover." She put a hand on my chest, gently exploring its firm contours.

"How come it's okay for a girl to do that to a boy whenever she feels like it, but if the roles were reversed it'd be all 'inappropriate touching'?"

"It just is. Double standards. Get used to it. And pecs aren't boobs."

"You make a fair point. But still, in the interests of gender equality, I think I should be allowed to squeeze back sometime."

"And maybe you'll get that chance."

She took a step back, however, so that I wouldn't get any funny ideas. The chance she was referring to wasn't going to come any time in the immediate future.

"You've been a hit with our visitors," she said. "Yours and Rama's circus act went down a storm. It's all anyone's talking about."

"I'm a born showoff. Just call me a performing

monkey. Why are these people here anyway? This is some sort of public relations exercise, right? A big old schmooze fest. India's our faith power station so we've got to keep its rulers sweet. Is that the deal?"

"Something like that," Aanandi said.

"So it's not? It's more?"

"Or less."

This peeved me. She could be so aggravatingly elusive at times.

"Why do you keep on keeping things from me?" I snapped. "I'm a deva now. I have the same clearance level as you. I'm in the loop. Is it too much to ask for some honesty?"

"'Honesty,' says the swipe card stealer."

"You can't hold that against me forever."

"I damn well can if I feel like it. What I can't do – won't do – is give you a straight answer if I don't think you're ready for it."

"Oh, and who decides that? You?"

"Yes. And keep your voice down. People are looking."

They were, most notably Lombard, and he was scowling, and I didn't want to piss him off, not on what was obviously an important occasion, so I did lower my voice.

"It's a business thing, then," I said, putting two and two together. "That's what the Trinity have wheeled their devas out for. We're not just the after-dinner entertainment, we're the merchandise."

Aanandi tried to keep her expression inscrutable, but this in itself was tantamount to a big fat yes.

"I'm right, aren't I? This is – it's a trade expo."

"Kind of." She sighed. "Shit, I shouldn't be saying anything. Not until the ink's dry on the contract. You promise you won't breathe a word to the others?"

"I don't know. Depends on what I'm not supposed to be telling them."

"You have to promise."

"Well, all right."

Aanandi drew me aside until we were in a corner where no one could overhear us.

"The Avatars will find out soon enough, once the deal's been sealed," she said. "I have a feeling Parashurama's figured it out already. He's a shrewd one. You think these bigwigs have come all the way from New Delhi just for shits and giggles? They want to sign the Ten up. They want to hire them."

"As what? Mercenaries?"

"Pretty much. This whole shebang, it's not just a meet-and-greet. Tonight there'll be negotiations, the Trinity and the Indian government around a table, thrashing out terms of lease."

"Can the Trinity do that? That's not what the Avatars are about, surely."

"Wrong. The Trinity can do whatever the hell they like, and the Avatars are about whatever the Trinity say they're about. There's serious money hovering in the air. Eight-, maybe nine-figure sums."

I whistled.

"India loves the Dashavatara," Aanandi continued. "The Indian government thinks recruiting the Avatars as an elite force of troops is a sound move.

It could well be, both politically and strategically. It'll cement the government's popularity with the voters, and there's an election in the offing so that can't hurt. But also, in defence terms, who can deny that a unit of super-powered commandos is just the ticket for dealing with India's enemies?"

"Which enemies? I thought India didn't have that many."

Aanandi rolled her eyes. "Typical Westerner geopolitical ignorance." She started ticking off a checklist on her fingers. "There's internal Islamist terrorism, for one thing. During the past couple of decades militant Muslims have set off bombs in Mumbai, Uttar Pradesh, New Delhi, everywhere, killing hundreds of civilians. Not to mention Sikh separatists in the Punjab and paramilitary insurgents fighting for independence for Assam. Then there's the troublesome neighbour to the north and the whole Kashmir dispute."

"Oh, yeah. Pakistan. That's not been good, has it?"

"Understatement of the century. After the Korean peninsula, Kashmir is the likeliest potential flashpoint for a nuclear conflict. Pakistan believes India has been unlawfully occupying half the region since Partition, India says much the same about Pakistan, and meanwhile most Kashmiris want to be shot of both of them and live in an autonomous state. There've been three wars over Kashmir so far, and there's constant civil unrest within its borders which threatens to spill across into northern India. And with Pakistan being held together precariously by a caretaker government and becoming ever more unstable, only a step away from yet another military coup or, worse, a Taliban takeover..."

"India would like something special in its back pocket," I finished. "Just in case. Something Dashavatara-shaped."

"The propaganda value of the Dashavatara alone – it's incalculable. It might even be enough to get the Pakistanis to back down and behave without a shot needing to be fired."

"Alternatively it might just escalate the situation."

"True," Aanandi said with a grim nod. "I'm questioning the wisdom of hiring the Avatars out to India myself, but then who am I? I'm just a monkey, not an organ grinder. No offence meant."

"None taken." Now was not the moment to crack a joke about grinding organs. "Is this why those Pakistani jets came after us that time?" The attack on the *Garuda* had been only a few weeks ago. I could hardly believe it. It felt like I'd lived a lifetime since. In a sense, I had. "The Pakistanis foresaw something like this?"

"Who's to say? Perhaps. The Pakistanis have itchy trigger fingers at the best of times, and this isn't the best of times. We just have to hope –"

And then, as if on cue, the missile hit.

25. DRONE STRIKE

THE MISSILE WAS fired from an unmanned aerial vehicle controlled remotely by a pilot in a military bunker in Karachi. The drone, a combat-capable upgrade of the Shahpar reconnaissance UAV, was Pakistan's homegrown answer to the Predator, and while no match for the American craft in terms of efficiency, performance or payload, it was deadly enough.

The missile itself was a laser-guided Baktar-Shikan, a variant of the Chinese-built HJ-8 anti-tank missile, modified for air-to-ground launch. It was light and compact, to suit the small drone, but it still packed a considerable high-explosive wallop.

It struck the flank of the outer ring, some one hundred yards from where the assembled company was standing. The building spouted flame. The concussion blast knocked several people off their feet. Rubble spewed outwards, showering over us in a lethal hail.

I couldn't understand why no one was moving out of the way. Bits of building were tumbling through the air – chunks of concrete, shards of glass, twisted fragments of steel – and people seemed to be watching it as though mesmerised. Why didn't they run? Why weren't they even ducking?

Then I realised that I had slipped into time dilation mode again. My reflexes and perceptions had hyper-accelerated in response to a threat. Seconds were passing like minutes.

I swept Aanandi aside, flattening her to the ground just as the wavefront of hurtling rubble reached us. Expressions – alarm, bewilderment, terror – shifted across her face as slowly as wax melting.

I spun round and launched myself towards a trio of the Indian VIPs, who were in the throes of dropping their drinks and cowering, reacting at last to the missile impact. I bundled all of them down behind a low wall. A length of rebar missed impaling the head of the Deputy Speaker of the Lok Sabha by inches.

The marquee flailed and billowed as debris ripped through it. Parashurama swung his axe and pulverised a piece of concrete the size of a football before it hit Bhatnagar, reducing it to a cloud of gravel that showered harmlessly over the arms dealer and the Cabinet Secretary next to him. Kurma shielded Lombard and the Minister of External Affairs with his armoured bulk. A tide of airborne rubble broke against his back, shattering to dust.

Silence followed in the wake of the explosion. Then screams erupted, some of pain, some of horror. Not everyone present had escaped injury. I saw a member of the Maldivian waiting staff clutching a deep gash in her leg, and one of the lesser Indian dignitaries was cradling a visibly broken arm.

I looked back at Aanandi. She appeared dazed but unhurt. I had saved her, as well as three of the Indians. Back of the net for Hanuman!

A second Baktar-Shikan struck.

This one landed further into the complex, the fourth ring. The island shook underfoot. A pillar of flame roiled upwards. Almost everyone was screaming now, human voices bleating in mad animal panic.

Above the hubbub Parashurama yelled orders. "Avatars! Round people up! Form a perimeter!"

Only we devas were moving. Everyone else was too terror-stricken to budge. Like cornered rabbits, they thought that if they stayed still and kept their heads down, danger might pass them by. We tried pulling them by their arms but they resisted. Even the military brass were having trouble processing what was happening. It had been a long time since any of them had seen action in the field, if ever.

"Be calm," said Buddha. "Be free of fear. Master your thoughts. Let go or be dragged."

His words cut through the paralysis that had seized people, pouring honey on their terror. They got up and meekly allowed themselves to be herded together. Parashurama positioned the Avatars around the stunned, huddled humans. We faced outwards, a living bulwark.

Rama squinted at the horizon. "Another one is incoming. Brace yourselves."

The third missile shrieked overhead and hit Mount Meru's hub, the tower housing the Trinity's private apartments. The impact rocked the building, shattering virtually every window in it. One of the upper storeys was gutted in an instant, and I fully expected that the tower would crumple in on itself and collapse. It didn't. Smoke poured from a gouge in the side, water from broken pipes jetted like arterial blood, but the tower remained erect.

Parashurama suggested that everyone should take cover inside, but Lombard gave the idea short shrift.

"There's no bloody air raid shelters on Meru. No basements, even. You've seen what these damn missiles can do. They'd pick us off just as easily indoors. Might as well stay out here where we can see them coming and have a chance of avoiding them."

Everyone scanned the sky intently. The three missiles had struck in fairly quick succession. As time passed and no fourth one arrived, it began to seem that the attack was over – although this could just be a lull while our unseen enemy regrouped and prepared for the next salvo.

Finally, after about a quarter of an hour, we all agreed that no more missiles were coming. For now.

Krieger, gazing at the central tower, moaned in dismay. "Straight into my goddamn living room! Son of a bitch! I have a Miró vase in there. My wife bought it for me."

"Never mind your bloody vase, mate," growled Lombard. Blood trickled from a tiny gash in his temple. "What about my collection of Miles Davis white label pressings? That's six years' worth of collecting there."

"They're on the floor above."

"Still, the chances of them surviving..."

"Records are replaceable. A Miró ceramic isn't."[1]

"Still, at least the tower's mostly intact," Lombard said. "Could have been worse, eh?" A look passed between him and Krieger.

"Yes," the Texan said. "When you put it like that..."

"Structurally sound where it needs to be. There are things more valuable than vases and LPs."

Bhatnagar joined his two colleagues, his arm around his wife's shoulders. Her sundress was grimy and torn, her whole body trembling. "Who?" he demanded. "That's what I want to know. Who in hell's name is firing missiles at us?"

"Who do you think?" Lombard shot back. "Pakistan. Got to be. And on the day we have guests from India. That's no ruddy coincidence."

---

[1] I know what you're thinking. I was thinking it myself, at the time. How could anyone bicker about possessions, having just narrowly survived a fucking missile attack? But then the rich aren't like the rest of us, and the ultra-rich *really* aren't.

"You say that, but without proof…"

"The timing is the proof. They've been keeping an eye on us. They know what this get-together signifies. This is a deliberate act of provocation."

"If you ask me, I don't think that's the intention at all," said Krieger. "They've hit us at the edge, in the middle and at dead centre. It's a demonstration. They want us to know they can get us any time, with some accuracy. It's the proverbial warning shot across the bows."

"Warning shot my arse," said Lombard. "Warning shots *miss*. Whoever's responsible, if it's Pakistan or someone else, they're calling us out. They're picking a fight."

The Cabinet Secretary, who had recovered most of his wits by now, joined in the debate. "Like you, Mr Lombard-ji, I suspect Pakistan of being behind this outrage. It stands to reason. Although our meeting has been carried out under conditions of stringent security and in the strictest secrecy, Pakistan's intelligence forces are as capable as our own. If not more so, since ours seem to have failed us in not anticipating the attack."

He broke off to direct a fierce glare at the two intelligence heads among the delegation. Both of them shrugged, part aggrieved, part contrite.

"We are aware that a state of hostility already exists between Mount Meru and the Pakistanis," he continued. "And of course they have been spoiling for a fight with India for a long time. Our presence at your headquarters has offered them a target too tempting to resist. Two birds with one stone. The Indian government, you can rest assured, will investigate thoroughly and punish the culprits."

"Thanks for that, but I think we can go one better," Lombard rumbled. He kicked a hunk of masonry that lay at his feet amid the splinters of a table it had wrecked. "I'm not the sort to bend over, spread my cheeks and take it up the freckle. Not from the Pakistanis, not from anyone. Mount Meru isn't just our HQ, it's our home. Any bastard wants a piece of us? Fine. He's got it. Screw the schedule. Screw negotiations. Gentlemen, ladies? The Dashavatara are at India's service. Deploy them where and how you like."

26. CHANDIGARH

THE GARUDA TOUCHED down at Chandigarh airbase on a humid, grey morning, taxiing to a halt outside the low breezeblock structure that was the main administrative building. Around the base stretched a green, tree-dotted plain, with the city of Chandigarh crouching beyond it, just visible to the north-east, a line of foothills biting into the overcast like jagged black teeth. We were on the fringes of the Himalayas, some two hundred kilometres from the border with Pakistan and a similar distance from Kashmir.

During the flight from Meru the mood had been tense and argumentative. The Dashavatara were broadly in favour of the Trinity's decision to loan them out to India, but there were dissenting voices. Buddha stated that violence was not always the most appropriate response to aggression. Varaha, meanwhile, was of the opinion that the Dashavatara were not a military unit or even a paramilitary one, and shouldn't behave as if they were.

"We slap down asuras when they rear their ugly heads, all right, no worries," the Boar said. "I haven't got a problem with that. It's our job. But diving headlong into an international conflict? Does anyone else see the potential for that backfiring? Or is it just me?"

"You're not an eco-warrior any more, Varaha," said Kalkin, who had recovered from his poisoning in Los Angeles, although his shoulder remained a little stiff. "You don't have to wring your hands over every little thing."

"Besides, they attacked us," said Vamana. "They threw the first punch."

"And we're certain it was the Pakistanis?" said Krishna. "It's beyond doubt?"

"They've more or less said so themselves, and India confirms it," said Parashurama. "India's RISAT-2 reconnaissance satellite tracked the heat signatures of three unmanned drones making a return journey to and from Karachi. They're calling it an act of war."

"One has to be sure," said Krishna. "My country's history is full of wars fought for no good reason, started by leaders who lie."[1]

---

[1] *Secret Origin:* Krishna was a Syrian by birth, name of Abdulrahman Ghazzawi. He was raised in abject poverty in a tiny village outside the city of Homs and won a scholarship to study at the Technological Institute of Agriculture at the Damascus University. He returned home with the knowhow and the zeal

"Join the club," said Vamana. "The Iraq War, anyone? The British Prime Minister and the imaginary 'weapons of mass destruction'? All politicians fib, and they fib the most where war's concerned. But there's no question here that the Pakistanis are to blame. They've all but copped to it, haven't they? What did their Foreign Minister say on television?"

"He called it 'a pre-emptive strike against a potential terrorist threat'," said Kalkin. "He didn't actually say who or where the so-called terrorists are, but he didn't have to. Once you say the words 'terrorist threat,' people pretty much stop hearing and start running around like headless chickens."

"He also omitted to mention the Indian government officials in his statement," said Matsya, "and how close they came to becoming collateral damage."

"This is a come-and-have-a-go-if-you-think-you're-hard-enough moment," said Vamana. "Lombard hit the nail right on the head. The Pakistanis are calling us out into the car park."

"But why rise to the bait?" said Buddha. "Isn't that exactly what they want? Why be so predictable?"

"Well, I for one am not letting them get away with it. Those missiles killed five people. You seem to be forgetting that, tubby. Too busy turning the other cheek. Catering staff, a couple of technicians – five innocent people."

---

to expand his family's smallholding into a thriving cattle farm specialising in both dairy products and biogas production. Then the Trinity came calling, seeking not just a cowherd to be their Krishna but an *educated* cowherd, one with an evident passion for bettering himself and the world.

"We're playing into their hands, though. Think how it's going to look if the Dashavatara start taking sides, favouring one nation over another. We'll lose all credibility. Besides, don't we want peace? Shouldn't we at least try to seek a nonviolent solution to the crisis?"

"Oh, no, Buddha, mate," said Vamana. "Don't you go trying your voice hoodoo on us. You know it only works on civilians, not your own kind."

"I'm not. But I could make it work on Pakistan's leadership, if we could just get them to come to the negotiating table and parley with us."

"Their military is already on a state of high alert," Parashurama pointed out. "Things have gone too far for talks. Pakistan and India have both poured additional troops into Kashmir. They're halfway down the road to war as it is, and I don't think anyone or anything is going to be able to stop them. Even you, Buddha. The effect of your voice isn't permanent. A half-hour after you'd sweet-talked them, they'd be back to getting ready to rumble. These things have their own unstoppable momentum. Fingers crossed the UN can achieve something, but...". He grimaced.

The United Nations was doing its damnedest to persuade the two sides to pull back from the brink. UN diplomats were shuttling back and forth between Karachi and New Delhi, trying to defuse the tension. India was playing the righteous victim, while Pakistan was putting on a front, claiming it had no knowledge of there being anyone other than "terrorists" in its crosshairs. The Pakistani leadership's rhetoric was going down well at home, largely because the politicians were skirting around the truth and positioning themselves firmly on the moral high ground. After all, if America could protect its sovereignty through drone strikes, why not anyone else? And if the ire of India had been roused, well, that was just too bad. Relations between the two countries had never been that cordial to begin with.

"We can't afford *not* to get involved," said Rama. He was busy assembling his bow from its components, slotting the carbon-fibre limbs into the aluminium riser. His lips were pursed pensively amidst his artfully razored chin stubble. "India itself is now in peril, and we have to help defend it or risk losing the main source of our siddhis."

"It's not often you hear a Brit say these words," said Vamana, "but I agree with the Frenchman. We're in this whether we like it or not, for any number of reasons."

"The best we can hope for is that our taking part will help bring about a speedy resolution," said Kurma. "If we end up fighting Pakistani armed forces, as we may well, the battle should be short and decisive."

"Amen to that," said Parashurama. "Let's be the weight that tips the scales firmly in India's favour."

You may be asking yourself how I, your humble narrator, am able to relay the foregoing conversation to you in such depth. The answer, obviously, is that

I was there. Rama had invited me to come along on the mission, despite objections, most of them from Vamana. The Archer was adamant that I belonged in the Avatars' company and that, although I was untried in combat, I could nonetheless be an asset to the team.

I wasn't so convinced of that myself. I was scared out of my wits at the thought of getting involved in actual fighting, with bullets coming my way and enemies hell bent on killing me. If it came to that, I could foresee myself dissolving into a useless, gibbering wreck.

On the other hand, I was Hanuman now, and my place was at Rama's side. Hadn't I rescued him and his brother Lakshmana when the demon Ahiravan took them captive and held them in his palace in the underworld? Hadn't I scoured the Himalayas for the magic herb that would heal Lakshmana after he was gravely wounded in battle? Hadn't I taken an arrow in the leg because I'd recognised it as one of Rama's, although it was fired at me in error by his younger brother Bharat? There's devotion for you, to let yourself be hit by a friend's arrow rather than jump out of the way.

I knew cognitively that I, which is to say Zak Bramwell, had done none of these things. But Hanuman had, and his identity was superimposed on mine. The two of us coexisted within me, Hanuman's exploits my exploits as well, his personality tingeing my personality. It was as though I was being haunted by a ghost, and the ghost was me. Does that make any sense? No? How about this, then? It was as though I had been driving along and pulled over to pick up a hitchhiker, and the hitchhiker, who from behind looked like a stranger, turned out to be someone I knew really well. Is that better? This deva business is tricky to explain to anyone who hasn't become one. Like trying to teach a blind person about colours or a deaf person about music.

At any rate, Rama had vouched for me. He'd insisted on me tagging along, to the point of refusing to go himself unless I did. The Avatars weren't exactly pleased, Vamana least of all. I wasn't going to be forgiven any time soon for kicking the Dwarf in the teeth and humiliating him. Rama's blackmail, however, couldn't be argued with. His flashy bowmanship made him the Dashavatara's star player, their MVP after Parashurama. If the Warrior was the *de facto* team leader, the Archer was definitely second-in-command, and what he wanted, he got.

We stepped out of the *Garuda* into the blowsy north Indian heat. A score of air force men lined up on the tarmac to form an honour guard, and we were met formally by a senior officer in full dress uniform with a chestful of ribbons and a heap of gold braid on either shoulder.

"Air Marshal Pradeep Venkatesan, commander in chief of Western Air Command," he said. "At your service, my lords."

"No 'my lords,'" said Parashurama, returning Venkatesan's crisp salute with an equally crisp one of his own. "Just call us by our Avatar names. What's happening? Give us a sitrep."

Venkatesan paused while a MiG-21 roared past on the runway and took off. A pair of pale brown Zebu cows in a pasture by the perimeter fence kept chewing the cud as the jet shot over their heads, unperturbed by the eardrum-shredding cacophony of its turbofans. Elsewhere there was activity, men scurrying urgently to and fro, ground support vehicles trundling between hangars.

"As you can see, we are in a state of high combat readiness. On the instructions of the IAF Chief of Air Staff, I'm sending planes out to patrol the northern border and conduct naked-eye reconnaissance sorties over Kashmir. The Pakistanis are doing much the same on their side, and there have been skirmishes, a few shots fired; so far without loss of life or aircraft, but it is surely only a matter of time. The situation is grave, Lord Parashurama – I apologise; I mean Parashurama. Very grave indeed. Basically we are awaiting orders to scramble all fighters and engage the enemy. The go command could come at any moment."

"What about on the ground?"

"Pakistani infantry and armoured divisions are massing along the Kashmiri Line of Control. UN peacekeepers have been recalled from the region, which is seldom a good sign. If the UN packs up its bags and goes home, you had better be ready for trouble. Furthermore, I have it on good authority that Pakistan is boosting its troop numbers all along

its border with us. The sabre is being rattled like there's no tomorrow – and there may well *be* no tomorrow, unless we are very careful, or very lucky, or both. Now, while the war drums beat ever louder, how may I be of assistance to you?"

"Well, the *Garuda* could do with refuelling."

"I shall get my ground crew onto it right away."

"And is there somewhere we could hang out? Rest up and get some chow?"

"My private quarters are at your disposal," said Venkatesan. "They are not far from the mess, where you will find the cafeteria more than adequate to your needs."

My stomach growled. I was looking forward to some nosh.

But then...

"Air marshal! Air marshal!"

A junior office came sprinting across the tarmac from a nearby building. He skidded to a halt, fired off a nanosecond-long salute, then said breathlessly, "Reports just in, sir. Pakistani forces have crossed the Line of Control."

"Where, corporal?"

"At three points, sir. The Haji Pir Pass, along the Sialkot-Jammu Road, and along the Indus Valley."

"*Madar chod*!" Venkatesan swore.[1]

"There may also be an incursion across the Siachen Glacier. That hasn't been confirmed."

"But it's likely. The glacier's always been a grey

---

[1] It means *motherfucker*, in case you don't know or can't guess.

area. No man's land." The air marshal removed his beret and ran a hand over his thinning, slicked-back hair. "Very well. War it is, then. Parashurama, esteemed Avatars, I'm afraid we are hearing the call to arms. You may still rest and refresh yourselves, if you require, but..."

"No," said Parashurama. "We're here to help, so help we will. Gas up the *Garuda* and contact your superiors to find out where we're best deployed."

"It would be my honour. You heard the man, corporal. What are you standing around with your mouth open for? Get on the phone to Western Air Command. Hop to it!"

The subordinate scurried off. Venkatesan settled his beret back on his head.

"Such a sorry business," he said with a mournful frown. "I pray that it will go no further than it did the last few times. Stay conventional, I mean. Not escalate."

"We're all hoping that," said Parashurama. "And if the Dashavatara have any say in it, it won't."

Venkatesan's amber eyes studied us, and I could tell what he was thinking.

We were devas. We were hardly what you might call *conventional*.

If we were introduced into the theatre of conflict, wasn't that in itself an escalation? Facing gods, wouldn't the Pakistanis feel perfectly justified in raising their retaliation to the next level?

27. THE BATTLE OF SIACHEN GLACIER

I'M NOT GOING to go into a full précis and analysis of the Fifth Indo-Pakistan War here.[1] Nor am I going to go into the rights and wrongs of it. I'm not a historian, and this isn't an impartial account of events. This is one man's first-hand experience, an insider's view. You want all the facts and figures, the stats and data, the timeline? Look it up. Better yet, write your own book. *I'd* read it.

I'll stick with telling you what I know, which is this. India's Chiefs of Staff decided the Dashavatara could do most good up at the Siachen Glacier,

---

[1] I'm not even going to get into a debate over whether it was the Fifth or Fourth, since the Kargil conflict in 1999 was never an officially declared war but is still counted as an Indo-Pakistan fracas.

which is situated in the eastern Karakoram range of the Himalayas and is the highest-altitude, arse-freezingest place I have ever been or ever want to be.

Their reasons for despatching the Avatars there were twofold.

First, it was the most porous part of the border between the two sections of divided Kashmir. It lay beyond the point where the rigidly demarcated Line of Control petered out, and both India and Pakistan laid claim to it but neither was really happy about maintaining a presence there, on account of the inhospitable terrain, thin air, treacherously steep mountain slopes, year-round arctic conditions, and general inaccessibility. The temperature in Siachen can drop to minus fifty Celsius. Who'd want to occupy that sort of territory for any meaningful length of time? So both powers planted outposts and just sort of pretended they controlled it, while neither did. And since Siachen was relatively unmilitarised compared with the rest of the Line of Control, the Dashavatara would have more or less free rein to confront the enemy in whatever way suited them best.

The second reason was that details about the Pakistani incursion across the glacier were vague, based on interception of phone chatter among local civilians about troops being sighted on the move, heading north to south. The Indians didn't quite know what they were facing, how many soldiers, if any, the Pakistanis had mobilised. A platoon? A regiment? A whole division? More? Reconnaissance was tricky,

so the rumours could not be substantiated. Blizzards and dense cloud cover could baffle even the highest-spec synthetic aperture radar satellite imaging system, and there were countless valleys and gorges where men could successfully conceal themselves from overflying spy planes. There could be thousands of Pakistani infantry flooding into Siachen, or just a trickle of dozens. Banking on it being the latter, the Chiefs of Staff felt that the Dashavatara, whose aptitude for widescale battlefield combat was as yet undetermined, belonged where the fighting was likely to be least intensive.

It was a tryout, in other words. They were breaking the Dashavatara in, sending them where the least harm would be done if things went arse over tit and their battle prowess did not match up to expectations. The Siachen Glacier lacked the strategic importance of the other three invasion points, so if for some reason the Avatars failed to hold it, no matter.

Which may sound a bit callous and cavalier, but to be fair to the Indian military, they were dealing with a completely new and unproven tactical element. They were well versed in their Cold Start doctrine, aimed at rapidly responding to any Pakistani offensive through a series of carefully coordinated counterstrikes. Nothing in the doctrine, however, made provision for the involvement of super-powered individuals. The Chiefs of Staff were drawing up plans on the hoof, integrating the Avatars into their asset structure as best they could.

The *Garuda* alighted halfway along the glacier, at the forwardmost point of India's nominal zone of occupation. Its spherical wheels crunched deep into the layer of snow covering the ice. We were in a flat-bottomed valley, chains of ragged peaks on either side. We stepped out of the aircraft and were immediately hit by the arid, numbing cold of the place; the oxygen-poor air literally took your breath away.

Venkatesan had lent us suits of extreme cold weather gear, including parkas, thermal mittens and insulated trousers, all in snow pattern camouflage. These helped, though not by much.

Matsya was the only one of us who didn't wear one. Subzero temperatures didn't bother him. He was full of antifreeze glycoproteins which inhibited the formation of ice crystals in his flesh and bodily fluids and protected him from cold damage. He could swim in the darkest ocean abysses, he said, and be unaffected.

Krishna's chariot wouldn't carry us at this sort of altitude, so we tramped on foot. Our rendezvous point was an Indian army camp on a small plateau a mile upslope from the *Garuda*'s landing zone, nestled against the base of a crag that afforded some shelter from the elements.

The camp consisted of tents and igloos, without the consolation of a rigid-walled structure anywhere, and was home to an infantry unit under the command of Captain Sawhney. He and his troops were a straggle-bearded, hollow-eyed bunch, their faces roughened and reddened with chilblains. They looked as though they had been up in the mountains, manning this hopelessly remote sentry post, for far too long. I saw a couple of them warming the barrels of their rifles over a kerosene stove to defrost them. I also saw a man squatting over a hole in the snow at the edge of the campsite, not caring that he was in full view of everyone as he took his dump.

"Welcome to the 'third pole,'" said Sawhney. "I would invite you to make yourselves at home but, as you can see, my friends, there is little in the way of home comforts here."

"Never mind that," said Parashurama. "The Pakistanis. Where are they?"

"We have scouts further north. They have spied Sno-Cats and snowmobiles, and a column of men, coming down the glacier. An estimated two hundred troops in all. We were told to wait until you arrived before engaging. Now that you're here, we can get down to business."

"How far away is this column?"

"Eight, ten miles."

"And how many men do you have in total?"

"Forty. Forty of the best. A little frostbitten and altitude-crazed, but they're as hardy as you could wish for, and itching for some action. This has been a long time coming. There have been phony wars and false alarms. Up here the Pakistanis are foolish and tend to shoot at anything. Their gunfire echoes all the time. They piss bullets away like they're one-rupee coins. But then they don't have the resupply issues that we have. Geography is in their favour. They have road access on their side, whereas we must rely on airdrops. So we sit tight and wait for them to calm down, and keep our safety catches on while they take potshots at us from across the valley. There's only so much of that a man can endure before he starts hankering for payback."

"Forty of you plus ten of us, against two hundred," said Parashurama. "Seems like a fair fight."

The Indian grinned. "With the Dashavatara in our corner, how can we fail?"

In short order Sawhney had roused his men and we were trekking northwards. The Indians joked and sang songs as they marched.

I quizzed one of them, a young private, about life in Siachen. He didn't speak great English but I gathered that his tour of duty had lasted a year so far, with several months still to go.

"Down in base camp, at foot of glacier, it is nice," he said. "Huts. Carpets. A hospital. Satellite TV. It is heaven. Here, hell. Very dangerous. I'll tell you a story. We are out on patrol, not long ago. My friend treads on snow. Looks like ordinary snow. Suddenly he is gone. Walking next to me, then gone, downwards." He mimed a steep plummet. "Into deep crack in ice."

"Crevasse?" I said.

"Exactly. Crevasse. No one sees it. Covered over by bridge of snow. My friend does not even scream. Too fast. We never find him. Too far down."

I watched my footing carefully after that.

A wind whipped up. Clouds sailed in, blanketing the blue firmament. They seemed so low overhead you could reach up and touch them. We moved across an expanse of rugged white ground, ridges of purple-black rock boiling up around us. Here and there the ice formed pinnacles, thrust up by the immense glacial pressures below. The landscape was so ugly, it was almost beautiful.

The wind brought snow. First a few flakes, like heralds. Then a thick onslaught, a blinding television-static whirr of white motion.

Our progress slowed to a trudge. Rama took point, peering ahead through the near-whiteout, looking for the first sign of the enemy. Nobody was singing or making jokes any more. The Indians kept their heads down and their mouths shut as the snow rimed their beards and eyebrows, turning them into yetis.

All at once Rama raised a hand. We halted. Sawhney, with a few gestures, directed his men to fan out and assume defensible positions. They scattered to either side, setting themselves up to deliver criss-cross volleys of enfilading fire downslope onto the approaching Pakistanis. Those with tripod-mounted heavy machine guns flattened out on the snow, adjusted the sights and fed belts of armour-piercing rounds into the breeches. The Avatars, meanwhile, spaced themselves out in a line that stopped just short of the Indians' field of fire.

The drone of far-off engines mingled with the mournful sough of the wind, sometimes faint, sometimes almost inaudible, but gradually getting clearer and more distinct.

I was in a quandary. Part of me wanted to run for cover behind the nearest rock and not come out until the shooting stopped. Another part knew I should be standing shoulder to shoulder with the Dashavatara, especially Rama. It was my rightful place.

As the pulses of engine noise increased in volume, I felt a quickening sense of excitement that made my fears seem pathetic and immaterial. Cowering behind a rock? What kind of feeble creature did that? Certainly not the Son of the Wind, the firstborn and favourite of Anjana the cloud spirit, she who was cursed by the sage Brihaspathi to take fleshly form but whose curse was lifted by the act of giving birth. Certainly not the adventurer, the trickster, the leaper, the laugher, the light-hearted one, Hanuman.

A pair of Sno-Cats emerged through the swirling flurries of snow, headlamps glaring. Captain Sawhney snapped an order over the shortwave band, and bullets strafed the two vehicles from either side. Windscreens shattered; holes were punched in bodywork. A caterpillar track broke in two and flailed around the drive wheels. Crossfire tracer rounds lit up the snowstorm like stroboscopes.

Pakistani troops scrambled out from the Sno-Cats, returning fire with German submachine guns and Type 56 assault rifles.[1] More Pakistanis bundled in

---

[1] Chinese-manufactured AK-47 ripoffs.

from the rear, joining their comrades beside the Sno-Cats and kneeling to shoot.

Snowmobiles arced out on either side of the valley, heading for the Indians' firing positions, hoping to outflank them. Each carried a driver and a pillion rider whose job was to blast away over the driver's shoulder. The snowmobiles' speed and manoeuvrability made them much harder targets than the lumbering Sno-Cats.

But that was all right, because the Indians had deva reinforcements.

Rama sent arrows through the goggles of three of the snowmobile drivers. The vehicles veered wildly, slithering to a halt.

Narasimha loped across the ground on all fours and sprang to intercept another of the snowmobiles. He snatched the driver out of his seat and was eviscerating him even as the two of them spun through the air.

Varaha lowered his head and charged straight at an oncoming snowmobile. He grabbed it by its engine shroud and flipped it over onto its back; the driver was bent double underneath and crushed to death, while the pillion rider was thrown free. He landed near Buddha and sprang to his feet, rifle raised, but with just a few words and a calming gesture, Buddha made him sit down and start etching pictures in the snow with his gun barrel. The soldier looked as happy as a kid in art class.

A snowmobile turned and made for Kurma, kicking up a peacock tail of snow behind it. The

Turtle stood his ground. Bullets pinged and whined off his armour. The driver gunned the throttle, fully intent on mowing Kurma down. The pillion rider egged him on, clapping him on the helmet. The snowmobile struck the Avatar head-on and exploded. It was as though it had run into a concrete pillar. Kurma stepped away from the heap of fiery wreckage, using handfuls of snow to damp down the splashes of burning fuel on his leg and chest.

Krishna commandeered one of the driverless snowmobiles and, with Parashurama on the back, set off at speed towards the main body of Pakistani infantry, who were coming up from the rear, some on skis, the rest on foot. Kalkin did the same, straddling his vehicle like the horseman he was, talwar aloft.[1]

Together, the Avatar-driven snowmobiles roared into the Pakistanis' midst. Parashurama's axe and Kalkin's sabre swung and chopped, their blades a glinting whirr of motion like dragonflies' wings. Men toppled, minus a limb, a head, even a heart, or else hewn evenly in two, trunk folding over legs.

Jumbo-sized Vamana grabbed one of the crippled Sno-Cats by the chassis and tipped it over onto the

---

[1] *Secret Origin:* His real name was Katsuo Arakari, born in Okinawa but raised in California, where he founded a riding school that taught the arts of bushido swordplay in conjunction with equestrianism. His Samurai Ranch in Sacramento attracted patronage from wealthy people the world over who were looking to get in touch with their inner horse-borne warrior. He even wrote a bestseller about it, *Kyuba No Michi – The Ancient Japanese Knight In The Modern World*, a mix of philosophical tract and self-help book.

group of Pakistanis crouching behind it, squashing them all.

Matsya wriggled like an eel through snow banks, popping up here and there to bring an enemy combatant down in an inescapable chokehold.

Meanwhile the Indians kept pouring bullets at the foe. The echoes of gunshots rippled around the theatre of conflict like endless thunder.

Two Pakistani soldiers ran screaming at Rama, sidearms drawn. He killed one outright with an arrow and transfixed the other's gun-hand with a second arrow. The man fell with a shriek, and Rama stepped in to deliver the *coup de grâce*.

He didn't spot the third soldier who had drawn a bead on him from behind.

Luckily, I did.

I leapt from a standing start, covering ten metres in a single bound, and came down on the Pakistani's back, driving him face-first into the snow. I pounded on him until I felt things break beneath my fists. I rose, bloody-handed, triumphant, exhilarated.

After that there was no stopping me. The threat to Rama was all I'd needed to galvanise me into action. Once I'd joined the fray, I was committed. I chased down enemy troops; I clubbed them with the stocks of their own rifles. I twisted their heads until neck vertebrae crackled. I throttled and I fractured. I was Hanuman, who could move as fast as his father Vayu, lord of the winds, blew. I was the cavorting, chattering monkey god who was your best friend and your worst enemy. You laughed *with* me, never at me. Either you danced to my tune or I danced on your grave.

From the Sno-Cat that still remained upright, Pakistani soldiers produced a pair of shoulder-mounted rocket-propelled grenade launchers. They managed to loose off one of the RPGs at the Indians. Its thermobaric warhead took out six men in a single tremendous flash that turned a patch of the glacier to steam.

They didn't get the opportunity to fire another.

I looked down on them from on top of the Sno-Cat. I had my legs apart, my hands on my hips. It was a self-consciously superheroic stance, but bugger me if it didn't feel right for the occasion.

"Gentlemen," I said, "you have two choices. The one that involves putting down that bazooka and surrendering, or the one that's completely stupid."

Good line, eh?

It's possible that none of the Pakistanis had any English, but they must at least have grasped from my tone of voice what I was offering them.

The guy with the RPG launcher aimed it at me all the same.

This next thing really happened. I have a hard time believing it myself, but it did.

The man holding the weapon depressed the trigger. The RPG round burst from the barrel. It was greeny-brown and shaped like a mace, stubby-ended. It sailed up at me and I caught it by the stem, just above its fiery tail, as though it was a Frisbee. I swung round through 360°. The power of a billion souls behind me, the faith of a billion believers inside me. I let the RPG go. It shot straight back to where it had come from. I back-flipped off the Sno-Cat's roof as two kilogrammes of explosive lit up a small sun and reduced men to cinders.

Not long after that, the Pakistanis laid down their arms.

Of the original two hundred, less than fifty were left. The Indians had contributed, but we devas accounted for the most of the dead.

Beaten and bewildered, the Pakistanis allowed themselves to be marched to the Indians' camp. A few choice words from Buddha kept them nice and docile. I did my bit as Hanuman by skipping around them, mocking and crowing. Then Rama called me over.

"*Tranquillement, mon ami.* You have been using your siddhis extensively. You must take things easy now, or risk crashing."

It was hard to calm down. I had seen battle. I had killed enemies who had been trying to kill me. As appalled as I was that I had taken lives, I was thrilled too. Hanuman was fearless. Hanuman was lethal. His speed and daring and ruthlessness were intoxicating. He paid no heed to consequences. He did what he had to, and he enjoyed it.

I had had my first taste of something very sweet. By God, I was liking being a god.

But I took Rama's advice, remembering how wretched that siddhi crash had made me feel. I slowed to a walk. I tried to be more Zak Bramwell, less deva. Mainly because I didn't want to crap out suddenly in front of everyone and lose face.

And that, folks, was the Battle of Siachen Glacier. A minor altercation in light of what was going on further down the Line of Control, but a decisive win for India, and there would be few enough of those in the coming days, on either side. There would be only stalemates and mutual massacres and then the ultimate Pyrrhic victory of a nuclear strike.

28. COLONEL ZEHRI

COLONEL ZEHRI WAS the name of the captive soldiers' commanding officer. He was the one who had put his hands up and surrendered, demanding that he and his men be accorded their full rights of protection as prisoners of war under the terms of the Third Geneva Convention.

At the Indians' camp, Zehri secured a promise from Captain Sawhney that his troops would be looked after, fed, and escorted off the glacier at the earliest opportunity. The sun was setting, and he realised little could be done to move them anywhere else now. However, they could not be expected to spend more than one night out in the open, exposed to the elements. That would be inhuman treatment.

Sawhney radioed base and arranged for a pair of

Mi-17 helicopters to come up the next morning to airlift the Pakistanis out.

"You lucky devils," he told Zehri. "Wherever you end up, it can only be warmer and more pleasant than here."

Zehri then asked to be introduced formally to the Dashavatara. He wanted to pay his respects to the victors, he said.

And so Sawhney led him over to the *Garuda*, where the Avatars and I were thawing out and shovelling food into our faces. We needed to replenish our reserves after the heavy physical drain of siddhi usage, so we were ploughing through our stocks of high-caloric energy bars and protein smoothies, specially devised by a nutritionist at Mount Meru. Disgusting stuff, tasted like sweetened sawdust and chocolatey clay, but we hoovered it up like crack addicts. There were supplies of amrita on board as well, but we had been advised against using that except in cases of emergency. Eating was the less drastic, old-school method of re-energising yourself. Shooting up with Korolev's salamander juice got instant results but the serum grew less effective with repetition, the body becoming increasingly desensitised to it with every dose.

Zehri stamped snow from his boots before entering.

"So, these are the ones they call gods," he said, looking round the cabin. "But from what I see, you're nothing more than men with an overinflated opinion of yourselves."

"Whoa, whoa, whoa," said Vamana. "You what? You reckon you can just walk in here and start slagging us off? I think you're forgetting, matey, we just made mincemeat out of your lot."

"Give me one good reason why I should not gut you where you stand," Narasimha growled, taloned fingers outstretched.

Credit to Zehri, he barely flinched. "I mean no insult. I speak my mind, that is all. I accept that you defeated us soundly. What I do not, will not, cannot accept is that you are gods, no matter what the newspapers and the television networks insist."

"Because Allah decrees that there are no other gods but him?" said Parashurama.

"No. I am as secular as a Muslim can be. I am little concerned with what Allah says or wills. But you see, I know what you are. Pakistan's intelligence services are better informed about you than you might think. We are aware that the Trinity Syndicate has been engaged in experiments. Theogenesis, is that the term? You may have most of the world believing you are Hindu devas reincarnated. We know better. You're genetically modified organisms, one step up from tomatoes that don't rot and mice that glow in the dark."

"Oh, this just gets better and better," fumed Vamana. "Next he'll be calling us Frankenstein monsters."

"You are, in a way."

"Who's this 'we'?" Kalkin asked.

"The upper tiers of government and military,"

said Zehri. "Why else do you think we have been harassing you at Mount Meru? What were those drone strikes for? To show you that we aren't fooled. We aren't intimidated. We know the truth, even if no one else does."

"What are you saying?" said Parashurama. "That we were your targets at Meru? That your fight is with us, not India?"

"With you *and* with India. There isn't much difference as far as we're concerned. We anticipated that you and our beloved neighbour would join forces eventually. It was inevitable. Your shared interests are too great. A decision was made in Islamabad to force the issue. If India were ever to utilise the Dashavatara in combat, Pakistan would most likely be on the receiving end. So Pakistan made it happen sooner rather than later. We wanted it to be when we were fully ready for it and best able to retaliate. The timing would be ours, not anyone else's, certainly not India's. We have been planning for this for months. The drone strikes were the final catalyst. The Pearl Harbor moment. All those Indian dignitaries visiting you on your island – it was the ideal opportunity. We couldn't resist."

"Playing into their hands," said Buddha. "Did I not tell you?"

"Buddha, make yourself useful," said Parashurama. "Is he telling the truth? If not, force him to."

"Colonel," said Buddha to Zehri, "a lie harms the liar more than the one who is lied to. Come clean. Keep no deceit in your heart, lest it taint your soul."

"I am not lying and have no reason to lie." Nothing about Zehri had changed as a response to Buddha's verbal handjob; he must be on the level. "I am telling you exactly what I know, freely and of my own will."

"He is," said Buddha. "Whether it's the genuine truth or not, he believes it to be."

Zehri seemed relieved, as though a matter of honour had been settled, his probity no longer in question. "You could consider this me delivering a message from my superiors. The order has come down that whoever meets you in battle should, if the opportunity presents itself, be frank with you about Pakistan's motivations for inciting war."

"Why?" said Rama. "To undermine our resolve?"

Zehri shrugged. "That may be one outcome, although I doubt it will work. But you do appreciate, don't you, that you have become little better than weapons? Whereas before you were ridding the world of demons, now you are being turned against human beings, like living artillery. What does that tell you? Who are the demons now? And ask yourselves this. Where did those asuras spring from? And where have they gone to? They used to crop up on an almost daily basis. Now, all at once, there aren't any anymore. The wellspring seems to have dried up. Why? Why do they stop appearing just when you're needed elsewhere, when battle opens up on a different front?"

"We don't need to listen to this bollocks," said Vamana. "Get this twat out of here before I zoom up to full size and drop-kick him over a mountaintop."

"Think back," Zehri went on, undeterred. "Is it not rather convenient that asuras started crawling out of the woodwork when they did? The moment you Avatars were on hand to deal with them, there they were."

"Karmic balance," said Matsya. "With the good comes the bad."

"Ah yes, 'karmic balance.' Very neat and tidy. Or was it more than that? Was it because the Trinity needed a handy way of introducing the Dashavatara to the public and demonstrating their skills?"

Vamana fronted up to Zehri, making himself just tall enough that he could look down on the Pakistani. "You, pal, are getting seriously on my wick. Think you can psych us out with all this misinformation propaganda tosh? Think again."

"Hurt me if you will," said the colonel. "All I'm saying is that you should take a good, long, hard look at yourselves. Are you proud at using your godlike gifts to slaughter enlisted men? Would true gods do that? Why are you even here in Kashmir? Do you belong in a human war?"

Vamana drew back a fist.

Parashurama grabbed his wrist, restraining him.

"No. Don't give him the satisfaction. Hit him, and he's won. He's got to you."

Slowly, reluctantly, the Dwarf nodded and lowered his arm.

"Colonel," Parashurama said, "you've made your point. We've heard you out. Now, please leave the *Garuda*."

"With pleasure. Thank you for your patience." Zehri exited down the steps.

He was twenty paces from the aircraft when Parashurama's battleaxe came spiralling out of the doorway. Zehri didn't see it coming. Perhaps, in the last split second of his life, he heard its whirling whirr behind him. Perhaps, albeit briefly, he understood what that sound meant.

The axe passed straight through his torso, cleaving him in two from shoulderblades to hips and embedding itself in the ground several yards ahead of him. Zehri keeled over, his chest split open at the front, ribs clawing outwards. A massive pool of blood spread out beneath his body, staining the snow crimson.

"What the – ?" Vamana spluttered. "You tell me not to thump him, then you cut the bastard in half?"

Parashurama didn't reply. He went to retrieve his weapon, shaking the blood off the blade as he came back.

He looked grim, grimmer than I'd ever seen him – and the Warrior was not known for being a bundle of laughs.

"That was uncalled for," said Buddha as Parashurama re-entered the cabin.

"Shows how much you know, Peacemaker," said Parashurama. "Man had to die. I just didn't want him knowing he was about to. Killing him the way I did, that was a mark of respect. He had balls, coming to us and saying his piece like that. I wanted him to go back thinking he'd discharged his duty and got away with it. But I couldn't let him live. Couldn't have him sharing what he knows with anyone else around here. Definitely couldn't have him reporting back to his superiors that he'd rattled us."

"Has he rattled us?" said Kurma.

Parashurama didn't reply.

"What he said," said Varaha, "is there some truth in it?"

Parashurama hesitated. "Yes," he said. "Yes, I'm afraid I think there is."

29. DEMONS AS SUPERVILLAINS

THERE WAS SILENCE in the *Garuda*'s cabin.

"The truth?" said Kalkin. He had a very idiosyncratic manner of speech, pronouncing each word precisely. "That we aren't gods? We know that already. It's a useful fiction that keeps public opinion on our side. It's harmless. A white lie. Besides, who's to say that we don't have the genuine spark of divinity in us? We receive power from worship. Isn't that the practical definition of a god? We're superior to ordinary people. Again, that's what a god is. Ask me who I am, and I'm likely to tell you Kalkin the Horseman. Katsuo Arakari is a set of clothes I once wore. My life as him feels like a dream I had, and I'm awake now. Science may have transformed me into Kalkin, but the net result is I'm still Kalkin."

A couple of the other Avatars inclined their heads in agreement.

"No, that's not what I'm referring to," said Parashurama. "The asuras. You guys must have wondered about them, surely. We are manufactured, manmade, and then demons appear out of nowhere, like magic? How does that stack up? Come on, I can't be the only one who's been thinking it's a little fishy."

"Hey, Matsya," said Vamana. "He said fishy. Do you think it's fishy?"

The Fish-man fixed Vamana with an imperturbable, glassy stare. "Ignoring your feeble attempt at humour, Dwarf, I must admit that there have been times when I have asked myself whether the asuras might originate from the same source as us. Might they not have been through the theogenesis process as well? Been human once, as we ourselves were?"

"Me, I've been having too much fun to care," said Vamana. "How about you, Narasimha? Bothered about where your prey comes from? Or are you just happy to be hunting?"

"I am divine anger," said the Man-lion. "I am the protector. I slew the blasphemous demon Hiranyakasipu when no one else could, and I did not think twice about it. Slaying asuras is what I am best fitted for by nature. I do not question it, any more than the lion questions killing the zebra."

"Oookay, so it's an unqualified 'couldn't give a toss' from Narasimha. Krishna?"

"I have... had doubts. But Parashurama, you are the Warrior. The soldier. The loyal one who follows orders. You have led us. And all along, you have not been certain we are doing the right thing?"

"No, that's not it," said Parashurama. "Taking down asuras – no question it's something that needs to be done, and we should do it. Lives are saved if we do, put at risk if we don't. But I'm not stupid. I'm not some dumb grunt who gets handed a gun and told where to point it and just goes along with that. I don't have any evidence to back up what I've been feeling, these suspicions I've had. But for a while my gut's been telling me that the Trinity haven't been wholly straight with us. And it's been telling me that even more strongly since this India business blew up. What if – *what if* – the asuras were only window dressing? Just a way of getting the world onside quickly and easily. A showcase for us. A commercial. Letting people, and especially the Indian government, know what devas can do."

"This is all very conspiracy theory all of a sudden," said Vamana.

"But it's perfectly possible that the Trinity created them too, so as we'd have something to fight. Something inhuman and obviously evil."

"Supervillains," I said.

"Huh? What do you mean?"

"Superheroes need supervillains," I said. "They're no good if all they have to defeat are petty criminals, smugglers, rapists, racketeers and so on. It's asymmetrical warfare. Too easy for them. They need equals – opponents with abilities to match their own, with similarly outlandish names, motivations and looks. If I'm following what you're getting at, Parashurama, you and the other Avatars were being presented with something similar, with the asuras. You couldn't be chasing down a gang of bank robbers or rousting a drug cartel. That's for the police to do. Demons, on the other hand – that's clearly a job for supermen."

Parashurama jerked a thumb in my direction. "Check out monkey brains here. Hanuman's nailed it. Demons as supervillains."

"Let's get this straight," said Vamana. "The Trinity set the whole thing up? They created the asuras? They planted them? Let them attack and kill civilians so that we could fly in and save the day? It's crazy. Crazy talk." He shook his head, but it was less a denial, more an effort to dislodge the idea from his mind before it stuck fast. "They wouldn't do that."

"The men who've lent us out to the Indian military wouldn't do that?" said Varaha. "Wouldn't turn dangerous creatures loose and send us in to mop up the mess and then exploit the publicity that results? Really?"

"Yes, thank you, Mr Sarcasm."

"Not sarcasm. Cynicism. Justified cynicism, I'd say. The Trinity are businessmen. This has been a business enterprise – theogenesis, all of it. We – we are *product*. It's so bloody obvious now. I was blind to it beforehand because I like to help people, I want to make a difference, I want to make the world a better place. Don't snigger, Vamana. Don't you dare. But I had my misgivings about us getting dragged into a war, even if we were the victims of an act of aggression. And in light of what that colonel just told us, and what Parashurama's been saying... Jeez. Ever get the feeling you've been taken for a ride?"

"Why wouldn't they have told us?" said Kurma. "The Trinity. Right at the start. Come clean with us. Why the subterfuge?"

"Don't be ridiculous," said Varaha. "Would you have signed on the dotted line if you'd known it was all going to be a massive con? 'You'll be fighting demons, but don't worry. They're bogus. We made them specially for you.'"

"When you put it like that, no."

"Exactly."

"What really sticks in my craw is that Pakistan seems to know more about us than we do," said Parashurama. "This whole situation stinks, and I'm saying we head back to base and get to the bottom of it. Who's with me?"

It didn't sound as though Parashurama was putting it to the vote. Rather, he had made his mind up and was expecting the rest of us to go along with him.

Myself, I was feeling a twisting in the pit of my stomach. There was betrayal in the air. Had we been fed a pack of lies? Were we, as Zehri had said, little better than weapons?

Back in the early 1990s, I spent a portion of my first paycheque from my very first *2000 AD* commission on a copy of *Uncanny X-Men* #137, the double-sized "Death of Phoenix" issue. It was a treat for myself, a pat on the back for finally scoring a professional comics gig after years of unpaid fanzine contributions and supporting myself with tedious freelance design jobs. *UXM* #137 is a classic, the culmination of everything that writer Chris Claremont and artist John Byrne had been working towards during their stellar 1980s run on the title. In those pre-internet days I bought it sight unseen from a mail order catalogue. It cost me £100.

The dealer advertised the comic as near-mint grade, and it was, and it came bagged and boarded to help preserve its integrity, too. But what he neglected to mention was that it was a UK edition, with the printed cover price in pence rather than cents. To collectors, a pence copy is worth way less than a cents copy.

I wrote him a letter complaining. He wrote back stating that he had never said in his catalogue that it wasn't the UK edition. The fault was mine for not checking. Besides, I should have been able to tell by the sum he was asking for it. A cents copy would have been at least £50 more expensive.

So technically he hadn't defrauded me. Morally, though, he had.

I'd only read the comic in a trade paperback collection before, and I'd always promised myself I would splurge out on an original once I could afford to. I wanted to cherish my *UXM* #137. I'd spent what should have been my rent money on it. It was a ridiculous extravagance.

But it had come with a catch. I had been swindled out of its true value. I don't recall what I did with the comic in the end. I may have sold it on, at a slight loss. By the same token I may have burned it, a symbolic cremation, a funeral pyre for my naivety. Knowing me, probably the latter.

Hey, you're thinking to yourself, *am I reading this right? Surely he can't be equating being stiffed by a dodgy comics dealer with the deception which appears to have been perpetrated on him and the Avatars by the Trinity. It's one thing to be disenchanted about a superhero comic, quite another to learn that you have become an actual, bona fide superhero on the basis of a huge, murderous con. Get some perspective, nerd!*

Dear reader, you may well be correct. The sensation was the same, though. The same sour taste in the back of the throat. The same painful awareness of others laughing at your idiocy and gullibility. The same dark, simmering resentment.

Only multiplied by a thousand.

30. EVEN A DEVA CAN DIE

ON THE WAY back to Meru the next morning we received a distress call from Chandigarh.

When we got there, the airbase was at full battle stations. Pakistani troops and armoured divisions had crossed the border and were storming into the Punjab. Indian forces had contained them at the Sutlej river, but further north the Pakistanis had encountered less formidable opposition. The cities of Amritsar and Ludhiana had fallen to them, and Pakistani tanks were now closing in on Chandigarh. A battalion of them, around fifty, was barrelling down National Highway 95 and would be within striking distance of the airbase in under an hour.

Air Marshal Venkatesan was the epitome of cool-headedness in a crisis. Yet beneath the unflappable exterior lay a man desperate for help – for anything that might give him a tactical edge.

"Sirs, I have no right to ask this from you, but if Chandigarh airbase falls, the Pakistanis will gain a stronghold and the Punjab is lost. I can put it no plainer than that. Will you fight alongside us?"

Though we had our own agenda to pursue, we could hardly refuse. Confronting the Trinity would have to wait. A few hours, what difference would it make? Venkatesan needed us. At the very least we could help hold the line until reinforcements arrived from Patiala to the south.

Venkatesan's MiG-21s were already strafing the column of tanks with air-to-surface missiles, but Pakistani jets – Mirages and JF-17 Thunders – were providing effective air cover and few of the Indian pilots survived to make a second run. An HAL light combat helicopter had also scored hits with Nag anti-tank missiles until it too had fallen prey to the Pakistan Air Force. The PAF's air superiority in the region was making it tough for Indian forces to curb their ground offensive.

Parashurama divvied us up into two groups. The majority went in Krishna's chariot to meet the Pakistani tanks head-on. Kurma, Rama and I, however, were tasked with depleting the PAF air cover.

What this translated as was: jumping out of the *Garuda* onto moving jet aircraft.

I know, right?

But when you're a fully revved-up, siddhi-enabled deva, nothing – even the craziest shit – is impossible.

With Captain Sylvain Corday, formerly of the Royal Canadian Air Force, at the controls, the *Garuda* ran rings around the PAF fighters. We soared above the theatre of combat and singled out individual Pakistani planes to home in on. Then either Rama would pull off some nigh-impossible shot using an arrow with a hollow, nitroglycerin-filled tip, sending it straight into the jet's turbofan with devastating results, or else Kurma or I would leap from the doorway and freefall onto the fuselage. In the Turtle's case this mean plunging straight through, breaking the aircraft in half. Me, I would land on all fours, smash open the cockpit canopy, and yank the pilot out. That or puncture the plane's aluminium skin and rip out some vital part of the avionics. As the plane veered wildly out of control, Captain Corday would bring the *Garuda* alongside and I would leap back aboard. Kurma had to face the indignity of falling the rest of the way to earth like a meteor. Each time, the *Garuda* would swing by and pick him up from the impact crater he created.

Between us we downed over twenty PAF warplanes. The first time it was my turn, I nearly bottled out. God knows how fast we were going. Several hundred miles per hour. I'd never even done a parachute jump, and now I was supposed to propel myself, parachute-less, out of one supersonic aircraft to alight on another?

But that was Zak Bramwell being a wuss. Hanuman couldn't give a shit about danger. Pouncing onto a fighter jet in midair was the sort of insane stunt he loved. Zak Bramwell might be wetting his pants, worrying about what if he overshot, what if he missed his target, what then? All Hanuman cared about was hitting his mark with style.

One time, atop a Mirage, I almost came a cropper. The pilot tried to shake me off by launching into a succession of barrel rolls. I lost my grip and went slithering aft along the plane, athough centripetal force kept me in contact with the fuselage throughout. I caught hold of the tail assembly and immediately set to work twisting off the rudder flaps. There was nothing the pilot could do after that except eject and watch his bird spiral into a nosedive.

Down on the ground, the other devas laid into the Al-Khalid tanks and the lighter, shorter Al-Zarrar tanks that were rolling east towards Chandigarh. I only have their testimony to go on, since I was kind of busy in the sky at the time, but by all accounts it was a fierce, hard-fought battle. The Pakistanis did not stint with their coaxial machine guns and 125mm smoothbore tank guns, but they were designed for disabling and destroying other armoured vehicles and causing maximum damage to infrastructure. They were not meant for deployment against individual human beings who presented smaller, nimbler targets.

I can piece together how it went down. Vamana switching between dwarf size to escape notice and giant size to flip a tank over onto its side. Varaha charging like his namesake Boar, hammering an enemy vehicle into submission with his tusks.

Narasimha tearing open the turret hatch of an immobilised tank and diving inside to eliminate the crew by hand. Parashurama lopping gun barrels in half with his axe. Matsya, though out of his preferred element, using the same vast strength that made him such a supernaturally swift swimmer to wrench machine guns off their mountings. Kalkin leaning out from Krishna's chariot as it swooped low, severing caterpillar tracks with precision-placed sabre strikes.

They worked their way along the highway, cutting a swathe through the tank column from vanguard to rear. Indian planes, dominance of the skies once more theirs, zoomed in to finish off the crippled, stationary enemy units.

A couple of Al-Khalids trailing behind the rest made a break for it. They veered offroad onto farmland, crashing through fences and poorly built breezeblock houses in their eagerness to escape.

The Avatars did not let them get away. They chased and hounded the tanks. The driver of one, panicking, steered nose-first into a deep irrigation ditch which he couldn't reverse out of. The other Al-Khalid headed for a copse to take cover, but Avatars caught up with it while it was still out in the open, halfway across a rice paddy. The crew, rather than remain confined in their vehicle to face their ends, bailed out and ran. Knee-deep in muddy water, they didn't get far. Matsya circled around them below the surface like a shark, picking them off without mercy.

It was only as the Avatars were returning to

Krishna's chariot that they realised they were down a man. Varaha wasn't with them any more. They assumed he must be back along the highway somewhere, mopping up the last of the tank crews. Krishna flew low beside the pockmarked road, past one wrecked, burning tank after another. Everyone kept their eyes peeled.

They found Varaha sprawled face down next to the charred hulk of an Al-Zarrar. A 7.62mm bullet had caught him in the torso, boring a hole through his latissimus dorsi muscle. The wound sucked and bubbled. The bullet had hit a lung.

Krishna rushed him to the airbase hospital at Chandigarh in his chariot. The *Garuda* touched down there not long afterwards, and Rama and I were at Varaha's bedside within moments, bearing an emergency amrita kit. We administered shot after shot, while air force medics swarmed around us trying to keep the patient stable and stem the bleeding.

After the fourth dose of amrita, Varaha went into convulsions. His vital signs dropped precipitously. The docs tried CPR and defibrillation. Nothing doing.

Around noon that day, Varaha the Boar was pronounced dead.

31. THE STONE LOTUS

To SAY THE Avatars took Varaha's death hard would
be an understatement.

It was so mundane. A random bullet. A lucky
shot. Such a prosaic way to go. Scarcely befitting
of a deva.

And if we hadn't stopped to help defend
Chandigarh, Varaha would still be with us. That was
the real kick in the nuts. Our further involvement in
the war, reluctant as it was, had got him killed. We
hadn't intended to keep fighting on the Indians' side,
not until our concerns about the Trinity Syndicate
had been settled one way or another. But neither
could we ignore Air Marshal Venkatesan's appeal
for assistance. That was what devas did, wasn't it?
Responded to cries for help? Answered prayers?

The irony was that Varaha had been the most pacifist among us, after Buddha. He had to some extent been the Dashavatara's conscience. Just as, in his former life as Stevie Craig, he had staged dramatic protests and publicity stunts to raise awareness about the damage mankind was inflicting on the ecosphere, so as Varaha he had tried to make his fellow devas think carefully about what they were doing.

In Vedic legend, Varaha killed the demon Hiranyaksha, twin of Hiranyakasipu who later fell prey to Narasimha. Hiranyaksha was indestructible, immune to harm from any human or animal – except, as it happened, a boar. Vishnu duly took boar form to challenge him after he kidnapped Bhudevi, the earth goddess. Their duel in the depths of the primordial cosmic ocean lasted a thousand years, and in the end the victorious Varaha carried Bhudevi up to the surface on his tusks and restored her to the rightful place on dry land, above the waters. They fell in love and married, happy ending. All together now: *ahhhh*.

Varaha was earth's lover and defender. So was Stevie Craig.

Now both were gone.

And we devas were angry.

We'd been angry already and now we were angrier, and there was no Varaha any more to check or temper that anger. Buddha was still with us as the voice of reason, but even he was having trouble processing Varaha's death. He could offer consoling words about Varaha's consciousness passing from one state to the next, his karmic energy destined to rematerialise in another form, his atman already on its way through the neverending cycle of life and death towards rebirth, perhaps refined by devotion and good works to the very highest pinnacle of self, which is to say the absence of self. What he could not do was make any of us feel better about there being one less Avatar in our ranks. The Ten had become nine. Something was missing now. The set was irredeemably incomplete.

Maybe, too – though no one said it out loud – we were upset because we were gods, and gods don't get killed. They especially don't get killed by something as banal as nine grammes of lead and cupronickel cast into the form of a bullet round. What we had here was cognitive dissonance. We knew we were supposed to be immortal, invulnerable. But we also knew we weren't, we were just souped-up human beings, stronger and hardier than most but still with human frailties. A bullet *shouldn't* kill us, but still could.

In fact, if anyone were to ask me to sum up in a single phrase what being a deva was like, that phrase would be "cognitive dissonance". What we believed about ourselves thanks to theogenesis and our conditioning in the Induction Cocoon clashed repeatedly with what our rational minds kept telling us. We were lab rats who thought themselves gods, or gods who could not forget they were once lab rats. We were creatures of ancient myth transposed into the 21st century, equipped with 21st century hardware and protection, immersed in 21st century environments and geopolitics, deities out of time. We were the unreal made real, legends brought to life.

No wonder what Colonel Zehri had said had freaked us out so much. Our inner equilibrium was precarious enough as it was, without us having to think that we were being dicked around further by the Trinity, that there were wheels within already wobbly wheels.

In short, Varaha's death was the capper on a crapper of a day.

Things didn't get much jollier when we arrived back at Mount Meru.

While Buddha and Krishna oversaw the respectful offloading of Varaha's body, Parashurama selected a delegation of devas whose purpose would be to confront the Trinity and screw some answers out of them. It was him, Kalkin, Rama and me. The others were considered too hot-headed to come along. The matter had to be broached with diplomacy and tact. Threatening the Trinity with a mauling or a stomping was unlikely to secure success.

Why was I included in the delegation? Good question. I think Parashurama understood that Rama and I were inseparable. You wanted the Archer, you got the Monkey too. But also, I was the one who had twigged to the superhero/supervillain dynamic of the relationship between devas and asuras. I had insider knowledge of the whole paradigm.

As Parashurama put it, "Everyone needs a geek on their team."

"No argument here," I replied. "The geek shall inherit. Nerd is the word. Who's got your back? The anorak."

"Okay, enough. Don't make me regret my decision."

"Can't help it. Like the Jews say at Christmas: happy Hanuman."

"Seriously. Do you want to come along or do you want to be benched?"

I mimed zipping my lip.

Our swipe cards could get us no further than Meru's second-from-centre ring, but dammit, we were devas. A little thing like a locked door wasn't going to stop us. A couple of swings from Parashurama's battleaxe, and hey presto, we were standing outside the complex's innermost section.

The tower rose seven storeys high. The damage inflicted by the drone strike near the summit had yet to be repaired, but tarpaulins had been stretched over the gaping holes to keep out the elements.

We were on a walkway that linked to it midway up. The storeys below us were windowless, an expanse of sheer blank wall, prison-like. I speculated whether they were empty, just a supporting structure for the Trinity's personal accommodation.

"They perch atop a hollow edifice," said Rama. "How apt." He had never sounded quite so French as then.

"What now?" Kalkin asked Parashurama. "We call them out?"

The Warrior nodded. "And if that doesn't get us anywhere, we bust our way in."

Nobody responded to our yells. Nobody came to one of the tower's many balconies like some billionaire Juliet or Rapunzel.

"Odd," said Kalkin. "They have to be in. No one's seen them anywhere else in the complex today."

"Oi, rich geezers!" I shouted up. "I've got some money out here. Interested? It's free."

No answer.

"Damn, I was sure that would work. Like cheese to mice."

We stared up at the solid, stalwart tower. The tarpaulins bucked like sails in the warm Indian Ocean breeze.

Parashurama crouched, thigh muscles bunching, then sprang. He landed on one of the lowest balconies. If I remembered rightly, this would be Bhatnagar's floor. Krieger's lay above, and Lombard's was at the very top. A hierarchy, even among the Trinity. They weren't such equals as they liked to make out. I wondered how they had settled on who got which level of the tower. By calling dibs? Drawing lots? Or maybe it was inverse alphabetical order. Or maybe according to net worth, Lombard out-Croesusing Krieger, and Krieger, Bhatnagar.

It didn't take Parashurama long to establish that there was no one home in Bhatnagar's apartment, nor in Krieger's or Lombard's.

"Weird," he said, leaping down to rejoin us on the walkway. "I've performed a full sweep of all three apartments. If I didn't know better, I'd say they've upped sticks. Something about the way things have been left... They didn't just go, they went in a hurry."

"No," said Kalkin. "I mean, where would they go *to*? Why would they desert?"

"Because they knew we were coming back. And they knew why." This was from Rama, and it was one of those statements that sound like the person speaking doesn't want it to be true.

"The lower floors," I said. "Let's try those. Could be they have a romper room down there, or a sex dungeon or something, and that's where they are."

There was a locked door at the end of the walkway, and just inside, a thicker locked door, this one made of steel, with the added safeguard of retinal and palm print scanners. Neither portal lasted long when Parashurama's big axe came a-knocking.

Now we were on a gantry with a metal staircase zigzagging down from it. Below us lay a chamber four storeys tall, its circumference lined with stacks of what I can only describe as giant specimen jars. Each was as tall as a man and full to the brim with preservative fluid, a solution of formaldehyde and seawater. Each, too, was illuminated from beneath by uplighters inset into the base.

Some of the jars had nothing in them but fluid.

Others were... occupied.

By the corpses of the asuras which the Avatars had fought and killed during the preceding weeks. The rakshasa from Grand Central Station. The albino vampires from Paris. Various nagas. Duryodhana. Rahu. Adi. Others. A demonic rogues' gallery. Their remains floating suspended in the dense, slightly cloudy fluid. Eternally still.

The formaldehyde stink made you feel like your nose hairs were being singed.

"Trophies," said Parashurama softly. "Goddamn."

"We brought them back here thinking they were going to be hygienically disposed of," said Kalkin. "Cremated, or incinerated, or whatever. Not this. Not *kept*. The Trinity definitely told us the bodies would be treated like chemical waste. I remember it. They would be properly dealt with."

"A falsehood," said Rama. "And where there's one falsehood, there are likely to be more."

"What's that?" I asked, pointing to the centre of the chamber.

There sat a raised dais, looked down on by the rows of pickled asuras in their glass coffins. It had a kind of display podium on it, a waist-high steel column topped by a clear dome.

We went down for a closer look, and found biohazard symbols plastered all over the column.

The dome itself was no larger than you might find covering a cake stand, although it was hermetically rubber-sealed around its base – and what lay inside was no Black Forest gateau.

It was a piece of rock.

But not just any old chunk of granite or schist or pumice.

It gleamed. It glittered. Tiny flecks of blue

crystalline matter reflected the glow from the specimen jars, like chips of sapphire.

And it had a shape.

It was a delicate arrangement of concentric layers. Seven of them. Like petals.

The rock resembled nothing on earth so much as a flower. A lotus, to be precise. Petrified.

"What the fuck?" I said, because someone had to. Someone had to say *something*, and you know Hanuman. Chatty as a chimp.

We all gazed at the rock flower, curious and a little unnerved. None of us knew what to make of it. We were like cavemen studying an iPhone. It was beautiful and strange. Even if we could have touched it, even if the dome and the biohazard symbols hadn't suggested how unadvisable that would be, I doubt we would have dared. To have touched it would have been to profane it somehow.[1]

The nape of my neck prickled. It didn't help that we were surrounded by dozens of dead asuras, all adrift in preservative, their skin stippled with millions of tiny bubbles. Monsters with the gashes and the amputations that spoke of how they died. Torn flesh flaring. Sightless eyes peering out between half-closed lids. A mausoleum of curiosities. Creepy much?

"Any of you guys feeling that?" whispered Kalkin.

"Feeling what?" said Rama.

"You know. That buzzing sensation." Kalkin gestured vaguely in the region of his head. "Inside."

---

[1] Deflowering a flower, ha ha.

"Now that you mention it..." I said.

Now that he mentioned it, I was aware of a buzzing sensation to go with the nape hair prickling. I'm not sure what precisely my cerebral cortex is, but that was where it seemed to be coming from. From some core component of my brain. The hypothalamus, the limbic system, the amygdala... Hell, I don't know. I'm a comicbook artist, Jim, not a doctor. One of those places. A nagging intracranial itch.

It worsened the more I looked at the stone lotus. It seemed as though the flower was sending out signals and something in me was responding to them like a radio picking up a broadcast.

In a spirit of experimentation, I leaned right up close to the dome, so that my nose was almost touching it.

Static squawked inside my head. Mental white noise.

I reared back.

"Shit," I breathed. "It's like... This is going to sound nuts, but it's like it *recognises* us. That piece of stone, it knows who we are. What we are."

"You're saying it's sentient?" said Kalkin.

"I'm not saying anything. I don't pretend to understand what's going on. But our presence seems to trigger a reaction in it. Or being in close proximity to it triggers a reaction in us. You try. See for yourself."

The other three copied what I had done, putting their faces next to the dome's glass. All three jerked back as though they'd touched an electrified fence.

"*Sacre bleu*," said Rama. Because sometimes French people do actually say that. "My brain, crackling."

"Like a Geiger counter," said Parashurama, "detecting strong rads."

"There's an association here," said Kalkin. "Between it and us. An affinity."

"Yes," I said. "That's it. The stone's speaking to us at some level. Communicating."

"It is even a stone?" said Parashurama. "Is it naturally that shape, or did someone, you know, make it? Sculpt it? Build it?"

"The lotus. Our Induction Cocoon visions. There's a connection," said Rama. "Somehow this thing ties in to how we were transformed. I can't think how, but I'm sure of it."

"I know someone who'd know," I said.

32. CAST ADRIFT

W<small>E WENT IN</small> search of Professor Korolev.

He, however, like the Trinity, was nowhere to be found.

We scoured the second ring, interrogating every technician and lab assistant we came across. None of them had seen Korolev since yesterday.

"This is getting all rather Scooby-fucking-Doo," I said. "Korolev's abandoned ship as well?"

We widened the scope of our enquiries to take in the third and fourth rings as well. Finally we found someone able to enlighten us. It was one of the security officers, the same guy who had courteously turned me back that time I'd tried to enter the middle ring without a swipe card. He was a freckled ginger Afrikaner whose face reminded me of Gert Frobe as Goldfinger, only a mite more jovial.

"Oh *ja*, the bosses have gone," he said. "Didn't you know? Went this morning, man, first thing. Seaplane came for them, took them off the island."

"Did Korolev go with them?" said Parashurama.

"The Russkie scientist? Yeah. And Mr Bhatnagar's family. The pretty Indian girl too."

"Aanandi?" I said.

The security officer nodded. "If that's her name." He held a hand level with his shoulder. "This high. Talks American. Very smart. It was kind of unexpected, you know? Us guys in security didn't get any warning. Normally we're told whenever the principals are on the move. Then we can arrange for close protection. No one gave us any notification this time, which is kind of strange, I suppose. Maybe there weren't any spare seats on the plane."

"Any idea where they went?" said Parashurama.

"Not the faintest. Need-to-know, obviously. Somewhere safer than here would be my guess. Those missiles must have really spooked them. Spooked everybody, to be honest. Me included. But that one that trashed their apartment tower – you can hardly blame the bosses for thinking it's time to make like cow dung and hit the trail. Hey, aren't you fine *laanies* supposed to be fighting a war right now?"

"We're, uh, awaiting further orders."

"*Ja, ja.* It's a bad business, that. I'm seriously worried, man. I'd be heading back to Jo'burg right now if that was an option. We're pretty close to the fallout zone here, if the balloon goes up. Another reason why the bosses hightailed it, I reckon. At least if worse comes to worst there's an emergency evacuation plan. Seaplanes on standby twenty-four seven, ready to shuttle all personnel over to Malé. We can have Meru emptied in under six hours, and charter jets can then take people on to Africa, Australia or even the US. Hopefully we won't have to implement it, but you've got to be prepared for every contingency, *nè*?"

"Good to hear," said Parashurama. "So there's absolutely no way of knowing where the Trinity are now? No way of tracking them? No phone number to call them on?"

"Not as far as I know. You'd have to ask someone further up the food chain. Try Tellmann. Chief of security. I can show you to his office."

Tellmann, though, wasn't much more useful. The Trinity's departure had come as a surprise to him too, so much so that he hadn't known anything about it until he was woken by the racket of the seaplane arriving. He'd run out in his pyjamas in time to see Lombard and the others climbing aboard. The plane had taken off before he reached the docks.

"I have their private cell numbers in my directory," he said, "and I have tried calling, but no one's picking up. Straight to voicemail."

"Screening," said Parashurama. "Or maybe blocking."

Tellmann didn't like the idea; it offended him

professionally and perhaps personally too. "It's important that they keep me in the loop. How am I meant to do my job otherwise?"

"Where do you think they might be?"

"Your guess is as good as mine. They've each got about sixteen houses, so maybe one of those?" He shrugged. "It's not like they left a forwarding address or anything. Mr Lombard keeps a Cessna Citation X at Ibrahim Nasir Airport on Hulhulé. Assuming they've transferred to there from Malé, they could easily be halfway across the world by now."

"Wouldn't they have had to lodge a flight plan with the airport authorities?"

"I see where you're going with this, but owners of private aircraft can file a request to have their flight plans kept classified from the public, so you'd have difficulty finding out. Hacking into the database at Ibrahim Nasir is a possibility, as is bribing someone in air traffic control, but even then, destinations can always be changed mid-journey. There's no guarantee they'd land where they said they were going to land. I know this from my time bodyguarding movie actors and musicians. If they're told there's a pack of paparazzi waiting for them at airport A and they're not feeling like facing them, they divert to nearby airport B at the last minute while still in transit. The paps never find out in time."

"So basically the Trinity are off the grid and incommunicado until whenever they decide to get back in touch with the rest of us."

"That's the long and the short of it," said Tellmann.

"If you don't mind my saying, it's kind of curious that you Avatars are as much in the dark about this as the rest of us. I'd have thought if the bosses were going to tell anyone they were relocating, it would be you."

"Yeah," I said, "we're pretty baffled about it ourselves. And then there's what we found in the –"

Parashurama gave me a sharp nudge in the ribs. Clearly we weren't discussing the asura mausoleum or the stone lotus with anyone else just yet.

"It must not have crossed their minds," he said to Tellmann. "Officially we're under Indian military jurisdiction, so I guess the Trinity don't consider us their responsibility at the moment. They've handed us over."

"Still, you'd think..."

"Thank you, Mr Tellmann. We appreciate your cooperation."

"No trouble. Always glad to help Avatars and" – the chief of security glanced at me – "whatever you are, Hanuman."

"Me? I'm the neurotic but cool one. The wisecracking hipster who makes the rest of the team approachable and relatable. The Spider-Man of this outfit."

Tellmann could not have given less of a shit. "Yes. Well. Like I said, glad to help."

We met up again with the rest of the Dashavatara and filled them in on our news.

"So they've done a moonlight flit," said Vamana. "The weaselly bastards. Where does that leave us?"

"More to the point, what is this flower object you describe?" said Kurma. "What is it for? What does it do?"

"I'm darned well not opening the case it's in to find out," said Parashurama. "Here's what I think we should do. Notify Varaha's next of kin. That's first and foremost."

"We've commandeered space in one of the kitchen walk-in refrigerators," said Buddha. "Not best practice in terms of culinary hygiene, but we've got to keep the remains cold somehow until Varaha's family can arrange for their collection."

"Good. Next, we need to decide whether we're going to try and work out the Trinity's whereabouts and go after them. There may well be an innocent explanation for them jetting off unexpectedly, but I'm hard pushed to think of one. I don't like being cast adrift like this. I don't even like *feeling* we've been cast adrift. Makes me very antsy. As though there's more to come."

General assent all round.

"Let's rest up and reconvene first thing tomorrow," Parashurama went on. "Just to be on the safe side, I'm going to spend the night aboard the *Garuda*. It's not that I don't trust Captain Corday. It's just that someone might give him an order he can't disobey, and then we'd be without a ride. *Garuda*'s our transportational edge. It gives us a real chance of catching up with the Trinity, overtaking them even. It's faster than anything they've got, and there's nowhere they can go that it can't reach. Without it we'd be pretty much marooned on Meru. Be a shame to lose it."

This, too, seemed like a sound plan. The Warrior thought of all the angles. It was good to have a trained military mind like his in charge.

We went our separate ways. The only benefit I could see from the shocks and setbacks we'd experienced that day was that they had helped bring the team closer together. We were united in our disaffection, bonded by our shared suspicion of the Trinity. We had no idea then of the full scope of their machinations, but the glimpses we were getting made us a very unhappy band of brothers, and our main aim now was to get to the bottom of it all.

33. THE UNCLE GABBY SHIRT

I DON'T KNOW why I ambled over to Aanandi's room that evening. I just did.

It was something to do other than watch the news on TV, which was what almost everyone else on the island was doing, the main preoccupation.

The situation on the subcontinent was spiralling into chaos. Pakistani forces had pushed as far south-east as Jodhpur and Jaipur and were dangerously close to New Delhi. Kashmir was entirely a war zone. China had closed its border with the region, as had Nepal, leaving Kashmiri refugees with nowhere to go, no sanctuary from the bloodshed.

India simply had not anticipated the ferocity and intensity with which the Pakistanis were attacking. Though Pakistan was by far the smaller of the two nations, it made up in sheer aggression what it lacked in troop numbers and firepower. India was firmly on the back foot, and flailing.

The UN Secretary-General had appealed for calm and was doing his utmost to broker a ceasefire with the UN ambassadors from both countries, but without success. The rhetoric spewing out of Islamabad and New Delhi was defiantly hawkish and belligerent. This was a war, it seemed, which needed to be fought, and which neither side was willing to back down from.

Neighbouring countries were voicing deep concern, as well they might. Iran and other Middle Eastern powers were offering support for Pakistan, as was Russia. At present they were confining themselves to vague expressions of sympathy and brotherhood, but the possibility of military aid or even direct intervention was not being ruled out if the crisis worsened. Israel, ever attuned to unrest in the region, heightened its alert status and tested a few long-range missiles for good measure. India, for its part, was looking west for allies and finding them in the US, largely among Republicans in Congress who deemed any enemy of a Muslim nation their friend.

Epic News had managed to embed journalists with both the opposing armies and was covering the fighting on the frontlines extensively. The channel also devoted airtime to the reaction back home in the States, where alarmed members of the public were panic-buying bottled water and non-perishable foodstuffs, stripping supermarket shelves bare like

locusts. All the major American cities saw a mass
exodus, long lines of traffic clogging the freeways
and toll roads leading out. As one anxious father-
of-three said from behind the wheel of a belongings-
laden family SUV, "If the nukes start flying, who's to
say where it'll end? Whole world could go bananas."
Meanwhile an enclave of doomsday preppers in
the Ozarks were feeling justifiably smug. "Always
said this day was gonna come," said the mulleted
patriarch of an extended clan who were all armed
with assault weapons, right down to the youngest
child, aged five. "Them ragheads wipe one another
out, don't make no never-mind with me, but they
ain't gonna take us down with them, hell no. We'll be
holding out in this here compound long after the rest
of the planet is glowing ash. All hail the Free States!"

Rumours that the Dashavatara had been sighted
in action on the battlefield were neither confirmed
nor denied by an Indian military spokesman. "What
I can tell you," he said, "is that the gods have been
on our side. Make of that what you will."

India's Chiefs of Staff had in fact been attempting
to re-establish communications with us ever since
the battle outside Chandigarh, but Parashurama had
refused to respond to their efforts to hail us over
the *Garuda*'s radio. Plaintive phone calls came from
them direct to Mount Meru but these, too, were
ignored. Whether the Indians tried contacting the
Trinity, I can't say, but I imagine they did and got
nowhere. The Trinity were stonewalling everybody.

Should we devas have set aside our own private

grievances and got involved again in the conflict? Might we have been able to stop it before it went too far? That's one of those great imponderables, a question that frequently comes to me in the long watches of the night and guarantees a sleepless hour or so. In my view, if we *had* gone back in I doubt we would have made much of an impact in a war that was already being waged on several fronts and spreading fast. Besides, the Indians had not shown a great deal of aptitude and imagination in the way they utilised us. I suppose they could have sent us behind enemy lines to carry out some black ops raid on the Pakistani high command, cutting off the head to bring the body to a standstill, but ethically we would have had problems with that. I certainly would have. Battling soldiers, tanks and planes was one thing, but assassinating generals in cold blood? That's the stuff of war crimes tribunals.

What it came down to was this. The war had cost us a teammate, and it was a price we begrudged paying. Our reasons for becoming embroiled in the conflict were tangential to begin with. We had no real sense of commitment. Neither patriotism nor ideology was spurring us. We'd participated mainly because the Trinity had told us to – and in the Trinity we did not trust any more.

So, in the end, we were content to relegate ourselves to the same status as almost everyone else on earth. We became uneasy spectators, following the progress of events on television with an appalled fascination, hoping for the best, dreading the worst.

Going to Aanandi's room was my way of taking a break from the unfolding international mayhem. I still found it hard to fathom why she had sneaked off with Lombard and chums. She didn't belong with them. Morally and spiritually, I mean. The Trinity were pure corporatism, greed machines, human on the outside but with dollar-green blood flowing through their veins. There was more to Aanandi Sengupta than that.

The door was locked, of course, but that was no obstacle, not to Hanuman. I went outside and monkeyed my way up the exterior of the building. The sliding door to the balcony was also locked, but a bit of deva-strength tugging snapped the latch, and I was in.

There had to be something in the room, some clue as to why she had left and maybe as to where she had gone.

That was what I told myself, at any rate. That I was there to solve a mystery.

But in truth, I was there because I was miffed and miserable. Hanuman might not care what a mortal woman thought of him, but Zak Bramwell did. I took Aanandi's abrupt departure personally. I felt we had a spark between us. Damn it, we *did*. So how could she just go, without giving me some explanation, some justification? Did I mean that little to her?

Her room was spick and span, as ever. Not a single thing out of place. She'd even made the bed before she went. Touch of OCD maybe?

I sat down on the bed and ruffled up the covers a little, to make the room look more lived-in. Now her absence wasn't quite so total. She hadn't left a complete vacuum behind.

I stayed there for ten minutes, breathing in ghosts of her scent.

Something caught my eye. I'd thought there wasn't anything out of place, but there was. One of the books protruded at an angle. The rest were in tidy rows like soldiers on parade, except for this one which leaned drunkenly out from the shelf.

It wasn't just any old book, either. It was one of Aanandi's own publications: *The Field Of Truth*. Her survey of the *Bhagavad Gita*.

I took it down and riffled through it.

There was something lodged between two of the pages. A sheet of paper.

I slid it out.

A handwritten note, beginning with the words "From A to Z".

"No way," I murmured to myself.

From Aanandi to Zak.

Had she left me a clue after all?

I read on and found that actually it was a whole lot more than that.

I'm betting you're going to break into my room. You've done it once, why not again? I know you. You're a nosey so-and-so. Can't leave well enough alone.

Well done, though, on finding this. A credit to your

powers of observation, or my arts of subtle direction. It was almost painful to leave something not straightened and squared away, but I had to. So you'd spot it. You and no one else.

Got a message a half-hour ago. Lombard wants off the island, pronto, and he wants me to come with. Duty calls. Can't reasonably say no. I haven't got much time. That's why this is so hurried and low-fi. If I could have done something cooler and cleverer, I would have.

There's more to Meru than you realise. More going on here than you can possibly guess. The game is bigger and reaches further. The Dashavatara were only ever the beginning.

I don't know why I'm telling you this. Probably I shouldn't. But you seem like what my dad calls a "pukka cove," and I hate to see you being used.

There's a second site. Another Meru. That's where we're headed. Lombard's old stomping ground. If I knew exactly where it was, I'd say, but I've not been there myself before. I know it's in a disused mine of some sort. That's all. Sorry.

I'm scared. What the Trinity have started, I don't think can be stopped. But I think it should be. I think someone has to stop it before it goes too far. I wish that someone were me, but I don't have the resources or the power. You and the other devas might.

There was a postscript.

> PS. Look in the top drawer of the vanity unit. A little gift.
> I ordered it in from the States. Had it made specially
> for you.

I opened up the drawer indicated, and inside lay a T-shirt. It was printed with an image lifted from a *Sock Monkey* comic by Tony Millionaire.[1] It was a blow-up of a single, intricately drawn panel showing Uncle Gabby, the titular sock monkey, puzzling over a Chinese finger trap. The speech bubble read: "It is an ingenious device!"

I chuckled. *Sock Monkey*, with its anthropomorphised animals and quaint Victorian-engraving look, was a weird read, as unnerving as a recording of a nursery rhyme played backwards. I liked it, but only in small doses.

Aanandi had left a second note with the T-shirt.

> You don't have a proper uniform of your own. I hope this
> will do.

I tried the shirt on. Looked cool, I thought. On the back there was a Sanskrit-style "10½" in a circle. My unofficial Dashavatara number emblem. I chuckled again.

---

[1] Not the name he was born with, surprisingly enough, although you can't fault cartoonist Scott Richardson for choosing a pen name that stated so nakedly what he wanted out of life. Then again, who am I to judge another's pseudonym?

Then I reread the first note, and a sombreness
settled back over me.

*What the Trinity have started, I don't think can
be stopped.*

War.

They had wanted this war all along.

They had meant for devas to fight in it.

Why?

That remained to be discovered.

But at least now we had some indication where
they might be holed up.

34. BIOLOGICAL WEAPONS

THE GARUDA ARCED high, heading south-east.

"'A disused mine of some sort,'" said Vamana. "That's it? That's all we have to go on? I hate to state the obvious, but Australia's a bloody big place. Must be hundreds of disused mines there. Thousands, probably. How the hell are we supposed to find the right one? Needle in a stack of needles, if you ask me."

"You must not dismiss what Hanuman has contributed," said Rama. "Before, we had nothing, no hint where the Trinity are."

"It's okay, Rama," I said. "You don't need to defend me. Vamana, I know you make it your business to be a prick to everyone."

"Not everyone," said Vamana. "Just people I

don't like. Which – newsflash – includes you, faeces flinger."

"But I'm on the squad now," I went on, somehow managing to refrain from smashing his stupid face in. "Like it or lump it. Also, I have siddhis myself. If I want to, I'm perfectly capable of twisting your bumpy little head off."

"You could try."

"Don't tempt me. I doubt anyone would stop me if I went over there and kicked seven shades of shrinky-dink shit out of you. They'd probably cheer me on, thinking you had it coming. The fact is, the way you keep trying to prove you're bigger than everyone else is becoming pretty tiresome. We get it. You've felt belittled all your life. You have something to prove. But right now there's more important stuff going on than your self-esteem. Two countries are on the brink of nuclear conflict, which the Trinity may have engineered, God knows why, and which is liable to spread across the world. So just get your priorities straight, huh? Snark at me all you like but *some other fucking time*, yeah?"

Vamana looked as though he could go one of two ways: either completely lose his rag with me, or concede graciously. I could see the inner debate raging. Which option, he was wondering, would do less harm to his standing with the other Avatars?

In the end he chose a middle path. He grated out a laugh, then said, "Point taken, Hanuman." His voice was syrup but his eyes were venom. "I do have a tendency to, well, overcompensate. I'm glad you've brought it to my attention that I can be a bit acerbic sometimes. I will strive in future to be a better person."

Which, translated from nicey-nicey language, meant: "Fuck you, matey. First chance I get, I'm going to screw you over so hard, you'll be limping for the rest of your life."

No one in the *Garuda*'s cabin was under any illusion that Vamana's contrition was sincere, least of all me. However, for the time being, it did seem he was going to be a good boy and behave. That was enough.

Parashurama said, "Turns out Aanandi's been a darn sight more helpful than even she thinks. The big clue is 'Lombard's old stomping ground.' We know the guy was born and raised in Queensland. His parents ran a cattle station outside a town called Cloncurry, which isn't far from the border with the Northern Territory. All this comes courtesy of his Wikipedia entry, which is so long and detailed you have to wonder if he didn't write most of it himself. It stops just short of worshipping the ground he walks on. Anyway, around about Cloncurry there's all sorts of mineral deposits – silver, lead, zinc, copper, phosphate rock, oil shale, uranium, you name it. Place is riddled with mine workings, some dating back to the mid-eighteen-hundreds. It's also about the hottest spot temperature-wise in all Australia, which is saying something. Of the mines, approximately half are still in use, the rest tapped out and shut down."

"Doesn't narrow it down much," said Kalkin.

"I grant you that. But it might be worth our while to focus on the immediate vicinity of the cattle station, and here's why. Lombard sold the farm off when he was just starting out in the media biz. Then a decade ago he bought it back, along with several thousand acres of adjoining land. Paid top whack for it, and some would say that was sentimental affection for the old homestead. Which is fine, and plausible, but what if he had an ulterior motive?"

"To build this 'second site' there?" said Kurma. "This 'other Meru'?"

"Precisely my thinking." Parashurama waved a printout of a map of the area. "Again the internet comes to our rescue. Because it just so happens that on one patch of land adjoining the cattle station, one of the extra bits Lombard bought, there is a disused copper mine. It wasn't a massive reserve, couple of million tonnes of chalcopyrite, copper sulphide ore. A local firm dug the lot out, then closed the pit back in the nineteen-eighties. Now I'd say, on balance, that this mine, the Golden Rocks Mine, is looking like a strong contender. Wouldn't you all agree?"

"It meets the criteria," said Matsya. "Is there any evidence of recent construction work?"

"None externally. I zoomed in as far as I could on Google Maps. Some derelict outbuildings, old unpaved road, the rest just scrub and sand. But that isn't to say there's nothing there. Could all be underground, a secret installation. You might also like to know that Cloncurry has an airport.

Runway's easily long enough to land a Cessna Citation on."

"Hanuman," said Kalkin, "isn't it just a little bit fortuitous that Aanandi left this message for you? One that provides just the right amount of information we need to locate the Trinity. Doesn't it seem somewhat of a breadcrumb trail? Like we're *supposed* to be following them?"

"You mean is this a trap?" I said. "That did occur to me. All I can tell you is my instinct says it isn't."

"Your instinct," said Vamana, "or your gonads?"

I shot him a look.

The Dwarf held up his hands, palms out, mimicking surrender. "All right, all right. Sorry. It's nice-guy Vamana from now on. Promise."

"Yes, I fancy Aanandi," I said. "I don't deny it. I like her a lot. But I'm not completely blinkered. She could be leading us on. This could all be a bluff, a cunning Trinity plot. Maybe there's no second site at all. Maybe we're being led a dance. Maybe they want us chasing after phantoms while they get up to something else, somewhere else."

"If what they want is us to get lost running round in circles in the middle of nowhere," said Buddha, "there are few better places for that than the Australian Outback."

"But," I said, "I don't believe Aanandi would be a party to that. Certainly not willingly. She's not like Lombard or Krieger or Bhatnagar, or even Korolev. She still has a soul."

But did she? Did I really know Aanandi Sengupta

that well? Or did I just like to think I knew her? Was I fooling myself? Was she using me? The book, the note, was it all an elaborate setup?

I hadn't had a great track record with women up to that point. I tended to fall in love hard, then soon start taking the object of my infatuation for granted, assuming my dazzling worship of her would blind her to my many personal shortcomings. I didn't have any great insight into the female mind or emotions. My *own* mind and emotions were still something of a mystery to me, for that matter.

I wanted to be right about Aanandi.

Trouble was, I couldn't be sure.

Captain Corday's voice over the intercom broke in on the discussion.

"Uh, gentlemen, quick heads-up. War situation bulletin. Pakistani President's just held a press conference. Foreign Secretary, bunch of military brass with him. He's delivered what he calls a final ultimatum to India. Says India should capitulate immediately. Claims it's used biological weapons against Pakistan. I'm guessing that's a coded reference to you guys, since there've been no reports of gas attacks or anything like. Says Pakistan's spatial, military, economic and, uh, what's the fourth one? Political. Its spatial, military, economic and political thresholds have all been breached. Red line time. Unless India surrenders, he's reaching for the button. This is all second-hand, you understand. I'm getting updates in dribs and drabs. Cross-chatter from air traffic controllers in Colombo, Singapore,

Jakarta and Perth. But shit, it's not looking good, fellas. Just thought you should know."

"Holy Mother of Christ," said Parashurama. "They're taking it right to the brink."

"I thought Pakistan was winning," said Vamana. "Don't you go nuclear only as a last resort? When your back's against the wall?"

"They *are* winning," said Rama. "That's why. They're pressing home the advantage. They're hoping to blackmail India into giving in. Preying on fears of mutually assured destruction."

"Must be a bluff," said Krishna.

"Even if it is, my homeland is not going to take a threat like that lying down," said Buddha. "It's more likely to launch a pre-emptive strike. Get its retaliation in first."

"I'm afraid you're right," said Kalkin. "Pakistan may just have miscalculated badly."

"And it's on us," I said. "We made it worse by being there. We've given them the excuse they need to ratchet things up a notch. Bugger, bugger, bugger."

"The Trinity," said Matsya. "They must be the key to preventing Armageddon. Aanandi's note seemed to imply that."

"Then it's all the more imperative that we get to them," said Parashurama with steel in his voice. "And most ricky-tick."

35. THE GOLDEN ROCKS MINE

WE BYPASSED CLONCURRY airport altogether, landing on a flattish area of desert equidistant between the town and the Golden Rocks Mine.

Matsya stayed aboard the *Garuda*. Arid, baking-hot air did not agree with him. He dehydrated easily, and his amphibian skin was better suited to moist, cold environments. Exposure to the Outback at the sun's zenith would have cooked him like a kipper.

The rest of us set forth in Krishna's chariot. It sped low over rugged red earth, hugging the contours of the terrain and whisking past stands of ghost gum and bottletree. A mob of kangaroos went hopping away in fright. As we crossed above a creek, a scarily large crocodile basking on the bank thrashed down into the shallows, taking refuge in the cloudy green water.

"Jesus, that croc looked like Matsya's second cousin," Vamana commented.

"You're only saying that because he's not here," said Kalkin.

"I'd say it even if he was. We have a love-hate thing going, the Fish-man and me. Plus, he's almost impossible to get a rise out of. I take it as a challenge."

"So much for 'nice-guy Vamana,'" I said. "How long did that last? A couple of hours?"

The Dwarf forked two fingers at his eyeballs, then at me.

I forked two fingers at my own eyeballs, then turned them into a V-sign.

Vamana smirked. "You watch your back, Tarzan of the Apes."

"Backs of my knees, maybe."

We circled the Lombard cattle station, which consisted of parched fields, broken-down fences, and a mean little tin-roofed shack surrounded by dilapidated barns and sheds. A rusted tractor stood beside the driveway, tyres long since perished to nothing. Weeds twined up through its axles and engine block.

"Uninhabited," said Parashurama. "No one's lived there in years."

"Lending weight to the theory that Lombard bought the land for the mine," said Kurma.

"My thoughts exactly. Krishna?"

"On my way."

The chariot swung out westward, heading for a rocky ridge on the horizon.

Over the other side lay the Golden Rocks Mine.[1] It burrowed into the side of a hill, and the pithead was marked by the skeletons of old machinery – cranes, conveyor belts, crushers, hoppers, sluices – which the mining company had seen no profit in dismantling and removing. A prefabricated hut, once the foreman's office, had half collapsed on itself. There were still deep ruts in the dirt road leading into and out of the site, from the wheels of a fleet of dump trucks.

"*Voilà*," said Rama, pointing.

Parked just inside the mine's mouth, deep in shadow, were a pair of four-wheel-drive vehicles, a Toyota Land Cruiser and a Land Rover Discovery. Though dusty in places, both cars were shinily, fulsomely new, in stark contrast to the tarnished, peeling relics around them.

"Bingo," said Parashurama. "Set her down, Krishna. Not too close."

Kurma and Narasimha went ahead as scouts. The former was the least harmable of us, and the latter had the sharpest senses and reflexes. The same applied for booby traps. Kurma was once a caver, too, so his expertise in subterranean matters might come in handy.

The mine's mouth swallowed them up in

---

[1] So called because chalcopyrite, in raw form, has a kind of golden sheen. But you probably guessed that already, or even knew.

darkness. We waited. The sun was hellish, seeming to pin everything down with an iron grip. Cicadas chirruped relentlessly in the desert shrubbery, making me think of the emergency signal from Jimmy Olsen's wristwatch which he would use to summon Superman whenever he got into trouble: *zee-zee-zee*.

Kurma and Narasimha re-emerged shortly and reported back.

"It goes in quite a distance, maybe half a kilometre," said Kurma. "Sheer rock. But then the tunnel shelves steeply downwards, and there's a freight elevator. Funicular; runs on a set of tracks."

"Does it look like a recent addition?" said Parashurama.

"Not as old as everything else around here. I'd say it's been there no more than a few years. Five, maybe six."

"The cars," said Narasimha. "The Trinity's scents were on them. Fresh. Also in the tunnel."

"That's the clincher," said Parashurama. "Okay, troops. Here's what we're going to do. We need to get Buddha down below so that he can work his magic on the Trinity, make them 'fess up to us. Buddha's our main asset right now. A group of us escort him. Keep him safe at all times. This all right with you, big guy?"

The Peacemaker nodded gently, eyes half-closed.

"The rest of us –"

But Parashurama didn't get to complete the sentence.

The prefab hut exploded. Fragments of plywood framework, composite wall panelling and honeycomb insulation showered outwards.

Something uncoiled from within.

Something enormous and glisteningly loathsome.

36. TAKSHAKA

IT WAS A NAGA, a snake-man, but it was far larger than any of the nagas the Dashavatara had faced up 'til now. It reared erect twenty, twenty-five feet, a huge humanoid torso atop a serpentine tail as thick as a tree trunk. Its head was hooded like an angry cobra's. Its markings were bands of red, yellow and black like a coral snake's. Hand-sized scales reflected the sunlight dully along its rippling length.

It was Takshaka, one of the nagas' tribal kings. I knew this because Hanuman knew it. The recognition was instant and primal. Takshaka, robber and poisoner. A nasty piece of work. The kind of monarch only snake asuras would allow themselves to be ruled by. Worst among equals.

He lunged straight for us, without hesitating,

without pausing to monologue or posture. He slithered across the dry soil with sinewy contractions of his tail, bearing down on us with freight train speed and power. His maw gaped, revealing a pair of upper fangs as long as sickle blades and dozens of lesser teeth serrating his gums. Sulphur-yellow venom oozed from the fang tips.

The attack took us all unawares. He could have had his pick of any of us. His mistake came in choosing Kurma as his target. He torqued his head sideways and bit the Turtle around the middle – the one deva present who could withstand those giant fangs.

There was a loud *crunch*. Kurma's armour buckled under the pressure exerted by Takshaka's jaws, but held. The fangs did not penetrate. Venom squirted uselessly down Kurma's front, sizzling in the dust at his feet.

Takshaka let go and recoiled, tossing his head, annoyed. His slitted gaze fixed on another of us, Buddha. You could see what was going through his mind. *That one*, he was thinking. *So much softer-looking. Plenty of flesh to sink my teeth into*.

Narasimha leapt to intercept.

Takshaka batted him aside with a backhand sweep. The Man-lion hurtled through the air and crashed into one of the hoppers, a massive drum which at one time would have held tons of crushed copper ore. He bounced away, stunned senseless. The impact rang the hopper like a gong.

Takshaka dived at Buddha, but now Parashurama

was there to protect the Peacemaker. The blade of his battleaxe collided with the naga king's head.

I was expecting the axe to draw blood at least, if not slice Takshaka's brow open to the bone.

But Takshaka's scales were made of sterner stuff, it seemed. Tougher even than tank armour.

He laughed, a gritty mocking sound like thunder in the hills, the promise of a storm.

Parashurama was fazed. Being the Warrior, however, he swiftly adapted, altering his plan of attack. He adjusted his grip on the axe handle, spreading his hands, and the weapon became a kind of quarterstaff with which he began clobbering Takshaka from all directions, left, right, up, down, a volley of blows that drove that giant asura back, back, further back, away from Buddha.

Realising I'd never get a better chance, I leapt in and grabbed Buddha. Sweeping him off his feet, I whisked him over to Krishna's chariot.

"You two need to make yourselves scarce," I said. "At least until we've put Hissing Sid over there down for good."

Kalkin joined Parashurama in the fight. He started hacking at Takshaka's tail with both his talwars, although he had no more success piercing the naga king's hide than the Warrior had.

With a lash of his tail tip, Takshaka sent Kalkin flying. The Horseman ended up like Narasimha, sprawled on the ground, semiconscious.

This asura was like no asura the Avatars had confronted yet.

This was a serious foe; one they might not be able to defeat.

Not that that was going to stop them trying.

Rama shot a flurry of arrows at Takshaka. His bowstring twanged and twanged. But the naga king was simply too tough. The arrows ricocheted off as though the Archer was shooting Nerf darts at him.

I bounded over to Vamana, who was in the throes of upsizing. When his body had finished distending and contorting and he was at his maximum height, I said, "Get me up there."

"You what? Up where?"

"Onto Takshaka's head."

"How? You want me to just walk up to him and plonk you on?"

"No. Throw me."

"And why would I do that?"

"Look at it this way. If you miss, I'll probably end up buried face first in the hillside behind him. So you can't lose."

"Well, since you put it like that..."

With a cockeyed grin, Vamana picked me up and leaned back like a baseball pitcher winding up for the throw.

"Why are you doing this?" he said.

"Trusting you?"

"Not that. What do you hope to achieve on top of that thing's head? If Parashurama can't even put a dent in it, what difference can you make?"

"Distraction. Give someone the opportunity to hit it really hard. Someone like you."

"*Oh*. Well then, do your worst."

And he hurled me.

"Fastball special!" I yelled as I flew through the air like a javelin.[1]

Vamana's aim was more or less true. I shot past Takshaka's head, but close enough to reach out and grab the rim of his cobra-like hood. I swung round, scissored my legs around his neck, and began battering his brainpan with both fists as though drumming on bongos.

Takshaka swung violently from side to side in an effort to shake me off. He clawed at me but I clung on. The stink of him was ghastly. His hide gave off a putrid musky odour, while his venom had the acrid stench of rotten cucumbers.

I transferred my attention to his eyes, hammering them hard.

Takshaka squeezed them shut to protect them. Enraged, bellowing, he slithered blindly backwards. Together we crashed against one of the conveyor belt units. His shoulders bore the brunt of the impact, but I barely managed to hang on. He sensed this and leaned forward in order to throw himself backwards again.

Then Vamana appeared. He had wrenched off the arm of a crane and was holding it out in front of him like a lance, broken end forward.

He charged, ramming the twisted tips of the crane

---

[1] Come on, you get the reference, even if you're not an X-Men fan. Fastball special? Wolverine? Colossus? Oh, never mind. Suit yourself.

arm spars into the naga king's belly. Takshaka roared in pain. Vamana drew the crane arm back and rammed it again. I heard – and felt – bones splintering inside Takshaka.

A third blow pinned the naga king to the conveyor belt. He was screaming and thrashing. Blood spurted from his maw, along with jets of angry venom.

Parashurama leapt, swinging his axe. A single, perfect strike shattered both of Takshaka's fangs. Venom sprayed everywhere, along with fragments of dentine.

Vamana stepped back, and Takshaka toppled to the ground, sobbing in agony. I sprang away.

The giant Dwarf raised the crane arm above his head and brought it down vertically like a pile driver. The spars were impaled into the earth on either side of Takshaka's neck. Vamana used his bodyweight to grind the arm further downwards, and the naga king was immobilised. His tail lashed, his fingers furrowed the dirt, but he couldn't for the life of him writhe free.

Parashurama came over lugging a boulder.

Viewers of a sensitive disposition should look away now.

"This is how we used to deal with rattlesnakes back home in Wyoming," the Warrior said. "They were a lot smaller, and so was the stone, but the principle's the same. Pin the rattler behind the back of the head, then bash it until it stops moving."

He pounded Takshaka's head with the boulder until brains came gushing out of his nostrils. An eyeball popped. The naga king's flat noggin gradually grew more and more concave until it was crater-shaped.

A full minute later, his tail finally stopped twitching and lay still.

We looked at one another, panting, sweating. None of us said what we were thinking: *That was a close one. And Takshaka may not be the only thing the Trinity have up their sleeves...*

Parashurama knew a pep talk was in order. "Good work, team. Especially you." He meant Vamana and me. "The two of you, working together. Miracles do happen."

"Yeah, well," grunted Vamana, "don't expect an encore. Wouldn't have done it, but I knew the Monkey wouldn't manage on his own."

"Aww, I love you too, ya big lug," I said. "Come over here and gimme a cuddle."

"In your fucking dreams, mate."

"Avatars!"

The shout echoed across the pithead.

We all spun round.

Dick Lombard was hailing us from beside Krishna's chariot. Krieger and Bhatnagar were beside him.

The chariot itself had four new occupants, in addition to Krishna and Buddha.

I recognised them. It was the quartet of shaven-headed goons who had kidnapped me off the street in Crouch End. There was Diamond Tooth, the leader of the pack, and Hillbilly Moustache, and Knuckleduster Ring, and Knuckleduster Ring's twin.

Knuckleduster Ring and Hillbilly Moustache had semiautomatic pistols pressed to the backs of Krishna's and Buddha's heads. Diamond Tooth had just finished fastening a ball gag over Buddha's mouth to prevent him speaking. He gave a signal to the other three, and all four of them plucked foam earplugs from their ears.

The Trinity did likewise.

Rama nocked an arrow.

"Come now, Archer," said Lombard. "There's no call for that. We're all friends here still, despite what you might think. Besides, you could kill one of us, maybe two, but not before Krishna or Buddha gets a radical brainectomy. You're fast but not that fast, and the four gents you see here are hardcore security professionals. Not like the rent-a-cops at Meru. This lot have black belts in not giving a shit about their personal safety or anyone else's. True, fellas? You aren't scared of dying, long as you get to take somebody with you."

The four goons didn't even crack a smile. That was how seriously they took the business of being badass.

"Pains me to say it, as a good Aussie," Lombard went on, "but if you want serious shitkicking troppos on your payroll, go British. Ex-British special forces, to be precise. Costs a buck or two, but worth every cent. And no, Narasimha. Uh-uh-uh!" He wagged at finger at the Man-lion, who had crawled back to his feet and was sizing up the distance between him and the Trinity. "I'm watching you. Same goes for you as for Rama. You try anything, and at least one of your Avatar pals is toast. Got that? You don't want to go losing another teammate, not so soon after poor old Varaha shuffled off his mortal dingdong."

"We haven't come for a fight," said Parashurama. "We've only come for answers."

"Yeah, we reckoned as much," drawled Krieger. "But you can't blame us for seizing the initiative, can you?"

"How did you know we were coming?" I asked.

"How do you think?" said Lombard. "What, you reckon you can just scoot around in the *Garuda* – an aircraft *we* built – and we wouldn't know where you were? You must think we came down with the last shower. We've got a GPS transponder on that thing locked tight, beaming us a signal constantly." He tapped his temple. "Pays to keep an eye on your assets at all times."

"Takshaka's ambush was just a diversion," said Bhatnagar, "so that our men could get into position to neutralise the most vulnerable and most dangerous of you – Buddha. If we're going to talk with you, we want it to be on our terms, without Buddha compelling us to agree to your demands."

"The playing field is levelled," said Lombard. "We have hostages and guaranteed command of our own free will. And that, my friends, is how you negotiate. In any business deal, you always make sure you're holding the aces so the other blokes can't have a lend of you. Doesn't matter how powerful they are, long as the upper hand's yours, you can't lose. Devas, corporations – it's all the same. It all comes down to leverage."

"Then as equals," said Parashurama, laying down his axe carefully and deliberately, "on a level playing field, let's talk."

37. DESCENT

THE FUNICULAR ELEVATOR sank at a ponderous pace into the bowels of the earth, thrumming and trembling as it went.

It was Lombard's idea to conduct discussions underground, out of the sun. "Outback heat'll fry the arse off you. More civilised to talk in the shade, and you'll be surprised how nice and cosy we've made things down below."

Riding on the elevator's platform were the Trinity Syndicate, the four goons, Buddha, Parashurama, Kalkin, Rama and me. The other devas remained at the pithead, in the mouth of the mine. If we didn't return in an hour, they were primed to come down and raise merry hell.

Buddha was still being held at gunpoint, and still

gagged. I was certain we could have freed him at any time and disposed of the four goons, but it suited our purposes to play along for now. The Trinity must have realised this. We were giving them the benefit of the doubt, pretending that they were setting the terms of the truce even though they, and we, were well aware who outgunned whom. Call it courtesy. Without the Trinity, after all, we wouldn't have had the siddhis in the first place. As a wise man once said, with great power comes great responsibility. Not to mention great self-restraint.

"Here's how it is," Lombard said. "You blokes are showroom models. You'll have figured that out by now. You're the poster boys for theogenesis. No shame in that. And we're damn proud of you. Isn't that so, fellas?"

Krieger and Bhatnagar nodded in assent.

"Look at you," the Australian went on. "Look at what you've done. Look how you *look*. You're just about perfect. We couldn't have asked for better."

"Stow the flattery," said Parashurama. "We're not in the mood."

"Right you are. But I thought you ought to know, you shouldn't feel as though you've been used, as though you've been exploited somehow. We were going to come clean with you soon enough. Eventually. When the time was right. Which is sort of now. So there's been a little economy with the truth, a little finessing of the facts. So what? No one minds really. Goes on all the time in business. You pretty much expect it. Nothing would ever get bought or sold if people were completely honest with one another. Guile oils the wheels of commerce."

"*Bien sûr*, but this is not commerce," said Rama. "This is us. Our bodies. Our identities. Our lives."

"Don't be so sensitive, mate. It's all commerce. Everything is commerce. Anyone who thinks otherwise is deluded."

"I pity you."

"Yeah, thanks for that, snail eater. Your condescending opinion means a great deal to me."

Rama's hand twitched towards his bow, or rather towards where his bow would have been, slung over his shoulder, if he hadn't left it up top. We had agreed to accompany the Trinity down minus any of our weapons – not that we were exactly harmless without them, but it made the Trinity feel that little bit safer and marginally evened the odds.

"So you lot are just the start of something," Lombard said. "Our showreel. Thanks to you and your asura-bashing exploits, we have the attention of the world – and especially of the governments of the world. It's fair to say that Epic News and my other media outlets have helped raise your profile and heighten brand awareness, but that wouldn't have happened without you guys out there strutting your stuff, corralling and conquering demons, and doing it with such style and panache too."

Still we descended, deeper and deeper. Wall-mounted service lights slid past at five-metre intervals, casting complex, gyrating shadows.

"Then came Kashmir. That was the decider, the

acid test. Our Avatars could handle spooky, snarling nasties from the pages of the Vedas, but what about troops on the battlefield? Tanks? Guns? How would they acquit themselves in a more practical, mundane situation like that?"

"The kind of situation," Krieger chimed in, "that nations have to face as a matter of course. War is a fact of life, and governments are constantly on the lookout for a military advantage over their enemies, anything that'll give them strategic dominance."

"Do you have any idea what the yearly worldwide spend on armaments is?" said Bhatnagar. "Even I don't, and I should. It's in the trillions. The American military alone has an annual budget of six hundred and eighty billion dollars. Defence is any country's single greatest expenditure. It's a big juicy pie, and who doesn't want a slice?"

"You proved yourselves equal to anything the Pakistanis could throw at you, and they're no slouches," said Lombard. "You demonstrated that devas could swing the pendulum in a conflict."

"So next on the agenda," said Krieger, "has been making sure every government on the planet is brought in on the picture. Knows what you devas actually are and where you came from."

"I've begun making overtures," said Bhatnagar. "Calling up all my defence department contacts, and they're extensive. Clueing them up. Telling them who deserves the credit for you, who created you. Most of them knew already, or had an inkling. Keeping anything a complete secret is so very hard these days. The reaction, so far, has been overwhelmingly positive."

"Phone's been ringing off the ruddy hook, to be frank," said Lombard. "Word's spreading fast. Everyone wants what we've got, from tinpot dictator to Pentagon grand high mucky-muck. Everyone's after a piece."

"A piece... of us?" said Kalkin. "You're proposing to hire the Dashavatara out. Sell us to the highest bidder. India was just your first client."

"No," said Parashurama, shaking his head in dawning realisation. "That isn't it, is it? Not us. What you're selling is the ability to make more like us. The theogenesis process itself."

"Bingo." Lombard touched his nose. "The Warrior has nailed it in one. Brains *and* brawn, this kid."

"We can't keep sending you people off to fight," said Krieger. "It was hard enough convincing you to go into Kashmir. You're not some rental car we can just lease out again and again."

"I'm glad to hear that," I said. "Here was I thinking you were treating us like a commodity or something."

"No," said the Texan, missing my irony, probably on purpose. "We're conscious that you have an altruistic streak, most of you. We selected you originally for theogenesis because each of you has, to some extent, a desire to do the right thing, to be better than average, to excel and set a good example. We needed, in effect, heroes, and heroes is what we got."

"Even with Kashmir," said Bhatnagar, "you wouldn't have got involved if Pakistan hadn't launched missiles at Mount Meru. It gave you the necessary impetus. Heroes avenge."

"Please don't say you set that up," said Rama.

"Hell, no," said Krieger. "But – full disclosure – we anticipated it, or something like it, was going to happen."

"You *knew*?" said Parashurama, teeth gritted. I daresay if he had had his axe on him, he would have brandished it then, maybe even used it. As it was, barehanded he could still easily have knotted any one of the Trinity into a human pretzel, and looked ready to.

In response, Diamond Tooth ground his pistol harder into the back of Buddha's neck. The other three goons also had handguns and were training them on us from the corners of the elevator platform. At any moment it seemed violence might erupt and bullets fly. We would undoubtedly win the altercation, but we might not all survive it.

Parashurama weighed up the pros and cons, and softened his stance.

"You knew," he said again, this time not a question.

"We anticipated," Krieger stressed. "The way the Pakistanis had been hassling us, their policy towards us, it was coming. It was all but inevitable. They wanted to draw us out. We let them."

"They could have killed us all. Everyone on Meru."

"Possible, but unlikely," said Lombard. "That would never stand up in the court of international opinion, a massacre like that, wiping out the entire island. A calculated level of antagonism, on the other hand..."

"A huge gamble nonetheless."

The Australian shrugged. "Life is risk. It's a risk when I have that extra egg for brekkie, that extra tinnie of lager at sundown. Will this be the one that gives me the heart attack? The one that rots a final, fatal hole in my liver? You roll the dice and, if you're lucky, it pays off and you can roll again."

"But the war is about to go nuclear. That's a risk you didn't take into account."

"Ah, it'll never happen," said Lombard, with a breezily dismissive wave. "They've been there before, those two, butting heads. One or other of them will back down. It's always the way."

"Not this time, I think. And they wouldn't be at the brink if it hadn't been for us 'biological weapons.' Us siding with India has turned a conventional conflict into something potentially far worse."

"Don't take it to heart," said Krieger. "This was always going to be a tricky moment, geopolitically speaking. Suddenly there's a new breed of human on the block, men like gods, soldiers equivalent to a whole platoon each. It was bound to cause some destabilisation, a bit of friction. Temporary, I'm sure."

The elevator was nearing the end of its long, slow slide. Bright illumination glared up from below.

"Year from now," Krieger continued, "everyone'll have adjusted and acclimated. There'll be a new status quo."

"Same occurred after the Yanks nuked the Nips at Hiroshima and Nagasaki," said Lombard. "The world was shaken for a while, but settled. People got used to the idea of an atomic age. They learned to, if not love the Bomb, at least accept it."

"What you're saying is we're seeing the beginning of a new arms race," said Kalkin.

"That's about the long and the short of it, yes."

"With devas in place of atom bombs."

"Devas, asuras, gods of every stripe, not necessarily Hindu. We chose the Hindu pantheon as our starter set because... Well, Vignesh, turban-top gods was your brainwave. You explain."

Bhatnagar met the barbed comment with a long-suffering nod. "The Hindu pantheon lent itself best to the goals of theogenesis. It met our criteria. The Dashavatara were the perfect way of showcasing what the process could do, the range of augmentations we could make, from amphibious Matsya to size-changing Vamana. There was also the sheer quantity of worship we could channel in order to provide power, thanks to the devotions of my countrymen. No other set of deities is as varied or as venerated in the modern age as the Hindus'. We considered the ancient Greek and Roman pantheons, the Egyptian gods too, but simply no one believes in them any more. Nor are they as formidably powered as devas, as intrinsically superheroic."

"But that isn't to say that individual nations won't be able to draw on their own indigenous pantheons if they want to," said Krieger. "It's possible that theogenesis could be used to recreate members of the Shinto Kami and the Chinese Celestial Bureaucracy, for instance. There are the orishas of the Santeria tradition in South America and the voodoo loas in the Caribbean. Older civilisations like the Inuit, the First Nations of Canada and the Native Americans still cleave to their ancestral belief systems, loaded with moon gods, trickster gods and such. Go looking hard enough, you'll find pockets of polytheism everywhere, ready to be explored and exploited."

"And it wouldn't be that hard to resurrect the dead religions either," added Lombard. "Enough Mediterranean Europeans would start worshipping Jupiter or Zeus again, or whoever, if they were convinced it was for their own good. Tell them the security of the region depends on it, their own theogenised fighting force is relying on them, and you'll see. They'll be pouring libations and sacrificing cows like nobody's business. It'd be as if Christianity never happened. You can count on it."

"Is this your sales prospectus?" I said. "The pitch you'll be using to flog your merchandise?"

"Something like," Lombard said with an amused smile. "How governments customise and tailor our process for their own ends, that's up to them. It isn't our concern. All we're after is signatures on contracts and big fat funds transfers."

The sheer avarice in his eyes, and Krieger's and Bhatnagar's, was both mesmerising and repulsive. It had a slick, greasy glow to it, like the rainbow sheen of spilled petroleum.

These three cared about nothing – nothing – except their bank balances. They were already wealthy beyond most people's dreams, and still they craved more, more, more. The world might burn, millions might die, but their pursuit of profit trumped all that. Money mattered. Anything else came a poor second.

The elevator juddered to a halt.

Everybody looked at one another across the platform. Hillbilly Moustache's finger tightened on the trigger of his gun. Parashurama glanced at him sidelong, then at Diamond Tooth and Buddha, gauging distances, angles, timing, trajectories.

Tense seconds passed. I braced myself for action.

Then Lombard said, "Come along. Let's give you the tour. There's heaps to see, and more to tell."

38. DEMON DEPOT

THERE WAS A broad central corridor, a main artery with dozens of narrower side corridors branching off at right angles. Everything was brilliantly lit and decked out with polished white tiling and smoothly rendered plasterwork. You might never have known you were a couple of thousand feet below the surface of the earth, but for the slight sense of pressure in your inner ear and the muggy warmth of the atmosphere which no amount of discreetly whirring air conditioning could quite dispel.

"Power comes from a geothermal plant," said Lombard, genial tour guide. "Cost a buck or two to put in, but it's free electricity for life. That's the living quarters we just passed. Humble but adequate.

Down there's our communications hub. What'd I tell you? All nice and cosy."

He was right. It was hard to imagine these corridors as tunnels, former mine workings where men had once toiled in dense heat and dust with drill and pickaxe. The place was tidy, well appointed, and spotlessly clean. We could have been anywhere, a research installation, an office building, some high-spec corporate HQ, you name it.

Until, that was, we came to the demon depot.

A couple of code-locked, bank-vault-solid doors gave access, via an antechamber, to a room lined with cubic cells. Each cell had a thick plexiglass front, and while most were empty, a couple of dozen of them were occupied.

Asuras prowled to and fro in the confines of these prisons – nagas predominantly, here and there a rakshasa or a vetala. Hunks of raw bloody meat littered the floor at their feet, alongside the digestive end products of the meat. The smell inside the cells must have been rank, although it didn't seem to trouble the demons.

Standing before the cells was Professor Korolev. He was carrying out some sort of inspection, tapping notes into a tablet. His shirt was sunset orange with repeating silhouettes of palm trees, cocktails and parrots.

He took in the arrival of devas, Trinity and gun-toting goons with scarcely a bat of an eyelid.

"Afternoon, gentlemen. Welcome to Yamapuri. My little joke. Is not really hell. But is home of asuras, yes, like Yamapuri."

The surprise on the faces of us devas must have been all too apparent, because he went on to say, "What, you are thinking they are just coming magically out of nowhere, like rabbits out of hats? You fell for that story?" A mirthless chuckle. "Well, why not? Is good story. 'Karmic balance. Can't have good without bad.' Hah! Asuras are manufactured, same as devas. Exact same procedure. Reverse transcriptase enzyme in aerosolised form, followed by session in Induction Cocoon. What works for gods works just as well for gods' opposites."

The asuras had noticed us and sprang to the front of their cells, pawing and pounding at the plexiglass. A cacophony of muffled thuds and growls filled the air.

"Down! Play nice!" Korolev barked at the demons. To us he said, "They don't like you. Is only to be expected. You are their mortal enemies. If that glass were any less strong, right now would be pandemonium in here. Asuras out for blood."

"Who are they, then?" I couldn't help but ask. "They must have been people once. Who would allow themselves to be transformed into something like that?"

"Allow themselves. You make it sound as if they are volunteering."

"They were forced into it?"

"Is simpler than that," said Korolev.

"They are, or were, the type that nobody'd miss," said Lombard. "People from between the cracks."

"Tramps, you mean. The homeless."

"Some of them. Real bottom feeders. Blokes

who've fallen so low, they don't even know how to get up again. Druggies. Alkies one bottle of meths away from complete renal failure. The dregs of society."

"But also mental patients," said Krieger. "The incurably insane. The ones who've been languishing in clinics and institutions since they were kids and would probably die without ever seeing the outside world again. We took them away from that."

"It's remarkable how modest the bribes were," said Bhatnagar. "The clinic directors didn't need much of an incentive to have these difficult, life-term inmates taken off their hands. They were happy to be shot of them. As I recall, the most we ever paid anyone was a brand new full-spec BMW."

"You could say we did the loonies a favour," said Lombard. "We gave them their freedom."

"Freedom to become your unconsenting patsies?" I said. "Freedom to be turned into monsters?"

"Not monsters," said Korolev adamantly. "Look at them. They are beautiful."

"And you're sick. Sick in the head."

The professor cut me a flinty stare.

"And the hobos," said Parashurama. "The 'bottom feeders.' You just kidnapped them off the streets?"

Lombard canted his head towards the goons. "We had snatch squads like these guys operating in five major cities. They worked quietly, discreetly, after dark. An alleyway, a bloke lying in an intoxicated stupor, the back of a van – it wasn't the hardest thing on earth to do. And the upshot? One less piss-soaked bundle of rags to trip over on your way to the office. One less waste-of-space dero milking the welfare system, pissing your and my taxes up the wall."

"If we made a naga out of a drooling cretin in a straitjacket," said Bhatnagar, "is that such a bad thing? Isn't that, in fact, simply repurposing? A clever use of resources?"

"Yeah," said Lombard. "And if a bludging tramp becomes a vetala, isn't that kind of fitting? Now he's literally a bloodsucking leech."

"It's all three of you, isn't it?" I said.

"What do you mean?"

"Singly, on your own, none of you would ever have done this. You'd never have had the nerve or the lack of scruples."

"You underestimate us."

"But together, as a threesome, you can somehow justify it. Justify anything. It's not so terrible when there's someone else to share the responsibility. The burden of shame gets spread out until it's light enough to carry. Each of you probably tells yourself you're not the bad guy, it's the other two. They're the ones who are doing wrong, and you're just going along with it."

"That's it, Hanuman. Bonzer, mate. You've sussed us fair and square. What are we going to do with ourselves, now that you've completely bulldozered us with your psychological insights?"

"The asuras we killed," said Rama. "Was it

absolutely necessary to keep them as trophies in the tower at Meru?"

"Necessary as a nipple on a tit," said Lombard. "Well, no, preserving them like that wasn't. That was just vanity. Like the vodka-swigging boffin here, we're proud of them. They *are* beautiful, in a fucked-up way. Incinerating them would have been a pity. A waste. So we made an exhibition out of them instead. Works of bloody art, they are, and why shouldn't we keep them and display them for our own personal enjoyment? Doesn't do any harm."

"The main thing was you guys always brought them back to Meru after they were dead, just like we told you to," said Krieger, "so there was never any physical evidence left lying around. Call it protecting our intellectual property. If a government or a rival company were ever to get hold of one of the corpses, they'd put their best scientists on it and have the thing dissected within hours."

"Which would open up the possibility of them figuring out the theogenesis process and reverse-engineering it," said Bhatnagar. "Then, at a stroke, we'd have lost our exclusivity. All our time, investment and effort would be for nothing."

"I still say theogenesis cannot be reverse-engineered," grumped Korolev. "Is impossible. Without crucial component..."

"The stone lotus," I said.

"You know about that?"

"If we know about the asura necropolis, then we know about the lotus too. Duh."

"*Da*, of course. But I am thinking you have no idea of its origins or how is connected with theogenesis."

"Maybe you should tell us."

"Maybe you've been told enough already," said Lombard. "Maybe we'd prefer to keep some secrets secret."

"What I'd like to know," said Parashurama, "is what you plan on doing with these live asuras here. I'm guessing you have no use for them any longer. Having us fight demons is off the agenda now. That phase of the masterplan is over, and this bunch are therefore surplus to requirements. We are certainly not going to cooperate any more. We are not going to go out and kill demons for you in public, not now we've learned what – who – they truly are. Makes me sick to think we believed we were slaying asuras when we were actually murdering innocent civilians. They weren't enemies but victims."

"Will you put them down like dogs?" said Rama.

"Bolt through the head like with a horse when it's past it?" said Kalkin.

"Couldn't you blokes just slaughter them for us right now?" said Lombard. "As a favour?" He laughed raucously. "Only joking. Crikey, the looks on your faces. Anyone'd think I'd asked you to go suck off a dingo in a dunny."

"The general idea is to let them go," said Krieger. "You're right, Parashurama. We don't need them. They've served their purpose. They've become spares. Leftovers. So we might as well set them free."

"Just offload a bunch of asuras onto the world?" I

said. "Release them into the wild? It's not like they're bloody baby alligators you can just flush down the toilet. They're marauding monsters!"

"Not monsters," Korolev insisted.

"We wouldn't turn them out as they are," said Bhatnagar. "What would be the point when we can restore them to their original state?"

"Oh," I said, startled. "I didn't think that was... Is that possible? I thought once you were theogenised, you were theogenised for good."

"Did someone tell you that?" said Krieger archly.

"Yeah. Aanandi. Well, at least, she said she believed it was permanent, and no one else said it wasn't."

I turned to the other devas to enquire if they'd known the process could be reversed. Their faces gave me my answer without having to ask the question. They were as taken aback as I was.

"You led us on," said Parashurama to the Trinity. "You had us thinking we'd be this way forever. Why?"

"Would it have made any difference?" said Bhatnagar. "You submitted yourselves to the process regardless. That's a true demonstration of your commitment, and we applaud you for it."

"But," said Krieger, "do you seriously think we'd let you walk around all revved up thanks to *our* technology, and not have a way of pulling the plug on you if we needed to? What if one of you went rogue? Decided to turn freelance? What if you went off the reservation and got yourself captured, or maybe tried to sell yourself to a rival syndicate? We have a fallback option. Of course we do. We're not stupid."

"The Lord giveth and the Lord taketh away," said Lombard, glib and gleeful.

"Show them, Gennady," Krieger said to Korolev. "Use one of the asuras as an example. Let them see how we can undo what we've done."

Korolev input a series of commands into his tablet. "Initiating reverse theogenesis in containment cube seventeen... *now*."

He gestured towards a cell holding a rakshasa. The jet-black demon was raging at the plexiglass, trying to hammer its way out.

Pale blue gas purled down from above, billowing around the rakshasa until the creature was obscured completely from sight. The thuds from the battering of taloned fists lessened, then ceased altogether.

"I am unwriting the rewriting," said Korolev. "A second virus, antidote to god virus, related but not same. Locates the altered DNA strands and neutralises the resequencing. Like theogenesis, is not painless. Coming down hill is no less arduous than going up."

It didn't sound it, either. The rakshasa's screams were audible even through the plexiglass. Bit by bit they became less raw-edged, less shrill, more familiar... More human.

"Extracting," said the Russian biochemist, and the gas was sucked back up out of the cell through the same vent it had come in by.

As the air inside the cell cleared, a naked man was revealed. He was on his knees, down amid the chunks of meat and the spatters of rakshasa filth. He rocked back and forth, sobbing. He had lank, matted hair and the scrawny, knotted physique of the long-term malnourished.

Slowly he became aware that his ordeal was over. He gazed at his hands as though unable to recognise them. Then he blinked up through the glass, surveying us with bloodshot, sunken eyes. He said something, we couldn't hear what, but his expression was perplexed and imploring.

I went to his cell. "Let him out. He can't stay in there. It's disgusting."

"Very well," said Korolev. "As you insist."

I should have sensed what was up. I should have detected the scent of treachery in the air. All of us devas should have. But we were still coming to terms with the Trinity's revelations. We were still feeling rocked by our own gullibility and culpability. We were, at that moment, more human than god. The Trinity had us on the back foot, and they knew it.

They had planned it that way.

They had planned it all.

Korolev tapped out a command which remote-triggered the cell's opening mechanism. The glass front rose, retracting into a recessed slot above.

The poor unfortunate inside stumbled out. I caught him. He stank of faeces, unwashed body and lifelong desperation.

Was he one of the homeless people the Trinity had

abducted, or was he a madman they had "liberated" from the medical professionals entrusted with his care and wellbeing?

It made little difference. If he wasn't insane already, his experiences of being a demon had robbed him of what few marbles he'd had left. He gibbered in my arms, spittle-froth flecking his lips. His eyes roved and rolled wildly. I tried to comfort him, but I don't think he was listening. I don't think he even heard what I was saying. He was long past that.

While this was happening – while I and the other devas were preoccupied with the former rakshasa – the Trinity had begun backing stealthily towards the door. So had Korolev and the goons.

Buddha failed to notice this, too, until it dawned on him that the barrel of a gun was no longer digging into his head. That was when he grunted out a warning to us, loud as he could through the ball gag.

Too late.

Diamond Tooth planted a 9mm round in the back of Buddha's head from a five-yard range. The Peacemaker's chubby features dissolved in a mist of blood, skull fragments and grey matter. The gag shot from his mouth and bounced across the floor like the rubber ball it was.

Parashurama yelled, "Get them!" but all of the goons opened fire, and it was bullets, bullets, bullets, blasting at us in a merciless hail.

We ducked for cover, not that there was much of it

available in that room. Kalkin bellowed in pain as a bullet thudded into the meat of his shoulder. Another winged him, ripping a gouge out of his thigh.

The Trinity and Korolev were already out through the first of the two vault-like doors. The goons were following in two-by-two formation, each pair laying down cover fire for the other pair, swapping out their spent gun clips with expert synchronisation. The door had nearly shut as Diamond Tooth and Hillbilly Moustache sneaked through to join everyone else on the other side of it. It slammed resoundingly. Bolts slid into place with heavy metallic finality.

"Shit!" I cried. "Shit, shit, fucking shit!" In the heat of the moment it seemed that Hanuman's legendary wit had deserted him and all he could do was swear impotently.

Worse was to come.

Not from me, I mean, although I did swear some more.

From the Trinity.

Because the glass fronts to all the cells began to rise, as one, and the asuras emerged.

39. A TWO-PART TRAP

KALKIN WAS INJURED, unable to stand. Rama and Parashurama were weaponless. We were facing a couple of dozen demons.

Screwed?

You might say that.

But not entirely.

Parashurama, axe or no axe, was still immensely strong and a never-say-die scrapper. Rama, bow or no bow, still had a deadeye aim. And I was still Hanuman, Son of the Wind, as swift and destructive as a typhoon.

I let out what I hoped was a rallying cry. "Are we not men? We are devas!"

Parashurama and Rama gave me blank looks. Obviously they weren't fans of American post-punk New Wave bands.

"Let's fuck their shit up."

This they understood.

And so, accordingly, we fucked the asuras' shit up.

We went easier on them than we would have previously, because we were now thinking of them as tragic, hapless victims, not simply the slavering, rampaging demons they appeared to be. We did our best to incapacitate and render unconscious, rather than to kill.

It wasn't always possible, though. The asuras, after all, weren't showing us the same consideration. They wielded their talons and teeth with the sole aim of tearing us to pieces and then tearing those pieces to smaller pieces, and several times the only way to stop them from succeeding was to strike a fatal blow.

Parashurama slugged away like a prizefighter crossed with a wrestler. I saw him shatter a rakshasa's ribcage with a single punch and grapple a naga to the ground and fasten it in a chokehold until it blacked out.

Rama found any object that wasn't nailed down and turned it into a throwing weapon. He cold-cocked a vetala at twenty paces with a computer keyboard, hurled ballpoint pens into eyes as though they were darts, and zinged a glass ashtray with the accuracy of a ninja flinging a shuriken.

Me, I was a whirling dervish, bounding this way and that across the room, caroming off walls, now in the asuras' midst, now behind them, now in front. I delivered harrying, commando-style strikes, a kick to the knee here, a kidney punch there, leaping out of reach before my target could retaliate. I softened them up, Parashurama and Rama took them down.

I don't know how long it took us to account for all the demons. Ten minutes tops. It felt like a fraction of that time, and an eternity.

But finally they were all on the floor, most of them comatose, a few dead.

On our side we had a plethora of brand new cuts, scrapes and bruises, but we were more or less okay. Kalkin still had that bullet in his shoulder and a chunk missing from his leg, but the rest of us had kept the asuras at bay and protected him from further harm.

I was, however, feeling swimmy-headed, as though I'd just stepped off the waltzer at the funfair. The fight, following close on our battle with Takshaka, had run down my inner reserves. Parashurama and Rama were, I could tell, in the same boat, in the early stages of a siddhi crash. The Archer sagged into a chair, fanning his face and sighing, "*Ouf.*" Parashurama, being a good soldier, refused to show weakness, but he was swaying a little where he stood, listing to one side.

"Sprang a trap on us," he muttered. "Those bastards."

This was the first time I'd heard even the mildest profanity from the Warrior's lips, and it was all the more shocking for that.

"No getting around it," I said. "The Unholy Trinity just gave us the sack. Nothing says 'contract terminated' quite like unleashing a horde of demons on you."

"Or a bullet to the brain." Parashurama went over to Buddha's body and knelt beside it for a few moments, head bowed. "Guy never harmed anyone. He wasn't a threat to them. That was cold. Stone cold. Like he was some sort of used Kleenex needed tossing away." He studied the Peacemaker's ruined face, fixing its hideous messiness in his memory. "I'm not going to forget this. There will be payback."

"We have to get out of here first," Kalkin pointed out. "No chance of payback if we let the Trinity slip away."

"Have to get you some medical attention, too," said Parashurama.

"I'm fine." But the Horseman's pinched grey face told a different story.

"I don't think that door can be opened from the inside," I said.

"If I had my axe..." said Parashurama.

"But you don't. So what are our options?" I scanned the room. "Maybe there's a ventilation system I could crawl through."

"That only works in the movies. Normal ventilation ducts are too narrow to fit a person inside."

"Narasimha and the others will come down once the hour is up and we have not reappeared," said Rama. "We could wait. They will find us eventually, and neither door will be a match for Vamana at full size."

"There is that," said Parashurama. "But mightn't the Trinity have a surprise in store for them too?"

"Another of their permanent severance packages?" I said. "I wouldn't put it past them. But my money would still be on our teammates. There's not much the Trinity could throw at them that they couldn't handle. *We* managed to beat all these asuras, don't forget, and that was unarmed."

"Yeah, which is bothering me."

"How so? I'd have thought it was a good thing."

"Well, surely the Trinity must realise there was a likelihood the asuras wouldn't finish us off."

"They wanted us busy so they could make a clean getaway."

"I wonder if that's it. What if this trap isn't done with us?"

"Don't say that," I said. "If you're worried, that makes me worried."

"If there's one thing I've learned lately, it's that you can never be too paranoid where the Trinity are involved." Parashurama got somewhat unsteadily to his feet. "These might not have been all the asuras they had available. There could be some of the bigger, even meaner ones lurking in the wings. Durga, perhaps. We haven't met him yet, here or anywhere. Or Prahlada. Or, God forbid, Kali. Look for a hidden door, one that connects to some other holding cells. Maybe there's a second part to the trap. If the first bunch of asuras were just the warm-up act, then the main attraction..."

He faltered. His voice faded to a whisper.

"Or it could be something else altogether."

He was looking at the cells with their wide-open fronts.

"Oh, you sons of bitches, you wouldn't..."

As if on cue, a hissing sound issued from inside the cells.

Not a fresh batch of nagas slithering out to attack.

The vent in each cell was in operation, fans cycling, the first faint wisps of blue vapour fingering downward from the ceiling.

"They're going to flood the room with antidote," said Parashurama. "They want to depower us. They're going to take our goddamn siddhis away!"

40. ANTIDOTE GAS

REASONABLY ENOUGH, WE did nothing for several seconds. We were too stunned. All we could do was watch in dismay as the blue gas tumbled into the cells, filling the cubes from edge to edge.

Only as it began to spill out into the room itself did we act.

Parashurama sprinted to the door and began hammering on its steel face with both fists.

Rama, meanwhile, searched desperately for some alternative exit.

As for me, I ran to a console in the corner. I was hoping to find controls that could stem the flow of gas, or at least close the cells.

All the console had, though, was a screen and a mouse. The keyboard which had previously been attached to it now lay in three pieces on the floor beside the head of a vetala.

I tried the mouse anyway, clicking frantically on desktop icons, opening one after another. Technical files, reams of data, complicated security software. Nothing looked like the master command system for the cells, and I probably wouldn't have recognised it even if I'd seen it. My savviness with computers extends no further than word processing, sending emails and doing artwork. To me they're pretty much a cross between a glorified typewriter and a high-tech Etch-a-Sketch.

Besides, I doubted Korolev would have left things so that the release of the gas, once initiated, could be overridden from this console. He wouldn't be that careless. He ran everything remotely from his tablet. He was, at this very moment, holding in his hands the only means of saving us.

I gave up. It was useless. Out of sheer frustrated spite, I put my fist through the screen and pounded the mouse to pieces.

Remember how I said before that we were screwed?

That went double now.

The gas crept across the floor like an oncoming fogbank.

"Up," said Rama. "We must not let it touch us."

He and I hauled Kalkin onto the console, where he lay awkwardly, one hand pressed to his leg to stem the bleeding. Then we clambered on it ourselves.

Parashurama continued pounding at the door. He had managed to put a number of shallow dents in it. Given time, he might even have been able to damage it enough to prise an opening.

But we didn't have time.

We had three minutes, tops. That was how long, I calculated, until the antidote gas rose higher than our heads and engulfed us, then started working its debilitating magic.

Aside from the console, there was nothing to stand on that would give us extra height, and even the console offered only a few further seconds of grace before we were fully immersed. Nor were the walls climbable. They were smooth, without any crevices or projections to use as handholds.

The blue tide of gas had reached Parashurama at the door and was lapping around his ankles. Still he kept clobbering away, futile though it was.

"I do not wish to go back to being Jean-Marc Belgarde," said Rama morosely. "To give a man a taste of divine power then tear it away – that is cruelty."

"And it's going to hurt and all," I said.

"Pain is temporary. Loss is everlasting."

The French. You've got to hand it to them. A nation of philosophers.

Parashurama was flagging. His knuckles were raw and bloodied. The door remained defiantly in place.

There seemed to be nothing for it but to brace ourselves and kiss our siddhis goodbye.

Then, with a *chunk* and a *clunk*, the bolts within

the door retracted. Miraculously it began to swing open.

On the other side stood Aanandi.

"Well?" she said. "What are you waiting for?"

Parashurama stumbled headlong through the doorway. Rama and I staggered after him, supporting Kalkin between us.

In the antechamber, I turned for a glance back.

The asuras on the floor had started to transform, their bodies writhing and contorting as the gas surged over them. Talons shrivelled to become fingernails. Fangs blunted to teeth. Complexions changed. Muscles shrank. Skeletons regained their normal proportions. Scales melted away, reverting to soft skin. The dead demons flexed and shuddered, their corpses lent a semblance of life by the physiological rigours of the process. The living ones moaned and mewled, but the fact that they weren't conscious spared them from the worst of the agony. Small mercies.

Then Aanandi slammed the door shut. Tendrils of the gas sneaked around our feet, dissipating, dispersing.

"Miss Sengupta," I said. "I could fucking kiss you."

"Not now, Zak."

"Later?"

"We'll see. First things first. You four need amrita."

"We need to go after the Trinity," Parashurama corrected her.

"And how far are you going to get, the state you're in?"

The Warrior conceded the point. He was teetering on the brink of physical shutdown, so close to a siddhi crash he could barely move his head to nod.

"Besides, the Trinity haven't hung around to gloat. How else do you think I was able to open the door and let you out? I wouldn't have got anywhere near it if they were still here. They're on the move already, making for the exit."

"Then the others'll stop them," I said. "They're up at the mine entrance."

"Different exit. There's more than one way out of this place. The Trinity have taken the secondary access shaft. I saw them head that way. It's a staircase, for emergency evacuation. It comes up about half a mile from the pithead."

"We can still..." Parashurama said weakly.

"You can't. Accept it. They're in the wind. You want them, you'll have to wait. Next time. Okay?"

41. PREADOLESCENT WISH-FULFILMENT FANTASIES

IN THE EVENT, Aanandi had to bring the amrita to us. That was how enfeebled we were. We couldn't even totter along a few hundred yards to where the serum was stored. Pursuing the Trinity would have been completely out of the question.

She dosed us up, Kalkin first, and ah, sweet, sweet amrita. Renewer of vigour. Remover of exhaustion. Knitter of wounds. The deva's salvation.

"You're good at injections," I told her. "I hardly felt it."

"Practice. My dad's a diabetic. As a little girl I learned how to give him his insulin shots, in case his blood sugar level dropped so low he couldn't manage it himself. He's squeamish about needles, so he used to make me inject him anyway sometimes, if

Mom wasn't around. He still does when I go home. I refuse, but then he guilt trips me about being a bad daughter, so…"

"There were times when I wouldn't have minded sticking a needle into my dad. Hard. In the eyeball. When he was being a bastard to my mum. Mind you, she could be as much of a bitch back. It was a match made in heaven."

"Poor you." She gestured at my T-shirt. "I see you're wearing it."

"I like it."

"I like that you like it."

As the other devas and I waited for our physical percentile bars to return to 100, we heard voices in the main corridor. Familiar ones.

"In here!" I called out, and shortly Narasimha, Kurma, Vamana and Krishna joined us in the antechamber, making it a pretty crowded space. They had Parashurama's, Rama's and Kalkin's weapons with them.

Parashurama brought them up to speed on recent events, and Narasimha and Kurma immediately hustled to the freight elevator and ascended up top again. They returned bearing bad news. In the time they'd been away from the mine entrance, the Toyota Land Cruiser and the Land Rover Discovery had gone.

"Damn," said the Warrior. "Once they got to the surface, they circled back and took the cars. They knew you guys were going to come down when you did, and timed it so that you wouldn't be there.

They knew exactly how long to wait before making their move, because they knew what we'd arranged. Those three are *sneaky*. Heck, I'd admire them, if I didn't want to stomp on their pointy heads so much right now."

"We could still go after them," said Krishna. "They do not have that much of a head start, and my chariot is swift, swifter than any car."

Parashurama was tempted, but said, "No. We're going to get them. Of that there is no doubt. But we're going to do it on our terms, at a time of our choosing, when we're at full strength and have full control of the situation. Wherever they're going, they can't hide forever. We found 'em once, we can find 'em again."

He turned to Aanandi.

"In the meantime, maybe you'd care to explain why you're helping us."

"Is there any reason I shouldn't be?"

"You're a Trinity Syndicate employee."

"So are you."

"A valued one."

"So are you."

"Debatable. But you came here with the Trinity from Meru."

"They told me to come. Not the same thing. And I couldn't see a way of saying no. They sign my paycheques. I have an obligation."

"Bait," I said.

"Yes," she said with a bitter, deflated sigh. "I know. They were using me. They told me to leave that note.

They wanted to leave a trail but didn't want it to be obvious. Mr Lombard virtually dictated what I should write. I hated doing it. I hated how they were exploiting our... friendship, Zak. Abusing your trust in me. But I had to go along with it. You give in to people like Dick Lombard. You can't disobey, no matter what your conscience is telling you. There's no telling what someone like him is capable of."

"I think we have some idea now," said Rama.

"Yes. True. And I hope I've managed to redeem myself by pulling you out of Korolev's 'Yamapuri' in the nick of time. I hope that proves where my loyalties really lie."

Aanandi was speaking to all of us, but I could tell – or chose to believe – that she was addressing me directly, personally.

She went on, "I'm not happy with the way the whole theogenesis project is headed. That part of the note was genuine. Things have been happening that I don't agree with and never signed up for. I've been kept in the dark about stuff, same as you have, and that doesn't sit well with me. The Trinity have gone too far already, and I'm scared they're going to go even further."

"What I don't get," said Vamana, "is who the fuck they're hoping to sell the technology to, if the missiles start flying. There won't be much of a market for devas once the world's a glowing radioactive ash cloud and everyone's dead."

"Oh, they don't believe the Indo-Pakistan situation is going to go nuclear," said Aanandi. "And even if it does, they reckon the conflict will stay confined to the subcontinent. It won't spread any further."

"That's naive."

"Or hubristic. Or optimistic. Or, just possibly, a fair assessment of the circumstances. Some say that any exchange of nuclear weapons will have a cascade effect, rippling out across neighbouring countries, drawing in the other nuclear powers, until everyone is launching their ICBMs left, right and centre, and we all fry. Others predict that the horror of one or two nukes exploding will bring all parties involved to their senses and stop a war dead in its tracks. Worked in 1945, didn't it?"

"Different age," said Parashurama. "Before proliferation. Nobody else but America had the Bomb back then, so there was no danger of things spiralling out of control."

"I'm not saying I subscribe to that idea. I'm just telling you how the Trinity are thinking. They're confident they can work the crisis to their advantage, however it plays out. That's the kind of men they are."

"And we're nothing more than loose ends now," said Kurma.

"As far as they're concerned, yes," said Aanandi. "Again, that's not something I'm happy with." She glanced at all of us in turn, but her gaze rested longest on me. "How casual they are about other people's lives."

"Buddha..." said Parashurama, with feeling.

"Scratch a plutocrat and you'll find a sociopath," said Vamana.

"Being ruthless is an asset in business," said Aanandi, "but those three take it to a whole new level."

Kalkin, who was sitting propped up against a wall, let out a soft groan. His leg was healing, but he still had a bullet lodged in his shoulder and there was little amrita could do about that. It needed to come out.

"Aanandi, is there anyone in this place with medical expertise?" Rama asked.

She shook her head. "Professor Korolev studied as a physician before switching to biochemistry, but he's gone."

"Plus, evil," I said.

"Not so much that as amoral. Solely in it for what he can get out of it. Either way, he's the only one who could have helped. There's maybe ten people onsite right now, aside from us, and none of them's a doctor or a nurse. Maintenance and ancillary staff. Cloncurry has a hospital, though. Kalkin could go there."

"Or one of you could dig the bullet out of me," Kalkin said. "Wouldn't that be quicker and simpler?"

"But a whole lot more painful," said Kurma.

"I played a surgeon once," said Vamana, adding, "But it was for a comedy sketch at the Edinburgh Fringe. Didn't exactly have to pick up any skills to make it look authentic. They just gave me this giant scalpel and I stood on a stool beside the operating table. Hilarious."

"Thanks for that," I said. "A useful contribution."

"Still a bloody contribution. What have you got to offer?"

"I know a little about combat casualty care," said Parashurama. "I guess I could have a go."

"Works for me," said Kalkin.

"I'm sure I can find a knife and some dressings," said Aanandi. "Give me a few minutes."

"Hurry, before I change my mind." The Horseman flashed a weak grin.

"Fancy some company?" I asked Aanandi.

She didn't say no, so I went with her.

Out in the corridor I said, "Thank you. For saving us back there. Pulling our arses out of the fire. If it wasn't for you, I'd be plain old Zak Bramwell again."

"And we couldn't have that."

"No, we could not. I love being Hanuman. I owe you big time for helping talk me into it, and for planting the idea in Bhatnagar's head in the first place. I wouldn't give this up for the world."

"It does seem to agree with you."

"Agree? It's a dream come true. Superheroes are basically preadolescent wish-fulfilment fantasies. 'If only I could fly. If only I could beat up the school bullies. If only nothing could hurt me.' Most people grow out of them and gain whatever status they can as adults to shield them against the unfairness of life. Me, I'm still stuck in childhood, secretly longing for some cosmic ray or irradiated spider to come along and magically make me a superior being. Only, I don't have to worry about that any more, because it's happened. Result!"

"What's nice is you haven't changed. Outwardly, yes, but you're the same person on the inside. Don't give me that look. I mean it. I was worried that becoming Hanuman would be the undoing of you. You'd turn into this, I don't know, power-crazed jock or something. But you've kept a level head. Kudos."

"That may be the kindest thing anyone's said to me. No girlfriend's ever called me level-headed before. Plenty of other things but never that."

Oops. See what I did there? It just popped out. *Girlfriend*. Complete accident. Aanandi wasn't my girlfriend. I wasn't sure if she was my anything. And now it sounded as though I presumed she belonged in that category, and how was she going to react to that? Not well, probably.

"I wasn't implying that you were my, er, you know, whatever," I said, hastily backtracking. "It came out wrong. Slip of the tongue. No girlfriend's called me level-headed, but that doesn't mean you're one."

She halted and turned.

She went up on tiptoes.

It wasn't a huge kiss. No tongues. No tonsil-sucking.

It was just a kiss.

But it was a hell of a kiss nonetheless. Warm, with just the right level of pressure. The kind of kiss that leaves your lips tingling and your head spinning for minutes afterwards.

She walked on. I stayed frozen to the spot.

"Are you coming?"

Like a happy zombie, I shuffled after her.

In the kitchen Aanandi located a first aid kit with bandages and wadding, along with a small sharp knife and some cooking brandy to serve as disinfectant. We took the stuff back to the antechamber, where Parashurama set to work. He did a good job, considering he wasn't trained for it and everything he'd learned, he'd learned from watching medical corpsmen at work on the battlefield. Kalkin acquitted himself well, too. He only screamed once or twice when the knife tip probed a little too deeply. Otherwise he was as stoic as one of the samurai he admired so much.

Parashurama applied a field dressing, and Kalkin wondered aloud if he could pass out now, and promptly did.

Aanandi beckoned me, and we set off along the main corridor again. "I have something to show you," she said, and I got excited, thinking she was leading me to a room in the living quarters where we could... oh, you know.

But it wasn't to be. The kiss was a marker, a promise, but we weren't going any further than that, not yet.

Instead, we ended up at a door marked R&D, which turned out in fact to be an armoury.[1] Prototype handweapons lay on workbenches, crafted in the same quasi-Mughal style as Parashurama's axe and Kalkin's talwars, all curlicued appendages and intricate symmetrical *koftgari* inlay.

"The Trinity had metalsmiths working on

---

[1] Here I could insert all sorts of saucy double entendres about wielding weapons, thrusting swords, shooting ammunition and so on, but that's just not who I am.

upgrades to the Dashavatara's existing arsenal, and new weapons for the devas who don't currently carry any," Aanandi said. "They discontinued the programme a few days ago. These ones you see would have been introduced as part of a second phase, had we all stuck to the original script. That club over there, for example, that's for Kurma. His power set is mostly passive, so it would give him offensive capability."

I picked up a pair of hollow discuses with lethally sharp edges. "Who are these for?"

"Matsya. And the J-shaped sword? That's called Nandaka, and it's meant for Krishna."

"I get anything?"

"As a matter of fact, no. Sorry. Only the Ten. You were an afterthought, remember?"

"I prefer 'a belated but vital addition.'"

"Yes, of course. Isn't that what I said? You must have misheard." Aanandi began gathering up the items she had already pointed out.

"Can I grab something too? If everyone else is getting a new toy, I don't want to be left out."

"Help yourself."

I went looking, and was drawn to a pistol crossbow. I liked the heft of it, the way it sat in my hand. Rama had his recurve bow. I merited something similar.

The pistol crossbow seemed easy enough to operate. Crank the cocking lever upward to draw back the string. Slot a steel-tipped bolt into the groove. Curl finger around trigger.

Ker-thwack!

The bolt embedded itself in the floor at my feet, centimetres from my big toe.

"Note to self. Hair trigger."

I shot a second bolt, this time taking the precaution of levelling the crossbow and aiming before shooting, and scored a direct hit on the side of a lathe.

"I am death to all metalworking machinery," I declared.

I was lining up a third test shot when a deep rumble echoed through the entire installation.

"What the – ? What *was* that?"

Aanandi's eyebrows knitted together. "No idea, but it didn't sound good. Earthquake? No, couldn't be. Not in the heart of Australia."

I hooked the pistol crossbow into my belt and scooped up as many of the bolts as I could carry in both hands. Then I rushed out of the room, alongside Aanandi with her armful of armaments.

All at once alarms started hooting, and another rumble reverberated around us, so profound it made us stagger. The overhead lights flared, then dimmed. Plaster dust trickled down from the ceiling.

We heard a cry, and some people in hard hats and overalls came sprinting past, looking distinctly panicked.

"The plant," one of them gasped as he went by, gesticulating wildly. "The flaming thing's gone haywire on us. We've been trying to contain it for the past half-hour, but every time we use a shutdown protocol it gets cancelled, and none of the failsafes are kicking in like they're supposed to. The turbines have stopped and won't restart. Flash steam is building pressure. We've tried venting. We've tripped every damn relay there is. No good. It's like we've been locked out of our own system. Like someone's sabotaged it."

"The plant?" said Aanandi. "The geothermal plant?"

"Yes!" said the man, dancing backwards to keep up with his fleeing colleagues. "It's overloading. Going critical. Everybody needs to get out of here. Now. It blows, and the whole site'll come crashing down around our ears!"

42. MCDUNN'S TAVERN

We legged it back to the antechamber, where the Avatars were already up on their feet and preparing to move. They might not have known exactly what the alarms signified, but anything making that raucous a racket was clearly not summoning people to dinner or prayer. The rumbles were their own kind of alarm anyway. The lights were flickering like crazy as well, another ominous sign.

Aanandi led us to the emergency staircase. The freight elevator was not a viable option, not with the electricity supply faltering. Besides, it was glacier-slow. We could move faster on foot.

The skeletal steel framework of the stairs zigzagged up a vertical shaft. Some way above us, multiple footfalls clattered. The site staff. We added our own clatter to theirs. Vamana had enlarged himself to the point where he could carry the unconscious Kalkin easily in his arms, but not so tall that he had to duck to avoid hitting his head.

We charged up that shuddering staircase with the earth groaning and bellyaching around us. The red glare of auxiliary lighting bathed everything in an all-too-appropriately hellish glow. The same forces that had been harnessed to provide the installation with energy were now being turned towards destroying it.

Onward we climbed, the staircase shaking ever more violently. Fissures were appearing in the shaft walls. Sedimentary rock flaked off and crashed at our feet. The air swarmed with choking dust.

Finally, a door; daylight. We rushed out one after another into the infernal blaze of an Outback afternoon. We didn't stop for a breather. The site staff, ahead, were still running, scrambling downhill onto open plain, and we took our cue from them. They must know what minimum safe distance was, and even if they didn't, even if they were just rabbiting, it seemed sensible to get as far away from the installation as possible. The rumble was continuous now, and loud, like a neverending roll of thunder.

Then, with a sharp, deafening detonation, something deep within the world broke. Part of the hillside behind us leapt, then slumped in on itself. Chunks of slope calved off and tumbled down onto the pithead, engulfing the rusted old machinery and burying the mine entrance.

The avalanche continued for some time, a slithering tide of boulders, scree and shale, as further sections of the ridge imploded in a kind of chain reaction. I imagined the installation's corridors caving in, the demon depot crushed under a million tons of rock, the bodies of the former asuras mashed to paste.[1]

The chaos subsided. The falls of debris slowed and settled. A dust cloud the size of a small town massed in the sky above the devastation, breezes tearing at its edges and beginning to thin it out. The ridge of hills sported a new depression, a jagged gouge in its otherwise undulating contours, as though God had taken a hatchet to it.

Parashurama was the first to speak. "Sound off. Everyone okay? Anyone hurt?"

We checked our limbs, inspected one another for injury. Other than a liberal coating of dust, nobody had much to complain about.

Except Krishna, who swore in Syrian Arabic, something evocatively guttural about a dog licking your mother or your mother licking a dog, I forget

---

[1] And in case you're wondering, there was no way we could have retrieved the surviving ex-demons and brought them with us to the surface. The room was clogged with antidote gas, remember? The only one among us who could have gone in there with impunity was Aanandi, and the task of dragging each dead-weight body out in turn by herself would have taken several minutes – time we didn't have to spare. It wasn't particularly noble of us to leave them behind, but there was no alternative. Besides, if the rakshasa which Korolev had restored to human form was anything to go by, none of them had much in the way of sanity left or much of a life to look forward to. So, all things considered, a quick painless death was perhaps the kindest thing for them. I think. I choose to think.

which even though he did translate the oath for me later on.

"My chariot," he said, with a mournful, angry look at the rubble-strewn disaster area that had been the pithead.

Somewhere beneath that mass of fallen rock, most likely mangled beyond all recognition, lay his nifty rocket-propelled sled. We wouldn't be zipping around in *that* ever again.

He was upset, and I sympathised. It was by no means the shittiest thing that had happened to us that day. The Trinity's betrayal, Buddha's death, four devas almost having their siddhis revoked – these all trumped the loss of the chariot. Not to mention the little matter of the underground installation blowing up and very nearly taking the lot of us with it, which only a fool would fail to realise had been the Trinity's doing. Who else could have triggered the overload in the geothermal plant? Who else could have nullified the shutdown protocols and made the failsafes fail? They sincerely did not want us devas around any more to queer their pitch.

But still, the chariot was the final insult, the kicker. It had been just a vehicle, a piece of machinery, but it had been a cool one, and its getting wrecked seemed a harsh and unduly capricious twist of fate.

Krishna, moreover, had been attached to it, and felt superfluous without it. "What good am I now?" he lamented. "A Charioteer without a chariot."

Aanandi stepped forward. It's a tribute to the woman's grit and determination that she was still carrying the weapons she had gathered from the armoury – the sword, the club, the discuses. She could quite reasonably have dumped them the moment the alarms kicked off. But instead she had clung on to them gamely. I still had the crossbow and bolts, too, by the way.

"Here." She proffered the J-shaped sword to Krishna.

"What's this?"

"Nandaka. Yours."

Bemused, he took the sword from her. He slashed it experimentally through the air. A small smile crept onto his face.

"I feel like... I feel I know what to do with this, even though I have never held such a thing before in my life. How is that?"

"Why shouldn't you? Krishna in the *Mahabharata* is a warrior, and Nandaka is his blade."

"Yes. Yes! Of course. I fought Rukmi with it on the battlefield and won. Rukmini, his sister, pleaded with me to spare his life, and I did, for she was then my fiancée, soon to be my wife. But not before I shaved off Rukmi's hair and moustache, like so."

He performed a few deft flicks with Nandaka, its tip at head height, the same manoeuvres he would have used to depilate his foe.

"That taught him!" he crowed. "Nothing conveys the shame of defeat like having all your hair shorn off."

Krishna's sour mood lifted somewhat, although we all still faced the prospect of a long trek back to the *Garuda* in fearsome heat and the full glare of the sun. At Parashurama's suggestion, we set off straight away. "No shade to be had hereabouts, and sunset's still several hours off. Might as well be moving as standing still. Going to broil either way."

Along with the site staff we formed a straggling line, trudging south. Rather than clamber over the hills eastwards to where the *Garuda* was parked, we circumnavigated them along the mine access road, a longer but flatter journey.

We had only gone a mile or so when what should come soaring majestically over the brow of the ridge but the *Garuda* itself. Captain Corday and Matsya had heard the tumult of the hillside collapsing and seen the dust cloud, and come to investigate. Spotting us, Corday changed course and alighted by the roadside, and soon we were inside the blissfully air-conditioned cabin and flying to Cloncurry.

We dropped off the site staff at the hospital so that they could have themselves checked out if they wanted. They all repaired to the nearest bar instead.

Then we called in at the airport a few miles outside town, only to learn that Lombard's Cessna Citation X had departed an hour earlier. Destination? The flight plan said Sydney, but the air traffic controller, who was more than a little awed to have devas quizzing him, confessed that the jet had made a sharp turn shortly after takeoff, diverting east. "Last I saw of her on the radar, she was making a beeline for the Pacific."

"It was a long shot," said Parashurama as we left

the control tower. "At least now we know where they might be headed."

"The States?" I said.

"There ain't much else that-a-way."

We couldn't go after them immediately; Captain Corday had already logged his maximum total flying hours for the day. "It just wouldn't be safe," he said. "I don't get my rest, chances are I'll nod off at the yoke, and no one wants that."

We all of us checked into a motel, charging the rooms to Aanandi's Trinity Syndicate credit card, ha ha. Apart from Matsya, that was, who took a cab to Chinaman Creek Dam just outside the town and immersed himself in the reservoir there for the night to rehydrate.

Corday went straight to bed. The rest of us cleaned ourselves up, split into groups and went out to see what Cloncurry had to offer, which, it being hardly a bustling metropolis, was not much. Dusk was falling as Parashurama, Rama and I wandered down the dusty four-lane main street, drawing inquisitive glances from passersby. I'd invited Aanandi to join us, but she had excused herself, pleading exhaustion. I think she was reluctant to associate with the Avatars, given her part in luring us to the Golden Rocks Mine. She felt guilty – unjustifiably, I thought.

We entered a tin-roofed pub called McDunn's Tavern.

"Bugger me," said the landlord, none other than McDunn himself. "I heard the circus was in town. Dashavatara, yes? Did I pronounce that right? So what can I get you fellas? We've got beer or beer. Or beer, if you'd rather."

Rama and I ordered beers. Parashurama, who was teetotal, asked for a Coke, which made McDunn's face crease up in suspicion.

"You're in Oz, mate. You've got to be careful. Me, I'm a liberal-minded bloke, but there's people who might get the wrong idea about a man who doesn't drink beer. Especially one who dresses like you do."

The Warrior gave the landlord a look that would have cowed a rampaging bull.

"Only kidding," said McDunn. "Just a spot of ocker humour. No harm meant. One Coke. Ice? Lemon? Dinky little cocktail umbrella?"

We sat down at a melamine-topped table on rickety plastic chairs. There were a dozen or so other patrons in the pub, all male. An Australian Rules Football game played on the TV, and they were pretending to watch it, but really they were more interested in us. It hadn't occurred to me how hard it was to be unobtrusive when you were a superhero – or at least when you were in the company of two people clad in superhero garb and known the world over. Hanuman wasn't famous himself, but the guys he was with most definitely were, and they were drawing constant sidelong looks.

Eventually a couple of the townsfolk ambled over to us, one of them a meaty Caucasian, the other an Aborigine. I wondered if there was going to be a challenge, the kind of confrontation that happens when outlandish-looking strangers arrive in a

remote, conservative town and visit a local watering
hole. McDunn's Tavern seemed like that kind of
establishment, where the resident yahoos didn't take
too kindly to weirdos from faraway parts. Damn it,
I'd seen *Priscilla, Queen Of The Desert*; I knew how
this was going to pan out.

These two looked intimidating. Maybe they were
drunk and thought they could beat us up – bring the
big bad devas down a peg or two, show them that
they weren't so tough. If that was the case, they were
in for a shock.

Then, all at once, they were grinning inanely and
asking for autographs. What I'd taken for menace
was in fact reticence, shyness. The Caucasian was
Barry; the Aborigine, Tommo. Parashurama and
Rama signed beer mats for them. Hanuman? They'd
not heard of me. They assumed I was just some
civilian hanger-on, an Avatar groupie. I didn't get
to sign a beer mat, even after I told them I was a
deva too. To them I was just some twat in a monkey
T-shirt. I didn't look the part, did I? No spandex.

Barry and Tommo asked endless questions
about fighting asuras, about having powers, about
everything, while the rest of the pub listened in, the
football game forgotten.

"Why're you here anyway?" Tommo wanted to
know. "Are there monsters on the loose nearby?"

"Only my missus," Barry said, and roared with
laughter. "Don't suppose you could get rid of her
for me, could you? Only I can't afford a bloody
divorce."

"Just Avatar business," Parashurama said cagily. "It's all sorted now. You've nothing to worry about."

They begged Rama to do some arrow tricks for them, but he had left his weapon in the *Garuda*, as had Parashurama.

"How about a dart trick instead?" he said.

The pub's dartboard was mounted on the wall not far from the TV set. Rama steadied himself at the oche, three darts in his left hand. The locals gathered round eagerly.

The first dart scored a bullseye. Everyone cheered, not appreciating that Rama could have made the shot from considerably further than eight feet away. Standing on his head. With his eyes shut.

He went all Robin Hood with the second dart, propelling it into the back of the first. Its point sank into the intersection of the other dart's flights.

The cheers were far louder this time. Beer slopped over the rims of glasses, drizzling precious amber nectar onto the floor. Beefy hands clapped Rama on the back. "Good on yer!" "Bonzer!" "Ripper!"

"The same again, *peut-être?*" Rama said, lining up the third dart. He was playing to the crowd, relishing the attention. And why not? Who could blame him? Our team had had a crappy time of it lately. It was good to be reminded that the public liked devas.

"Five bucks says he screws up!" someone shouted.

"You're on!" someone else shouted back.

Others joined in the betting. Banknotes flapped in the air.

Rama focused. Brought the dart up to his eye. Levered back his elbow.

The dart flew.

Thunk!

And missed the board altogether, embedding itself in the wall instead.

There was silence, then uproar. Mocking laughter. Men demanding their winnings. "Bad luck, mate," Rama was told. "Nice try."

I couldn't believe he had missed. Parashurama's expression said likewise. We looked closer at the Archer, and saw that his gaze wasn't on the dartboard. He was oblivious to the fuss going on around him. He didn't appear to care that his shot had gone wild.

He was staring at the TV.

On the screen, the words BREAKING NEWS blared in capitals. A grave-looking newscaster was saying, "...if you've just tuned in, we're interrupting the Swans versus Bulldogs game to bring you an important announcement. We're getting reports, so far unsubstantiated, of a large, a very large explosion in Kashmir which occurred at seven thirty-five Eastern Standard Time. We don't know as yet that this is indicative of a nuclear detonation, but the evidence suggests that it is. The blast appears to be centred on the city of Srinagar in the Kashmir Valley, which lies in the Indian-administered area of the state. The Prime Minister is due to make a statement outside Kirribilli House in a few minutes, and we'll have that for you, live, when it happens. In the meantime, let's go over to our defence correspondent..."

43. RED HOT MONKEY GOD SEX

WE DIDN'T GET much sleep that night. Who did? Like everyone else, we stayed glued to the television. McDunn's Tavern was far from the worst place in the world to watch apocalyptic events unfolding. At least there was alcohol, and McDunn was prepared to keep serving it long after the licensing laws said he shouldn't.

"Let the cops try and bust me," he said. "All the good it'll do them. This could be the end of civilisation. *Mad Max* time. What do I care about losing my licence? If ever there was a time for everyone to get completely bloody shitfaced blotto, it's now."

Take note, however. He didn't start doling the drinks out for free.

Gradually the evidence of a nuclear strike mounted up, until it was irrefutable.

A US Geological Survey field unit in Kabul had recorded a seismic event 400-odd miles away, its epicentre in the Kashmir Valley. It had registered 4.0 on the moment magnitude scale, a level consonant with a one-kiloton above-ground nuclear explosion.

Then some very shaky phone footage came in from a Swiss mountaineer halfway up Mount Kolahoi in the Himalayas. It showed what appeared to be a mushroom cloud on the horizon, although the distance made it hard to tell for sure. It could just have been a lone, oddly shaped cumulonimbus.

Rumours began to circulate about a power blackout in the area surrounding Srinagar, which suggested either that several electricity generating stations had been destroyed or that an electromagnetic pulse had caused voltage surges and knocked out the power grid. Most likely it was a combination of both. The rumours were corroborated by reporters in the region.

What remained unclear was which of the two sides in the ongoing conflict was responsible for launching the weapon. Srinagar had fallen to Pakistani forces the previous afternoon, and the Indian prime minister had responded by giving Pakistan twenty-four hours to withdraw from the city or 'reap the consequences.' Was this him making good on his threat? The Pakistanis had begun to pull their troops out, however, so it was possible that they had capitulated but, in revenge, subjected Srinagar to a scorched earth policy.

Experts speculated. Pundits pontificated. Worry was etched deep into every face onscreen.

Meanwhile stock markets plummeted like suicides leaping off a cliff. Trillions were wiped off share values. Only gold and other precious metals prospered, as investors shunted what was left of their money into solid commodities.

The United Nations convened at dawn in New York for a special emergency session, but the ambassadors from India and Pakistan didn't show up. This left everyone else with little to do except spout off at one another across the chamber in their native tongues, a Babel of impotence. The security council passed a resolution calling for an immediate cessation of hostilities, after which all the delegates went home to be with their families.

The question of who launched the nuke continued to confound the media. The governments of both countries would neither claim nor deny responsibility. Each refused point blank to give any public statement beyond saying that they were assessing the situation and considering an appropriate response.

That was the new global reality. Never mind who started it; it had happened. Atomic fission had been used in anger for the first time in seventy years. Millions were dead. Images taken from an overflying plane showed the incandescent wasteland that Srinagar and its environs had become. Firestorms blazed in the darkness. A

2,000-year-old city had been erased from the map, its monuments gone, its inhabitants incinerated in a single, terrible flash. There was nothing left but burning irradiated rubble.

We watched well into the small hours. Nothing changed. The horror could not be undone. Srinagar could not be unbombed.

But eventually fatigue set in. There was only so much reportage, analysis and conjecture the mind could take. Repetition numbed the tragedy to a dull nothingness. That or the many beers I drank. Doubtless both.

I don't recall much about staggering back to the motel through downtown Cloncurry. I think I may have had a run-in with a semi-feral cattle dog chained up in somebody's front yard. The hound either didn't like the cut of my jib or it had been unsettled by the febrile mood that had overtaken the humans in town. Maybe it had something against monkeys, or devas. I don't know. Woof bloody woof.

Anyway, canine close encounter aside, I made it to the motel unscathed, and into bed, and within moments of passing out on the pillow – or so it seemed – there was a knock at the door and I was letting Aanandi in.

She had been crying. She had just got off the phone with her parents in Boston. Her father was putting up a brave front but he was scared, she could tell, very scared. The Senguptas had relatives back in the old country, of course; Mumbai mainly, but also down south in Bangalore and Chennai. He was frightened on their behalf, he said, fearful that the entire subcontinent was about to go down in flames.

Aanandi in turn was worried for her parents, living as they did in one of America's major cities. They had not abandoned Boston as so many others had during the early stages of the crisis. They had stayed put in their brownstone condo in leafy Brookline, but life was not easy for them now. The neighbourhood was mostly deserted. Many shops were shut, food stocks running low. People were trying to carry on as normal, maintain the civilised veneer, keep the social contract alive, but there had been spillovers of looting and street violence from rougher areas like Dorchester, Mattapan and Roxbury. Gangs roamed at night. The police were stretched thin trying to maintain order.

"And it'll only get worse now," she said. "Breakdown, mass panic. Law of the jungle. I've told them not to leave the apartment unless they absolutely have to, but my poppa, I know he won't listen. He'll head out to the grocery store, try and get in supplies. 'Must think of your mother, 'Nandi. *Mataji* is not as strong as she once was. I must look after her.' Stubborn ass."

Fresh tears flowed.

"Zak," she said. "Will you hold me?"

It wasn't a request I was going to turn down, was I?

I held her. I felt her body through her clothes, the warmth of it, the pliancy. Her breasts pressing against my chest. Her shoulderblades flexing under my palms. It was wrong to be aroused, but I was. Couldn't help it.

She felt what was happening. She pulled back just a little.

"Really?" she said with a crooked smile, sniffing.

"Afraid so. Sorry. Reflex. Out of my control."

Her hand went down and gripped. The pressure she exerted was painfully exquisite.

"I don't think you have anything to apologise about. Not judging by what I'm holding."

Without letting go, she thrust her mouth against mine, sinking her tongue in urgently. I pawed her breast, homing in on her nipple through her blouse and bra. She made a desperate, compliant noise in the back of her throat.

Clothes flew. The bed creaked under the weight of two bodies suddenly dropping onto it, as it must have done on countless occasions before. A motel mattress and frame, well used to passion.

Within moments we were both perspiring in the humidity of an Australian night. Damp skin slithered against damp skin.

"P-protection?" I stammered.

"We could be dead tomorrow," she whispered in my ear.

Hardness found a home in hot wetness. Slamming into place. Aanandi arched. Her lips formed a shape, a perfect O, while her eyes narrowed to slits.

I'm writing about it here because it was the best bloody shag I've ever had. I mean it. Zak Bramwell had sex, but Hanuman – he had sex to the power of a hundred. It was to ordinary intercourse as Dom Perignon is to Babycham, as an Aston Martin is to a Smart car, as Alan Moore is to just about any other comics writer you care to name. It was Jack Kirby lovemaking – epic, grandiose, excessive, dynamic, complete with fizzing crackles all around it.

I'm talking from my own point of view. Hanuman had senses and sensitivities way in advance of Zak Bramwell's. He experienced, he *felt*, far more intensely than his non-deva alter ego ever had. When he came, it was an almighty, earthquaking *ka-blam!*

But I don't think Aanandi had anything to moan about, either. Or rather, she did. Plenty. And not just moaning. Yelling. Screaming. Howling. Yes, you read that right. Howling. I reckon she would have woken up every other guest on the premises if they hadn't been awake already and watching the news on TV or jamming the telephone exchanges with anxious calls to loved ones or doing what Aanandi and I were doing – coupling as if that could somehow stop the world falling apart.

And the monkey god had stamina, you betcha. After the second go-round, Aanandi couldn't believe I was up for another almost straight away, and neither could I, but that didn't stop us from having thirds.

I hadn't been that randy, or that quick to recover, since I was a five-wanks-a-day teenager.

In the aftermath, Aanandi and I spooned. She dozed off. I lay awake, fused to her by sweat and

AGE OF SHIVA

other secretions. The aroma of our cumulative funk was pretty pungent, but in a good way.

I thought of my past, my effortful and dissatisfied life, the troubled childhood I'd escaped by losing myself in comics and superhero dreams; and I thought of my present, the metamorphosis I'd undergone, the place I had earned alongside the Avatars, the powers I now possessed.

I also thought of my future.

There *had* to be a future. I knew this because I could feel it. Literally touch it. It was lying next to me.

"Aanandi?"

"Mmm?" She stirred. Her voice was thick with sleep and tiredness.

"We're going to stop this."

"Stop what? You mean you and me?"

"No. Fuck, no. The war. The Trinity. Everything that's wrong. No one else can but us. Me and the Avatars. What's the point in being devas – superheroes – and just standing on the sidelines twiddling our thumbs? We need to raise our game. We need to make a stand. We've been puppets. We've been blinkered. We've been lagging one step behind the whole time. This is where it all changes. This is when we finally come into our own and fight back."

"Sounds good. But do you think you can get the Avatars to go along with that?"

"I know I can. Parashurama's there already, just about. He might take a little convincing, but not much. The others will follow where he leads.

But we need you, too. Your expertise. Your inside knowledge. We can't do it without you."

"They don't trust me."

"They will. You'll make them."

She rolled over. Her eyes shone in the silvery pre-dawn light stealing around the edges of the blinds. She cupped my face with a hand.

"You're going to end the end of the world?" she said. "Devas save the day?"

"Damn right," I said. "We've had enough of being the ball. Time to start being the bat."

44. KALI YUGA

The *Garuda* flew east, California-bound.

Parashurama had agreed with me that enough was enough. We couldn't just let the Trinity flog their merchandise wantonly across the world. The existence of the Dashavatara alone, a handful of devas, had sparked a nuclear conflagration. Multiply that by a hundred, a thousand... It was unthinkable.

"We've got to limit this thing," the Warrior said. "Stop it proliferating. Once theogenesis goes global, all bets are off. Let's assume Kashmir doesn't become a worst-case scenario. Tempers cool. There's a truce. What happens next? The Trinity sell to all bidders, and suddenly, super-troops. Every military organisation starts fielding their own deva battalions. You give generals a new toy, sure enough they're going to want to start playing with it as soon as they can. There'll be war again. More wars. Super-wars."

He convened the Avatars, and it didn't take him long to win them round.

"It's not proliferation I care about so much," said Vamana. "It's getting even with those lying, cheating bastards. They tried to fucking kill us. They had Buddha shot – shot like a dog. I want some bloody payback."

Grunts of assent, loudest from Narasimha and Kalkin. Vamana was speaking for all of them.

So it was with a mixture of altruism and self-interest that we boarded out multiplatform adaptable personnel transporter and ascended into the skies above Queensland. Refuelling the *Garuda* racked up a sizeable sum on Aanandi's expense account, but her card had plenty of credit still left and the Trinity hadn't seen fit to cut her off yet. Presumably they hadn't bothered because they thought she was dead along with the rest of us, another loose end neatly snipped.

The fact that the *Garuda* was airborne and on the move might have tipped the Trinity off that we were still alive, but Captain Corday had combed carefully through the vehicle and found the GPS transponder they'd been using to keep tabs on us. It was a small piece of tech secreted amid the navigation avionics, something you would easily overlook unless you were familiar with every inch of your aircraft.

The transponder was now lodged behind the cistern in a cubicle in the men's toilets at Cloncurry airport, beeping out the location of nothing but Aussie males relieving themselves and perhaps a funnel-web spider or two.

Aanandi was the one who had suggested we make California our first port of call. R. J. Krieger owned a clifftop mansion at Point Dume, one of the most exclusive areas of real estate in Malibu. Neither Lombard nor Bhatnagar had property on the West Coast. Krieger's house was the nearest Trinity residence to Australia and could serve as a useful bolthole, so that was where we should try before looking further afield.

It was a slender thread to be pursuing, but it was *something*. Going to Cloncurry had been a long shot but it had paid off, after a fashion. No harm in pushing our luck a little harder.

Aanandi sat at the front of the cabin, the Avatars towards the rear. The gap between was small but represented a clear separation, a gulf of scepticism. She hadn't yet proved her trustworthiness to them. I even overheard Vamana mutter that she could be leading us into a second trap. I thought about setting him straight, pointing out that Aanandi had been double-crossed too and could have died with us in the installation. In fact, she had led us to safety, lugging weaponry for Matsya, Kurma and Krishna with her. What more did she have to do to redeem herself? Disembowel herself with a ceremonial sword? Pull us all off in a mass bukkake session?

But I realised it was no good me arguing her case, especially not to someone as boneheaded as the Dwarf. The Avatars would learn to appreciate soon enough that her loyalty no longer lay with the Trinity – it was firmly with us. Her actions would speak louder than my words.

Without shame I joined her, plopping myself down beside her. She and I were in the exact same seats we had occupied when I first flew in the *Garuda* weeks earlier. So much had happened since then, so much had changed, that I could scarcely believe it, looking back. A cynical, lovelorn, somewhat callow comics pro had become a superhero. He had fought battles. He had had brushes with death. He had Got The Girl.

Who says dreams don't come true?

Mind you, I could have done without the copious bloodshed. Not to mention the world teetering on the brink of Armageddon. Those things kind of took the shine off the cherry.

Aanandi was frowning at her smartphone screen, scanning news sites. Over her shoulder I caught the headlines as she thumb-scrolled down: *Indian Cabinet And Military Hold Crisis Meetings. Pakistan Threatens Nuclear Strikes, With Backing Of Arab League. UN Envoys In New Delhi And Islamabad Urge High-Level Bilateral Peace Talks. American Secretary Of State Warns Of "Unmitigated Disaster" And "Global Repercussions." Death Toll Mounts. Prevailing Winds Turn Path Of Fallout Towards Abbottabad.*

Lombard's own Epic News took a slightly different tack, opting for less sombre and ominous wording:

"Worst Over," Experts Say. Both Sides Likely To Back Away From Further Hostilities. Reconciliation Still Achievable. This was a surprisingly measured – one might go so far as to say optimistic – response from a media outlet famed for its sensationalism, and I detected the hand of its CEO in the tone of the reporting. Dick Lombard needed the war to end so that the Trinity could get on with the business of peddling theogenesis. For once, it served the interests of Epic News to pour cold water on a conflict rather than fan the flames, even if that meant content that was less attention-grabbing than its rivals'.

Aanandi stroked my gibbon fringe of arm hair absentmindedly.

"Penny for them?" I asked.

She grimaced. "What can I tell you? It's obvious, isn't it? Millions could die. Billions. And I feel so helpless, so small."

"Me too. I've downed a jet fighter in midair with my bare hands, which I'm still freaking out about a little bit, and now along with everyone else I'm just hoping and praying that sense prevails. All these siddhis we have, but there are some things bigger than even devas."

"I can't help wondering..."

"What?"

"This is going to sound stupid, but I've been asking myself, could we be seeing the end of the Kali Yuga?"

"I don't know what that is. Is it bad?"

"It's worse than bad. It's the end of everything,

as predicted in the Hindu scriptures. The ages of human civilisation go in cycles. They're called the yugas, and there are four of them. Each is said to last forty-eight centuries, although there's some dispute about the figure. You start with the Satya Yuga, which is a golden age, literally the 'Age of Truth,' when mortals are ruled by and guided by the gods. The *Mahabharata* says that there is 'no hatred or vanity, or evil thought' during the Satya Yuga. Through worship and good works, everyone achieves a long, healthy life and a state of blessed perfection."

"Sounds good."

"Then comes the Treta Yuga. Evil rises. Demons walk abroad. People's devotion to the gods wanes by twenty-five per cent. This is symbolised by the Dharma Bull – which represents morality – standing on three legs now rather than four as it did in the Satya Yuga. The legs are austerity, cleanliness, compassion and truthfulness. One by one they go as the yugas pass."

"Until finally the Bull falls over."

"More or less. In the third age, the Dvapara Yuga, it's down to two: compassion and truthfulness. People have become jealous and competitive. They're liars, and that leads to disease – sickness of body and spirit."

"And in the fourth age, the Kali one, the Bull is balancing precariously on a single leg."

"Yes. The rishi Markandeya – the ancient prophet and sage – said that during the Kali Yuga spirituality will have declined to such a level that it has more or less died out. There will be widespread hatred, a general ignorance of the dictates of dharma. Children will not honour their elders and betters. We'll see mass migrations – starving millions on the move, searching for food. Fornication, drinking and drug-taking will be rife."

"So, not all bad, then." I waggled my furry capuchin eyebrows.

Her laugh was hollow. "Lust and intoxicants have their place, but Markandeya's point was that they will have become goals in themselves, obsessions, lifestyle choices. He also said that our leaders will no longer be reasonable, just or fair. They'll impose extortionate taxes and become a danger to the world."

"If that doesn't describe modern politicians, I don't know what does."

"The Kali Yuga is supposed to have begun in 3100 BCE, give or take, and if you do the math..."

I mimed counting on my fingers and mumbled about dividing by the square root and carrying the one.

"It's now, dumbass," she said. "The forty-eight centuries are up."

"And what comes next?"

"Destruction. Fiery catastrophe. Everything is obliterated so that the cycle can start again and the world begin afresh."

"Pressing the reset button."

"The yugas are an allegorical way of looking at history, explaining why things invariably turn to shit and justifying why the world is such a mess. They're a philosophy, not literal, empirical fact. All the same... You look at what's going on and you do start to think whether there might be some truth in it."

"This Kali," I said. "Is that the six-armed goddess with the swords?"[1]

Aanandi shook her head. "Same name, different entity. The Kali of the Kali Yuga is a doglike demon, the source of all evil, anger incarnate. He's an asura king who hangs around gambling dens, brothels, graveyards and slaughterhouses. Wherever there's sin or death, there's Kali."

"I don't suppose Korolev has made one of him, has he?"

"Let's hope not. A Kali would be worse than any demon you've faced."

"Worse than Takshaka?"

"Infinitely. That's another good reason to catch the Trinity before they go any further. The world does not need a Kali. Or a goddess Kali either, for that matter. She's as deadly as they come. She lives to kill demons, but when she's in one of her battle frenzies, woe betide anyone who gets in her way."

"I can't believe you just said 'woe betide.'"

"It's a nice phrase. What's wrong with it?"

"Nothing. Just – who says that, these days?"

---

[1] I remembered her vividly from *The Golden Voyage Of Sinbad*, which I saw on TV as a kid: the stop-frame animation figure attacking Sinbad and his crew in the cave, a masterful piece of work by Ray Harryhausen. She had scared the bejeezus out of me with her sinister dancer-like movements and her remorseless, stony-faced implacability.

"I do, obviously. I must have caught it off my poppa. He used to use it a lot when telling me his Veda stories. He was old-school that way. He'd even start them with 'Once upon a time...'"

I'd managed to lighten the mood, but thinking of her father reminded Aanandi of her concerns about him and her mother. Worry clouded her face again.

"Can't we do *anything* about the war?" she asked.

"Directly?" I said. "No. I discussed it with Parashurama. How do we decide who to fight for? Or against? More to the point, how do we stop nuclear weapons? With swords and punches? We can't. It's out of our league. We handle what we can handle, and that means the Trinity. But it's possible that fixing them will fix everything else."

"How?"

Parashurama and I had roughed out a plan over breakfast and then shared it with the other devas. I couldn't see the harm in running it past Aanandi and seeing what she thought. The plan hinged on several variables – not least, whether or not we caught up with the Trinity – but if by some miracle it worked, it solved everything in one fell swoop.

"It isn't public knowledge yet that devas are manmade," I said. "Same goes for asuras. Hardly anyone outside the Trinity's immediate circle knows that the demons are, for want of a better word, artificial, created by the same process that gave the world us. We're the good guys, but we're still basically a lie, a con job, operating under false pretences. Were the public to learn that..."

"The Dashavatara would be completely discredited."

"Yes. That would be a difficult enough pill to swallow, but knowing that theogenesis can lead to demons as much as it can to gods, that would be even more difficult. So the Trinity made a mistake, revealing the truth about asuras to us."

"They presumed you wouldn't be left alive to do anything useful with the knowledge."

"Still, it was foolish, because it's given us ammunition we can turn against them. The other group that would be discredited, you see, is the Trinity themselves. If word got out that they were the ones who unleashed Kumbhakarna in Moscow, Duryodhana in Venice, Rahu in Mexico City, and all those rakshasas and nagas and vetalas, responsible for so many deaths, there'd be an outcry. It would be hard for them to sell theogenesis anywhere."

"Though not impossible."

"Quite. There'd still be takers. Reputable governments would perhaps be forced by public opinion not to do business with the Trinity Syndicate, but there are plenty of *dis*reputable ones around. It'd be black market, but that's still a market. So we'll have to make sure that the technology is eradicated somehow. But mainly we'll have to make sure that the Trinity themselves, and Professor Korolev, end up behind bars, judged and found guilty of criminal acts, utterly disgraced and humiliated."

"There are some of the Avatars I can't see going for that. Vamana, Narasimha, Kurma... Those guys' dander is up. They're out for blood."

"Parashurama's got them to see sense. He's no Buddha, but he's charismatic nonetheless. The whole point is that justice should be served. The Trinity are put on trial at the Hague or wherever. They don't get away with what they've done. They certainly don't get to cream off billions from this new arms race they're going to kick-start."

"And jailing them de-escalates the war how exactly? It could be months, years probably, before a trial gets heard, and we don't have that long. We have days, maybe only hours."

"Ah, that's the beauty of it," I said. "If we can do this thing quickly enough, drag the Trinity kicking and screaming into the light *right now*, then it puts a whole new slant on the war. It gives both India and Pakistan a perfect get-out clause."

"I don't see."

"At the moment neither side is willing to back down. One or other of them has dropped a nuke, neither's prepared to own up to it, so they're stuck, deadlocked. The only way forward for them that doesn't involve a critical loss of face is to ratchet the situation up and take the next step – more nuking. But..."

"But if they can scapegoat someone else, a third party..."

"By George, she's got it."

"Then no loss of face."

"They can say, 'Well, it was the Trinity's fault. They came up with the Avatars. If that hadn't happened, maybe there'd have been no war.' Then the relevant politicians can shake hands and kiss and make up, everyone agreeing that the world would be a much better place without those nasty billionaire tycoons messing it up for the rest of us."

"That's... That's..." Aanandi was momentarily dumbfounded. "That's so ridiculous, it can't possibly work."

"And yet it might."

"I know! That's why I'm having trouble with it. I want to think it's crazy and impractical and unrealistic – but, holy shit, it really could be the way out of this situation."

"Desperate times call for desperate measures. Loony measures, even. And the Trinity are the perfect fall guys, aren't they? Everybody hates a crooked businessman, especially governments. Politicians like nothing more than to point the finger at people who are worse than they are, the corporate villains who no one elected, who are hard to hold to account. India can say, 'If we'd known what Lombard, Krieger and Bhatnagar were really like, what they were really doing, why, we would never have agreed to use those Avatars of theirs in combat', while Pakistan can say, 'We suspected all along they were up to no good, that's why we fired missiles at their island, and now we've been proved right, so we're not so aggrieved any more'. Both sides get to park their arses on the moral high ground, which makes it easier for them then to pull back from the brink of all-out, empty-the-silos nuclear bombardment. Earth breathes a sigh of relief. Happy ending."

"Not for the citizens of Srinagar," Aanandi said. "But yes, it's the best outcome we can hope for. You devas, though, aren't going to be popular. Especially in India. You've been passing yourselves off as Hindu gods, and to shatter that illusion…"

"It needs shattering. Both Parashurama and I are in agreement on that. 'Living a lie is no life at all,' he said to me, and I agree."

"And I can understand why he, of all people, would think that."

"Why?"

Aanandi glanced back down to the rear of the cabin. "Another time."[1]

"Anyway, I think people would come to understand after a while," I said, "and sympathise. We're the Trinity's victims as much as anyone."

"Zak." Aanandi took my hand. "You're a genius."

"I have my moments. The plan was mostly Parashurama's, though."

"Even so. Thanks to you both, we have a chance again. The world has a chance."

Seeing the renewed brightness in her eyes, I was loath to admit that I thought it was a very slim chance – a snowball's chance in hell. By now the *Garuda* was at its apogee, high over the mid-Pacific,

---

[1] I learned subsequently that Parashurama, a.k.a. Major Tyler Weston, had fallen foul of the Pentagon's notorious "don't ask, don't tell" policy. He had earned himself a dishonourable discharge after propositioning a master sergeant whom he wrongly believed was on the same sexual wavelength. The 3rd Ranger Battalion lost one of their best ever recruits, while Tyler Weston lost all faith in the institution which had been a central pillar of his family life for three generations.

and our bodies were light, partially weightless. I chose to enjoy the respite from gravity, the distance, the perspective. The ocean shone like beaten metal. The planet's curved edge was as hazy as a half-remembered dream. We had a plan. We had hope. I chose to believe that that was enough.

45. MRS R. J. KRIEGER

WE LEFT THE *Garuda* on Zuma Beach.[1] The strip of sand was all but deserted, no one jogging or dog walking or sunbathing, just the odd surfer bobbing far out to sea where the rollers broke. The weather was glorious but the unsettled geopolitical climate was keeping most Californians indoors, in the comfort of their own homes.

A mile to the south lay a bluff crowned with modern mansions – Point Dume. The houses were all cubes and curves, as though made of architectural Lego. One of them, though we couldn't see it from here, belonged to R. J. Krieger.

Parashurama split us up into two groups for a

---

[1] It's where they filmed the closing scenes of *Planet Of The Apes*. "Goddamn you all to hell!" etc.

pincer movement. One lot would approach the Krieger residence from the front, scaling the high wall that shielded the house from the street. The other lot would approach from the seaward side.

The latter group consisted of Narasimha, Vamana, Matsya and me.

There was no time to waste. The four of us hustled down the beach while the rest followed a zigzagging access road up to the main highway.

Matsya was carrying his discus weapons. He was itching to try them out. Parashurama had warned us that he wanted the Trinity taken alive if possible. Any bodyguards, however, were fair game. "Especially the guy with the diamond tooth who shot Buddha. He's a case for involuntary euthanasia if there ever was one."

Krieger's house was one of the largest on Point Dume, perched on the south-western sweep of the promontory. Its views of the Pacific were uninterrupted and panoramic. I couldn't begin to imagine how many millions a mansion like that must have cost – and yet the asking price would still have been pocket change to someone as loaded as Krieger was.

The cliff below was steep but not sheer. Looking at it with Hanuman's eyes I could see a dozen routes up, clear pathways of handhold and toehold, to me as easily scalable as a kids' climbing frame.

I ascended first. Narasimha was close behind, digging his talons into the volcanic rock for purchase. Vamana, meanwhile, grew to full height. He and

Matsya were under orders to wait on the beach until we gave them the sign to follow. A giant springing up to the brow of the cliff with an amphibious man on his shoulders would somewhat ruin the element of surprise.

Stealthily, Narasimha and I crept through the undergrowth that fringed the outer rim of Krieger's back garden. The house looked quiet. Most likely it was empty and this entire trip had been a wild goose chase. The Trinity were not here and never had been.

Narasimha's leonine nostrils flared. "A scent," he whispered.

"How many?"

"Just the one person. A woman. Outdoors."

"A woman?" Krieger had a wife. "Anyone else? Indoors?"

"I cannot tell until I am closer."

We padded across an impeccably lush green lawn, skirting cypresses and lollipop-shaped orange trees.

There was a swimming pool sitting snug against the rear of the house, surrounded by sun loungers and parasols. As we neared, I saw a woman floating in the water on a transparent inflatable. She had a drink in her hand, huge sunglasses on her face, and iPod buds in her ears. She also did not have a stitch of clothing on, her bare skin glistening with a sheen of tanning lotion.

Narasimha and I halted in our tracks. The woman was oblivious to our presence, very likely fast asleep. Flaxen curls fanned around her head on the inflatable's pillow, but from the tiny, tidily sculpted strip of pubic hair on display, it was apparent that she was not a natural blonde. Her breasts did not seem entirely natural either, remaining pert as she lay.

The Man-lion gave me a look: *what do we do?*

I shrugged. I reckoned we would have to secure and restrain her somehow before we ventured into the house. I hadn't anticipated having to deal with anyone but the Trinity and their goons. None of us had.

Narasimha and I could have stood and stared for a good while longer, paralysed by indecision. But then the woman stirred. She raised her upper half slightly from the inflatable to bring her drink to her lips. That was when she caught sight of us out of the corner of her eye.

"What the...?"

Narasimha moved like a cheetah on steroids. He dived sleekly into the pool, bundled the woman off the inflatable, and leapt out the other side with her in his arms. She had time to let out a startled, strangulated yelp, and then his hand was over her mouth and he had her in an unbreakable hold. She writhed but didn't stand a chance against his sinewy strength. Her sunglasses slipped off to reveal eyes bulging with alarm and indignation.

I motioned to her to take her earbuds out. She did so. Music issued tinnily from them – Lady Gaga, if memory serves. "Bad Romance."

"We mean you no harm," I said, as softly and reassuringly as I could. "Do you know who we are?"

The woman nodded. She might not have a clue about me but she surely recognised Narasimha.

"Then you'll know that our job is to protect the public."

She didn't seem convinced, and I can't blame her for that. I wasn't sure myself if that was our role any more.

"Just answer a couple of questions and we'll let you go, unharmed. That's a promise. Are you alone? Yes or no?"

She hesitated, then nodded.

"Is that the truth?"

She nodded again, more emphatically.

"Are you Mrs Krieger?"

She rolled her eyes. *Who else would I be?*

"Tiffany, yes?"

Another nod.

"And your husband isn't here? Or any of his business partners?"

She shook her head.

"I do not think she is lying," said Narasimha. "I am listening hard. All I can hear, apart from her music, is the Avatars on the other side of the house. From the sound of their footsteps, they are closing in. If people are inside, they are keeping very still, very quiet. This near to the house, I would surely be able to hear their breathing, and I cannot."

"Okay," I said. "Let her go."

"Yes?"

"Yes. But please, Mrs Krieger, no histrionics."

As Narasimha released her, Tiffany Krieger shot us

both a filthy look, then snatched up a towel to wrap round herself.

"Who the hell do you think you are, coming onto my property like this?" she said. "That's trespassing, mister. I could call the cops and have you dickwads arrested."

"I said no histrionics."

"Oh, this isn't me being histrionic," Mrs Krieger said waspishly. "Trust me, you don't want to see histrionic. This is me being calm as all hell."

Trembling – I think more with outrage than fright – she strode to a rattan-shaded bar and fetched herself a fresh glass to replace the one that had dropped into the pool when Narasimha scooped her up. She filled it with bourbon and ice and drank deep.

"You're Avatars, right?"

"He is," I said. "I'm... Well, I'm Hanuman."

"R. J.'s pet project. I know about you guys. The Trinity Syndicate's gambled about a gazillion bucks on you. What are you doing here? Aren't you supposed to be on Mount Mary or whatever the damn place is called?"

"Things have... changed."

"Changed, huh? How so?"

"Let's just say your husband and his friends, they're not the people we thought they were."

Tiffany Krieger coughed out a laugh. "That's a familiar refrain. R. J. comes across like a Texan gent, sweet as molasses, but Christ, deep down, that man is cold. Cold and hard." She helped herself to another generous portion of whiskey. I got the impression that she and booze were no strangers to each other. The evidence was there in her puffy cheeks, her bruised-looking eyes. "I don't know much about how the man does business, but if it's anything like the way he does other stuff, it's brisk, efficient, over quickly, and he gets out of it whatever he can get out of it and screw anyone else. How else do you become a billionaire? Not by playing nice and fair, that's for damn sure." Her face took on a certain cruel amusement. "So he and his pals have fucked you over?"

"Kind of," I said. "Pretty much."

"Ha! Well then, more fool you."

There was a crash from within the house.

"That your friends? Hope it was just them busting in through a window or door. We've got some priceless pieces of sculpture lying around. I collect. Hate to think somebody bumped into one of the Brancusis or the Modigliani and knocked it off its pedestal. The Hirst skull, on the other hand, that I don't care about so much. It was only an investment. Wouldn't object to the insurance payout."

Moments later Rama and Krishna emerged from the French windows overlooking the poolside, soon followed by Parashurama and Kalkin. The Horseman was still plagued by the injuries he'd received at the Golden Rocks Mine installation, his arm and leg both stiff, but he was doing his best not to show it. Bushido bravado.

"Nobody in," said the Warrior, disappointed.

"Except me," said Mrs Krieger. "You're the boss of the outfit, right, big guy?"

"I guess so."

"Then you explain to me why you've come barging uninvited into my home. And make it good."

"We're looking for the Trinity," Parashurama said.

"I get that, but what makes you think they'd be here? R. J.'s hardly ever around. He's always off somewhere, wheeler-dealering, checking on his minions, making his millions. I get to see him once a month, if I'm lucky. Lately it's been less than that. Most of the time I have the house to myself. Can't say I mind too much. He's not what you'd call an attentive husband, but as long as the housekeeping account's topped up and my credit card bills get paid off, who's complaining? And as for the conjugal relations side of things... Well, Ramon the pool boy does more than backwash the filtration system, if you get my meaning. Or is that too much information?"

She giggled and slugged down yet more bourbon. Now that she knew her life was no longer in danger, Mrs Krieger was enjoying being the centre of the attention, surrounded by all these men, and her with only a bathing towel to preserve her modesty. The booze was lowering her inhibitions, too, and making her talkative. I glimpsed a vivacious girl beneath the brittle woman, someone with brains who had lived an interesting and fairly racy life before settling down to become a trophy wife.

"Do you have any idea where your husband might be?" Rama asked.

"You people really are in a pickle, aren't you, Frenchie? Chasing after him. Can't find him. Why should I help you? Even if I knew anything, which I don't. Seems like you're out for blood. Why am I going to sell out R. J. if you're only going to kill him?" She pouted winsomely, like Marilyn Monroe doing her little-girl routine. "My own darling hubby-kins. My sweet Southern sugar daddy. I'm not that kinda gal."

"Your 'hubby-kins' is a lunatic who's used us, lied to us and did his level best to murder us," said Kalkin.

"That does sound like R. J."

"He's also key to saving the world, we believe," said Parashurama.

"Really?"

"Yes, ma'am."

"Ooh, 'ma'am.' I like that. Tell me more."

Parashurama outlined our plan to use the Trinity as a lever to shift India and Pakistan away from war. Mrs Krieger listened intently. Her eyes were glassy and pink and she was swaying a little as the alcohol worked its way into her system.

"Well, shit," she said. "So that's how the land lies, huh? The Trinity are the black hats and you're the sheriff's posse going to bring them in and save the good folk of Dodge. Puts me in kind of an awkward situation, as you can imagine. On the one hand, a wife doesn't rat on her husband. On the other hand, when your husband's clearly a rat, is it ratting? Doesn't the one cancel out the other? Oh, the dilemma."

We waited. Mrs Krieger's mind was already halfway made up.

"What the hell. I've got a solid gold pre-nup. If he wants a divorce after this, he'll pay through the ass. And he is, no doubt, a bastard. I love him the way you love a shark: you've got to admire the way he moves through the water and the other fish clear a path, but you know damn well he's going to take a chunk out of you if you're not careful. I lied just now." She looked at Narasimha, then at me. "When the Lion King and Monkey Business were holding me prisoner. Sorry, fellas. I said I was alone. What I didn't say is that I *wasn't* alone earlier today. R. J. dropped by this morning. Literally just called in on his way from LAX, grabbed some things, left again. Came and went so fast, we barely spoke. He told me him and his buddies – Dick and Vignesh – they'd be travelling for a while. I wasn't to try contacting him. He'd be off the grid. Work to do, places to go, people to see. Quick peck on the cheek and he was away again. Limo out front. Bodyguards. Gone in a cloud of dust."

"That didn't strike you as suspicious?" said Parashurama.

"What are you, a cop? There's no 'suspicious' where R. J. Krieger is concerned, pal. He does what he pleases. If he's staying on the down low, he has his reasons. Could be he's running scared, what with the Dashavatara hot on his tail."

"As far as he knows, we're dead."

"Is that so? Maybe he thinks otherwise. R. J. is

many things, but dumb isn't one of them. You don't get to be a master of the universe without smarts and guile. If he thinks there's even a chance you people are still alive, then of course he's going to take precautions, go to ground if he has to."

"You said he 'grabbed some things,'" said Kalkin. "What sort of things?"

"Just stuff. A suitcase, some fresh clothing. R. J.'s careful about his appearance, you've got to have noticed that. Dapper. I guess, since he was passing close to home, he didn't see the harm in taking a couple of minutes out of his schedule to stop in and raid his wardrobe, get a few clean shirts, et cetera. Underwear. Deck shoes. Also, say hi and goodbye to the little lady. He's a bastard but he's a courteous bastard. His mommy taught him manners."

"So the Trinity are flying off again," said Parashurama. "Probably airborne already. They've got a head start and this time we can't even guess where they're going. Could be anywhere."

"We're buggered," I said.

Vamana appeared, clambering up over the cliff edge with Matsya riding pillion on his back.

"Got bored of waiting for the signal," the Dwarf said, depositing the Fish-man on the lawn. "What's up? I'm guessing, from the looks of things, the Trinity are a no-show."

Parashurama brought the two of them up to speed.

"She knows more than she's letting on," Vamana said, pointing a finger the size of a loaf of bread at Mrs Krieger.

"Keep those jumbo hands to yourself, buster," she retorted. "You don't intimidate me. I've come clean, told you everything I can. The only thing I haven't mentioned is the *Makara*."

"The what?"

"It's Vignesh's big-ass yacht. Moored at Marina Del Rey. Hell, don't any of you know anything? Vignesh has been keeping it there for the past four years. Now, the three of them might be on Dick's plane, but they can get around just as well by boat. Not as fast, but a darn sight less cramped and more luxurious. The *Makara*.[1] You should see the thing. She's about a hundred feet tall, got two swimming pools, Jacuzzi, more cabins than I can count, couple of motor launches. Best of all, she's lower-profile than a corporate jet."

"How so?" I said. "A floating gin palace like you've just described, it's not exactly a subtle mode of transport."

"Yes, but – the Trinity are laying low, yeah? But they still want to do deals, meet clients and so forth. The *Makara*'s got a helipad, so guests can fly in and out. It's also got switchable privacy glass in every window and a sensor shield that sweeps the area looking for cameras, then dazzles the lenses with laser bursts. Something to do with detecting electrical charges. Paparazzi can't take a shot of anyone on board. No guarantee of that when you're disembarking from a plane at an airfield."

---

[1] Named after a sea leviathan in Hindu mythology.

"You're saying this yacht is where they'll be?" said Parashurama.

"I'm not promising it, tall, dark and handsome. What I am saying is if I were R. J., that's what I'd do – take to the sea. A boat's harder to pin down than an airplane. It can go anywhere, put in at any harbour, any bay, or just get lost for days in the middle of the ocean. It's more secure. It's more private. More comfortable."

"You also mentioned deck shoes," said Rama.

"I did, didn't I? Salty seadog R. J. in his handmade blazer and canvas loafers. Frankly, if I were y'all, I'd go to Del Rey and check Vignesh's landing slip. If the *Makara* isn't there, that's your answer."

She drained her glass.

"I'm no crazy lady," Tiffany Krieger said. "I don't want to see the world blown up any more than the next guy. If you think R. J. and friends are the solution to the crisis, then go get 'em. Please don't hurt R. J. if you can avoid it – I'm still enough of a loyal wife to ask for that – but at the same time, I wish you luck. Be stupid not to. You're weirdos and a bit messed up, but your hearts are in the right place. We have that in common."

46. THE HUNT FOR THE *MAKARA*

BY MID-AFTERNOON WE had established that Bhatnagar's five-hundred-foot, half-billion-dollar giga-yacht had put out from Del Rey Landing in Santa Monica shortly after ten AM. The *Makara*'s four diesel engines together yielded 95,000 horsepower, allowing her to achieve a top speed of thirty knots, around thirty-five miles per hour. She could be anything up to a hundred miles away by now, either far out in the Pacific or hugging the coastline.

It was a vast search area, a semicircle of roughly fifteen thousand square miles, and getting larger by the minute. All we could do was begin scouring it and hope for the best.

To increase our chances of success, Matsya took to

the ocean, equipped with a waterproof, ruggedized mobile phone bought from an army surplus store. Swimming at top speed, he used the phone's GPS to help him make a systematic sweep of the southern sector of the search area. The *Garuda*, meanwhile, quartered the northern sector, flying low enough that the *Makara*'s profile would show up on radar. Eagle-eyed Rama kept lookout in the cockpit beside Captain Corday.

It was a damn big boat, but then fifteen thousand square miles was a damn big amount of sea to hide in.

To our advantage, Matsya's hearing was perfectly adapted to a subaquatic environment. He could detect whalesong, the echolocation clicks of dolphins, all the low-frequency noises that travelled far through water – including boat propellers. He had a lobe in his brain that was sensitive to sound in the 100+ megahertz range. So whenever he picked up the rumble of screws churning and the cavitation of air bubbles, he would veer off in that direction to investigate.

In the *Garuda*'s cabin, the divide of suspicion remained – Aanandi and I at one end, the Avatars at the other.

Then Parashurama, bless him, took a significant step. He came forward and sat next to us. Ostensibly this was so that he could pick Aanandi's brains, but he was obviously sending a message to the others at the same time.

"I've been meaning to ask," he said. "You might know the answer to this."

"Shoot," said Aanandi. "Anything I can to help."

"So we found this stone flower in the central tower at Meru..."

"The Harappa lotus, yes."

"What the heck is it? It made our heads go all fuzzy when we got close to it. Made them hiss like a radio picking up static."

Aanandi nodded. "You're not the only ones. But no surprise it should affect devas more strongly than most. That lotus – it's the true source of theogenesis. Without it, you, what you are, would not have been possible."

"Is it something Korolev invented?"

"He wishes. No, it's older, much older, something the Trinity brought to him and he extrapolated from. It's the basis of his entire process. What it actually is... Well, there we enter the realms of speculation."

"Go on."

"Long story. How much time do you have?"

Parashurama shrugged. "Until we locate the *Makara*. I'm not doing anything else right now, so..."

He settled back in his seat and gave a short, sharp whistle, to get the other Avatars' attention. "Guys? Listen up. I think we're about to learn a thing or two."

47. A NATION OF GODS

AANANDI SPOKE HESITANTLY at first, then with growing confidence. I found myself picturing her speech as a sequence in a comic; a succession of tableaux overlaid with narrative captions.

She began by telling us that there are some Hindu scholars who theorise that the gods of the Vedas aren't just embodiments of abstract philosophical concepts. They aren't nebulous mythical entities, ideas given human form, fictitious characters playing roles in moral parables.

The Hindu gods are – were – real.

At one time, many thousands of years ago, they walked the earth.

The Indus Valley Civilisation is often dubbed the cradle of modern mankind. While the rest of the world was still mired in the Stone Age, learning how to domesticate animals and use crude tools, around the Indus river basin – situated mostly in what we now know as Pakistan but extending into India, Afghanistan and Iran – there was a flourishing, sophisticated society.

These people had advanced metallurgical skills and a profound grasp of mathematics. Their arts and crafts were of astonishing quality, particularly their elegant terracotta figurines. They had dentistry, plumbing, sanitation. Contemporary cultures in Egypt and Mesopotamia were backward by comparison.

There's more, though. It's reckoned that the people of the Indus Valley had access to technology of a kind we're only just beginning to be able to replicate today, and that the proof of this lies in the Vedas.

The most prominent example is the "vimana chariot." It's mentioned time and again in Vedic texts – a flying vehicle capable of great speeds. In the *Ramayana*, the asura king Ravana scoots about in an "aerial and excellent chariot" that looks like "a bright cloud in the sky," while in the *Mahabharata* another asura king, Maya, pilots a flying disc twelve cubits in diameter. The *Rigveda* depicts "golden mechanical birds" that can carry passengers up to the heavens, and then there's the Rukma Vimana, which is a kind of conical floating fortress, and the Tripura Vimana, an airship said to be able to travel as fast as the wind.

References to vimana aircraft in the Hindu

scriptures are numerous and consistent. Some are named after birds like the kingfisher and the ibis, others after larger animals such as the elephant. They're said to draw on some form of antigravity power source called laghima and be constructed from materials that absorb light and heat. There are even suggestions that they permit interplanetary travel. The *Ramayana* describes a trip to the moon and an airship battle which took place above the lunar surface.

The Indus Valley people also had extensive knowledge of the solar system and astronomy in general, and their proficiency with medicine was remarkable even by modern-day standards. It's thought that there was no disease – up to and including cancer – that they couldn't cure through a holistic regime of diet, exercise and herbal remedies.

The story of the nymph Tilottama, in the *Mahabharata*, implies that they could build robots, too. Tilottama is an artificial woman studded with gemstones and created to be so beautiful that anyone who sets eyes on her falls immediately and hopelessly in love. She was used to cause a rift between the demon brothers Sunda and Upsunda so that they would stop terrorising the world. It worked: they killed each other arguing over her.

Is it so hard to believe that these humans, with their extraordinary technological and medical prowess, were considered godlike by their primitive neighbours? Is it not even possible that they weren't human at all but a non-terrestrial race, visitors from another world, born under a distant star, who were venerated as though divine?

Hinduism famously has thirty-three crore gods. *Crore* is Indian for "ten million," so we're talking about 330,000,000 gods in total.

That's not a pantheon. That's a *nation*.

And what if this nation of space gods made its home, or at least set up an outpost, a colony, here on earth, in the northern region of the Indian subcontinent? What if the Hindu scriptures aren't so much a religious creed as a historical record?

If so, then the epoch of these god-beings came to an abrupt, violent end. The evidence is there in the ruined ancient cities of Mohenjo-daro and Harappa. In both places archaeologists have found deep strata of green glass – the result of clay and sand being fused at high temperatures and hardening.

There's also Rajasthan, west of Jodhpur, where scientists have identified a three-square-mile area with a greater than average incidence of cancer and birth defects. The level of background radiation is inexplicably high. Ruins nearby show signs of buildings that have been flattened. The skeletons of half a million bodies have been unearthed. Etchings on a temple wall attest to a fear of a "great light" that had the potential to devastate the region.

Northwest of Mumbai sits the Lonar Crater Lake, one kilometre across, many thousands of years old. It is not a meteorite impact site. There are no traces of meteoric material in the vicinity. Tiny spheres of fused basalt glass in the soil point to a burst of massive, intense heat and a pressure shockwave in excess of half a million atmospheres.

The *Mahabharata* speaks of a projectile "charged with the power of the universe" that exploded with "the might of a thousand suns." Robert Oppenheimer, head of the Manhattan Project, father of the atomic bomb, firmly believed that Vyasa, the author of the epic, was referring to a thermonuclear device. Oppenheimer once told a student that he had not invented the first atomic bomb but, specifically, "the first atomic bomb in modern times."

The Indus Valley Civilisation, in other words, destroyed itself in a spasm of nuclear fire, leaving nothing behind but rubble and a half-remembered dream of men who walked like gods, or gods who walked like men.

Which brings us to the Trinity's stone lotus.

It was discovered about fifteen years ago by a team from the Archaeological Survey of India who were excavating in and around Harappa. The lotus turned up amidst a cache of pictographic soapstone seals in the vault of what had apparently been some kind of administrative building. It was put on display in the National Museum in New Delhi for a while, where it baffled the curators, who couldn't decide whether it was merely a fancy ornament – a paperweight, a corbel, a candle holder – or had a greater significance and purpose. Night watchmen reported that sometimes in the silence of the empty building it seemed to give off a low, pulsing hum that made them nauseous, but the phenomenon remained anecdotal, never conclusively proven. Visitors to the museum likewise commented that the Harappa lotus was unnerving; they felt uneasy in its presence, detached, some said it was as though they were hearing voices in their heads when they looked at it.

Beautiful artefact though it was, the stone flower repelled people rather than attracted them, and eventually the museum's board of directors voted to offload it. A number of Indian and overseas universities were keen to take it off their hands, but all of them were outbid by Vignesh Bhatnagar.

Bhatnagar, with his abiding fascination with Hindu myth, believed the Harappa lotus was an important relic of the Indus Valley Civilisation. More than that – it was connected in some way to the godlike qualities they were rumoured to possess. Might it be radiating some kind of energy, presently unknown to science, which had a disorientating effect on sensitive people? Could that account for the complaints of nausea and "hearing voices"?

He passed it on to R. J. Krieger. There was no Trinity Syndicate back then, but the two men had met several times at the Bilderberg Conference in Davos, Switzerland and had struck up a friendship.[1] Krieger got his scientists working on the lotus, mainly as a favour to Bhatnagar but in part because

---

[1] The Bilderberg Conference is the annual shindig for top-level politicians and high-net-worth individuals where the fate of the world is thrashed out, or so the conspiracy theorists would have us believe. Others think it's just a big knees-up for the ultra elite.

there was a chance the artefact might have some property he could exploit, some undiscovered biological or chemical element he could extract and derive revenue from.

The whitecoats got busy sampling, analysing, poking around. The results were inconclusive.

It was Gennady Korolev, king of the lab, who made the breakthrough.

The lotus, he realised, exuded an energy field that responded strongly to faith.

Korolev had studied the results of all the various tests on the artefact, cross-referencing them with the human resources files on the scientists conducting the tests. The data overview showed that the lotus gave off higher electromagnetic readings whenever it was being worked on by an employee who adhered to a religious belief system.

Not all scientists are atheists. Many have found ways to reconcile empiricism with faith. Others retain the imprint of a sternly devout upbringing, although in adulthood they affect agnosticism. Religion has deep roots and can survive below the surface, if only subliminally, in even the most rational minds.

Correlating experiment with experimenter, Korolev deduced that the Harappa lotus set up a kind of sympathetic resonance with people who, consciously or not, put their trust in a higher power. To back up his hypothesis, he assembled a random selection of college-student guinea pigs and, using single photon emission computer tomography, took images of their brains as he introduced them into the lotus's presence. Proximity to the artefact stimulated certain regions of the brain associated with religious experience. There was a increase in blood flow to the temporal lobe and a matching decrease in blood flow to the parietal lobe, considerably more marked in the test subjects who professed faith than those who didn't. This was in accordance with the findings of experiments in the field of neurotheology which have demonstrated how prayer and meditation augment temporal lobe activity, bringing greater concentration and focus, and lessen parietal lobe activity, meaning a decline in spatial awareness. Religious trance or ecstasy, the sense of being "out of one's body," is neurological in origin. By contemplating the divine, you can go to a higher plane of consciousness within yourself.

What Korolev then noted, however, was that the blood flow alterations in the brain declined sharply after a minute or so. The human guinea pigs would start to complain of light-headedness, dizziness, occasionally headaches. At the same time, the lotus's energy field would intensify.

It was as though in some way the stone flower was leeching power from the people nearby. It was absorbing their faith, sucking it up like a sponge and projecting it out again.

Korolev took his startling findings to Krieger, who shared them with Bhatnagar. Together the two plutocrats discussed what the Harappa lotus's strange qualities might mean and how they could develop it into something marketable.

It was Krieger who proposed bio-engineering gods, superhuman beings charged and sustained by the power of faith. And it was Bhatnagar who sketched out the blueprint for the Induction Cocoon, a machine to distil worship and install it in a human body.

They brought Dick Lombard in on the scheme because of his globe-spanning media empire. His tentacles reached everywhere. He could channel electronic imagery from any corner of the planet and draw it down into a single location. The faith of billions was swarming around in the infosphere, just waiting for the person with the right infrastructure, the right connections, to milk it. A reservoir begging to be tapped – and Lombard owned the drilling equipment.

Which isn't to say he was easy to convince. When Bhatnagar and Krieger approached him with their idea, Lombard dismissed it as "the most harebrained load of old cobblers I ever heard in all my born days." But when the potential profit level was put to him – an income stream pouring in from the defence budgets of just about every nation on earth – he soon changed his tune.

And so the Trinity Syndicate was born.

Korolev was given the task of somehow developing the Harappa lotus's properties into a reproducible process that could refashion men into gods. He was promised a sizeable cut of the proceeds if he managed it, which was more than enough of an incentive to do his utmost to succeed.

He quickly ascertained that the bright blue glinting flecks in the flower were crystalline structures, basically organic in nature. A single tiny fragment could be cultured in a gel medium derived from hydroxyapatite, a mineral found in teeth and bones. The artificially grown crystals could then be atomised and inserted into a protein cage structure – his "god virus" – which housed and bonded with the crystal molecules and was able to "infect" the tissues of a host body with them.

Abracadabra, theogenesis.

It wasn't too great a deductive leap to suggest that the crystals and laghima, the vimana power source, were associated. Perhaps the Indus Valley god-beings fuelled their aircraft with their own minds, their own faith. They believed their vehicles could fly, and thus they flew.

The Harappa lotus, then, was nothing other than an exotic battery which operated on a closed-loop system with every vimana pilot. He fed it with his faith – his imagination – and it in turn supplied energy to the flying chariot's antigravity propulsion drive. A larger vessel such as the Rukma Vimana might require a hundred minds working in unison to keep it aloft, like the oarsmen of a Roman galley all pulling together. As long as everyone on board was convinced it would stay airborne, it would.

As for the Indus Valley Civilisation's drastic demise, one can conjecture that the society went through a decline and fall as most societies do. It began with a golden age and, millennia later, ended in a dark age.

Reading between the lines of the Vedic texts, there was fragmentation, a fissuring. On one side the devas – enlightened, gifted, abiding by the rule of law. On the other side the asuras – devious, dangerous, malcontent. The faultlines were pre-existing. Mistrust and hatred had festered for centuries, one faction chafing against the other. In the end, the mutual antagonism got too great. Tempers flared. Deities waged war against demons in a string of escalating battles until finally the ultimate weapons were unleashed. All died, leaving behind nothing but ruins and a regional race memory which, over time, evolved into epic tales of gods and monsters and, ultimately, into a creed.

48. MAGIC ALIEN JUJU DUST

"So THAT'S WHY, when we leaned close to the lotus, it had a reaction to us," said Parashurama. "Like it recognised us."

"Yes," said Aanandi. "Some sort of feedback. A resistance. Like pushing the same poles of two magnets together. You and it are essentially full of the same stuff."

"Freaky."

"The freaky part for me is the advanced ancient civilisation bit," I said. "I thought all that Erich von Däniken *Chariots of the Gods* bollocks was thoroughly debunked years ago. Shows how much I know."

"You're the proof that von Däniken was on to something," said Aanandi. "All of you are. The

Trinity Syndicate have resurrected a long-lost technology and put their own spin on it, and you're now carrying it around inside you."

"I dunno," said Vamana. "Is it better or worse, knowing we've got magic alien juju dust running through our veins? I think I preferred it when it was just the prof's virus. That at least was science. This is science fiction."

"Anyone else seeing some uncanny parallels?" said Kalkin. "A race that vaporised itself to oblivion with nuclear weapons? History is about to repeat itself."

"Cycles," I said to Aanandi. "The yugas. From Satya to Kali."

She acknowledged it with a glum nod. "Maybe the sages of old were on to something. It seems the world needs a regular purging. No society, however mature, can last indefinitely. Ripeness, then rot."

"It doesn't have to happen," said Kurma. "Not this time."

"Unless we can find the Trinity, it may. And even then…" She sighed. "Talk about grasping at straws."

The *Garuda* banked left, beginning a turn. I assumed we had just completed a pass and were coming about to try the next. In other words, still no sign of the *Makara*.

But then, over the intercom, Captain Corday said, "Gentlemen and lady, we've had a ping from Matsya. Seems he may have struck gold. I'm heading for a rendezvous with his co-ordinates. Keep your eyes peeled."

He poured on speed, and within twenty minutes

we sighted a gargantuan motor yacht, closer to a cruise liner than any private boat, white as an iceberg in the azure ocean expanse. It had seven tiers of deck, a helipad just like Tiffany Krieger had said, a huge radar array, and a superstructure silhouette that combined humpback whale with space rocket.

Corday circled the yacht, and the name painted on the stern confirmed once and for all that we had found our objective: MAKARA.

He then matched the *Garuda*'s course to the *Makara*'s and began decelerating.

"Expect resistance," said Parashurama. "They'll surely have drafted in more bodyguards."

Krishna drew his sword, Nandaka. "I'm ready."

Kurma tightened his grip on his club. "So am I. Bring it on."

Narasimha flexed his taloned fingers like a pianist warming up. He said nothing.

Rama came aft from the cockpit, shouldering his bow and quiver. "Corday will hold position above the helipad so that we can jump out."

"What about Fishface?" said Vamana. "Is he going to join the party?"

"Matsya is submerged alongside the *Makara*. He will resurface when he sees us board."

"Good luck, guys," Aanandi said. "I mean it. You know what's at stake. Do it right."

The outer door opened and wind rushed in. The helipad's huge white H lay some twenty feet below, lurching slightly as the *Makara* ploughed through the Pacific swell.

Parashurama dropped first, hitting the helipad with his knees bent and ankles together and then rolling, paratrooper-style. Rama was out next, followed by Krishna, Kurma, Kalkin, Narasimha, me. Vamana stepped out growing, so that he was somehow almost stationary as he fell. He hit the boat at nearly full height, crouching on his giant haunches.

The *Garuda* peeled away.

"Perimeter," said Parashurama, and we moved in pairs to the helipad's edges and looked over.

Nobody in view.

"They must know we are here," said Narasimha. "So where are they?"

"Hiding?" said Vamana. "Cowering in the bilges? Who cares? Let's go dig the fuckers out."

"Easy there," said Parashurama. "I don't like this."

"Please don't say, 'It's quiet. Too quiet.'"

"Well, it is, Vamana. No obvious defensive measures. It's like they're lying in wait. Like we're right where they want us."

"Paranoid much? This is three businessmen and a handful of ex-special-forces squaddies, not the ruddy Taliban."

"After the Golden Rocks Mine fiasco, I have every right to be cautious. How many darn traps did they spring on us there? I know from dangerous, and these guys are it."

The Warrior padded down the steep flight of metal stairs from the helipad to the top deck, his axe held warily at an angle in front of him.

The rest of us never saw the door open and the gunman emerge. We heard the shot clearly enough, though, a sharp *crack!* above the hiss of the waves cleaving under the *Makara*'s bows.

The bullet struck Parashurama in the arm. He reeled under the impact, but recovered swiftly and lunged at the shooter. His axe blade embedded itself in the man's gut.

I leapt down to the Warrior's side. "Shit. How bad is it?"

He inspected the ragged hole in his arm. "Missed the artery. Hurts like crazy, but I'll live."

He leaned over the gunman, who lay on the deck with a wedge of entrail protruding from the gash in his stomach. A puddle of blood glistened on polished teak planks.

"Unlike you, buddy. How many of you are there? Tell me."

The man coughed wetly and redly. He was dressed in a black battledress jumpsuit, Kevlar tac vest, holsters and webbing galore, ammo belts, grenades, combat helmet. He wasn't one of the four goons, but he was clearly military. Mercenary.

"I can make it quick," Parashurama told him. "Put you out of your misery. Or you can lie there bleeding out, long and slow. What's it to be?"

"You are so screwed," the dying man gasped.

"How's that?"

"Dozens of us. And that's... that's not just any bullet."

"What do you – ?"

Parashurama staggered. His dropped his axe and clung on to me for support.

"Parashurama? You okay?"

He didn't look okay. His face had paled. It seemed thinner, too. In fact, all of him seemed thinner.

"Hollowpoint fragmentation round," the gunman said, weirdly, serenely smug. "Got some sort of... juice inside. Makes you super creeps... not so super any more."

Parashurama slumped to the deck. "Korolev's antidote."

"You've got to be kidding," I said.

He looked up at me, sunken-eyed. His musculature was shrinking, flesh seeming to melt away. The Warrior was reverting to his former self, still well built but slender, a shadow of the bulked-up beefcake he had been.

"Dammit," he seethed. "So weak. Dammit, dammit, dammit."

The gunman gargled repeatedly in the back of his throat. He was laughing, gloating, even as he drowned on his own blood.

"'Dozens of us,'" I said to him. "So there's a private army on board."

A crimson grin. "That, and worse. Guys who hired us... don't fuck around. They know how to... protect themselves."

There was activity on every deck. All at once, below us, around us, we could hear doors opening, boots thumping, the *click-clack* of cocking levers being ratcheted.

Parashurama had almost completed the transition from deva back to human. He sat slumped against the base of the stairs, Korolev's antidote coursing through his bloodstream in liquid form. He was half the size he had been, and his wound was doubly serious now. The arm hung limp by his side, useless.

"What do we do?" I said. "Do we bail?"

"Heck no." A wave of pain made him grit his teeth. "We've come too far, we're too close, for that."

"But you're our leader."

"And as your leader I'm telling you don't give up. I may be no good to you any more, but you're still devas. You still have your siddhis. Use them. Show these scumbags what you're made of. Here."

He slid his axe across.

"I can't take it," I said.

"It's no use to me. You, you've got two working arms."

The clatter of approaching footfalls was loud. The Trinity's private army was coming up to engage.

"Go on," Parashurama urged. "You'll get the hang. You're Hanuman, a born fighter. A warrior too."

Was I?

I was.

I grasped the axe by the handle. I hefted it. It felt comfortable. Well weighted. Right.

"Okay," I said. "Think you can make it up to the helipad? Good. You should be safe there. Avatars?"

The others were grouped round us. I rose to my feet.

"This is going to be harder than we thought," I said. "But we do not stop. We do not falter.

Somewhere on this boat are three men who we need to take alive at all costs. Everyone else is just in the way. Collateral damage. Do not get shot. Even a flesh wound will turn you back into who you used to be and leave you vulnerable. Apart from that – go for it. Let's give these bastards hell."

I caught Vamana's eye. For once, the Dwarf wasn't giving me that arch, superior look of his.

"Not bad, Mighty Joe Young," he said. "Nice speech, well delivered. Rousing."

And then mercenaries appeared, each clutching a stubby submachine gun at chest level.

And so began the fight of our lives.

49. AN ENGLISH THING

I WAS THINKING of Krystyna the Polish barista as we battled our way down through the boat.

I was thinking of Herriman my cat, and Mrs Deakins my busybody neighbour, and Francesca my ex.

I was thinking of my parents, now living at opposite ends of England, my dad in Cornwall, my mum in Northumberland, as far away from each other as they could be without crossing borders or water but still in contact via email and getting on better than at any time during their doomed-as-Uncle-Ben marriage.

I was thinking of the comics industry pros I'd hung out with at conventions and laughed and got drunk with, and also the fans who'd queued at a publisher's booth for a signed sketch or my autograph, their admiration like a drug, heady while it lasted but always followed by a guilty comedown crash, as though I didn't deserve it, a hollow high.

I was thinking of the people I liked and loved, the people who meant something to me, who had significance – Aanandi Sengupta foremost among them – and of all the people whom those people liked and loved, a network of personal connections, relationships that extended across nations, branching to all quarters of the globe, the thing that made seven billion separate humans a race.

The world had more uniting it than dividing it.

That was worth preserving.

That was what we were fighting for.

I swung Parashurama's battleaxe as though I had been practising with it all my life. Mercenaries attacked. Mercenaries fell before me like scythed wheat.

Chatter-bursts of gunfire ripped the air. Rama's arrows flew in showers. Kurma's club bludgeoned and pummelled. Narasimha tore. Vamana crushed. Kalkin and Krishna slashed and stabbed. Blood spattered the decks and walls of the *Makara*. Stray bullets ricocheted off metal bulkheads and sent chips of fibreglass and aramid composite flying in all directions.

Up on the helipad, Parashurama – Tyler Weston – defended himself with guns taken from the body of the man who'd shot him. One-armed, he blazed away at anyone foolhardy enough to poke their head up over the top the stairs.

On the dive deck at the stern, Matsya whirled through a throng of opponents, his bladed discuses parting skin and flesh. Droplets of seawater and blood glistened on his scales.

The Fish-man was the next to lose his siddhis. The mercs overwhelmed him with sheer numbers. Rama and I struggled to reach him but were pinned down by suppressing fire. Windows above us shattered, spraying us with glass fragments as we crouched behind a bench seat.

The mercenaries wrestled Matsya to the floor and one of them casually lodged a bullet in his thigh. Then they all stood back to watch him transform. His scales faded away. His gill slits receded, closing up like gashes healing in fast motion. His glassy black eyes became the eyes of an ordinary man. The webs of skin between his fingers and toes shrank to nothingness.

The mercs laughed at this belittling, this humiliation. In return Klaus Gottlieb, professional aquanaut, cursed them in German, spitting out his fury and defiance. There was no question that they had deliberately chosen to wound rather than kill. They wanted to see him become normal, human, at their mercy.

The same mercenary who had shot him in the leg now pressed the barrel of gun to his forehead. Gottlieb went calm and still.

"Any last words, Kraut?" the man asked.

AGE OF SHIVA

"Yes. Enjoy the rest of your life while you still can."

"Eh? What the hell's that supposed to – ?"

The merc looked round, following Gottlieb's gaze, in time to see Vamana leaping from one of the upper decks down to the dive deck. The entire yacht rocked as the Dwarf landed right in the mercenaries' midst. His gigantic arms swiped left and right, scattering the black-clad men, knocking many of them overboard. His expression was a leer of pure rage.

"Leave! Him! Alone!" he bellowed, snatching up the mercenary who had Gottlieb at gunpoint.

The man turned his weapon on Vamana, but the Dwarf popped his hand off at the wrist as though twisting an apple from a bough. As the mercenary screamed, Vamana grasped his head loosely and slammed a fist into it, squashing it into a mangled mess. He then used the corpse like a flail, threshing the other mercenaries with it.

"You know, I'm beginning to like that arrogant wanker," I said to Rama. "Who knew he actually cared about Matsya?"

"Vamana would rather pour scorn than say what he really feels. Isn't that an English thing?"

"Touché."

"Duck!"

I did, and Rama planted an arrow right in the eye of a mercenary who was trying to sneak up on me from behind.

I returned the favour a moment later as a mercenary pounced on the Archer from the deck above. The axe caught the man between the legs and continued upward, cleaving him neatly in two. The halves fell to the deck like sides of beef.

The opposition dwindled, crumbled. Soon the *Makara* was littered with the bodies of its defenders.

A handful of the mercenaries, having seen the tide of battle turning, made an escape bid in one of the yacht's motor launches. They didn't get far. An arrow from Rama struck the powerhead on the outboard, crippling it. A second arrow, this one explosive-tipped, found the launch's fuel tank and – *boom!* – that was all she wrote.

Some thought it would be okay if they surrendered, but Narasimha was having none of that. By the time he had finished with them, his talons were clogged with gore. Prisoners of war? Geneva Convention? Fuck that shit.

So now we were down to seven, Parashurama and Matsya both alive but depowered, and the *Makara* was ours. Nothing more stood between us and the Trinity Syndicate, wherever they were on board, except their bodyguards.

We went inside through a set of sliding doors, to find ourselves amidships in a three-storey atrium with a spiralling glass staircase around the edge and a geometrical modernist chandelier overhead. Gilt-flecked marble flooring, and mahogany fixtures with gold accents, added to an air of over-the-top opulence. The Palais de Versailles looked tastefully restrained by comparison.

The atrium was so well soundproofed, we couldn't hear the crash of waves and spume outside. Nor could we feel the *Makara*'s pitch and yaw; gyroscopic stabilisers compensated, giving a smooth ride in all but the roughest conditions. In fact, the only thing reminding us that we were on a moving boat was the faint burr of the engines detectable through the soles of our feet.

We advanced slowly. I motioned to Rama and Krishna that they should split off and take the stairs. They obeyed without demur. I didn't realise until then that I had somehow become leader. From "eleventh man" to captain. From comics nerd to head of the herd. It must have been the axe – Parashurama's signature weapon, still charged with his authority, a baton symbolically passed on. That or nobody else wanted the position and it had fallen to me, dumb chump, by default. I like to think that maybe, too, I had gained the Avatars' respect. Surely they wouldn't be deferring to me otherwise.

As Rama and Krishna ascended, Kurma, at my instruction, took point for the rest of us. We crossed the atrium in a wedge formation, the indestructible Turtle at the front, a bulwark against any foe.

A door burst open.

Burst – as in splintered into a thousand pieces.

And out stepped an asura so grotesque, so hideous, we stopped in our tracks.

He had to bend low to fit through the doorway. His massive frame was sheathed in a pelt of matted mud-brown fur. Whiskery jowls hung from his face, flapping and covered in slobber. Two lower fangs rose either side of his muzzle like a warthog's tusks. The smell of him – godawful. And his eyes were jutting crimson orbs, alive with savagery and contempt.

He had long, powerful arms, and from the paw of each protruded a scimitar that was larger, broader and more fearsomely curved than Kalkin's talwars or Krishna's Nandaka. His bearlike belly heaved imperiously as he surveyed us. His feelings were plain: he did not think much of what he saw.

Radiating off him was a sensation of horror, depravity, wickedness, so strong it was almost a physical force. Here was a creature steeped in the ugliness of the world. Everything that was wrong with human nature was embodied in this shambling, vile, doglike beast. What good people loathed, he loved. What decent folk abhorred, he embraced. He moved where the dirt was thick, darkness's patron saint, a lord of vice and squalor.

He was evil. Let's not beat around the bush here. He was all that's foul and bad, and sin fed him, sin made him grow fat and strong, sin in his gut, sin in his sinews, the sin which starved infants in the Horn of Africa and stalked the slums of Mumbai and chained women in basements and groomed pre-teens online and paid the obscene bonuses of bankrupting financiers and oppressed democratic uprisings and gushed oil into the Gulf of Mexico and left the Aral Sea a toxic wasteground, the cumulative abuse and avarice of mankind, and it was all in him.

He was evil, and he was awesomely strong, and he was the end of days, and his name was Kali.

50. KALI

KALI LET HIS aura of utter malevolence wash over us for a few more seconds, and then he struck.

He took three steps forward and booted Kurma into the air like a football. The Turtle pirouetted helplessly almost all the way to the chandelier, and as he descended Kali readied both of his scimitars, pointing them perpendicular, a pair of deadly pillars.

I distinctly remember thinking, *It's Kurma. The armoured one. He'll be all right.*

Then Kurma fell onto Kali's blades, back first, like a fakir onto a bed of nails, and they impaled his torso clean through, piercing both the supposedly impenetrable armour and the supposedly impenetrable flesh beneath.

With little more than a shrug, Kali flicked Kurma away. The Turtle's lifeless body flew straight at Narasimha, who didn't quite dodge in time. His reflexes were lightning, but he was still reeling from the shock of seeing Kurma killed, as were we all.

The *snap* of bones breaking was audible across the width of the atrium. The Man-lion managed to disentangle himself from Kurma and stagger back to his feet, but he was clutching his chest and wincing. Two ribs had been shattered by the weight of the Turtle's armoured bulk, a third fractured.

Vamana reached up and grabbed the chandelier by its support chain. He yanked the dazzling mass of glass free from the ceiling and flung it down onto Kali.

But the asura spun his swords over his head like a helicopter's rotor vanes, whittling the chandelier to pieces. He was the eye of a storm of glass shards that sprayed outwards around him. When he was done, the chandelier was just a ring of twinkling ice on the floor, Kali at its centre, unharmed.

Vamana rushed at Kali, arms open to crush him in a bearhug. Kali sidestepped, and a scimitar flickered, and all at once the Dwarf was a crumpled heap, clutching the back of his knee.

"Aargh! My fucking leg! Cut the fucking tendon!"

He lashed out with his good leg, but Kali was already moving on, focusing on his next target: Narasimha, who growled and straightened up as much as his injured ribcage would allow.

Kali's scimitars became a flashing cyclone of

thrusts, feints, jabs and slashes. Narasimha bobbed and wove, evading one blow after another. Even unhurt, it would have been all he could do to keep from being hit. Kali didn't give him any opening for a counterattack.

Rama, on a mezzanine halfway up the staircase, loosed three arrows. Kali barely even paused from his assault on Narasimha. One scimitar did the work of deflecting all three shafts. Then the onslaught against the Man-lion resumed in earnest.

"We're getting our arses kicked here," I said to Kalkin.

"No shit. Whatever gave you that idea?"

"The bastard's unstoppable. What do we do?"

"It's all right, Hanuman." Kalkin unsheathed his talwars. "*You* don't do anything. Leave this to me."

The Horseman stepped forward, resolute. I could see in his eyes the fulfilment of the bushido code he so loved: the virtues of honour, loyalty and courage, even unto death.

At that moment, a couple more asuras arrived to join the fray. Hanuman recognised them instantly, their identities surfacing in my brain from the monkey god's deep pool of memories. These two were Koka and Vikoka, brothers, Kali's generals. Neither was as large as the master they served, but they were no less ugly. They were conjoined at the flank, like Siamese twins. Koka carried a kukri dagger in his right hand; Vikoka had the same in his left.

They came down from the head of the staircase,

meeting Rama and Krishna on the mezzanine. Tongues bared, they swung their kukris as one.

Krishna countered Koka with Nandaka. Rama, who had emptied his quiver with those last three shots at Kali, used his bow like a shield to ward off Vikoka's strike.

"They need your help," Kalkin told me. "Kali is mine."

I knew the truth of this just as Kalkin did. The Horseman, with his talwars, was made for fighting Kali.

He yelled out Kali's name, and the demon broke off from harrying Narasimha. Canine contempt filled his face, and he charged headlong at the Horseman. Blade met blade, twice over. Steel clanged ringingly against steel.

I sprinted up the staircase to Rama and Krishna, who were holding their own against Koka and Vikoka but only just. The twin demons moved with a supple grace, four legs working as one. Their daggers' flame-shaped blades darted, fast as snakes' tongues.

Spotting a gold sovereign ring adorning Koka's hand, I knew where these asuras had come from, who they had been. The Trinity were throwing their bodyguards at us, the four goons. This was a last-ditch attempt to beat us. They had exhausted all other avenues.

The thought reinvigorated me. It meant we were almost there. We had ploughed through the Trinity's defences, battered down every obstacle they had put in our way. Now they were sacrificing their final pieces on the board. This was what we had reduced them to.

I leapt between Rama and Krishna. There seemed only one logical way to combat the seamless twin terror of Koka and Vikoka, and that was divide and conquer.

The battleaxe descended, and Koka was unzipped cleanly from Vikoka and vice versa. The severed demons, blood pouring from their sides, fought on, but they weren't nearly as efficient apart as they were together. Krishna ran Koka through with Nandaka. Rama clubbed Vikoka's brains out with his bow.

Back down on the atrium floor, Kalkin and Kali were going at it hammer and tongs. The swordplay was almost impossible to follow, so blazingly, blisteringly fast did the lunges and thrusts and parries and ripostes come. Narasimha and Vamana looked on from the sidelines. There was no room for anyone else in this contest. Kalkin and Kali were locked in mortal combat, perfectly matched adversaries, Kalkin smaller but nimbler, Kali larger and stronger but a fraction slower. The space between them seemed latticed with steel. The clashes of blade on blade were drum-tattoo swift, as though there were a dozen duellists in the room rather than just two.

"Let's go," I said to Rama and Krishna. "Kalkin's buying us time. I don't think the Trinity are going to hang around. They never stay put if they can run."

We barged through the door at the top of the staircase, the one Koka and Vikoka had come in by. A short corridor led to a second door. We barged through that too.

Beyond lay a theogenesis chamber, a cramped, bonsai version of the room in the second ring at Mount Meru. There was an upright plexiglass tube with vents that could flood it with aerosolised god virus. There was an Induction Cocoon in the corner. All the kit you needed to build your own gods on the go. Doubtless the Trinity had intended to perform demonstrations here for visiting dignitaries, showing just how quick and easy it was to make men supermen.

Professor Korolev looked up, startled, as we slammed our way in. He was busy strapping the fourth goon to a steel table in preparation for dosing him up with god gas. Diamond Tooth, Buddha's killer. Presumably Vikoka was Knuckleduster Ring's brother, twins in demonhood as well as in life; by a process of elimination, Kali was Hillbilly Moustache.

Korolev hoisted his hands straight into the air. He wasn't daft. Against three devas, he didn't stand a chance. Abject surrender was the only realistic option available to him.

Diamond Tooth strained against his bonds. "Don't just stand there, you idiot," he snarled at Korolev. "Untie me. I can take them."

"No," I said evenly, "you can't. Krishna? Rama? Which one of you wants to do the honours?"

To his credit, Diamond Tooth didn't sob, he didn't

plead, he didn't beg for his life. The game was up. He faced his end with bravery and bravado.

"Shit," he sighed as Krishna loomed over him, Nandaka aloft. "Well, if you've got to go, might as well be a god that does it. Come on, you blue-skinned cunt. Don't faff around. Let's be having you."

Krishna beheaded him with a single clean chop.

Korolev said, "You're too late, you know. Is all over. No point executing me as well. The situation has changed more than you realise."

"What have you done?" I demanded.

"What have I done?" The Russian biochemist chuckled coldly. "What I was asked to do by Trinity. I am making Kali, Koka and Vikoka only to run interference, giving time for other lot of theogenesis to bed in."

"What other lot of theogenesis? Who else have you zapped with your fucking gas?"

"Who else is there?"

"I don't know. The crew of this boat?"

"They are on the bridge, still sailing it."

"More of those mercenaries."

"Not them."

"Domestic staff?"

"Down below, confined to quarters for their own safety. You really are being dense, Hanuman."

"The Trinity themselves," said Rama.

"Well done, the Archer. Bullseye."

"You theogenised Lombard, Krieger and Bhatnagar?" I said, incredulous. "Jesus fucking

Christ, how stupid is that? Those three are certifiable madmen."

"I disagree. Is sane act, to give themselves siddhis as final layer of defence against you."

"What have you transformed them into? Please don't say asuras."

I had visions of the Trinity as nagas or maybe vetalas, on the loose, rampaging, causing all kinds of havoc. It didn't seem a stretch of the imagination at all. Billionaire businessmen as snake monsters, as vampires – they were made for it. Vocational determinism.

"Why not see for yourself?" Korolev nodded to a door behind him at the far end of the chamber. He gave a smile that was eerily beatific. "They are just through there, in the stateroom. Companionway, up one deck. They are waiting. I would even say they are expecting you."

I walked past him.

"So I get to live?" he said, casting a glance at Diamond Tooth's decapitated corpse. "I am co-operating. Not resisting. I am not such a bad guy, huh? Just scientist, with scientist's curiosity. I research. I discover and create. I advance human understanding. Is not so wrong. Is no crime."

"Curiosity isn't a crime," I said.

Korolev visibly relaxed.

"But almost everything else you've done is."

I swung the axe backhand. It's fair to say he never saw it coming.

51. THE TRIMŪRTI

IN THE STATEROOM, a semicircle of windows faced the bows. There were plush cream leather sofas and armchairs and a carpet soft as mink. Recessed LED lighting cast a muted ambient glow. The wallpaper had a lotus pattern, white on gold.

The Trinity greeted us calmly as we entered.

They weren't themselves any more.

Dick Lombard had pale blue skin now, like Krishna, and an extra pair of arms. He perched on one leg, with his left heel lodged against his right knee, exquisitely balanced. The corners of his mouth were permanently turned up in a hint of a smile.

R. J. Krieger was even odder-looking. Instead of one head he had four, each facing in a different direction as though to the cardinal points of the compass. Like Lombard he also had an extra pair of arms, but next to the multiple heads that seemed almost normal.

Vignesh Bhatnagar, meanwhile, sported a third eye in the centre of his brow that moved and blinked in synchrony with the other two. His triple gaze was even and haughty and timeless.

All three men were naked save for loincloths. They stood absolutely, serenely still, neither cowed nor aggressive. I turned to Rama and Krishna. We all recognised the gods before us. We didn't know what to do. Bow? Genuflect? Attack? Retreat? What?

The Trinity were the Trimūrti, Hinduism's holy triumvirate, the three-as-one who rule over all. Lombard was Vishnu, the maintainer, he who preserves. Krieger was Brahma, the creator, he who bestows life and form. Bhatnagar was Shiva, the destroyer, he who brings about change.

A media magnate, upholder of the status quo. A biochemist with his hands on the building blocks of life. An arms manufacturer whose product was responsible for countless deaths.

Now *that* was vocational determinism.

"Please," said Vishnu, "Hanuman, Rama, Krishna, all three of you, lower your weapons." Lombard's abrupt Australian tones had been replaced by something mellower and more neutral. "Violence benefits no one."

"It's a pleasure to see you again," said Brahma. "Our children. Our creations."

"We know your desire," said Shiva. "We see how it burns inside you, an all-consuming flame. Let it expire."

"You don't want to fight?" I said. "You're not resisting? Are you scared of us?"

"Not scared," said Vishnu. "How could we be scared of you when we are everything – the beginning, the middle and the end? We are the universe in three aspects. Nothing you can do holds any terror for us."

"We were, we are, we will be," said Brahma.

"Ceaselessly in flux," said Shiva, "and thus, in our natures, unchanging. The eternal Trimūrti, united, interleaving, everlasting."

They all three spoke with the same slow, dreamy inflection, their native accents and intonations erased, as though their individual personality traits had been overwritten, replaced by those of the gods who now inhabited their bodies.

It was both creepy and beguiling. These were *our* gods, the deva's devas, supreme even to us, the threesome from which everything was born and lived and died. Yet they were also still Lombard, Krieger and Bhatnagar, whom we'd pursued halfway across the world and wanted – needed – to expose for the criminals they were.

"You revere us, you resent us," said Vishnu, as though reading our thoughts. "We understand."

"You regard us as your enemies," said Brahma, "yet you know you owe us your allegiance as well."

"Conflict and confrontation," said Shiva. "Such

has been your lives. But what if there is another way?"

Rama levelled his bow accusingly. "You have done unspeakable things," he said. "You would do worse if we allowed you."

"That *was* us," said Brahma, all four of his heads nodding at once. "But that *is* not us. We have transcended what we were. We have become so much more. You know that. You see it."

The Trimūrti moved closer together. They didn't so much walk as float.

Hovering in a triangle formation, back to back, the soles of their feet inches off the carpet, they began to revolve in the air like a child's bedroom mobile turning in a breeze. When they talked, their voices joined together, overlapping, finishing each other's sentences. It was hard to tell which one was addressing us. Sometimes all three of them were moving their lips but only one voice could be heard.

"We regret what has transpired."

"The past is past."

"We have sown confusion and pain."

"Gain was our watchword."

"Discord our legacy."

"The world teeters."

"Kali is unleashed."

"Cycles turn."

"The axis pivots."

"What brought ruin once may bring ruin again."

"We feel no joy over that, only sorrow."

"If you were to seek revenge on us, to punish us

for our misdeeds when we were mere men, we would not stop you."

"It is deserved."

"We would submit."

"We are capable of erasing you from existence with but a thought."

"We choose not to."

"You continue to live because we will it."

"We are not vengeful. There is no hatred in us."

"Only compassion. Only understanding."

"Our deaths would be just another part of the tapestry of existence."

"Meaningless and acceptable."

"We place our fate in your hands."

"We are at your mercy."

"But what purpose would it serve, killing us?"

"When there is good we can do."

"Hope we can bring."

"Peace we can restore."

"Wait, whoa, hold on, what?" I said. "Peace you can restore? What's that mean?"

"We can end what we began," said the Trimūrti in pure unison. "We can return order to the world. Kali Yuga can become Satya Yuga, the age of harmony between men and gods. It is within our power. You know this. As easily as breathing we can halt the march of war and re-establish equilibrium, undo what has been done. We can make these words deeds with no more effort than it takes to say them. On condition that we live, we can guarantee that the world lives too. All will be as before, but better."

"You're willing to save the world? You can do that?"

"Have we not just said so? Do you not believe us?"

The thing was, I did. As the Trimūrti twirled uncannily before us, exuding sheer omnipotence, I believed firmly that they could make everything right again. At that very moment billions of people were praying for divine intervention, fearful of apocalypse. All that faith was crackling in the atmosphere like spiritual lightning, and these three could catch it and channel it and use it.

"We promise a future where the human race accepts our guidance," they said, "where their worship sustains us, where we influence all that happens. There will be peace and accord and all manner of fine things."

"Ah," I said. "So there's a catch. Quid pro quo. This is in fact a deal. All this talk of transcending, but you're still businessmen after all."

"A deal in which nobody is the loser. A deal to the benefit of all parties."

"You get blind devotion. The world gets a golden age."

"Precisely. With us overseeing the transition from hostility to tranquillity."

"At a price."

"What price peace? Peace is surely priceless. You cannot put a value on it."

"But the alternative is we kill you, right here, right now," I said, "and the human race gets to muddle along as before, making its own way, its own mistakes."

"Our survival is mankind's survival. But if that is not your wish…"

Simultaneously, all three made a gesture of submission, heads lowered, hands held out to the side.

Parashurama's battleaxe hung heavy in my grasp. Its blade dripped blood onto the carpet, as did Nandaka and Rama's bow.

The Trimūrti were presenting us with a very simple, take-it-or-leave-it choice. End them, and the human race could go on its merry way, perhaps continuing to stumble down the short rocky path that led to extinction. Let them live, and there would be no more dissent or hatred. People would be as one under the Trimūrti. It would be an age of Vishnu, an age of Brahma, an age of Shiva, where independence of thought, free will, would take a back seat to the dictates of gods.

I could only stare at Rama and Krishna, wondering what the solution was. The pair of them looked as nonplussed as I felt. Such a responsibility. Such a decision. What was the right thing to do?

Minutes ticked by.

The Trimūrti patiently awaited.

Their surrender, or ours?

52. DEICIDE?

So ALL-OUT THERMONUCLEAR war was averted. You
know that. It didn't happen. India and Pakistan
pulled back from the brink. They managed to settle
their differences by negotiation, with the UN gamely
egging them on.

Neither country owned up to the obliteration
of Srinagar, and there are compelling arguments
for guilt on either side, and for innocence. Lately
we've seen the incident classed as an "accident" in
several quarters, a catastrophic blunder rather than
a deliberate act. A rogue commander in the field, a
misinterpreted order, an itchy finger on the button,
the fog of war, all that. It doesn't bring back the
many hundreds of thousands of dead, it doesn't
console their grieving relatives, it doesn't mend

the scorched, irradiated disaster zone that lies at the heart of Kashmir, but what it does do is help ease the process of reconciliation. The wound heals more quickly and less painfully when there is no recrimination to salt it.

The Dashavatara continue to exist, but severely depleted. They're down to Narasimha, Vamana, Rama and Krishna. Not forgetting Kalkin, of course; the Horseman's battle with Kali was long, drawn-out, gruelling, but victory ultimately was his. He still bears the many scars inflicted by Kali's scimitars, even after treatment with amrita. He wears them with justifiable pride. Vamana and Narasimha bear their own scars too. Vamana limps with every step. It doesn't do much to improve his temperament. He's still the same insufferable little twerp he always was. But he's *our* insufferable little twerp.

Aanandi says it was Kalkin's destiny to slay Kali, just as it was Kali's destiny to be slain by Kalkin. According to the Vedas it happened before, so was due to happen again. What was poetry became reality – and it was a fairly messy reality, let me tell you. The *Makara*'s atrium looked like a slaughterhouse when Kalkin was finished. That huge dog demon had a lot of blood to shed.

We've retreated to Mount Meru, we devas, while we debate our next move. We lost much of the trust we'd gained when we took part in the Indo-Pakistan conflict. People are treating us with a great deal of scepticism now. We are less than we first seemed, is the general feeling. In the media, in the online forums, in the bloggers' opinions, we're not spotless idols any more. We're tarnished.

That's fine. We accept that.

It started out as superheroing, but then it changed and became darker and more complicated. Murkier. A game of lies and compromise.

Such is life. Like a tube of toothpaste, everything starts out orderly, the stripes all in neat rows, but by the end, when you get down to the dregs, it's a mixed-together colourless mess. The Dharma Bull begins life with all its legs, then in due course it's lying on its side in the mud with four stumps. Austerity, cleanliness, compassion and truthfulness have vanished one by one.

Some of us reckon it's time to 'fess up. Tell the world everything. I've spent the past few weeks writing this book for that very reason: an honest, first-person account of the strange, traumatic months we've just been through, telling how a noble dream turned out to be a corrupt nightmare. Publishing it would explain a lot. It would, I hope, humanise us and enable others see us in a fresh light.

If we make a clean breast of it, maybe we'll be forgiven. Then we could start over, put our siddhis to use again, do some genuine good. We could – I don't know – obtain a UN mandate to assist with rescue and relief work. Humanitarian stuff. Help out in trouble spots. Escort aid convoys into volatile regions and disaster zones. Protect Red Cross officials from harassment and intimidation like super-powered minders.

As long as we're never seen to take sides, we never ally ourselves with one country or other, wouldn't that be all right?

It's an idea. Our discussions on the subject are long and in-depth. Aanandi leads them. She is our conscience, our compass. I think, if we listen to her, we are unlikely to go wrong.

In the meantime, we guard the secret of the stone lotus and theogenesis. Meru is abandoned, unoccupied except by us. Half of the technicians and domestic staff scarpered off home when everything went to hell in Kashmir. The rest quit shortly afterwards when their salary payments abruptly and mysteriously stopped and it became apparent that the Trinity Syndicate was no longer a viable going concern. Sand drifts between the complex's seven rings, rattling against the windows on breezy days. It's still our secret lair, but it's a sun-bleached ghost of itself, once bustling, now all but deserted.

Tyler Weston and Klaus Gottlieb are still with us, still on the team, and if we can figure out how Professor Korolev's theogenesis machines work, perhaps Parashurama and Matsya will one day be reborn. Perhaps we can find other willing volunteers, too, and the Dashavatara can become ten again; there can be a full complement of Avatars.

So far, since India and Pakistan signed their peace agreement in Moscow, the world has been a remarkably calm and sanguine place. It's as though the horror of Srinagar has sobered everyone up. Moves are afoot to implement a freeze on all weapons of mass destruction, a moratorium paving the way to a worldwide ban that will see stockpiles systematically decommissioned until there are none left. There is even talk of all standing armies being demobilised, troops put out to pasture. War no more.

Will that come to pass? Anything's possible, I suppose.

Is this the dawning of a new Satya Yuga? Are we taking the first steps towards an age of true enlightenment?

If so, could that be because there be supreme beings currently circling the oceans in the giga-yacht *Makara*, exerting their influence on us? Are people's actions being determined by them, as yet without anyone being aware of it? Are all mortals their unwitting thralls, in return for a guaranteed future of co-operation and nonviolence?

Or did Rama, Krishna and I raise our weapons and kill the Trimūrti, as they offered?

What did we choose? Did we decide to commit deicide? Or did we, by doing nothing, submit to a higher authority on your behalf?

What do *you* think?

JAMES LOVEGROVE'S *PANTHEON* SERIES

THE AGE OF RA

UK ISBN: 978 1 844167 46 3 • US ISBN: 978 1 844167 47 0 • £7.99/$7.99

The Ancient Egyptian gods have defeated all the other pantheons and divided the Earth into warring factions. Lt. David Westwynter, a British soldier, stumbles into Freegypt, the only place to have remained independent of the gods, and encounters the followers of a humanist freedom-fighter known as the Lightbringer. As the world heads towards an apocalyptic battle, there is far more to this leader than it seems...

THE AGE OF ZEUS

UK ISBN: 978 1 906735 68 5 • US ISBN: 978 1 906735 69 2 • £7.99/$7.99

The Olympians appeared a decade ago, living incarnations of the Ancient Greek gods, offering order and stability at the cost of placing humanity under the jackboot of divine oppression. Until former London police officer Sam Akehurst receives an invitation to join the Titans, the small band of battlesuited high-tech guerillas squaring off against the Olympians and their mythological monsters in a war they cannot all survive...

THE AGE OF ODIN

UK ISBN: 978 1 907519 40 6 • US ISBN: 978 1 907519 41 3 • £7.99/$7.99

Gideon Coxall was a good soldier but bad at everything else, until a roadside explosive device leaves him with one deaf ear and a British Army half-pension. The Valhalla Project, recruiting useless soldiers like himself, no questions asked, seems like a dream, but the last thing Gid expects is to find himself fighting alongside ancient Viking gods. It seems *Ragnarök* – the fabled final conflict of the Sagas – is looming.

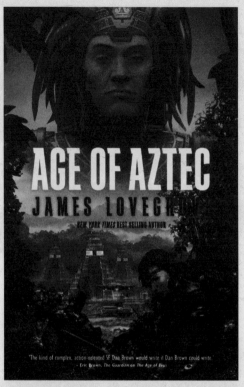

AGE OF AZTEC
JAMES LOVEGROVE
NEW YORK TIMES BEST SELLING AUTHOR

'The kind of complex, action-oriented SF Dan Brown would write if Dan Brown could write.'
– Eric Brown, *The Guardian* on *The Age of Zeus*

UK ISBN: 978 1 78108 048 1 • US ISBN: 978 1 78108 050 4 • £7.99/$7.99

The date is 4 Jaguar 1 Monkey 1 House; November 25th 2012, by the old reckoning. The Aztec Empire rules the world, in the name of Quetzalcoatl – the Feathered Serpent – and his brother gods.

The Aztec reign is one of cruel and ruthless oppression, fuelled by regular human sacrifice. In the jungle-infested city of London, one man defies them: the masked vigilante known as the Conquistador.

Then the Conquistador is recruited to spearhead an uprising, and discovers the terrible truth about the Aztecs and their gods. The clock is ticking. Apocalypse looms, unless the Conquistador can help assassinate the mysterious, immortal Aztec emperor, the Great Speaker. But his mission is complicated by Mal Vaughn, a police detective who is on his trail, determined to bring him to justice.

WWW.SOLARISBOOKS.COM

Follow us on Twitter! www.twitter.com/solarisbooks

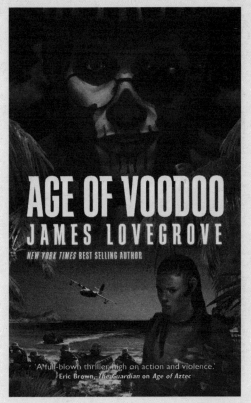

'A full-blown thriller, high on action and violence.'
Eric Brown, *The Guardian* on *Age of Aztec*

UK ISBN: 978-1-907519-40-6 • US ISBN: 978-1-78108-086-3 • £7.99/$8.99

Lex Dove thought he was done with the killing game. A retired British wetwork specialist, he's living the quiet life in the Caribbean, minding his own business. Then a call comes, with one last mission: to lead an American black ops team into a disused Cold War bunker on a remote island near his adopted home. The money's good, which means the risks are high.

Dove doesn't discover just how high until he and his team are a hundred feet below ground, facing the horrific fruits of an experiment blending science and voodoo witchcraft. As if barely human monsters weren't bad enough, a clock is ticking. Deep in the bowels of the earth, a god is waiting. And His anger, if roused, will be fearsome indeed.

 WWW.SOLARISBOOKS.COM

Follow us on Twitter! www.twitter.com/solarisbooks

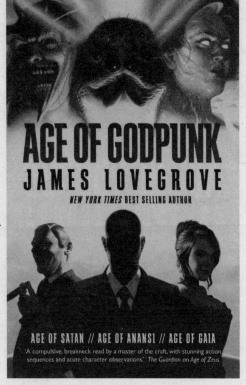

AGE OF GODPUNK

JAMES LOVEGROVE

NEW YORK TIMES BEST SELLING AUTHOR

AGE OF SATAN // AGE OF ANANSI // AGE OF GAIA

'A compulsive, breakneck read by a master of the craft, with stunning action sequences and acute character observations.' *The Guardian* on *Age of Zeus*

UK ISBN: 978-1-78108-128-0 • US ISBN: 978-1-78108-129-7 • £7.99/$8.99

'Lovegrove is vigorously carving out a 'godpunk' subgenre —
rebellious underdog humans battling an outmoded belief system.
Guns help a bit, but the real weapon is free will.' *Pornokitsch*

Age of Anansi: Dion Yeboah leads an orderly, disciplined life... until the day the spider appears, and throws Dion's existence into chaos...

Age of Satan: Guy Lucas travels the world, haunted by the tragic consequences of a black mass performed as a boy, but the Devil dogs his steps...

Age of Gaia: Energy magnate Barnaby Pollard has the world at his feet, until he meets Lydia Laidlaw, a beautiful and opinionated eco-journalist...

WWW.SOLARISBOOKS.COM

Follow us on Twitter! www.twitter.com/solarisbooks